THIRST

BY

TEAGAN BRODY

ISBN: 978-1-946547-12-5
eBook ISBN: 978-1-946547-13-2

ALSO BY TEAGAN BRODY

Awakening

Fugue

Awareness

For Mike, Geoff, Bill, Kelly, Darrin and Jesse – You were the best friends anyone could have wanted and I miss you all more than you will ever know.
And as always,
For Tarod – every moment with you is the greatest blessing of my existence.

"Sometimes you have to look real hard at a thing to understand it. It can take even more time to realize that that thing is absolutely necessary." – *Teagan Brody*

"Life is not perfect, other than being perfectly imperfect." – Joss Tobin

Prologue

It was not quite dawn as we lay in bed, each of us staring blindly up at the ceiling, lost in thought. You know it is the only way, *Ana's voice silently whispered in my mind.* They will have to get the whole story, not just the bits and pieces you and I can give them.

I stewed over her words. I knew she was right. But like the dilemma Sephor *Mikhail had once faced, I feared too much for Ana's safety to agree to send her on such a mission on her own. It was simply too dangerous, especially since I could not go with her to protect her. Regardless, there was no guarantee it would even work, for the mercurial being she meant to seek shunned society at the best of times. What if she put herself through all the dangers only to be rejected... or worse?*

No. I could not allow her to go.

You do not own me, you know?

I turned toward her, desperately searching her eyes as I countered, No, I depend on you. If we have learned anything from yesterday, it is that I cannot survive without you. And that is why I cannot allow you to do this thing.

So, you're placing your needs over the needs of these people? *she asked with feigned innocence.*

I sighed in resignation. She was using my own words against me, the spiteful Jess! *I had used this very same argument to plead my case for coming to the* Samarean *in first place and she well knew it. Still, the words were as true now as they had been mere days ago and I knew she had won.*

A tremor stole through my entire being and I reached for her. How could I do what had to be done whilst constantly worrying about her safety?

We have our link, *she softly reminded me.* They cannot take that from us.

I hugged her closer. So much was riding on this and should anything happen to her, I knew my life would mean nothing.

Don't even think such things, my love.

I pulled back and smiled at her. She was right – again. I must keep a positive outlook; if not for her and myself, then for my people. This had to work and – if I were being honest with myself – I would admit there were simply no other options at this point. The people were proving more difficult to convince than I had expected, especially that Jarba, and I knew only solid proof would convince her of the veracity of my tale.

They're coming, *Ana silently whispered as she eased out of our embrace and climbed off the bed.*

A chill stole over my skin and I felt them too, now. Reaching out, I caught her hand and squeezed tight for a moment. She glanced down at me, her face the very picture of love as she poured as much of her energy as she could spare into my hand clasped around hers. Just before the knock on the door sounded, she withdrew her hand and stepped away from the bed.

"Come," I said. I cast my eyes downward as the Samarean guards entered the room. Best not to look again upon Ana's retreating figure for fear of alerting them to her presence.

The two guards came to an abrupt halt a yard into the room, looking left and right before demanding, "Where is your Jess?"

From the corner of my eye, I saw Ana sneak safely out the door behind the two. Only then did I raise my gaze and say, "She had to leave."

It was a phrase I would repeat numerous times over the next few hours as the alarm was sounded and the entire area was searched top to bottom as I was interrogated time and time again. When finally the top interrogator joined my guards and me, she was incredibly hostile. "She lied," was her opening statement as she entered the holding chamber where I was being kept.

"It may appear thus," I explained, "but I assure you, she has not."

Jarba grabbed a chair and turned it around,

straddling it and crossing her arms along the top of the back. "She vowed to remain to protect the Prince. Now she has gone. How is that not a lie?"

Looking her directly in the eyes, I informed her, "I have gathered enough energy into myself to protect him until her return. You have nothing to fear."

Jarba was quick to counter my statement, demanding, "And what of the energy you require? Do you have enough for that? For as I recall, you collapsed at the same time the Prince did. Or has that slipped your mind?"

"The Prince and I both will be fine until she returns," I assured her again.

Jarba sighed in frustration. She had reviewed all of the footage of the room where the two Jus had slept for the evening, and neither she nor the monitoring team could explain how the two guards in the room had failed to notice the Jess simply walking right around them and out the open door. She herself had interrogated the two and shown them the same footage. Neither had believed his eyes. Neither had given an explanation as to how he could have missed her, for she had been clearly visible on the monitor. In fact, she had been clearly visible all the way down the hallway and even past it.

It appeared the whole escape had been right in front of everyone's eyes and yet not a soul had seen her leave.

As Jarba watched the Joss now, she was struck by one thing: she believed him. Every instinct in her told her he was telling the truth. Yet how could she trust him? He held the future of her entire race in his hands and without his Jess, there was no guarantee he would even survive – let alone the Samarean Prince!

She buried her face in her hands, rubbing hard across her eyes as she made her decision. She needed to know what had happened so she could figure out a way to get back to the others. And this Joss held all the answers. Only by allowing him to finish his tale would she be able to learn the information needed to ensure that could happen.

Sitting back up, she nodded, saying, "Very well. Let us return to the round chamber where you will finish your tale."

"I assure you," I said sardonically, "There is no possible way to finish the tale yet."

Jarba threw a suspicious glare my way before standing and leading the way out of the room. Two new guards brought up the rear with me walking in front of them.

As soon as I had taken my seat and she had the attention of every occupant in the room, Jarba began her interrogation once more.

"On the yester, your Jess left off with a group of hybrids and Jus in the earth-bound home of a Toti couple who claimed to be Juish, themselves. Let us begin there."

Without reservation, I shook my head. "My Ana will have to continue that side of the story when she returns for her insight and memory of the happenings throughout that period will be far more accurate than my own. Instead, I will continue where I last left off – at the Badlands Complex, where Thomas was about to come upon a horrific scene..."

Chapter 1

Thomas started, waking violently from the dream only to discover that it felt like he was still immersed within it. His mind was sluggish and he had difficulty pulling himself upright. Getting up from the bed was a colossal chore, but something was calling to him and he knew he had to move. He felt almost as if there was some kind of monster waiting for him, but the thing – whatever it was – was still calling to him and he forced himself up and out of his room.

He stumbled out into the hallway, weaving and bumping into the stone walls as he struggled to make his way through the dimly-lit passageway to the master suite. An urgency set in. He had to get there. He *had* to. But it felt like there were heavy weights attached to his feet keeping him from reaching his destination, each step costing more energy than a mere step should.

There were no Kurr in attendance as he opened the main door to the suite, and he stumbled unheard into the receiving room. He passed over to the bedroom his mother and Mikhail shared, not even bothering to knock as he turned the handle and practically fell inside.

There, he stopped dead in his tracks. His eyes nearly bugged out of their sockets at the scene confronting him. Mikhail and his mother were both lying on the floor of the room, just at the foot of the bed, each one writhing and twisting in agony as they gasped desperately for breath. Their mouths were agape and they clawed frantically at their own throats, their bloodied fingers digging deep into the soft flesh there. Thomas stared in mute horror as blood gushed from the claw marks each made.

Finally, he snapped out of his horror-induced shock and ran to his mother's side, grabbing her hands and pulling hard to tear them back from her throat. She fought him, even though her eyes were rolled up into the back of her head. Still she gasped and gagged, as if she couldn't breathe. Her mouth was wide open, but no air was getting through!

"Mom!" Thomas screamed. "Mom! M'khail!" Over

and over he screamed as he fought for control of her clawing, bloodied hands. "M'khail! Mom!" Mikhail clawed at his own throat over and over, the blood flowing freely all over and around his writhing form. His eyes were also rolled back into his head as he gasped and gagged.

Each writhing adult made sick gurgling sounds, as if liquid was running down their throats and into their lungs. In some dim recess of his mind, Thomas realized it must be blood from where they had gored themselves in the neck. He yelled their names a couple more times, but received no response from either of them. Then inspiration struck and he changed his call, yelling instead for the one person who might actually be able to help him.

"Nera!" he screamed, as loud as he could. "Help me, Nera! Help!" There was no response. Tears were now flowing freely down his cheeks, but Thomas did not care. His mother was no longer struggling with him and Mikhail's fingers suddenly stilled their clawing and dropped off to his sides. Both of them closed their eyes and then they both stopped moving.

That was when Thomas felt it... *something was approaching.*

He had never felt anything like it before. He could almost hear it as it neared. It sounded like a heartbeat, but heavy and low. It made the very air around him vibrate with each beat as it grew closer and closer to the room.

Was it Nera? Thomas swallowed and prayed that it would be, and that she was coming to help them.

He tensed as the doorknob turned and the heavy wooden door slowly swung open.

It was not Nera. Instead, it was the tall one with the deep voice that boomed and frightened Thomas. This one hated him and Thomas knew it.

Baphomet entered the room with Lisa in tow, his eyes widening in shock as he took in the scene. Anger blasted through him as at first, he thought the creature kneeling beside his brother's mate had done this. But Lisa's voice was immediately in his mind saying, *No, my love. Look at him. He's crying. He's scared. I don't think he knows what's going on here anymore than you or I.*

Baphomet's eyes narrowed and he took an abrupt mental step back to reassess the scene. He let go of Lisa's hand for a moment and stepped out of the room. Out in the hallway, he yelled for help. It was only a moment more before a couple of Kurr came running, their hair all askew from sleeping and each one in night dress.

Baphomet pointed to one and ordered, "You, go fetch Hantsushept." Without waiting for a response, he turned to the other Kurr and ordered, "You, get in here and help." The first Kurr had already disappeared, off on his quest to fetch the Kurric physician, Hantsushept, as Baphomet and the second Kurr rushed back into the suite. As they entered the bedroom, Baphomet noticed his mate was crouching next to the boy creature and a part of him cringed at the thought of her being anywhere near it.

Then the boy-like creature looked up at Baphomet and softly asked, "C-can you help them?"

Baphomet felt the first stirrings of compassion for the thing as he nodded and said, "If they can be saved, we shall do it." He rushed over to Mikhail's side and knelt, reaching a hand out to grasp his brother's forehead. Focusing in on any activity within his brother's mind, Baphomet detected a faint whirling of vibration inside that seeped through as if it was concealed behind some sort of buffer Baphomet's mind couldn't breach. But the activity, whatever it was, meant Mikhail still lived and this was a great sign.

Lisa, having watched and learned from what her mate had done, immediately leaned forward to test for activity within Sarah's prone form. Amazingly, she caught it. It was very slight and, like Baphomet with Mikhail, she could not get a clear reading on the thoughts or whatever activity it was. Nevertheless, she could detect activity and that was what mattered.

"Sheely can't breathe," the creature kneeling next to Sarah said urgently to no one in particular. "She's dying!"

Baphomet tensed. He had lost five offspring with the

human, Lilith. He would be damned if he was going to allow anything to happen to Mikhail's daughter!

"Where is that damned physician?" he demanded, already rising and turning toward the door.

Just then, Hantsushept and two of his medical aides rushed in with the Kurr who had been sent to retrieve him. The physician initially headed for Mikhail's prone form, thinking to save what he knew as the head of the Lorim first. But Baphomet cut him off and redirected him toward Sarah.

"Take care of the child," he commanded. "It is what both of them would want."

Hantsushept wasted no time with argument. He turned and focused all of his attention on the fetus trapped within the unmoving form of its mother. "We shall have to move her to the clinic as quickly as possible. I do not have the equipment here needed to sustain the child once it is removed."

"You're going to take it?" Lisa asked incredulously.

"If she is to live," Hantsushept nodded.

Baphomet nodded once and moved toward Sarah, saying, "I shall carry Sarah and the others can carry Mikhail."

"Shouldn't we use our shields?" Lisa asked as she moved to make room for him by Sarah's side.

"I would rather you did not," Hantsushept immediately cautioned. "I could not tend to her during the flight and there are any number of things that could happen during transport. Please," he continued at their solemn stares, "let us make haste."

Baphomet bent and carefully picked up his new sister, uncaring of the blood now staining his clothing. Lisa grabbed hold of his upper arm, but didn't say anything. They had been separated physically too long now as it was. The others would be able to handle moving Mikhail's heavy form.

Lisa, Hantsushept and Thomas followed as Baphomet carried the unconscious form of his brother's mate through the house and then outside. The small group moved as one through the night with their precious cargo, making their way as quickly as possible to the small Medical Facility. Baphomet would have preferred to use his shields to get his sister to the Medical Facility more quickly, but Hantsushept had made a valid point about the many things that could go wrong while they were transporting her. Besides, Baphomet knew he wouldn't have been able to carry Lisa, Sarah, Hantsushept and the creature all at once. So they made their way through the dark night as quickly as possible, while even more Kurr ran ahead to ensure everything was prepared for their arrival.

Once there, intravenous lines were immediately installed into the arms of the two unconscious victims and the medical team went to work on both. Hantsushept never once left Sarah's side as he worked feverishly to rescue the suffocating fetus from within her. There appeared to be no signs of life coming from either of the bloodied bodies lying atop the stretchers at either end of the room, but no one was giving up yet.

Baphomet and Lisa watched in fear as the Kurr worked on Sarah, each of them wondering if the future of *their* unborn child was now being revealed in the scene playing out before them. Baphomet slid an arm around Lisa's shoulders and hugged her close. He would not allow anything to happen to her or to their baby. It simply would not happen!

The door to the operating room flung open unexpectedly and Suriyah strode into the room, frantically demanding, "Where is he?" It took all of two seconds for her to take in the scene before her and, without additional comment, she made her way over to where Mikhail lay.

Baphomet knew she would be able to help their brother with her Jinn healing abilities and he turned his attention back to what was going on with Sarah and the baby. A second later, a blinding light erupted from within the center of the table where Sarah lay as the fetal sack was opened. Everyone had to look away, but Hantsushept reached in anyway and retrieved the tiny fetus from within the womb.

"Clamp!" he barked and one of the attendees placed the metal device onto the umbilical cord just above the physician's hand and then another. Another attendee quickly brought forward a small blanket and wrapped the tiny glowing form of the baby in it until barely any light showed. Finally able to look upon the thing, Hantsushept cut the umbilical cord and then went to work getting the infant over to an incubator where he administered the remainder of the care the infant would need to survive its first moments outside its mother's womb.

The rest of the team continued working on Sarah and Mikhail without interruption.

The only sounds within the room were those made by the medical team. The baby did not cry. It looked completely blue, from what could be seen of it. There was no movement from either it, Mikhail or Sarah. Baphomet, Lisa, and the creature, Thomas, all sat unmoving as they watched and waited.

He's afraid, Lisa's voice said in Baphomet's mind. She meant the boy-creature sitting closer to the table where Sarah lay.

Baphomet was unused to playing the good guy, but he understood his mate obviously thought he should comfort the creature somehow. He hesitantly disengaged his arm from around her shoulders and stood. Approaching the boy, he reached out a hand and touched its smaller shoulder in what he hoped would be construed as a gesture of friendship.

Without warning, a brilliant flash of light speared through Baphomet's consciousness and he was momentarily overwhelmed with a flood of visions – strange places, even stranger creatures, and things he had never before encountered in his wildest dreams. It was too much to take in and Baphomet had to sever his connection. He broke away from the creature and gasped for air.

The creature itself appeared shocked by everything that had just flashed through both of their minds and it, too, gasped for air in great heaving breaths before, all of a sudden, it simply slumped and crumpled to the floor.

Baphomet stared in open-mouthed shock at the creature's unmoving form. It lay there, utterly motionless.

"What did you *do*?" Lisa asked, her voice quiet but stunned, as she crouched down next to the creature and stared. She didn't touch the child, but reached up and took Baphomet's hand in hers.

It took a moment, but then Baphomet shook his head and whispered brokenly, "I-I did *nothing*. He simply fell." They both stood stark still, their eyes trained on the still creature, waiting for it to awaken. It didn't.

Finally, one of Hantsushept's aides took notice of this new victim lying on the floor and rushed over to help. One look at the Kurr's face, however, as she detected no pulse, spoke volumes.

No one else said a thing as they continued with their work. The aide went for help and was soon directing another Kurr to carry the body toward another part of the Medical Facility. The rest of the team concentrated on the task at hand. There was no time to spare on thoughts of what could have happened to the one they all knew as Thomas. There were three lives to be saved this night. The boy was now gone. There was nothing they could do about that. The three struggling to stay alive were in this room and they needed all the attention they could get in order to make it through to sunlight.

Baphomet and Lisa returned to their seats, their thoughts mingling in each other's head as they waited for whatever else the night would bring.

***

Sarah pushed against the thick blue substance surrounding her. Was this water? It felt too thick to be water and she wasn't entirely sure it was liquid. All she knew was that it was everywhere. There didn't appear to be any end to it, either. Which way was up and which down, she did not know.

She was quickly running out of air as she held her breath and feared she would soon drown in the cloudy blue substance. She reached and kicked as forcefully as she could. She let out a mouthful of breath, hoping against hope she would be able to tell which direction the air bubbles went. Unfortunately, it appeared the dark, smoky-blue substance was gaseous, not liquid, and her breath was immediately swallowed by the thick cloud. So no help there.

Another minute passed and she frantically kicked out, waving her arms in desperation. Her chest ached and things were starting to go dark around the edge of her field of vision. She couldn't wait any longer.

Her breath gushed out of her and she greedily sucked in, expecting to choke. Instead, she found she could breathe. Even as thick as the substance was, it entered her lungs as if it was nothing more than regular air. She gulped in great lungsful of the substance, hoping it was not damaging, for Sheely needed oxygen as well.

Sarah ceased her struggling against the substance and allowed herself merely to float along through whatever current there was. She could not tell if there was movement or if she remained in stasis in the same place. She heard nothing other than her own breathing. There was nothing and no one around other than the blue, swirling substance in which she floated. It was utterly silent. The eeriness of the silence made her feel so alone that she shivered, a surge of fear streaking through her as she wondered if, like Alice, she had fallen into some hole nobody had been aware of and she was now stuck somewhere where no one would ever be able to find her.

That could happen, right? After all, there were definitely rifts between the human dimension and the Loric dimension that were known. Perhaps she had fallen through an as yet undiscovered rift into some other dimension.

She tested her voice, calling out hesitantly at first, but then strengthening the volume as she finally called out in a fierce cry, "Mikhail!" Over and over she cried out, hearing no echo and no response. The blue swirls of smoky substance swallowed her cries immediately, but she had to continue. She had no clue where she was, nor how she had gotten there. But she was bound and determined to find Mikhail so she and Sheely could get out of there.

After what seemed like hours or even days, with her voice cracking and her throat aching more with each new breath she took, Sarah finally caught what she thought was another voice. It came from what sounded like somewhere far off to her left, though there truly appeared to be no left or right or any other type of direction in the dense fog of the blue substance.

"Hello?" she called now. Her voice was hoarse and it cracked when she tried again, but she finally managed another cry. "Hello!"

"Sarah?" a male voice called from far off.

"Hello!" she called again, wishing she could find some way of moving toward the voice. It wasn't Mikhail's voice, but it sounded familiar. That's when it hit her. This was Gabriel's voice! "Gabriel?" she called out. "Gabriel! Where are you?"

"Sarah!" he cried, closer this time.

Sarah narrowed her eyes in search of his form. "I'm over here, Gabriel!" she called.

"Sarah!" He was really close, but still she could not see him.

"I'm here," she said more softly. She reached out, feeling with her hands for anything of substance. There was only the thick blue fog surrounding her. The space around her became warm and Sarah whipped around, reaching out all around her as she waved her arms, her fingers spread wide. Her heart rate increased and a current of fear raced down her spine. "Where are you?" she called.

"I am right here," Gabriel said.

Then Sarah felt his hands on her arms, the old familiar tingle of his energies racing up her limbs from where his skin came in contact with hers, working to calm her nerves a little. She still couldn't see him. Why couldn't she even see his hands on her arms?

"I can't see you," she said tremulously.

"You have to concentrate to see anything," he said.

Sarah looked down at the spot on her left arm where she could feel his hand touching her and she focused. Instantly, his fingers and then his entire hand appeared. She reached up and grabbed hold of his hand, taking it in both of hers. With just a little more concentration, she found she could see his arms, his chest and shoulders, and then, finally, his head and face.

A smile of utter relief flashed briefly across her features as she threw both arms around his neck and hugged him, squeezing fiercely. Her heart was still racing, but she at least had someone familiar with her now.

"Where are we?" she asked as she pulled back from him. She didn't let go of her hold on him, but she did manage to put a little space between them in case he should be overwhelmed by her energies.

"I do not know," he said honestly. "I cannot recall how I came to be in this place. The last thing I recall is sitting at a table outside a small café near the hotel where I was staying in London. Past that, everything is a blur."

Sarah thought for a minute. She remembered writing in her new blog. Did she finish the entry? Yes. Yes, she did finish and she had emailed her siblings. What did she do then? There was no recollection there at all. She remembered sending the emails. Did she turn off the computer? She did not know. It was as if someone had come in and erased everything that had happened after she had sent the emails.

"Are you okay?" Gabriel finally asked.

"Y-Yes," Sarah stammered. "I'm just freakin' out 'cause I have no clue where we are and I can't seem to get in touch with Mikhail."

Gabriel's eyes narrowed in confusion and he said, "Sarah, Mikhail is right here." He motioned just to his left.

Sarah saw no one there, only the thick blue mist. She concentrated as she reached out, searching with her hand for her mate. "Mikhail?" she called, her throat seriously raw now. "Mikhail, I can't see you! Mikhail!" Not only could she not see him, she could not feel him near her either.

"What do you mean, you 'cannot see or hear her'?" Gabriel asked of no one in particular. "She is right here holding onto my arm."

"Can you see him?" Sarah asked, her voice urgent.

Gabriel turned his attention back to her and nodded, explaining, "He is immediately to my left, but it appears he is unable to see or hear you as well." He thought for a moment and then shook his head. "This must be some type of dimensional shift, I think."

Sarah gave him a look of utter confusion and he continued. "For some reason, I am able to see and hear both of you, but the two of you must be in slightly separate dimensions and, therefore, are unable to detect one another."

Sarah didn't understand how such a thing could be possible, but she wasn't about to argue with him. "So how do we get back to the same dimension?" she asked instead.

Gabriel shook his head and then held up a staying hand in the direction in which he had said Mikhail was located, saying, "Yes, yes." He turned more fully toward Sarah and said, "He wants to know how you and Sheely are doing."

Sarah took a deep breath to calm her nerves as she looked down to where Sheely's glow could regularly be seen shining through the skin on Sarah's lower abdomen. There was no glow. There was nothing. Immediately, Sarah raked up the hem of her shirt, exposing the skin underneath. She felt along her midriff, but there was no extra warmth there. A cry escaped her now-raw throat and she bent over to get a closer look at her own abdomen, desperately searching for the familiar little light that should be showing through there.

"Sheely!" she wailed. "Sheely!"

Gabriel's eyes widened and he immediately took her in his arms.

"Sheely!" Sarah cried. "Sheely!"

"I do not know!" Gabriel barked, supposedly to Mikhail. "There is nothing there." He hugged Sarah close, rubbing his hands up and down her back and arms.

Sarah sobbed and continued screaming out, "Sheely!" with every new breath she drew. She let him hug her, but it was of little comfort. "Sheely!" she wailed.

Gabriel just held her, soothing her with his hands and whispering "It is all right. Everything is going to be all right," to her again and again.

Eventually, Sarah's throat was too raw to make even the tiniest of whispers and she merely leaned her forehead against the hot wall of Gabriel's chest and let the flow of her tears continue unchecked. After what seemed an eternity, she whispered as best she could through her hiccoughs, "T-Tell him she's g-gone."

Gabriel hesitated only a moment before looking over to what still looked like empty space to Sarah and saying simply, "She says to tell you Sheely is gone."

Sarah heard no response, no noise at all other than Gabriel's and her own breathing. If Mikhail wept, she could not comfort him. If he had questions, she could not hear them to answer, not that she would know the answers, anyway.

Gabriel continued holding her, soothing her with his soft words and his gentle hands. "We shall get through this," he told her.

Sarah felt empty inside and could only tighten her grip on his arms as her tears continued to flow. What difference did it make? She and Mikhail were in separate dimensions and now Sheely was gone and there was no way she could get back to Thomas. Everything, it seemed, had been taken from her and she couldn't even remember how it had happened or why. The calamity of the situation was simply too much and her mind fell blank.

Closing her eyes, she allowed a waiting sweet oblivion to claim her consciousness.

***

Azra'il raced as fast as his shields would carry him. He had instructed his team to go to the place on the map where he showed them he had detected the two human energy tethers, but there they were to remain, hiding without taking any action until Azra'il rejoined them. For the moment, he was not concerned with the humans, nor even with Sarah Baker.

The old Kurr, Garnabiel, never did tell him which of his siblings was in mortal danger, but Azra'il wasn't the type to wait around to figure things out. If he could stop one of his siblings from dying, he was bloody well going to do so. He concentrated on the strongest energy source he could find as he whizzed through the night sky, hoping beyond hope that he would arrive in time to save whichever one it was. A complex of buildings finally came into view on the darkened landscape below him and he lowered himself upon his approach, searching for the source of the main energy concentration.

The difficulty with him showing up out of the blue was that he might not be welcomed by whomever was there when he arrived. Azra'il decided he should remain hidden within his shields up until the point when he could determine what needed to be done and for whom. As he approached, he could feel the strongest concentration of energy coming from a three-storied building off to his left and he lowered to it, slowing his speed as he penetrated the walls of the building, passing through room after room on each floor until he came upon a very crowded room on the lowest level, where he nearly revealed his presence in his shock.

There, lying on one gurney to his right was Mikhail, though very little of his brother showed through in the visage of the creature lying on the tall, thin hospital bed. This thing was unbelievably powerful and had a glow of energy radiating off it to such a degree that Azra'il nearly had to look away to keep it from hurting his eyes. Its hair was snow white and long, hanging limply off the edges of the table to nearly touch the floor.

Across the room, on another tall gurney, lay what might once have been the human Sarah Baker. The creature there very much resembled Mikhail's figure, except that it was much smaller in stature. There was a tremendous amount of blood covering both creatures and Azra'il wondered what on earth could have happened to two such powerful beings to put them into such a state.

Off to his left sat two more glowing creatures and Azra'il was momentarily stunned as he realized the larger of these two was his brother Baphomet, who had been banished from Lorim City nearly fifteen millennia ago. The female sitting with him looked to be the same type of creature as Baphomet, though her skin carried a dark pigmentation to it that suggested she was of a different race.

To his right, Azra'il noticed Suriyah, his sister, diligently working on Mikhail's form. Her Jinn healing abilities were the most legendary in the Loric Realm. Azra'il watched in fascination as she touched their brother here or there, instructing the aides working with her as to where to concentrate their efforts or how to proceed with patching up the throat.

He became a bit nervous, but instantly stilled as Baphomet and the female sitting with him suddenly looked with brightly-glowing white eyes directed right at the spot where Azra'il was hiding over by the wall. After only a moment's concentration, the two looked away and Azra'il was able to relax a little again as he watched and waited. He noticed an older male Kurr working over in the far corner of the room and decided to move closer to get a better look at what was going on there. Once he approached, he felt a sickeningly strong pull on his energies and was stunned yet again as he looked at what the Kurr was doing.

There, in what looked to be an incubator of some kind, was an infant. But this was no ordinary infant. This thing had no tether. No. All of its soul energy resided already within its tiny little body and *it* was what was pulling on his energies, he was certain! The glow alone coming off the child would have confirmed that it housed the entirety of its own soul. But the energy emitting from within its small form could be felt a mile away and Azra'il stared in amazement at the tiny bundle. It made not one sound, but Azra'il could both feel *and* hear its frequencies and tones, and it sent chills up and down his spine just being this close to the little energy-sucking bundle in the blanket.

As he watched the male Kurr touching the creature, a strange feeling overcame him and Azra'il had to mentally restrain himself from reaching forward to physically knock the Kurr aside so that he could take the child up into his own arms to care for it. Was he *crazy*? This thing, he didn't even know what it was or where it had come from and he could still feel it pulling on his own energies. The thing might suck him dry if he were to touch it. What on earth was he thinking believing he could survive touching it, let alone to be able to give it better care than the medical professional currently tending to it? To that end, why he should even care?

Shaking his head to clear his thoughts, Azra'il decided to put some distance between the alien-looking infant and himself and quickly returned to the farthest point on the other side of the room from it. From there he would be able to keep an eye on everyone and everything that was going on. He pulled his shields more tightly around himself and settled in against the wall to wait.

That was when he realized that Israfil and Djibril were both missing from the assemblage and he wondered where the remaining two of his siblings might be. Perhaps they had not taken refuge with Mikhail and the human, Sarah Baker – if she could be called human anymore. Azra'il supposed it was possible his other two siblings had chosen a different path and had finally learned the error of their ways in trusting Mikhail. If that was the case, then Azra'il would happily allow them back into Lorim City immediately, assuming they agreed to follow his command.

He missed them all so much. Just being in this room with the three siblings he had forced himself not to think about made him want to reveal himself. He wanted to help. He wanted to be a part of their family once more. *He* felt like the outsider, when it was *they* who had transgressed. Why should he feel ashamed as if *he* had done something wrong, when it was *they* who had broken the One Law, *they* who had defied the Designers' decrees?

But he couldn't help it. A yearning so deep within him sprang to life, urging him forward and clawing for release with such an intensity that Azra'il was not certain he would be able to resist it. As he stood there against the wall struggling against the urge to drop his shields to alert them all to his presence, he realized he simply could not do it. He could not reveal himself to them.

The realization settled upon his shoulders similar to the weight of the world settling upon those of Atlas. He had a function to perform here and he would perform it with as much integrity as was housed within his soul, no matter the emotional cost to himself. The people of Lorim City were counting on him to ensure no humans remained within the Loric realm and that justice was done to those who had created the chaos within their dimension in the first place. Azra'il would not let them down.

He pulled from his massive well of will power and fought the temptation to reveal himself, finally defeating it as he slumped back against the wall once more. When all of this was over and he returned to Lorim City, then and only then would he finally sit down and take out his feelings to examine them. Only then would he deal with his guilt and loneliness. Only then would he deal with the fact that he would forever more be the one remaining Lori in Lorim City, alone, for his siblings had chosen to abandon the righteous path and, therefore, had abandoned Azra'il.

***

Baphomet started as he suddenly remembered the reason why he and Lisa had ventured over to the main house this night and turned to Lisa to see if she could detect any signs of Israfil nearby. She concentrated a moment, but then shook her head and narrowed her eyes in confusion. Where could their most trusted brother be?

Their minds were instantly refocused on the room, however, as movement and a strangled gasp from their right caught everyone's attention. Mikhail was regaining consciousness and Baphomet stood to get a closer look. He wished he knew how to heal so that he could help, but he was Shaitan. He knew nothing about healing.

Then Mikhail's thoughts came to him and he was momentarily swamped with random thoughts and visions. It was difficult to make out anything with any clarity and Baphomet was glad that Lisa came to lend her strength, both physically and mentally. As he relied on her to help him remain upright, Mikhail's whizzing thoughts and visions brought on a temporary wave of dizziness that nearly caused him to lose his balance and fall. Fortunately, Lisa was also somehow able to buffer the amount of information coming at him so quickly from within Mikhail's now wide-open mind, and Baphomet was soon able to get enough of a grip on the situation that he was able to sort through at least some of what was swimming around inside Mikhail's brain.

"He has been with Djibril, but I cannot tell where," Baphomet said as he sifted through the thoughts. Several of the others stopped to watch as they waited for more information from him. Finally, he shook his head and said, "It is too muddled. I cannot decipher the images. They are all of some dark place and there is much fear associated with it and an overwhelming sadness." The others returned silently to their individual tasks, each wrapped in his or her own thoughts.

Mikhail jerked all of a sudden and gasped. His eyes sprang open wide and he grunted. In a flash, he was struggling with those attending him as his eyes frantically searched around the room. "S-Sarah!" he rasped, his damaged throat allowing only the slightest whisper to escape.

"Calm yourself!" Suriyah commanded, but it was all for naught and he continued his fight.

His attendees raced to control the IVs still attached to his arms as Mikhail bolted off the table, nearly falling directly to the hard tile flooring as he finally spied Sarah from the corner of his eye. He catapulted across the room to where her blood-covered form lay unmoving on the other gurney. Those attending *her* quickly moved out of Mikhail's way as he reached her and grabbed hold of her hand and held it to his lips. "Sarah," he whispered. He could barely stand due to the amount of blood he, himself, had lost, but he didn't pay any attention to that. Instead, he merely stared in rapt concentration at her and the glow emitting from within his eyes appeared strangely subdued as he silently wept for his mate.

He looked down at the place where his offspring had been before this whole ordeal had begun. One hand reached out to touch the area he and Sarah had come to know as Sheely's spot and a sob tore from within him. He collapsed onto his knees beside the table, burying his face against his mate's side as he sobbed.

Just then, a peculiar sound reached him and he jerked to attention. He looked around, searching for the source of the sound, and that's when he saw Hantsushept. A glimmer of fearful hope sprang to life within his eyes as he stood, releasing Sarah's hand and cautiously approaching the incubator where Hantsushept worked with two other Kurr.

A gush of breath rushed from his lips as he beheld his daughter for the first time in his life and the pain in his chest became so great he thought he would die right there on the spot. She was so small. He reached to touch her, but Hantsushept pushed his hand away. Mikhail immediately made to protest, but the old physician would have none of it. "You may hold her after we are done, my Lord. We must ensure it is safe and that she is in stable condition before anyone handles her," he announced. "For reasons I cannot understand, she is still alive and I mean to keep her so."

Hesitating only a moment, Mikhail nodded, for he knew the Kurr was right. He stood back, watching while Hantsushept and his two assistants continued working on his daughter. After a moment, he decided it would be best if he returned to Sarah's side until the physician informed him everything was okay with Sheely. He could hear her breathing, so that was what was important. He *couldn't* hear Sarah, however, and that was more frightening than anything.

He took Sarah's hand in his again and looked around for somewhere to sit. One of the attending Kurr pushed a stool right up behind him and he gave her a tremulous smile of thanks as he settled down onto it next to Sarah's limp form. She was so cold, so much more so than normal, and her body felt lifeless. There were tubes stuck in her everywhere and she was almost completely covered in blood. There were nasty gashes all over her throat. The team worked furiously to repair the damaged tissue, though it appeared a few had already healed somewhat on their own.

This was a good sign, Mikhail told himself. If her body was still healing itself, it meant death had not yet gotten a grip on her. He hoped that reasoning made sense. He wished he could communicate with her to let her know that Sheely lived. Wherever they had been, Mikhail recalled Djibril informing him that Sarah had said Sheely was gone. The agony of that moment would remain with Mikhail for the rest of his days.

He had prayed for death when Djibril had told him the

news and yet, he had suddenly found himself alive and awake back in the Loric realm. Now, with no clue as to where Djibril and Sarah were, or how they had even gotten there, Mikhail could only wait and hope that Sarah would somehow find her way back and pull through.

He thought of what he had been doing just before he found himself in that strange alternate dimension, but he still could not recall anything of any significance. He knew he had been monitoring Djibril and that Sarah had gone off to work on her new blog, but that was as far as his mind went. Past that, there was only darkness until he had come to in that alternate dimension with Djibril. He had no idea how long they had been there before Djibril had heard Sarah's calls, nor how long Sarah had been there before they had found her. He just wished she would wake up now.

As Mikhail rubbed his lips across the back of Sarah's hand, Hantsushept suddenly announced the all clear where Sheely was concerned and Mikhail left his mate once again as he went to hold his daughter for the very first time.

She was so tiny, so fragile, and Mikhail worried that he would drop her. He listened carefully as an aide instructed him on the proper manner in which to hold an infant. She placed Sheely's tightly bundled form into his arms and then stepped back out of the way. Mikhail gazed down upon the most beautiful face he had ever encountered in his very long life. Surprisingly, two very bright ice-blue eyes stared right back up at him, as if Sheely knew who he was and couldn't wait to get a look at him. Mikhail didn't think newborn infants were able to see – especially those who were born so prematurely. But her eyes were definitely open and she stared quietly up at him, looking him directly in the eyes.

"Hello, my beautiful daughter," Mikhail finally whispered. "I am your father."

Sheely blinked and yawned, then went back to staring up at him. For a moment, Mikhail thought he had heard someone from the other side of the room make a sound like that of a gasp of surprise and he cautiously turned to see who it was. He saw no one there, however, and turned back toward Sarah, walking the short distance over to where she still lay on the hospital gurney. He tilted his shoulders so that Sheely would be able to see Sarah's form and whispered, "See her? That is your mother."

Again, Sheely blinked and then went back to staring up at him. She didn't make a sound, not even mentally. But Mikhail could hold her now, could feel her and protect her and he knew she would be okay. He bent to gently rub his nose against her little cheek and inhaled her scent. She smelled of vanilla, it seemed to him, and he smiled as he straightened back up. Her bright ice-blue eyes were still focused on his face, though she yawned again.

Mikhail took the seat next to Sarah once more and just stared down at his daughter. She stared right back up at him. Sarah had to wake up now. Their daughter needed her. Mikhail prayed to whatever beings in the Universe that controlled these things that this would be the case.

Those watching the scene quietly wiped tears from their eyes. All this time, none of them had believed anything like this could even be possible. But here sat Mikhail, holding his daughter, as he watched and waited for the medical team to perform whatever miracles they could to bring Sarah back from the brink of death.

Even Azra'il, who still stood silently against the wall on the other side of the room hidden from view, wiped away moisture that welled and then spilled from his eyes as he watched his sibling. He wished he knew what had happened here, as the feeling that what he had thought was going on just might not turn out to be reality after all, set in. The one thing he did know was that he was going to stick around until he discovered the truth of this matter, starting with whose child it really was that Mikhail held, for Azra'il still could not bring himself to believe the creature was actually Mikhail's offspring, for that would mean...

Chapter 2

The blue swirling substance remained quiet and flowing as Djibril held Sarah close, even though she had been asleep for what felt like a very long time. He hated to admit it, especially since Mikhail was sure to be lurking about somewhere nearby, fully capable of listening in on his thoughts, but Djibril truly enjoyed feeling needed by someone, even if that someone didn't belong to him. It wasn't that he was fantasizing about Sarah, but the idea of having a mate who needed him as Sarah so obviously needed someone right now was almost more than Djibril could bear thinking about.

He sighed heavily as he realized the bent his thoughts had taken and he decided he had best talk with Mikhail to let him know what was going on before his brother got the wrong impression. "Mikhail?" he softly called. "Mikhail?" When there was still no response, he called out a little louder, "Mikhail, where are you?"

Sarah stirred against his chest and he quit calling to his brother for fear of disturbing her further. Where could his brother be?

Sarah stirred against him again, hugging him tighter as she rubbed her face against his chest. Then she frowned as the tones coming from him suddenly registered and she woke, pulling back a bit, looking around for something. She must not have found whatever it was she was looking for because she sighed and finally looked up at him. "How long have I been asleep?" she asked as recognition finally set in, her hoarse voice barely above a whisper.

"A while."

She blinked a few times. "Did anything happen while I was out?"

"I do not know that anything *could* happen here, wherever here is." Immediately after he had spoken, he regretted the thoughtless comment. One very big thing had already happened.

She was silent for a few minutes, and then she asked, "Is Mikhail still okay?"

Djibril hesitated. She had already lost Sheely. If he suddenly told her he could no longer detect Mikhail's presence, it might send her over the edge again, if not worse. "I will ask," he finally said, deciding on deception for her sake. He could always tell her later that Mikhail had suddenly disappeared. For the now, however, he was going to make her feel safe and secure. "Mikhail," he said, pretending, "Sarah wants to know if you are well." He waited for a response that would never come, pretending to be listening to his brother's voice. "He says he is well and that he loves you very much," he finally told her. He didn't enjoy lying to her. He just didn't want to see her suffer anymore.

She closed her eyes for a moment, her shoulders slumped and her head bowed.

The blue substance swirled silently around them, creating an impenetrable wall of silence, cocooning them within it.

Sarah still held onto one of his hands and Djibril gave her much smaller hand a gentle squeeze. "Did Mikhail ever tell you about the time he and Baphomet decided they were going to see if Lorim could use their shields to go beyond the atmosphere of the planet?" he asked.

Sarah slowly shook her head.

Djibril regaled her with story after story for the next few hours of the adventures he had experienced with his siblings. He would stop every now and then to pretend he was conversing with Mikhail, asking questions and even arguing with his absent sibling in order to make his performance more believable. Whatever it took to keep her calm was what he did.

Sarah asked but a few questions. Mostly, though, she simply held Djibril's hand and listened, her face a mask of barely-concealed sadness. After a while, she said, "I wonder how long we've been here."

"I cannot tell," he said. "It could have been any length of time. The time difference between the human dimension and the Loric dimension is remarkably noticeable when traveling from one to the other, I know. What passes as a day in the Loric realm, for example, spans the space of several days in the human realm. What interests me more than how long we have been here, however, is how we came to be here in the first place and where exactly *here* is."

Sarah sighed in frustration. "I'd like to know the answers to those questions, myself," she said. "I've tried my darnedest to remember what I was doin' just before I woke up to discover I was in this place. But it's like somebody just came along and vacuumed those memories right out of my head." She thought about it some more and then shook her head, saying, "I still can't figure out why Mikhail's stuck in a different part than me, either, or why you can see an' hear him an' I can't." Her lower lip quivered and tears pooled on the rims of the bottoms of her eyes as her thoughts turned again toward Sheely.

Djibril took her in his arms again, gently squeezing her shoulders and laying his cheek atop her head. "I do not know, either," he told her softly. "But I promise you, we *will* find a way out of this place. We shall discover the answers to all our questions and then we shall find ourselves back where we belong. We just have to stick together and have faith."

Sarah pulled back a little to look up at him, a slight smile playing at the corners of her lips as she softly said, "You know, I've never really had much experience with faith."

"Well," he said, smiling warmly down at her, "we shall have to see about changing that for you."

She quietly chuckled, but then her eyes grew serious once more and a little frown formed between her brows as she whispered, "Thank you, Gabriel."

"For what are you thanking me, my dear sister?" he asked seriously.

She blinked and then smiled and said, "For bein' such a good brother, such a good friend. I don't know how I could've made it this long without you. You've been my rock, an' if that man of mine hasn't told you how much you're appreciated yet, you should threaten him within an inch of his life because I think you've been just wonderful."

He gave her a lop-sided smile, nodded and blinked back his own tears, feeling guilty for his deception now. "You are very welcome, Sarah," he finally told her.

Sarah's smile actually reached her eyes and she placed a hand onto Djibril's chest in her gratitude. Then, as she happened to glance at the ring she wore on the third finger of that hand, her smile was suddenly replaced by a deep and worrisome frown.

***

Mikhail sat next to the bed where Sarah lay. Sheely was tucked up close to his chest in one arm, sleeping peacefully, while Mikhail held onto Sarah's limp, cold hand with his other hand. He tried not to look at her face too often because of all the bandages and tubes sticking out everywhere there. It made for a pretty gruesome scene so he chose to concentrate on the little hand he held.

He'd never felt so useless.

The wounds on her throat had healed by now, but she was still having difficulty breathing. Hantsushept had informed him that was probably due to blood in her lungs. He had said it was just a small amount and that it should clear up on its own over time. Mikhail had no choice but to take the Kurr's word for it. Suriyah was working right alongside the old physician and had been since Mikhail had come back to sit beside Sarah. If anyone could heal Sarah, Mikhail knew it would be Suri.

Of course, Suriyah wasn't the only one of his siblings there. Baphomet and Lisa had not left since Mikhail had awakened. They still sat along the back wall holding hands, just waiting.

As Mikhail sent a grateful glance their way, Lisa nodded toward the quiet little bundle he held and softly said, "She's beautiful."

Mikhail looked down onto the face of his new daughter. Sheely was the epitome of an Angel, even in sleep. There was a glow about her that made a body feel all warm inside when one looked at her. He smiled as he looked back over at Lisa, whispering, "I think she is getting stronger."

"Of course she is," Baphomet intoned quietly. "She is my niece."

Mikhail's smile widened.

Miriam, who had appeared earlier and had been silently sitting a short distance along the wall from where Baphomet and Lisa sat, now rose to come and collect Sheely from Mikhail. He disliked having to hand her over to anyone else, but he was still very weak from his ordeal and still didn't know how long it would be before Sarah's condition improved enough that he could stop worrying about her. Sheely didn't even stir as the old Kurr took her from her position against his chest.

"Thank you both for being here," Mikhail softly said to Baphomet and his mate after the old maid had gone.

Lisa gave a caring smile while Baphomet merely nodded once.

After a couple of minutes, Mikhail said, "You do not have to stay here. I am sure you must be exhausted after sitting here for such a long time."

Baphomet and Lisa exchanged confused glances and then Baphomet explained, "We are fine. It has only been a couple of hours, though *you* should probably get some rest."

"What has been only a couple of hours?" Mikhail asked in confusion.

"Since we found the two of you," Baphomet said.

Mikhail frowned. He had spent what felt like days in the blue dimension with Djibril before his brother had even heard Sarah calling out. Then, they had all been semi-united for what had seemed like at least another full day, if not longer. "So no one thought to check in on Sarah and me for the past few days?" he asked, his ire rising. He was glad Miriam had taken Sheely from him, for he was certain the sudden pounding of his heart against his rib cage would have awakened her.

Again, Baphomet and Lisa exchanged confused looks. "Mikhail," Baphomet said carefully, "according to your staff, you were last seen about three hours ago, just before they turned in for the night. Thomas told us he had only just discovered the two of you mere minutes before Lisa and I came on the scene." After a brief pause, he continued, repeating, "It has only been a couple of hours since we first discovered you."

Mikhail gazed off at something only he could see as his thoughts captured his attention. The old maid Miriam returned and silently reclaimed the seat she had occupied earlier.

Baphomet ignored the old Kurr, instead leaning closer to Mikhail, cocking his head to the side and softly asking, "How long was it where you were?"

Mikhail whipped his gaze back to his brother and frowned. After a couple of seconds, he nodded and said, "A lot longer."

Baphomet nodded. Lisa looked a little confused for a moment, but then her face cleared as understanding dawned with the onset of Baphomet's thoughts in her mind.

"Were you alone there?" Baphomet asked.

"No," Mikhail said. "Djibril was there and, after a while, he claimed to hear Sarah. From the conversations I heard on my side of things, she was there with Djibril in some way as well. But I could not see or hear her." He paused a few minutes and then said in a low voice, "The last thing I remember was Djibril comforting her because she could no longer sense Sheely. Then I awoke here."

Suriyah's head popped up suddenly and she asked, "Djibril was with you?"

Three pairs of eyes swung around to look at her. Mikhail frowned and nodded.

Suriyah's gaze dropped off, falling to the floor as tears welled in her eyes.

"Suri?" Baphomet asked hesitantly.

The tears overflowed as she looked back up at them and swallowed a heavy lump in her throat. "Just before I returned," she explained, "I had a vision in which I saw one of our brothers die in the human realm. I could not tell from the images I received which one was involved. But if what you say is true, then that can only mean…" Her voice trailed off as they all drew the same conclusion.

Baphomet and Lisa exchanged a sad look. "Baphomet felt something was wrong," Lisa said quietly around the tears forming in her eyes, "but we couldn't figure out what it could be. When Iz didn't come to check to see what was troubling us, we *knew* something was wrong. That's why we went to the Main House in the first place, to see if perhaps Iz had gone there. We heard Thomas' screams even from outside and we rushed in." She turned to look at Mikhail and continued, saying, "The two of you were lying on the floor of your bedroom with blood all over because you had each clawed so hard at your own throats."

Mikhail frowned as he worked to piece together the puzzle as to what had happened. "Why would we have clawed at our throats?" he finally asked.

"For that matter," Baphomet asked, "where do you think Djibril could be? I mean, might he also have clawed at his own throat as well, since he was in this other dimension where you and Sarah were?"

"I think wherever Djibril is found, we will also find..." Suriyah just stopped there. No one wanted to think about the fact that Israfil was most likely the one Suriyah had seen in her vision.

After a moment, Mikhail spoke, declaring, "As soon as Sarah is safe, we shall all go to find them both." All three of the others solemnly nodded in agreement. "Until then," Mikhail continued, "I need to make sure things here are okay." He turned to Miriam, saying, "Please inform my son that I am recovered and that I would like to see him immediately."

"Brother," Baphomet said, but then he paused. Lisa tightened her grip on his hand and gave him a reassuring nod when he turned his gaze on her. He swallowed hard and took a deep breath before returning his gaze to his brother's face. "The creat – your *son...* he is gone," he quietly said.

Mikhail frowned. "Gone?" he asked, his face a mask of confusion.

Baphomet prepared himself for a fight and then said, "Dead."

Mikhail's jaw dropped in his astonishment before he

finally recovered enough to speak. "And you waited *this long* to inform me of this?" he demanded.

"He collapsed almost immediately after we managed to get the two of you moved here from the main house," Baphomet explained. Mikhail was clearly enraged and Baphomet demanded, "What would you have done had you known earlier? There was nothing any of us could do. He was gone and we had to make sure Sheely and you and Sarah were safe."

His world now completely upside down, Mikhail fought for control. "H-How?" he brokenly asked.

This was the part that shook Baphomet. Mikhail would be sure to believe the Shaitan King had killed the creature as revenge for what Mikhail had done to Suriyah and him millennia ago. But Baphomet knew he could not lie to his brother. "I touched him."

Mikhail merely frowned. The words made no sense in his mind.

"He was frightened," Baphomet continued. "I tried to comfort him. That was all – I swear it. But the moment I touched him, it was like a whole universe opened in both of our minds and, when I pulled away, he simply fell to the floor and was gone."

Mikhail was silent. This was too much. First, he and Sarah had lost Sheely. Then he wakes to find that Sheely is alive, but Sarah may not survive. And now he discovers that his son, and probably his brother, are dead? It was too much!

Out of the blue, a name popped into his mind. Nera.

Nera had told Mikhail and Sarah she was some kind of protector to Thomas. Surely, she would not have allowed him to die! Had she taken him – taken his soul? She could do something like that, right?

Mikhail had to believe that Nera had something to do with what had happened to Thomas. It was a crazy idea – unfathomable, even. But whatever the case, it was a string of hope in an otherwise impossibly bleak day and Mikhail would take whatever he could get. He might not know *where* his son was, but he had faith in the idea that Nera would.

The question was why. Why would she wait until this

happened to take him? What significance did that hold? Nera had told Sarah and him precious little about why she was here, nor what she connection there was between Thomas and her. But Mikhail had at least thought Thomas' presence here was tied in some way to Sarah. Did Thomas' disappearance mean Sarah might not recover? Mikhail's heart set up a rhythm beating triple-time as this thought gripped his mind.

A warm hand grasping his shoulder suddenly brought him out of his reverie as Baphomet stood next to him and softly said, "Have faith, my brother. She *will* pull through this."

Mikhail remembered the last time something this bad had happened. Sarah had nearly died then. He had wanted to die then, too, the pain had been so great. There had been Thomas to consider then. Now there was Sheely. Almost as if she had read his thoughts, the faithful old Kurr Miriam stood and went to the door of the room. Another Kurr was there with Sheely. Miriam gently took the newborn and brought her back over to him.

He took the little bundle in his arms again and drew her close. She didn't even stir. Mikhail bent and buried his nose inside the blanket covering her tiny form. She now smelled like Sarah, he noticed. Pulling back again, he studied her. He could see the light from her natural glow and he wondered how something so small could contain so much energy without burning itself out.

She was so very beautiful. He bent to place a tender kiss upon her tiny forehead. She had only been out in the world for such a short time, but she already held his heart around her tiny fingers. But he could *not* raise Sheely on his own. Sarah *had* to return from that awful blue place. She simply had to. Sheely needed *both* of her parents.

Mikhail adjusted the sleeping child in his arms and returned to his former position, taking Sarah's limp, unmoving hand in his again as Sheely slept soundly against his chest. There was nothing coming from Sarah's mind. She may as well have been a billion miles away. "Please come back to me, my love," he whispered. "Our daughter needs us both more than ever now."

Suriyah went back to her position at the head of the bed so she could continue working to break through to Sarah on a psychic level. Baphomet returned to his position along the wall beside Lisa. The Kurr, Miriam, merely sat watching them all in silence.

Not one of them were any the wiser to the stunned and suddenly quite frightened Azra'il standing nearby watching all of them.

Chapter 3

Everything was all set. The bodies in the underground parking structure had been stripped of all identification, any personal effects, and especially any copies of the Qur'an. The burning of those was the most cherished part of the job to the black-clad figure. All that was left now was to move the one here in the stairwell into the same area as the others, clean his body of anything and everything, and then quit the scene.

Squatting down to better search the body's pockets, the black-clothed figure paused half-way through its task. There was no identification of any kind on this one. A quick check in the shoes revealed nothing, either. A deep frown formed on the brow beneath the black hood covering the figure's head. Suddenly, a sound caught the figure's attention. It was an odd, pitiful sound and the figure leaned forward toward the corpse's head.

This was no corpse. The bastard was still alive!

The black-clothed figure whipped out the jade-handled katana again, ready to do what had obviously not been taken care of properly the first time. But then the idea to look upon the man's face, to touch it with one's bare hand, struck the mind of the black bandit. After a lengthy pause during which the figure merely stared with intensity at the man's body, the katana was re-sheathed and the bandit's gloves were slowly removed. Moving cautiously, the figure removed the nearly-dead man's own hood to gaze upon what had to be the strangest creature the figure had ever beheld. The man's skin actually appeared to glow, even though the man himself was unconscious.

The urge to touch that glowing skin became too powerful and so the figure reached its left hand out. A millisecond later, the black bandit jerked the hand back, as a tingling sensation unlike anything the figure had ever experienced danced up the arm of the hand that had touched the man. In a flash, the little figure had whipped off its black hood, uncaring that the long, braided red ponytail flopped suddenly onto the filthy ground.

On the other side of the stairwell, hiding in the shadows, the one watching in secret nearly gasped aloud at his first sight of the fiery red hair and alabaster skin of the beauty crouching over his injured brother. His eyes narrowed as the beautiful young woman reached to touch his brother's face again. Her skin glowed with far more than mere health. She had much too much soul-energy radiating from within and the watcher knew what he was witnessing. He pulled his shields more closely about his frame, his eyes riveted to the scene. He would stay until he was sure his brother would be safe.

The young woman crouching beside the body that struggled for each breath touched a device on her throat and quietly said, "Lyss, I need you to get down here now!" She reached out to the body's neck, barely allowing her fingertips to touch the skin. When another hooded, black-clad figure silently appeared at the base of the stairs, she turned and said, "Help me get this one upstairs. He's coming with us."

The new arrival whipped off the masked hood of her outfit and the unseen one watching from the shadows *did* gasp aloud. They were identical twins!

The two young women stilled instantly as their keen senses picked up on the noise. They both stared without even seeming to breathe for the longest time, and the watcher feared that either he would be discovered or that the two young women would pass out from a lack of oxygen. When no further sounds came from the shadowy stairwell, the new arrival turned back toward the one bending over the body. "Chris," she quietly said, "this is not part of the plan. We've got a flight to catch in less than two hours. Clean the bodies, *all of them*, and let's get out of here as planned."

"Lyss, you don't understand," the one named Chris said. "This one has to come with us."

"Why?" Lyss demanded.

Chris stared at her. She couldn't explain and so she simply shrugged, shaking her head.

"So, what? We're just going to waltz onto the plane with a dead body?" Lyss snapped. Then she jerked back in sudden shock as the body lying beneath her twin softly gasped. "You didn't *kill* him?" she demanded. "Why the fuck didn't you kill him?"

"I thought I had done!" Chris snapped at her sister. "The blade struck true, even got stuck in his spine."

"Then how's he still breathing?"

Shaking her head, Chris explained, "The only thing I can think of is that the cut was so clean that everything was able to continue functioning and even some healing was able to get started. I mean, look at the wound on his neck."

Lyss came forward finally, sighing in frustration, and checked out the wound on the man's neck. The skin there was red and puckered, like an angry keloid scar, but it didn't appear the cut had been very deep, and certainly not all the way through to the spine. "What, did you garrote him?" she asked.

"No," Chris snapped again. "I told you. My blade sliced right through to the bone. It even got stuck there and I had to jerk it out."

Lyss looked at the wound again and raised her eyebrows. "Well, it's the damnedest thing I've ever seen," she said. "Did he have any identification on him?"

"Nah."

After a second, Lyss asked, "Well, so what? Cut his fucking head off an' let's get going before that rozzer comes back through!"

"We're not leavin' him!" Chris declared.

"You're gonna risk prison for a fuckin' sand nigger?" Lyss asked.

Chris looked down at the man's face. "I don't think he's one of them," she said. "He wasn't in there with the rest of them and he – I don't know. I just don't think he was with them, somehow."

"Then who is he?" Lyss asked impatiently.

"I dunno," Chris said. "But he's comin' with us, so help me get 'im upstairs."

Lyss sighed heavily and then shook her head, exclaiming, "Fine! But if we get caught, I'm *not* related to you!"

Chris flashed a wicked grin at her twin. As if anyone would ever believe the two of them were not related.

The twins managed to get the gargantuan body upstairs along with all the identifications and personal effects Chris had collected from the nine other bodies she'd decapitated. Next, she piled the Qur'an copies all together, sprinkled them with lighter fluid from a small container she had tucked into a carrying case attached to her utility belt, and then lit the fire. She and Lyss didn't stick around to watch them burn, but instead they returned upstairs and disappeared.

The one still hiding in the shadows of the stairwell listened for a while, tracking his brother's strengthening energies as the twins transported his body to Heathrow Airport, he assumed. It felt like they were headed in that direction.

Before long, the policeman the one twin had mentioned made his way down the stairs, presumably on his rounds as a security guard. That's when he found the dead bodies of the others, along with the undetonated device they had obviously planned to use to destroy the building above. The man called in the crime on his little hand-held communication device and the silent watcher knew it was time to go. One last check on his brother's energies assured him the twins had indeed somehow managed to get him aboard an airplane and were all three now in the air headed due west.

With that confirmed, the watcher pulled his shields tightly around himself and rose, passing through the concrete flooring of each level of the parking structure until he was out and in the air above it. He then headed east toward a nearby natural rift he knew. He wanted to get home, now that he knew his brother was safe. Passing through the barrier separating the dimensions, he breathed a sigh of relief. He was almost home.

***

"What is wrong?" Djibril asked. Sarah was staring at the ring on her finger, looking for all the world as if she was once again on the verge of tears.

"No-Nothing," she hesitantly said. She took a deep breath, as if looking for courage. "I'm fine," she finally said. "I just need to learn to do what you said, to have faith." She gave a slight chuckle, one corner of her mouth lifting as she explained, "I quit believin' in all the accepted faith-based norms a long time ago, you know? It just didn't make sense to me. It seemed cruel, even, considerin' the idea that *if* there was a god, it created bein's for the sole purpose of sufferin' simply so that *it* could have someone to worship it. I couldn't live for a creature like that. I couldn't worship it."

Djibril thought for a moment and then said, "I have lived the past fifty or sixty thousand years believing I was serving my Creators. Suri and Baphomet were never quite on board with giving blind faith to those who claimed to be our Designers, and then the last time the Designers were here there was the whole issue with Suriyah having had some sort of vision about them. She never fully explained to me what her vision had shown her. But I was never accepting of the punishments that were suggested for my brother and her afterward, and I let Mikhail know it when he asked my opinion on the matter."

After a moment, Sarah said, "I think that in the end we just have each other, that we must have faith in each other in order to survive. I've noticed that people become pretty invincible when they have someone who believes in 'em. So that's what we need to do."

He hugged her close again and she hugged him back. It felt so good to have someone here who understood and was just as vulnerable to the effects of the blue mists surrounding them. Suddenly, however, Djibril felt a tingle prickling the skin of his neck where Sarah's hands were. The tingle rippled throughout his entire body in a way it should not have done and he quickly disengaged himself from their embrace. Sarah gave him an odd look, but said nothing.

The tingling throughout Djibril's body continued and he didn't know what to do. Very soon, Sarah might possibly be able to see the result of the tingling sensation on his body and he had no idea how he was supposed to explain *that* to her. Oddly enough, he had never had to deal with this type of problem.

What was going on? A part of him was suddenly going nuts over the fact that he was stuck in this dimension with Sarah and now, there was no Mikhail. Another part of him was railing at the fact that something had to have happened to Mikhail for him to have left Sarah alone in this place with Djibril.

How could Djibril even contemplate what was going through his mind? Mikhail would not have left Sarah purposely. Djibril knew that in his heart and he knew too that *he* would do whatever it took to take care of Sarah for Mikhail. Now, though, Djibril was feeling Sarah's energies in a way he shouldn't be able to feel them.

Mikhail was gone. Sarah was alone.

Djibril decided if the energy feeling continued, then he would proceed toward offering Sarah the truth of their situation. She was trying so hard to be strong, stuck here in this place without anything familiar except for Djibril. He didn't want to shatter the platform of hope she was trying to maintain by rushing her, but he knew he wouldn't be able to continue comforting her the way he had up to now if her energies kept having this kind of effect on his body.

"Gabriel?" Sarah's voice suddenly interrupted his thoughts.

"Forgive me," he said as his attention finally turned back to her.

"Was Mikhail talkin' to you?" she asked.

Of course. Her thoughts would naturally stray toward Mikhail.

Djibril knew it was time to tell her. He took her hand in his. The tingling sensation immediately raced up his arms. He remembered the first time the two of them had touched. It had been outside the university she had attended in the human realm. Her touch had not disturbed him this way then. It had tingled, yes, but there it had ended. He had never felt anything more for her. Now there was more, so much more, and Djibril's eyes filled with tears as realization dawned. With Sarah's energies working on him in this new manner, and the fact that Mikhail had up and disappeared, it could only mean Mikhail was truly gone, as in dead and gone forever.

"Sarah," he whispered.

"Gabriel, what's wrong?" Sarah's eyes filled with concern as she realized he was on the verge of tears.

"I-I have something to tell you," he said.

She reached up and laid a hand against his cheek. Djibril felt it all the way down to his toes, among other places. No wonder Mikhail had reacted the way he had when he had first encountered Sarah. If Djibril had ever felt anything like this before, he would have ripped apart any male who ever came near her. He didn't know how his brother had handled it all this time, but Djibril now felt a ray of hope. There were no other males here. He had nothing to worry about as far as being jealous where she was concerned. But, first things first.

"I can no longer contact Mikhail," he said. "I have not been able to see or hear him for a while now."

"What do you mean?" she asked. "Y-You were talkin' with him just a while ago. You told me so."

"I know what I told you," he said, shaking his head. "I did not want to hit you with one more thing to worry about when you have had so much preying on your mind since we came to be in this place."

"So you thought it was better to *lie* to me?"

Djibril bowed his head. Finally, he looked back up, explaining, "I did what I did because I believe my brother is... dead."

Sarah paled instantly. She slowly backed away from him, shaking her head. "No," she whispered.

"I am not just making assumptions here," he said, reaching a hand out for her. "I have my reasons for believing him to be gone."

"What?" she demanded. "Because you can't see or hear him anymore? We don't know anything about this place! We don't know anything at all!" She was sobbing again now.

"I can *feel* you!" Djibril barked suddenly.

Sarah's breath caught in her chest and she stared at him, fear and confusion written all over her face.

"I-I did not want it to be true, either. I love my brother. I *love* him!" he declared vehemently, his fist hitting his chest hard in his exclamation. "But since he disappeared, my senses have switched to a much higher level where your energies are concerned. I do not understand it myself, but I cannot touch you now without feeling, without feeling... *ach!*"

Sarah looked away from him, frightened of what he was saying and embarrassed. "Wh-What if it's just this place, though?" she asked. "I mean, we *really* don't know anything about where we are at all. There's no tellin' what could've happened to Mikhail. Maybe he found a way out an' he's doin' everything he can to get us out, too!"

"Why would I suddenly respond to you this way then?" he asked simply. "I have never experienced anything like this before when we have touched. Even after we came to be here. When Mikhail was here with us, my body never once reacted to your touch the way it is doing now. In fact, I could only just sense your energies then and they were a little frightening, the same as always."

"I-I don't know," Sarah finally replied, slowly shaking her head. "But I refuse to believe Mikhail is just dead and gone."

Djibril thought for a moment. "Then let us test it," he said, determined to prove his point to her. He could *feel* her. He could damned near feel every breath she took, almost as if she was touching him even now and the ache in his groin was becoming almost unbearable.

"What do you mean?" she asked hesitantly, a slight frown marring her features.

He, himself, hesitated. Dare he suggest it? "Allow me to kiss you," he finally said quietly.

Sarah stared at him in utter silence as the blue substance swirled around the two of them in thick mists that looked as if you could catch them up in your hand and hold onto them. She looked down at the ring on her finger and swallowed a lump in her throat. The tiny little stone there was as dull and lifeless as could be and Sarah was suddenly swamped with a feeling of utter solitude. Mikhail couldn't be near if the stone was all cold and dull as it was now – she knew this. He had told her it would always glow with his essence as long as he drew breath.

Djibril waited with bated breath. He wanted her so badly now he felt as if he might explode then and there.

Sarah looked back up at him as a single teardrop crept over the rim of her eye and slowly coursed down her cheek. She shook her head, whispering, "I-I can't."

He moved in toward her, seeking only to comfort her as he reached out with both hands now, and saying, "Sarah…"

Sarah turned immediately, willing herself to move forward as quickly as she could through the blue mists, yelling, "No!" In an instant, she was swallowed whole by the thick blue mist.

Djibril remained still, stunned. He could still feel her energies. "Sarah!" he called. She had been so afraid of him. He didn't want to hurt her! He never could. Why couldn't she understand how precious she was to him?

An odd noise, seemingly from somewhere far away, caught his attention. He frowned as he moved through the mists in the direction the noise had come from. He heard it again. It was a voice, a female voice.

Oh, gods! She was in trouble! Djibril blasted forward by will alone toward the area from which her voice had come. "Sarah!" he called. Another voice sounded, he thought, and he was suddenly very confused.

The blue substance surrounding him became cloyingly thick and he couldn't breathe. In fact, his lungs now felt as if they were on fire! It felt like the blue mists were eating at the sponge-like cells of his lungs each time he inhaled and Djibril fought it as he continued moving toward the area where he believed Sarah to be. He gasped for air once, twice, desperately trying to reach her, until finally, a blackness completely devoid of pain eclipsed his mind and the blue dimension simply faded away into utter obscurity.

***

"Captain, he is not coming back," the Kurr said to his superior. "The humans must have killed him, too!"

"Quiet!" the captain of the small elite Guardsmen unit ordered. "We were ordered to wait here and that is precisely what we will do." He would not tolerate dissention within the ranks. His teammates were the best of the elite and there was no way a handful of humans could take them. A handful of Lorim, however, was an altogether different story. Even the captain wasn't stupid enough to play the odds in *that* match-up. Lord Azra'il had instructed the team to wait at this location for his return. The captain planned on doing that and that alone.

If he thought about it, he would have to admit that he couldn't blame his team members for their fears. He, too, recalled the dead bodies of his recently-fallen comrades within the elite Guard. Some had even appeared to have had their innards completely dissolved, as if someone had injected them with acid. Grown Kurr who had had years of training – some of whom the captain, himself, had trained – now gone. The captain didn't want to think about the Kurr he had known all his life but who were now gone forever. "We wait for Lord Azra'il," he quietly said.

"And if he does not return?" the same Kurr asked.

The captain merely turned away. Lord Azra'il *had* to return. The alternative was simply too horrifying to contemplate.

Chapter 4

Israfil was happier than he had been in a very long time. As he made his way across the still-sleeping landscape of the Loric realm far below, he replayed the past few hours in his mind. After all, it had only been a short while that he had been gone, but so much had happened.

Of course, he was exhausted now. His body felt like it had not slept in weeks, but Israfil had been preparing for bed when he had first sensed something slightly off-kilter with the energy flow of those he had trained his mind to monitor at all times. The difficulty had been to figure out which one needed assistance. Surprisingly, Israfil had found his mind turning toward the human realm and he had immediately released his shields and taken flight. He hadn't even thought to alert anyone that he was leaving the Complex grounds.

Everyone else had either already been abed or they had been preparing for it, so he hadn't wanted to disturb his other siblings. He truly hadn't known what the problem was, either, so it would have been pointless to alert anyone when he wouldn't have been able to tell them what was going on.

True to form, as if this was all some tragic story someone had written in a novel, Israfil had arrived in time to see that his brother, Djibril, was about to lose his head – literally! Israfil had immediately thrown out a protective buffer around Djibril without a thought as to the consequences of those actions. He had only thought to keep his brother from being beheaded. Fortunately, Fate had played a hand in keeping Djibril alive as well by making sure the sword's blade became stuck in the cervical bones of his neck. This had kept Djibril's head from actually being sliced completely off his body.

Israfil had been so enraged he had contemplated killing the black-clad figure whose blade had done the damage to his brother's neck. But then he had caught just the slightest taste of the sword-wielder's energies. Normally, human energies stayed within a certain frequency range and Israfil tended to ignore anything below a certain level. This one, however, emitted frequencies in a range far beyond that which normally constituted the maximum for humans and Israfil had stilled his upper shields, which had been in the process of unfurling in anticipation of striking the human down for its actions.

Israfil had remained in the darkest part of the stairwell while the black-clad figure disappeared into the space beyond for a few minutes. Then the figure had returned and done the oddest thing. It had searched Djibril's entire form, as if looking for something.

During this process, Israfil had subtly implanted the idea that the figure should look upon the face of the one it had almost killed, to actually touch the purity of his brother's skin so that the person would know the horror of what it had almost done. The figure had suddenly realized Djibril was still breathing and then it had chosen to obey the suggestion that it remove its black hood, revealing fiery red hair wrapped in a tight, thick braid atop a beautiful face of pure alabaster.

A part of Israfil had sensed, even at that point, that there was something special about this human having made physical contact with Djibril. A few minutes later, however, Israfil had known he was witnessing a miracle as he had realized Djibril's neck was healing with hyper-speed. This could only mean the human's higher frequency energies were helping to elevate and improve his brother's natural regenerative abilities, and Israfil had smiled at the implication *that* realization offered. Fate was a cruel jokester, Israfil thought, as he grasped what had happened. This was Djibril's true mate. Against all odds, the two of them had found each other. Of course, she had tried to *kill* Djibril, but Israfil couldn't really blame her for that. His brother's anal tendencies often had Israfil wishing for some way of shutting him up as well.

As he continued watching, Israfil had been preparing to leave, believing everything was proceeding as per Fate's design, when he had gotten quite a shock. The human had called for assistance from someone, which made sense, for Djibril, like all Lorim, was quite tall and muscular. The human female was fairly small by comparison and there would have been no way for her to transport him up and out of the stairwell on her own.

Another human had come down the stairwell to help. But what had shocked Israfil so much was the fact that this new human had turned out to be the first human's identical twin sister. He couldn't tell the two apart by just looking at them or by listening to them, and he had nearly blown his cover, too, when the twin sister had removed her own hood to reveal the exact same red flaming hair atop the exact same alabaster face. He had finally realized the only way he would be able to tell them apart would be to concentrate on their energy emissions and the differences in the tones and wavelengths coming from each.

It had been a tense couple of minutes after the two sisters had apparently heard Israfil's gasp of surprise. He had nearly left then and there, but he had wanted to make sure Djibril got out of this situation safely. The twins hadn't wasted any time. They had done their homework on the building's security and had managed to get Djibril out before security at the place had made its round of checks. That's when Israfil had finally felt it was safe enough to leave.

The energies from the first twin had been powerful enough to breach the buffer Israfil had erected around Djibril before she and her sister had taken him away. Israfil's senses indicated Djibril was now well on his way toward full recovery. If the female stayed with Djibril, which Israfil figured would happen now that she had had physical contact with him, then Djibril should progress normally and return to the Complex with his new mate within a short period of time.

Israfil smiled again as he neared the Complex. The human was a red-head and seemed as if she had the temper to match, judging by what he had heard of her exchange with her sister. Israfil wondered with glee how much fun it was going to be to watch how his staid and steady-as-a-rock brother handled her.

Heading toward the house he shared with Baphomet and Lisa, Israfil yawned and allowed his senses to stretch out so he could check on the two of them. But he pulled to a halt mid-air, hovering in place just above the tree line, as he realized they were not currently in the house. He stretched his senses out to include the Main House of the Complex, believing Baphomet and his mate may have gone there for some reason during the night. Contrary to his expectations, though, he only caught lower Kurr energies emitting from within the entirety of the Main House.

Now Israfil was concerned. He expanded his sensory net to include all structures on the Complex grounds. In seconds he had located his siblings, what seemed like all of them, at the Medical Facility and he raced through the air, through the walls themselves, to get to his siblings as quickly as possible, his heart pounding. Only an emergency would have caused them all to gather within the Medical Facility and he cringed as he pushed his energies to their fullest extent, cursing himself for taking his time in returning to the Complex.

He came to the single room where everyone was gathered and he landed, dropping his shields instantly. Several gasps sounded around the room and Israfil looked quickly around to discover what was going on and who all was hurt.

Baphomet, Lisa, and the old Kurr, Miriam, were to his left. Mikhail was sitting in a chair in front of Israfil holding what looked like a baby. Sarah lay unconscious on a table, or what might possibly be a gurney, and had all manner of bandages, tubes and monitor wires all over her. Suriyah stood at the head of that table, her hands on either side of Sarah's head. The old Kurric physician, Hantsushept, was standing near the head of the table on the other side from where Israfil now stood. And along the wall facing Israfil, his shields wrapped tightly around himself stood…

"Azra'il?" Israfil asked.

Everyone else in the room gasped again as Azra'il suddenly dropped his shields and stepped toward the gathering of his siblings.

***

Christiana Harrington, or Chris as the few who knew

her called her, carried the stack of bed linens into the guest bedroom of the beach house she shared with her twin sister Alyssana, or Lyss, on Long Island. Their new houseguest was much too tall for the standard queen-sized bed they currently had in the room, but at least they could make sure the bed linens were fresh and comfortable on the part of the bed he *was* on. She and Lyss had finally managed to get the huge man into the bedroom and onto the bed from the coffin they had had him in for transport from London to New York. Chris had been amazed at the sheer weight of the man. She and Lyss trained constantly and considered themselves pretty strong, but this guy must be *all* muscle because he weighed a veritable ton and had not an ounce of fat on him. At least they had had help with moving the coffin from place to place, but after they had gotten the coffin into the house, everything had been up to them.

Chris really had to hand it to Lyss. The whole coffin idea had been a stroke of genius to get their unexpected travel companion from London to New York with no identification and no questions. Chris never would have thought of it. Lyss was a whiz with the computer, though, and she had quickly arranged everything online, even before they had left the site with the body.

The man was still barely breathing by the time they got to the airport, so it had been no problem getting his body into the coffin. Money always made everything possible and Chris and Lyss had learned at an early age how to use their God-given feminine charms to get mostly whatever they wanted. When they had showed up with a coffin at the military transport they had previously arranged to travel on back to the States, all they had had to do to ensure the coffin was allowed to accompany them with no paperwork and no questions was to flirt with the appropriate grunt in charge and offer him the right price. In mere minutes, the coffin had been loaded onto the plane along with the two women and they had been off.

Now, Lyss helped Chris roll the giant man's body over onto his side at the edge of the mattress so the bed sheets could be changed. It was a struggle, especially since

Chris was doing whatever she could to keep from touching the man any more than necessary, but they finally managed to get everything changed out. Chris couldn't stand the tingling sensations that shot up her arms and then throughout the rest of her body whenever her skin came into contact with the man's skin, nor could she understand why Lyss didn't experience the same sensations whenever she touched him. It was uncanny because everything *always* affected them both the same way.

Chris didn't care. Just as long as she didn't have to touch the guy, she was fine. At least he was breathing better now. The wound encircling most of his neck would probably always be visible, Chris guessed, but the cut must have been razor thin because it had healed so quickly. She gathered up the old bed linens as Lyss inserted an intravenous line into the back of the guy's hand and started a drip.

"Tell me again *why* we're doing this," Lyss said as she adjusted the drip rate.

Chris stopped and stared at the unconscious man. After a moment, she shrugged and said, "I dunno. I just – I just couldn't leave him there."

Lyss stared at her hard and then said, "But you were supposed to kill him, like the others."

Chris slowly shook her head and quietly said, "No…, no."

Without another word, she left the room with the bundle of old bed linens.

Chapter 5

It was Miriam who broke the momentary astonishment of everyone in the room as she suddenly moved to collect the sleeping Sheely from Mikhail again. Azra'il watched with narrowed eyes as the old Kurr exited the room with the child whose energies he could still feel, as if the infant was touching him physically, even though she was now not even in the same room as he. It was crazy, but Azra'il couldn't think about that at the moment. He was now face-to-face with the most fearsome creatures he had ever encountered in his life and he knew he would have to tread carefully.

The last time Azra'il had seen Mikhail, he had been too stunned at first to react to the changes he had observed in his brother and then he had been affected by the strange state of utter confusion he and the entire council had experienced that day. Azra'il had no idea how Mikhail had pulled *that* off, but he believed it *had* been his brother's handiwork and so he was going to be very cautious around such a powerful being, brother or no.

A deep chuckle sounded to his right and Azra'il looked over to see Baphomet fighting a grin. Azra'il hiked a brow in question and Baphomet smiled, explaining, "I think you will find that if Mikhail had been the one responsible for your... *confusion* of that day, you would most likely still be suffering from its effects."

Azra'il frowned. Baphomet had just revealed that even his *thoughts* were not safe from his powerful siblings. He didn't know what to make of that fact and was momentarily frozen inside. Was he defeated by these powerful beings even before he had begun getting reacquainted with them?

Mikhail suddenly asked, "How long have you been here?"

Azra'il returned his gaze to Mikhail and said cryptically, "A while."

Silence reigned once more as each member of the entire group did his or her own bit of sizing up of their opposite siblings. Azra'il had no idea who the dark female was with Baphomet, nor even *what* she was, for she seemed to be like Baphomet and Mikhail, but Azra'il knew that was impossible. Suriyah was the only female Lori on this planet, always had been, and he knew also that his siblings and he were the only male Lorim on the planet. The female sitting with his outlaw brother had no tether and she sported the same glowing eyes and radiance as Baphomet, even though her skin's pigmentation was of that darker shade. Azra'il narrowed his eyes as he observed the couple's clasped hands.

Baphomet looked down to where his hand rested on his thigh as it held onto Lisa's, their fingers entwined as usual. One corner of his mouth lifted in a half-grin and he said, "Azra'il, I do not believe you have been introduced to my Lori mate, Lisa Murdoch." He turned to Lisa, momentarily ignoring Azra'il's look of utter astonishment as he continued, saying "Lisa, my love, this is my other brother, Azra'il."

Lisa smiled haltingly at Azra'il as she gauged the myriad emotions going on inside Baphomet's mind.

Azra'il, himself, finally managed to ask simply, "H-How?"

Everyone started as Suriyah suddenly cleared her throat very loudly and said, "Excuse me for interrupting the family reunion, but I think we are all overlooking a more important matter here." As all the others stared uncomprehending at her, she explained, "Israfil is now standing here with us, which can only mean the one in my vision was…"

All other thoughts were set aside as realization dawned and the mood of the room became very somber again.

A second later, however, it changed to one of confusion as Israfil announced, "Djibril lives."

Suriyah frowned and Baphomet said, "But Suri's vision?"

"If her vision showed what I think it did, it was not incorrect," Israfil explained, "merely the interpretation of it."

Mikhail stood, still holding onto Sarah's hand, as he

said, "That would help to explain how he could be in the same place with Sarah and me, wherever it was."

Israfil frowned, asking, "What do you mean?" Then he turned his gaze to Sarah and asked, "And what has happened to Sarah?"

Mikhail clasped the hand he held within both of his, saying, "We do not know what is wrong with her. It is as if she is simply not there anymore."

Israfil spared one more glance at Azra'il before turning back to Mikhail and asking, "What did you mean when you said Djibril had been somewhere with Sarah and you?"

Mikhail frowned. "I do not know how to explain it exactly," he said, shaking his head. "Before waking in this room, I was someplace else with Djibril."

"Describe it to me," Israfil immediately ordered.

Mikhail thought about the place where he and Djibril, and supposedly Sarah, had been. A moment later he shook his head again, explaining, "All that was there was this thick blue mist. It was everywhere. When I first came to be there, all I could see was the blue mist. I called out to Sarah, but I received no response. Hours passed during which I simply floated along alone. Every now and then I would call out, hoping anyone would respond. Finally, when I called out one last time, I heard Djibril call back. We kept calling to each other until it seemed we were right next to each other. We still could not see one another, only the blue mist. It took what seemed like a few hours before we discovered we *could* see each other if we concentrated on doing so. Several hours later Djibril heard Sarah calling out for me, or so he said. I never heard her or saw her, but it seemed as if he was truly conversing with her."

Israfil chewed on that information for a minute. Then he turned to Baphomet and hiked a brow, suggesting, "Dimensional shift?"

Baphomet nodded and said, "That is what I thought, but how did he get to a different dimension without even trying?"

Israfil rubbed his chin, deep in thought. Then he

turned back to Mikhail and asked, "Would you mind if we linked?"

"Of course," Mikhail said. "Anything to get Sarah back."

Israfil pulled a chair over, turned it around and straddled it so he and Mikhail were sitting face-to-face.

"Mind if I tag along?" Baphomet asked.

Mikhail and Israfil both nodded once.

Azra'il frowned. He couldn't believe they were about to do what he thought they were about to do and he tensed. His three siblings went completely still as Mikhail and Israfil stared into each other's eyes. As Azra'il watched and waited, his heart rate increased. What had happened here? His siblings, save for perhaps Baphomet, had never displayed such abilities as Azra'il was currently detecting in them. Even Baphomet's supposed mate was emitting a far too powerful energy signature and Azra'il had the feeling she was somehow linked mentally with Baphomet on some sort of permanent basis. Such power was unheard of!

Azra'il threw a nervous glance in Suriyah's direction, glad to have at least one sibling who still appeared normal, even if she was an outlander.

Suriyah paid him no heed as she concentrated on what was happening with her other siblings.

Israfil, Mikhail, and Baphomet sighed suddenly as they appeared to return mentally to the room. Israfil nodded once to Mikhail and then stood. He approached the head of the table where Suriyah stood, her hands still positioned on either side of the unconscious Sarah's head. He lifted a brow and Suri quietly stepped aside. Israfil took over her position, his hands on either side of Sarah's head, and closed his eyes in concentration.

Baphomet and Lisa turned to give each other a serious glance and again Azra'il had the impression that the two were communicating on a psychic level somehow. Mikhail, he noticed, merely stared at Israfil.

Again, Azra'il waited.

***

I'm scared of him, Lisa's soft voice said inside Baphomet's mind.

He looked over at her concernedly and wrapped a protective arm around her shoulders. *Do not worry, sweet Lisa,* he silently told her. *I shall not allow him or anyone else to harm you.*

She squeezed the hand she held, but then thought to him, *He's so powerful, even as just a regular Lori. And he hides many of his thoughts, like Israfil.*

I have noticed, Baphomet thought back to her.

Azra'il's power was abundantly clear to Baphomet now and he wondered if his most distrusting sibling had always had such strength. Baphomet hadn't seen Azra'il for nearly fifteen thousand years and Baphomet's own abilities had grown since meeting Lisa, so he wasn't sure if Azra'il had always been this powerful or not.

He could sense Azra'il's energies still working to help guide humans' soul-energies back up along their tether lines when their physical bodies died, even as his brother stood in the room with all of them concentrating on what was going on with the others. The power and control it took to work cross-dimensionally like that was astounding for a Lori, especially one that had yet to transform, and Baphomet shivered as a dart of concern suddenly raced down his spine.

His brother's thoughts, the ones Baphomet *could* catch, revealed that he still thought of all of his siblings as outlaws. Baphomet wondered what might happen if Azra'il was to ever meet his own true mate and evolve.

His sense of devotion to the false Designers was overwhelmingly evident, even now, and Baphomet worried that Azra'il might someday choose to do more for the Designers than just act as a guide for human soul-energies. Might he someday become executioner for them? They had utilized Lorim in such a capacity before. Would they not be even more inclined to do so with an evolved, more advanced version of Lorim?

Don't go borrowing trouble, Lisa's voice soothed in his mind. She tightened her grip on his hand. *Those awful Designers haven't come back yet and, until they do – if they do – we're just going to deal with what's going on here. We have to, for Cabal's sake.*

He hugged her closer, bending a little to catch a glimpse of the patch of light that was their son inside her lower abdomen. Cabal's glow had increased dramatically since Baphomet and Lisa had moved to Israfil's house on the outskirts of the Complex grounds and they were encouraged by how much stronger he was becoming each and every day. He still tended to shy away into hiding whenever others' thoughts encroached, as he was doing now, but Lisa and Baphomet kept mainly to themselves and rarely lost physical contact with one another. When they did choose to break their physical link, it was never for more than a few minutes.

Another shiver raced down Baphomet's spine at the thought of the wall of voices that would descend upon all three of them if Lisa and he lost physical contact for any great length of time. Even Baphomet wanted to hide from that, so he couldn't blame Cabal for being so frightened of other people's thoughts. After all, the first few days of his existence had been plagued with those uncontrollable incidences when the voices would take over completely. It wasn't until then that they had realized what was going on and how to control it.

Baphomet's mind returned suddenly to Azra'il as he wondered what ability or abilities his brother might develop if he ever did meet up with his natural mate. Baphomet assumed it was bound to happen sometime soon, since both Mikhail and he had already met theirs and, according to what he had learned when he had linked with Israfil and Mikhail, it seemed Djibril had most likely already met *his* now.

Suriyah's vision from all those many thousands of years ago had indicated they would all mate up very quickly once things started, so Baphomet believed his remaining three siblings would soon be evolving into whatever they were all meant to become.

There was some little detail that niggled at his mind at this thought, but the meat of the detail eluded him and he shrugged it off, returning to the thread his thoughts had woven before. He wondered what Djibril's mate was like.

The only impression Baphomet had gleaned from his semi-link with Israfil had been of red hair. If she turned out to be anything like Djibril, however, Baphomet knew she would be very anal and obsessive about every single detail. Djibril had always been that way. It was one of the things Baphomet found most annoying about his brother.

You know, Lisa's voice said as it drifted across his mind, *for someone who has his own fair share of hang-ups, you certainly are judgmental of others.*

Baphomet's lips twitched slightly. *Yeah*, he silently responded, *but you love me anyway.*

Lisa's eyes smiled up at him and he sighed as he rubbed her arm and returned his gaze to Azra'il. It had to be difficult for his brother, he realized. After all, even when he had first been banished from Lorim City, Baphomet had still had *one* of his siblings with him. He and Suri had lived together during the first one hundred or so years of their banishment until they had decided to break apart and build separate lives for themselves. Even then, though, Baphomet had visited Suri quite often. They both loved each other; they simply hadn't chosen the same paths in life. But each knew the other was always available should either of them have need of the other.

Whom did Azra'il have?

He had been living in Lorim City with none of his Lorim siblings for a while now. Baphomet couldn't imagine how lonely that must have been for Azra'il.

He chose that path, my love, Lisa's voice softly said in his mind.

Baphomet understood that, as he believed each individual to be responsible for his own path in life, along with all its rewards and consequences. He still disliked the idea of his brother living alone in the City where everywhere one looked there were reminders of all that had once been.

Baphomet didn't believe Azra'il to be evil, even though a part of him still felt the desire to get back at his brother somehow for the role he had played in having Suri and Baphomet banished from Lorim City. He ignored that part of himself. It was petty and mean-spirited and it had happened such a long time ago. Baphomet believed that anger would eventually fade away into obscurity, as had his anger toward Mikhail.

Of course, that had only happened *after* Baphomet had discovered from Israfil that Mikhail had never wanted to banish Suriyah and Baphomet in the first place.

That thought brought Baphomet back to the subject of Israfil and he turned his gaze to the brother in question. Baphomet had thought by tagging along during the mind-link between Mikhail and Israfil earlier that he would have a chance to learn more about his most elusive brother's abilities. He had been wrong.

Well, that wasn't entirely true. Baphomet had learned that Israfil had played a role in the fact that Mikhail, Djibril, and most likely Sarah, had all ended up in some other dimension – somewhat together. This, in itself, revealed that Israfil was far more powerful than even Baphomet had thought. The fact that he was still unable to break through the buffer Israfil maintained constantly around himself, however, told Baphomet there was much more beneath the surface when it came to Israfil. Consequently, what had been mere curiosity on Baphomet's part before was now a raging thirst for knowledge. He wanted to know what Israfil was hiding behind that well-maintained buffer.

***

Israfil ignored Baphomet's questing mind as he concentrated on the task at hand. He knew he would have to deal with telling everyone the truth soon enough, but for the now he just wanted to fix the problem he had inadvertently created. Who would have guessed Djibril would be being monitored while he was in the human realm, or that said monitoring would have led to such a mess? Why had Mikhail and Sarah been monitoring their brother anyway? Israfil wanted to get back inside Mikhail's mind to discover the answer to this last question, for his own instincts told him it was important. But he needed to find Sarah first.

When Israfil had thrown out the buffer he had created to protect Djibril from both the pain of the attack on his neck and from certain death, he had had no idea of the impact his impulsive act would have. Djibril's life had been spared, mostly due to blind luck when the blade had become lodged in the cervical vertebrae near the top of his spinal column, but Israfil believed the buffer must have helped to keep it from passing all the way through his brother's neck in some way, too.

Also because of the buffer, Djibril's energies, for the most part, had been displaced into some alternate dimension. The fact that Mikhail and Sarah had been secretly linked with Djibril when this had happened meant their energies had been displaced into the same dimension – kind of. The only thing Israfil could think of to explain what had happened was that there had to have been a buffer already in place between Mikhail and Sarah when they had each been drawn in separately. Otherwise, they would have been able to see and hear each other within that other dimension, as well as Djibril.

Of course, this new discovery merely heightened Israfil's curiosity by posing the question as to why there had been a buffer in place between Mikhail and his mate in the first place. Israfil made a mental note to himself to remember to revisit this issue when all of this was said and done. He already knew Sarah had been the one to erect the buffer, though. Mikhail's energies were still too uncoordinated, too uncontrolled for such an undertaking. Israfil could feel it.

He realized suddenly how off track his thoughts were getting and he gave himself a mental slap to get back on target.

There were an infinite number of dimensions where Sarah's energies could be residing and Israfil had little to go on as far as how to identify the one she was in when and if he should come to it. All Mikhail had been able to give him were images. Israfil had seen thick blue mists and nothing more. It was not much to go on, but he would work with it somehow.

Sarah's body was not breathing on its own, which meant she had almost fully vacated it. However, Israfil had caught just the faintest hint of her tones still emitting from within her body as he had completed his assessment of her state of being, so he knew she was not yet completely gone.

He was once again happy for the fact that the old physician, Hantsushept, had been around to recognize the baby was in mortal danger. If he hadn't taken Sheely when he had, Israfil believed the child most likely would have died. That, Israfil believed, would damn near have killed his brother Mikhail. As it was, Israfil knew he held the lives of both his brother's mate *and* his brother in his hands as he searched for Sarah's energies. The two of them were so closely linked that Israfil knew without a doubt Mikhail would never survive without Sarah.

Israfil understood.

He pushed a sudden onslaught of grim memories from his mind and concentrated. Sarah's energy frequencies were very specific. Israfil had learned some time ago how to recognize them and he concentrated more intently on the ones he could detect now. A pattern, faint and minute, suddenly captured his attention and he plunged headlong toward it, hoping he had found her at last. As soon as he entered the dimension from which those particular frequency patterns were emitting, Israfil knew he had found her.

He fought against the cloying, blue mist as he allowed a part of himself to settle in there. He could only withdraw a portion of himself in order to alert Mikhail that he had found her for fear that he would lose the dimension's location if he left it entirely. Instead, a tiny part of his energies was allowed to be sucked in and controlled by that dimension while the remainder of his energies returned to his body, still residing within the Loric realm.

Israfil raised his head and opened his eyes, a glazed look about them. He looked over at Mikhail's tense features and nodded once, faintly whispering, "I have found her."

Mikhail's eyes widened and a ray of hope suddenly flared into life within him; he then closed his eyes and concentrated.

Chapter 6

Djibril awakened lazily from a very deep nothingness. He lay there listening, not opening his eyes, not moving in any way, just listening – and feeling. He stretched out his senses.

She was still hiding from him, he knew, because her energies were not very close. But Djibril could still feel her. He could even hear her tones now and then and a part of his soul thrilled to this knowledge, while another part was saddened by it. It could only mean that Mikhail was truly gone, dead, never to return.

Djibril had told Sarah, but he wasn't sure that even he, himself, had believed it until now. As Sarah's energies became more and more detectable, however, Djibril knew it was so. But he would not waste time grieving. His beloved brother would not have wanted that.

Instead, Djibril was determined that he would work with Sarah, talk with her, and, most of all, be patient with her. He would do whatever he had to do to be the next one in her life. She was going to need a friend at first for support through her grieving period. Djibril realized now that that was where he had erred before when he had suggested she allow him to kiss her. She had only just discovered Mikhail was dead after having already lost Sheely. She probably had not even believed it. Djibril knew things would change over time, though, and he knew how to be patient.

Sarah belonged with him now, not because he had chosen it, but because Nature itself had chosen for them by making Djibril's body so very susceptible to Sarah's soul energies. It was pointless to go against Nature, Djibril knew, so they were simply meant to be together. No matter how long it took, Sarah would have to learn to accept that fact.

Djibril felt a little jump in his heart rate as he suddenly realized Sarah's energies were getting much stronger and coming physically closer to him. This excited him, for he knew she was looking for him. He opened his eyes.

Nothing happened.

Djibril tried again. Still there was nothing. Was he lost in some place of pitch blackness? Were his eyes even open? He reached to check, but realized his arm hadn't moved. He tried again. Still, no movement occurred. His heart rate increased. What was happening? He tried to yell out, to call to Sarah, but no sound came. How could this be? A small part of him recognized the fact that Sarah's energies were close, virtually on top of him even. But Djibril's mind was now consumed by the fact that he appeared to be trapped within his own body, unable to move or to call out or to do anything other than breathe.

He panicked.

He was paralyzed!

***

Sarah cleared her mind, allowing the blue mists to consume her form. She had run from Gabriel as long as she could, but then had decided it would be better to just stop and hide within the thick mists. She no longer heard his calls to her and she had stopped crying a while ago, so now there was only silence within her little corner of the blue dimension. She merely floated this way without form through the mists for a long, long time. She thought about the past, about the time she had spent with Mikhail. She wouldn't allow herself to think about Sheely or Thomas. If what Gabriel had told her was true, then Thomas would now be alone.

Sarah concentrated on her hand and it eventually appeared before her. The ring she wore on the third finger there still contained only the cold, dull stone. Mikhail had told her the stone had become infused with his soul energy and that *that* was why it had glowed when he had given the ring to her. He had said his soul energies would continue to glow as long as his soul existed on this planet, so she would always have a part of him wherever they were. The fact that the stone was now dull and without any type of glow whatsoever confirmed what Gabriel had said.

Mikhail had to be dead.

Sarah allowed the mists to take over again. She didn't want to see the ring or to think about that. She didn't

58

want to think about anything. She just wanted to stop being, to allow the blue mists to claim her mind as it had her body. But she couldn't. She had to survive for Thomas... for Thomas... Thomas. The name repeated over and over in her mind until she realized it was more a question. Thomas? Thomas? Thomas, who? Who?

Confusion set in. Who was she thinking about? She couldn't recall. A slight ache began in her head and her heart and she closed her eyes and simply let go.

Suddenly, from far off it seemed, there was a disturbance in the mists. It was a sound, a familiar sound, and Sarah opened her eyes and concentrated. This was crazy! She was now imagining she could hear someone's voice calling to her. It had sounded almost like... Mikhail. Sarah shivered. She had finally completely gone off her rocker.

She closed her eyes, letting go again, hoping the mists would consume her mind quickly so it would have no further opportunities to wreak havoc with her memories. She didn't want any memories. Down that path lay too much pain.

The call continued, getting closer. Sarah decided she would just let the voice wave wash over her and then it would be gone. Then she would be able to simply fade away into nothingness. She concentrated on seeing the ring one last time.

A brilliant glow suddenly illuminated the blue mists as her hand came into view.

Sarah was stunned! Then she heard the voice again and she screamed aloud. She didn't know how any of this could be, but she wasn't going to waste time thinking about it. Somehow, Mikhail had found her, even from beyond the grave. Now, as she concentrated on finding him, on moving toward his voice and his energies, she knew an elation she had never known before. She rushed forward through the mists, trusting that this wasn't some trick her mind was playing on her, simply because she had no other choice.

Without warning, she couldn't breathe. There was a horrible pain in her throat and there was something holding her hands down as she fought against it to reach her throat.

Something was very wrong here! It felt like something was being ripped out of her throat and Sarah thought she would puke right then and there.

"Sarah?" she heard Mikhail's voice ask right next to her. "Baby?"

She gasped and opened her eyes. Her entire body tingled painfully and she could feel blood rushing in a painful way throughout each and every part of her.

Ugly fluorescent lights glared down upon her, hurting her eyes and momentarily blinding her. She struggled to move when she realized she was lying on some sort of gurney. That's when realization finally dawned. This was the Medical Facility at the Complex. She was home! She opened her eyes wide at this point, uncaring of the pain from the lights as she searched for the one face she needed most to see. He was right there, standing just to her left, holding her hand.

Sarah leapt up into his arms, pain ripping through her abdomen and her right arm. She didn't even bother looking to find out what was causing it. Her screams, she knew, were horrible. She couldn't help it. She wailed and wailed as she threw her arms around his neck in a powerfully tight grip.

"Shh, baby," Mikhail whispered in her ear. "It is okay. You are safe now."

Still she wailed. Other voices sounded, but she paid them no attention.

"Please calm down, love," Mikhail pleaded as he held her tightly against his chest. Sarah merely continued wailing. His hands rubbed her back and her hair as her wails continued.

Eventually, the wailing quieted merely because she had reached her energies' limits. She didn't let go of the stranglehold her arms and hair had around his neck and back, but her hiccoughs took over for her sobs and then, exhausted, she lost consciousness against him.

***

Azra'il watched in absolute astonishment. He had seen the ends of this Sarah's hair moving seconds before she had regained consciousness and he had been completely confused. What had happened to the human Sarah? This one had opened eyes that glowed as brightly as Mikhail's now glowed. The old Sarah's eyes had not glowed. For that matter, neither had her hair been this long and white in color.

Something had happened to Mikhail *and* Sarah. The same thing had happened to Baphomet, and Azra'il was willing to bet the female he had introduced to Azra'il as his Lori mate had not always looked the way she currently did. Azra'il had lived on this planet for a million years and had only ever encountered one female Lori. Now he was to believe there just happened to be two more on the planet and that they had been in hiding in the human realm? That was ridiculous!

What had happened to his brothers? This couldn't be natural, could it? The blessed great Designers had never discussed anything like this in the histories they had taught the Lorim. Of course, never had the Designers mentioned anything about Lorim mating with humans other than to decree it was never to happen, that it was taboo. Was this why? Were the changes his brothers were experiencing because they had mated with humans some type of precursor to a developing cancer or some other type of incurable and fatal disease? Had these evil human, or what used to be human, females found a way to rob his brothers of their immortality?

One look at his two infected brothers and Azra'il knew their brains had been completely taken over by their illness, if that was the case. In order to find out if there would ever be a chance for recovery, Azra'il would have to have blood samples from both of them so he could have his medical team back in Lorim City analyze them to see if a cure could be found. It was quite obvious to Azra'il now that his brothers were suffering and he had a responsibility to find some way of helping them.

Azra'il had noticed the head of the medical team Mikhail had on staff here and he wondered if the Kurr could be persuaded to supply any information or samples he had on file so that Azra'il's staff could begin their research more quickly. The old Kurr appeared gruff and business-like, but everyone here appeared to defer to Mikhail's opinion without question, so Azra'il believed they all respected him. Someone like that would most likely be a loyal servant. Perhaps it would be best to sneak into the physician's offices himself for the samples and records? At least that way no one would be alerted to the fact that he was working toward a cure for his brothers.

A part of him wept inside for his brothers' suffering. After all, they were living under the delusion that it was okay for them to mate with human females, that they were allowed to breed offspring with these creatures. As he observed how very much involved his two brothers were with their mates, another part of Azra'il felt the oddest feeling of – what... *envy*? Why should Azra'il feel envious of them? They were delusional, obviously. They were ill, also obviously. So why should Azra'il feel such an emotion?

It must be due to his lack of contact with his siblings for so long. Seeing them, most of them at least, gathered here together where they could support one another as they all had done for hundreds of thousands of years, Azra'il could feel that sense of family tugging at his heart again. He had been missing that a lot lately and, now that he was back among his siblings and their supportive energies, his yearning for inclusion gnawed at him even more incessantly than ever before. He would have to take care not to allow that strange discontentment to color his judgment where his brothers' mates' punishment was concerned. His siblings could not be blamed. It was quite obvious they suffered from a terribly debilitating, mind-altering disease. Once Azra'il's medical staff discovered a cure for them, they would return to normal. Surely the council would understand and agree to that!

Before he had left the council last, he had promised to mete out a just and suitable punishment for those who had caused all the recent disturbances within the Kurric society of Lorim City, including his brothers, if necessary. Now, however, it was quite obvious his brothers had had no intentional involvement in any of the disturbances their people had suffered. Indeed, it was obvious to Azra'il that his brothers were victims.

The ones to blame here were the humans, as Azra'il had originally suspected. He had come here to see just how bad the situation had become and to arrest and pass judgment on those who had transgressed against the One Law laid down by the blessed Designers. What he hadn't anticipated, however, was how powerful the humans in question had become. These females were unbelievably powerful and Azra'il knew he would have to tread carefully until he could discover some way of controlling the two.

As he gazed at Baphomet and his mate, Azra'il developed a plan. It was devious and most despicable to any sane mind, but Azra'il was running out of time and options. He could sense how very powerful the two females were and he knew they were fully capable of fighting off even his best Guardsmen. He would have to hit the females where it hurt the most in order to be able to separate them from his brothers. Only then would he be able to get his brothers to safety where they could be treated and healed of their disease.

The little glowing patch on Baphomet's mate's abdomen – that was what had given Azra'il the idea. He could sense that Baphomet's mate – Lisa he believed Baphomet had said her name was – this Lisa, she appeared to care a great deal for Mikhail's mate. Azra'il could almost believe this Lisa looked up to this Sarah. If that was the case, then Azra'il needn't worry with Lisa. Get to Sarah and Lisa would follow.

That meant Azra'il would have to use Mikhail's supposed unsanctioned offspring as leverage. Azra'il settled back against the wall again as his mind went to work on the details of a horrible plan.

Chapter 7

"Whatchya doin'?" Lyss asked as she changed the drip bag on the man's IV. She had noticed her sister, Chris, sitting in the room with the man when she had walked in.

"What's it look like?" Chris asked as she held up the hunters' goods catalog she was reading. She was sitting on the chair in the corner facing the bed where the stranger lay. One leg was thrown over one arm of the chair and the other was stretched out onto the floor as she leaned her back against the other arm of the chair. She had been sitting in this same position, staring at this same page of the catalog, for the past hour, though she would never admit that to Lyss.

For some reason, she had felt an overwhelming need to watch over the stranger this morning after she had worked out and showered. So she'd grabbed a banana and had gone into the room, snagging the latest catalog she had purchased for something to do while she guarded him. She was always on the lookout for better equipment for Lyss and her to use when they went out on jobs and this particular catalog carried the top of the line brands of goods they used.

"Well, let me know if he wakes up," Lyss said. She checked the settings and readings on the various monitoring devices she had hooked up to the stranger. The damned things were acting twitchy for some reason, but they were still putting out legible readings. Everything looked okay, so she left.

Chris allowed her gaze to stray over to the stranger again.

What was it about him that called to her so much? He was attractive, sure. Many of the men she and her sister killed could be thought of as physically attractive, she supposed. They were all Muslims, though, so she didn't normally pay any attention. But somehow, this guy was different.

Chris laid down the catalog and got up to go and stand next to the bed. The stranger breathed in and out in a normal rhythm. No other part of him moved, just his belly as his diaphragm lowered and then raised, lowered and then raised. Chris wondered if he would awaken soon. It was odd to her that he wouldn't have awakened once during their entire journey from London to the house on Long Island. Maybe he *had* awakened during their journey. If he had awakened during his time in the coffin, might he now believe himself to be dead?

Chris pursed her lips and frowned at this thought. One would have thought the guy would have fought and yelled if that had been the case. Chris believed *she* would have done whatever she could, for as long as she could, had she been in such a situation. She looked down upon the man's face. He was probably like the majority of the others she had come across, no morals, all fired up about some cause somebody who was absolutely insane had preached to him about, believing that by killing a bunch of innocent people (and himself) he would earn a place of redemption in Heaven.

Jesus Christ! It made her sick just thinking about it. What had happened to men being men? What had happened to honor and integrity? Was it completely gone from the world? Chris and Lyss had been born and raised in England, but their parents had always taught them about honor and integrity. When the two had been just sixteen, their parents had been transferred to the New York office of the company they had both worked for and so they had all moved to America. There, they had fallen in love with the American idealistic way of thinking – Alexander Hamilton had become Chris' hero from the history books she had been required to read. Although he hadn't been born an American citizen, he had embodied the American spirit so much that Chris had soon come to think of him when she thought of her beloved America. And so, a couple of years later, Chris and Lyss had each officially become American citizens.

Over the last few years, however, Chris had noticed a degradation of society occurring around the world, including in her precious American society. No one taught morals anymore. Children weren't taught to be respectful to their elders or to strangers. They had no manners, no honor, no tradition, and no values. It seemed all there was inside any of them these days was an overwhelming desire to have whatever latest gadget or electronic gizmo that had been put on the market, and none of them wanted to work to get it.

Of course, Chris silently smirked, *once one got a job, it was hell to keep from losing it by saying the wrong thing or backing the wrong political team.* She personally believed her beloved America was nearly gone and that it would take another civil war, if not another world war for it, to even have a chance of rebounding. The majority of those in Washington would have to be kicked out, on both sides of the aisle, along with some in the White House. A new regime would have to be put in place. New laws would have to be written, along with a new Constitution. Those who worked in Congress and the Senate would actually have to *work* for a living for a change and, more importantly, would have to live by the same rules as the *rest* of the country.

The difficulty with that, however, was that there appeared to be no George Washingtons or Alexander Hamiltons left in this world. There were no great visionaries who still lived by an honor code and who were truly able to think on behalf of their countrymen, who could see hundreds of years down the road in such a fashion so that they could create a document like the Constitution that would be able to withstand the necessary societal changes a growing and thriving country would need.

There were no more *real* men left who were willing to stand up for what was right, to lead, to take *responsibility*. Instead, they were all asking what would be in it for them and telling everyone to just let the government take care of it. No one expected others to, oh, Chris didn't know, actually *work* for what they wanted. No, go on public aid. That's what one needed to do. It was a new twist on history that read, "Ask not what you can do for your country, but what your country can do for you." Either that, or one could join the other side and live with constant media attacks and threats to one's life.

It sickened Chris' heart, just thinking about it.

She and Lyss would be fine, she knew. She had been a double major at NYU – finance and political science – and she had made sure to set up everything she and her sister owned under an LLC so they could never be touched and never lose anything that was theirs. She regularly invested in real estate holdings and made sure their investments never dipped below 20% return yields per annum.

She knew her business and was offered positions with the top Manhattan finance firms on a regular basis. Of course, she never entertained the offers. The jobs she and Lyss did were not for the money. Although that was certainly a nice perk. What they did was strictly for personal reasons.

The stranger's breathing pattern changed all of a sudden. It was subtle, but Chris noticed it. Was he awake? Why were there no other signs? Should she call Lyss? Chris didn't know what to do. On a whim, she knelt down next to the low bed and placed a hand on the man's arm. Instantly, a zing of electricity shot up her arm, this one much stronger than when she had touched him before. She managed not to jerk her hand away this time, though only just. It was so odd the way that happened whenever she touched him. Lyss had said Chris was crazy when she had told her sister about the zinging sensation, but it still happened every time she touched him.

"H-Hullo?" she whispered just next to his ear.

"*What* are you doing?" Lyss suddenly asked from the open doorway.

"Nothin'," Chris said as she quickly stood back up from her kneeling position by the bed. "I-I think he woke up, but he's not responding."

Lyss checked a couple of the read-outs from the monitors. "Looks like somethin's goin' on in there, but I can't really get a good reading. These damned old machines are actin' up," she said.

"Well, why isn't he, you know, waking up?"

"From what you said, your blade cut almost all the way through his neck, genius," Lyss said sarcastically. "I'd be shocked if he ever wakes again. If he does, he'll most likely be completely paralyzed, you realize?"

Chris stared down at the man. He had been so warm when she had touched him. Now she finds out he's probably paralyzed for *life*, and that it's *her* fault? "So I've basically killed him?" she quietly asked.

"Look," Lyss said. "If what you said is true, then your blade had to have severed almost all of his major arteries, nerves, veins, and some serious muscles, not to mention his throat. That would be an indication of death, yes. If, as you also said, the katana got lodged in one or more of his cervical vertebrae, there's no *telling* what kind of damage was done there. I have to tell you that it is difficult for me to believe what you've told me simply because of the evidence before my eyes. I mean, people don't normally survive having their head sliced nearly all the way off, and they certainly don't heal as fast as this one had to have done in order for your story to be true."

She held up a hand as Chris started to protest, asking for silence as she continued. "But I have never known you to lie to me before and I cannot for the life of me imagine why you would lie about this," she said. "So, I'm willing to give you the benefit of the doubt."

"Oh, gee. Thanks!"

Chris watched as her sister adjusted this knob here and another setting there, wishing she could let Lyss know just how confused she felt inside. She looked back down at the stranger. It was as if his whole body was calling out to her with some secret code and she felt as if she would die if she didn't respond.

"Why are you doing this?" Lyss suddenly asked from the opposite side of the bed. "I mean, he's one of *them*. We kill his kind. It's what we do. We hate them and all they stand for." She stared hard at Chris.

Chris just stared back, blinking.

"Let *me* kill him," Lyss finally said softly.

Immediately, Chris reached out to cover the man, her head shaking violently as she yelled, "No!"

"Why not?" Lyss whipped out. "He's a dog of Islam, one of the most insane religions ever to exist on the planet! Should he ever wake, he would treat you like a cur – no, *worse* than a cur."

Chris remained in her guarded stance.

Lyss sighed. "They took everything from us, Chris – everything," she said with tears clogging her throat. "And now you want... what? To nurture this one back to health for some reason? You think he's different from the others somehow?"

Chris slowly shook her head, whispering, "I-I don't know."

"What?" Lyss demanded.

"I don't know!" Chris shouted. She looked up at Lyss once more, tears forming in her own eyes, and said, "Everything you've said makes perfect sense and I know it. But there's just something about him, something... *important* that's keeping me from harming him any further."

Lyss thought for a moment. Then she shook her head and said, "Well, the point is probably moot anyway. Judging from the readings, he won't make it through the night."

Chris' tears slipped over the edge and slowly made their way down her cheeks.

Lyss pursed her lips and rolled her eyes. Then she appeared to soften a little as she said, "I'll check back in an hour or so."

Chris merely stood there, silent and staring down at the stranger as Lyss left. Why *had* she done this? This man, this dog of Islam as Lyss had called him, was *nothing* to her. He was *beneath* her. Yet, she knew even now that she could not allow anything to happen to him. It was as if his soul called out to hers on some spiritual level.

She closed her eyes and sighed, wondering why her soul couldn't decide to hook up with someone like Brad Pitt.

All of a sudden, she felt as if the stranger was calling to her – literally. She opened her eyes and looked back down at him. He still showed no signs of movement, but she could swear she could hear a very masculine voice calling out, asking, *Where are you?*

She knelt down beside him once more, careful not to jostle him any as she leaned over him. She took his hand in both of hers, almost enjoying the electricity zinging up into her arms now from his touch. "I'm here," she softly said.

Where? she thought she heard him ask. *I cannot find*

you.

He sounded panicked and she rubbed one hand along his forearm. "I'm right here beside you and you're safe. It's all right. I'm right here." She held onto him like that, whispering and soothing him for the next hour. She was still kneeling beside the bed, holding onto his hand, when her sister returned to check in on him. Lyss frowned at what she saw when she entered the room, but then she went directly to work checking the read-outs from the monitors. She quietly cursed at the dilapidated machines as she gave one of them a good whack, and then silently left the room a few minutes after having entered.

Chris figured the man must have fallen asleep now because she heard no more calls from him. Still, she knelt by his side, never breaking contact with him. After a while, her knees and back became stiff and she looked around the room for a solution. There was only the one overstuffed chair in the corner. It was inviting, but even if she moved it over to the bed, it was too big to allow her to comfortably maintain physical contact with the stranger.

She looked down at the bed.

The very idea was insane! She could hurt him somehow if she did it, she believed. Lyss would think Chris had gone absolutely bonkers if she came in and caught her. Of course, she had already said there was no way he was making it through the night, hadn't she? What would be the harm then?

The bed felt a lot smaller and had a lot less room with him in it, but Chris managed to crawl up next to him under the covers. She was still completely clothed, save for her shoes and socks, so she figured she was safe. A part of her mind smarted off, saying, *The guy's paralyzed. What do you think's gonna happen?*

Chris was glad she and Lyss had insisted on central air as well as central heating when they had moved into this joint. The man had to have a fever, he was so hot!

It took a few attempts, but Chris finally managed to find a comfortable position where she was pressed entirely along the side of his body with one arm thrown over his chest for protection. Within minutes, she fell sound asleep.

Chapter 8

Mikhail started slightly as Baphomet suddenly rose to help Lisa stand.

"We need to go get something to eat," Baphomet whispered softly. "Cabal is starving."

Mikhail nodded his understanding and watched silently as the two left the room, quietly closing the door behind themselves. He had stopped rubbing his hand down Sarah's back a while ago when she had finally eased into a deep enough sleep that the hitches in her breathing had subsided. Now, as he adjusted his arm to a more comfortable position, he discovered his hand had been entirely wrapped up in her hair. It slowly adjusted its grip on his hand so he could move it. Mikhail looked up in time to catch Azra'il watching the interplay with wonder.

"Why have you come here?" Mikhail softly asked his brother.

Pursing his lips, Azra'il decided sticking as close to the truth as he could was the best policy and he said, "I came to discover why you would choose to give up the life you had in Lorim City for a life in exile."

Mikhail merely stared at his brother for a long time. Finally, he asked, "And so have you found your answer?"

Azra'il turned his gaze upon the still-sleeping Sarah. "I have seen that this one has affected both your mind and your body," he said. "I do not pretend to understand the mechanics of it, nor the reason behind it. But I do believe she is the root cause of all the evil that has happened within our realm."

Mikhail looked into Sarah's face as it lay on his left shoulder facing toward his neck. She slept on and Mikhail gently reached over to place a tender kiss onto her forehead before turning his gaze back to Azra'il and saying, "You know nothing, my poor brother."

Azra'il merely hiked a brow at his brother's words.

"You are very much alone in your City and I feel a great deal of pity for you," Mikhail baldly stated, putting Azra'il on edge at how close his brother was to reading

Azra'il's innermost feelings. "You still hold to things which were given to us under false pretenses." When Azra'il merely frowned, Mikhail said, "Do you not see? The false Designers deceived us. They did not want us to mate with humans because they knew we would become more powerful and that we would also have powerful offspring."

Azra'il could not deny the fact that it appeared both Mikhail and Baphomet had become much more powerful than they had been before, and he had both seen and felt how unbelievably powerful Mikhail's newborn child had been before the old Kurr had removed it from the room. He even imagined he could still feel the slightest trace of the infant's energies now, although she had been gone for a few hours.

"It is my greatest wish," Mikhail said, "that you find your one true other half someday so that you will come to know exactly how wonderful being joined together is."

Azra'il hiked his brow again and pursed his lips.

Mikhail fell silent.

Baphomet and Lisa chose that moment to return. They brought several Kurr laden with food trays back with them and all was quiet chaos for a few minutes as drinks and food stuffs were distributed throughout. The medical team was appreciative and Israfil and Suriyah both wolfed down their food without speaking. Azra'il sniffed at a sandwich one of the serving Kurr had handed him and eventually he ate it. He didn't say anything, though. When everyone had eaten, the serving Kurr cleared everything and left, just as quietly as they had come. Hantsushept made a little more than half his staff leave to return to their homes and then everyone remaining settled in again to await Sarah's reawakening.

Israfil suddenly turned toward Azra'il and asked, "Can you tell if she is improving or not? I mean, can you see how thick her tether line is?"

Azra'il blinked a couple of times and then turned back toward Mikhail and Sarah and announced quietly to the room, "I have never before encountered creatures such as these, these humans who either disguise themselves as something resembling a Lori or who actually suffer from some ailment that changes the very physical make-up of their bodies, I suspect until it destroys them." When he heard a couple of gasps around the room, from Kurr, Lorim, and whatever Mikhail, Baphomet, and Lisa had become, he paused before continuing. "However, I see no tether on her. I see no tether on Mikhail or Baphomet or his companion, either. I see only the glow from the soul-energies fully contained within your bodies, Sarah included. Whatever ails her now is within her body or mind."

"So she will live?" Mikhail asked hopefully.

Azra'il tilted his head and hiked a brow as he said, "Such as she can." He said nothing more and none of the others appeared inclined to say anything else, and the room settled back into silence as everyone waited. Azra'il wondered if what he had said was actually the truth. Could these physiological changes be killing his siblings' mates? If that was the case, then might the same changes be affecting his brothers similarly? Might they not burn out at some point?

Then there was the question of his brothers' offspring. Azra'il could detect the energy flow coming from the entity housed within Lisa's womb and knew it too possessed its soul in its entirety. And he *could* still hear the soft tones of Mikhail's child, could still feel its frequencies. The patterns were becoming clearer, more distinct, and Azra'il was virtually itching for a chance to examine that one more closely.

What could that creature be like? If he could feel the thing when it wasn't even in the same room with him, how unbelievably powerful would it eventually grow to be? What about when it hit puberty and all those hormones kicked into gear? How would *anyone* be able to control such a being?

Azra'il had no idea what he was going to do, but he knew he could not leave, not yet. There were far too many questions to which he needed answers before he could even think about leaving. His plan of earlier was still a viable one, he believed, and he went over the details of it within a hidden part of his mind as he waited silently with the rest of them.

***

Djibril woke again, though this time he could actually feel a little. This wasn't necessarily a good thing because whatever he did feel was pretty painful. He remained calm, as calm as he could, and attempted to open his eyes. He felt his lids lifting, but no trace of light leaked in. Cautiously, he reached a hand up to feel his face, to make sure his eyes had actually opened. It hurt to do it, but his hand finally touched his face clumsily and, after a few fumbled attempts at control, his fingers confirmed his eyes had actually opened, but that he was still unable to see.

In that moment, he heard what sounded like a door opening and then a female's voice screeching, "*What* the fuck is going on?"

Suddenly, Sarah's energies exploded into life next to him and he felt her body disengaging from his where they lay. He was powerless to do anything, he found, as even his voice would not work.

"What the *bloody hell* were you doing in bed with that sand nigger?" the angry female voice demanded.

Then an odd thing happened. Djibril had been expecting Sarah to defend him immediately and he *was* defended, except the voice defending him did not belong to his Sarah.

"You will lower your voice this instant!" hissed another female voice. "He's scared and confused enough without having some stranger come in screaming at him and calling him all kinds of names!"

"I'll solve that little problem for him right now, shall I?" the angry voice demanded. "I'll rip his fucking head off like you should've done in the first place."

"You come one step closer and I'll rip *your* head off, Lyss. I promise you!" his defender vowed.

"Chris," the one called Lyss finally managed in utter confusion. "Over one of *them*?"

"I mean it," Chris said. "Now get out!"

A moment later Djibril heard the door close softly somewhere close to his head. Then she was beside him again, touching him, and the whole world could have disappeared for all he cared. He had no idea why Sarah was pretending to be someone named Chris, nor why she was using a British accent, nor how there came to be this angry and vulgar Lyss person in the blue dimension with them, but none of that mattered. Sarah was with him and was touching him and his heart soared. Her sweet tones lifted his spirits while her frequency patterns did things to his body he had never felt or experienced before. Of course, Djibril had not endured his entire existence without having carnal knowledge of others, even a human or two, before the Designers had declared it forbidden.

This, however, was something far beyond anything he had ever experienced. This was home. He had finally found where he belonged and he felt it through all the way to his very soul.

He tried to speak her name, to tell her he was awake and that he could feel her. But the only sound he heard was a warbled low whisper that had no real substance and no words at all.

Her hands were immediately on his chest and face. "Shh," she softly said. "Everything is all right. You're safe now."

Djibril reached for her and then he felt her clasp his large hand in her smaller one. The tremendous energy coming off her in waves went up his arm and spread throughout his entire body. She was cool to the touch, but Djibril didn't care. What he cared about was staying physically connected with her. For some reason, there was apparently something wrong with his body, for he couldn't see, couldn't speak, and could barely manage to move. Yet he knew Sarah's energies would help his body to heal. He could feel them working on him already, for the hand and arm she held didn't hurt anywhere near as much now as they had mere moments ago when he had first reached for her. Assuming that angry Lyss person didn't return, Djibril believed he could be completely healed by Sarah's abundant energies in no time at all.

He was amazed at the strength and voraciousness of

her essences as they coursed throughout his body. He had had no idea of the magnitude of all the energy housed within her tiny frame. But he certainly felt it now.

His entire body tingled as each and every nerve ending was jolted by this new electricity. It ran along the neural axons and set fire to any area that needed mending. Djibril's throat was immediately aflame and he gasped at the hot sensation suddenly ringing his neck. The back of his neck exploded in pain next and he seized up, wondering what on earth could have happened to have caused this much internal damage to his person.

"Shh," Sarah soothed again. "It's all right. You're safe. I won't let anyone hurt you."

Djibril gasped at the pain again as it spiraled down his spinal cord. He could feel the neurons enervating his shields coming to life again and he hoped they wouldn't slip out from the sensation. He didn't know if he would be able to control them or not in his exhausted state. Having all of this foreign energy coursing through his limbs had completely taxed whatever energy reserves he had had on hand and he wanted nothing more than to fall right back to sleep.

As if she had read his thoughts, Sarah whispered close to his face in that British accent, "Go to sleep now. I'll protect you."

Djibril sighed and lazily drifted off as Sarah's energies continued their work. A part of his mind remained conscious of the fact that she was still there with him, stretched out alongside him wherever they lay. Another part of his mind went to work dreaming.

There were two beautiful little human girls in his dream. They were identical twins with fiery red hair and hazel eyes. Each loved their parents fiercely and they were always trying to gain the parents' approval with everything they did. If the father even mentioned having no son, each one of the twins would go out and learn how to do something boys did, just so they could allow him to experience something close to what he would have had if he had had a son in real life.

For example, one became quite good at football – had

even been on track to qualify for nationals before they had moved. And the other, well, she had become best all-around in her division of Mixed Martial Arts. Her father had particularly enjoyed the abruptness of this sport and he and she had spent many nights discussing different moves and exercises she could use to improve her technique.

As for their mother, the girls always wore the dresses she picked out for them without complaint. They attended the teas, music lesson and elocution classes to learn all the manners of polite society the way proper young women should. They were perfect daughters, the two of them. Even after they had moved from their beloved hometown of Bamford, England, they had remained as loyal and loving to their parents as two daughters could be.

Then everything changed.

Djibril suddenly woke to find himself lying in a room that had been tastefully decorated in subtle shades of cream and dark greens. It was a little less masculine than he would have preferred, but as he looked down at the cream eyelet lace coverlet someone had pulled up over most of his chest, he realized it wasn't Sarah lying next to him. Instead, the woman pressed closely up against his side had a thick cascade of natural fiery red hair spread out over most of her body and half of her side of the bed.

Djibril blinked in confusion. His brain took note of an IV bag hanging off to his left and several monitoring machines of some sort as well. Of course, none of these things were working due to their proximity to him and Djibril knew suddenly he was not in the Loric realm. He was no longer in the blue dimension either, apparently, and that only left the human realm as a possibility.

Moving as little as possible in order not to disturb the sleeping woman beside him, he turned his head to take in more of the room. There was a comfortable looking overstuffed chair in the far corner, a very old wooden wardrobe with a full-length mirror on one half of the front of it, a ceiling fan, two double doors that presumably led to a closet, and a wooden door in the other far corner that was half open. Djibril could see what looked like a toilet and sink beyond the door, but nothing more. He heard what sounded like waves crashing onto a beach, but the one large window in the room opposite the bed was closed and too high up for him to see out it to confirm this place was near a beach.

Suddenly, within his mind he heard that same British-accented voice, the nice one, calling his name. *Djibril!* she called. *Where are you?*

He looked down at the face of the woman lying beside him. Her great mass of hair almost completely concealed her face from view and he reached over to push it gently off her silken skin, thrilling at the energy that shot up his fingertips the moment they touched her. Confusion eclipsed all thought immediately thereafter as his hand was knocked away and he was subjected to the woman suddenly straddling his chest while her hand took a death grip on his still-sore throat.

"What the hell do you...?" she snarled, but didn't finish. He had clearly startled her awake from some deep sleep. Now, as she frowned, she climbed off his chest and let go her grip on his throat. She remained on the bed with him, sitting with her knees bent and her bum on her heels as she stared down at him. Her left leg was pressed up against his side.

"H-Hullo," she finally managed.

Djibril eyed her cautiously. He wasn't quite sure what to make of this situation. Sarah was not in the room, yet he could feel her energies. But for some reason, it appeared the energies he was feeling came from *this* woman. He swallowed a huge lump in his throat and asked in a very gravelly voice, "Sarah?"

The woman's hazel eyes narrowed and then she asked suspiciously, "Who's Sarah? Your wife? Your girlfriend? One of your *harem?*"

This last sounded particularly vicious and he was reminded of the angry voice belonging to the one called Lyss. His mind raced and he recalled all he had heard and seen in his dream and, frowning, he asked, again in that gravelly voice, "Chris?"

She was shocked. How had he known her name? She

backed off away from him a little and asked, "Who are you?"

"My name is Djibril," he said.

Chris blinked a couple of times. "From my dream," she softly said. "I saw you in my dream. You were in a cave with a man, teaching him the ways of Islam."

He nodded. "Yes."

She got up off the bed and walked over to the window. After a moment, she turned back to him and accused, "Then you *are* one of them – a Muslim."

Djibril frowned. "No, I…"

Just then, the door to the room opened and there stood Chris, or rather Lyss, as Djibril realized this had to be Chris' twin. She stepped into the room, but kept her distance from him. "I thought I heard voices," she said as she stared accusingly at him.

Djibril didn't know what to think. Both pairs of identical hazel eyes in identical beautiful faces surrounded by identical fiery red hair were staring at him like he was the sum of all evil in the Universe. He wondered what on earth he could have done to earn such hatred from total strangers.

He could remember nothing past when he had been searching for Sarah in the blue dimension after she had run away from him. Past that, all he could recall were her energies being near him and then inside him, healing him. Though now that he thought about it, he wondered if perhaps those energies hadn't belonged to Sarah after all. He looked back at Chris, frowning as he worked to figure out this puzzle.

There she stood, her soul-glow increasing with every passing moment, making the glow coming off her far brighter than that which emitted from Lyss, and Djibril suddenly knew. Somehow, Chris had found him. He didn't yet know how or why or even when. He simply knew she was his one true mate and she had found him and saved him from the blue dimension. And that could only mean…

"Oh, Sarah," he whispered aloud as he covered his eyes with one hand and rubbed hard at them. He would have to find some way to get back there, to the blue dimension, so he could find her and – and what? He didn't know how *he* had come to be in that place, let alone how to return there in order to help Sarah escape it.

"Who's this fucking Sarah person?" Chris suddenly demanded angrily from her position by the window.

"Do not speak in such a manner in my presence again," Djibril quietly ordered, lowering his hand from his eyes. He was unaccustomed to hearing any man speak with such vulgarity as this, not to mention a female.

"Fuck you, you Muslim bastard! I'll speak however the fuck I please," she informed him with a challenge in her voice and one brow raised in anticipation of the fight to come.

Djibril would have none of this. His voice might not be working right, but he could feel that the rest of his body had returned to its usual state, if not an improved one, and he whipped out his shields and rose into the air to hover visibly above the bed. The two were immediately shocked and quickly backed as far away from him as they could, each heading toward separate corners of the room as they took up defensive stances and stared in disbelief at the thing floating before them.

"Wh-What *are* you?" Chris finally managed to ask.

He narrowed his eyes on her and announced, "I am Lord Lori Djibril, though you may know me as Gabriel. An Arc Angel, I believe is how you would know me, and I will not tolerate such disrespect from anyone – not even *you*."

"M-Me?" Chris asked.

Djibril nodded once.

"Because she saved you?" Lyss asked.

Djibril turned his gaze on Lyss and, instead of answering her, asked, "How did she save me?"

Haltingly at first, the two women told him of how they had discovered him alive in the stairwell of the underground parking garage in London and of how they had then arranged for him to be flown to New York with them. "I thought you were dead because of the wound on your neck," Chris explained. "But then I noticed you were still breathing and, well, I couldn't just leave you there."

"What happened at the garage?" Djibril suddenly

asked urgently. He remembered being there now, in the stairwell. He had been watching the men in the parking area as they had prepared their device. He remembered hearing a noise behind him and then... nothing. Everything had gone blank. The next thing he recalled was waking in the blue dimension, then hearing Mikhail's voice calling Sarah.

Chris and Lyss spared a quick glance at one another before saying in unison, "Nothing."

"But there were men there with explosives," he said. "Did they succeed?"

The twins shook their heads.

Djibril sighed in relief at this news, but he was still very confused. Perhaps Israfil would be able to help him. He rubbed at his forehead and eyes again. He was exhausted once more. He wanted to lie back down on the bed below with Chris to allow her powerful energies to replenish his store, but there was no time. He needed to get back to the Complex as quickly as possible. Sarah's life depended on it. He only hoped Israfil wouldn't be too grief-stricken over the loss of Mikhail to help find her, wherever she might be. Djibril almost dreaded finding her, for he believed wherever she was, surely Mikhail's body would be found there as well.

He looked at each of the twins. They both deserved an explanation, but again there was no time. Instead, he would take Chris now. After everything was taken care of back in the Loric dimension, she and he could return to explain things to Lyss. Djibril moved slowly forward and lowered himself down to stand directly before Chris. "Come," he said, his arms spread wide. "We must make haste."

Chris relaxed from her ready stance. She felt nothing from him that called for caution. But as she stepped closer into the waiting circle of his arms, she frowned in confusion, asking, "Isn't Lyss coming, too?"

Djibril turned with a cautious look toward Lyss. Hesitantly, he said, "It would be better if you and I go now and then we could return later for you to see your..."

Immediately, Chris stepped away from his embrace. At his look of confusion, she announced, "Either Lyss comes with us, or I don't go."

The twins looked again at each other. Lyss was clearly confused by everything that was going on and even a little fearful. It was crazy. If she hadn't seen the guy float up into the air like he had done, she would've thought *he* was crazy. But he *had* floated up into the air and even she could feel something coming from him now. It felt like a soothing and almost sad energy or aura and Lyss kind of understood why her sister would be so keen to go with him without question. A part of her wanted to go just to find out what kind of adventure might lay ahead.

Djibril knew time was of the essence and he could feel the weight of Chris' words. He was certain she would not waiver from her decision, should he choose not to allow the sister to accompany them to the Loric dimension. He knew everyone would accept Chris' presence in their realm since she was to be his mate, but Lyss? She was just a human. There could be danger in taking her to the Complex without anyone's permission and that could spell trouble for Chris and him.

Mikhail had brought Sarah's family over without first consulting with his brethren and look what had almost happened to them. Would he be able to provide protection for the sister sufficiently enough before he and Chris mated and gained whatever abilities they were to gain? Djibril did not know the answer to that question, but he was out of time and unwilling to return home without Chris.

"You will accompany me if your sister is allowed to come?" he asked.

Chris swallowed hard and nodded before quickly stating, "That is the condition."

Djibril nodded once and then spread both arms wide, inviting, "Then come. We must hurry."

Lyss threw a concerned look at her sister, but she moved forward into the waiting arms of the strange creature.

As the man's arms drew the twins in close, each locked eyes with the other. With close to two decades of Catholic Church behind them, a sudden thrill of fear streaked through each twin. "Are we dying?" Chris asked in a small voice, as she pressed her body up against his for protection.

"No, my heart," Djibril said. "But someone very important may die, if we do not hurry." With that, he released all six of his shields, enclosing the twins and himself within their protective shell and rising up through the ceiling of the house. He noted absently that the house *was* situated on a beach, but then he concentrated on reaching any one of the rifts Mikhail had found for him and Suriyah at the outset of this whole fiasco of a journey. A little while later, he felt the pull of one. He paused in the air near it. Looking down at his mate's fear-filled face, he knew he could not subject her to the sting of the rift. Instead, he concentrated and within seconds, the two silent twins were sound asleep in his arms and he knew it was safe to cross the barrier.

Chapter 9

Mikhail adjusted his position, taking care not to move any more than necessary. Sarah had been asleep for hours and, although he was starting to feel concerned that perhaps she was sleeping too long, he was loathe to wake her in case she needed the sleep to recover from her time in the blue dimension. The difficulty was that she had been in the same position on his lap for the past several hours and his body was starting to protest at being forced to remain in the same position for so long.

He moved his other leg to ease a cramped muscle and Sarah suddenly started, as if coming out of a dream or a very deep sleep. She sat up and looked confusedly around the room. She paused as her gaze settled on Azra'il and a look of apprehension crossed her face.

"Sarah, sweetheart?" Mikhail softly asked. "Are you all right?"

She turned back to him and reached up to touch his lips with one hand. "Mikhail?" Her hair slowly wound itself around his shoulders and upper torso, entwining with his hair and caressing his body.

Mikhail reached up to wipe a belated tear away from her cheek and said, "Everything is all right."

Sarah laid her head back down on his shoulder and snuggled her nose up against his neck. "I thought you were dead," she said in a soft little voice.

Mikhail pulled her close and caressed her cheek. "I am not dead, sweetheart. We are both fine," he said.

For a moment, she was silent. Then, however, memories of her time in that other place returned and Sarah's face crumpled as a wave of sadness engulfed her. She buried her face against his neck and whispered, "Sheely."

"Shh, sweetheart," Mikhail eased in a low voice. "Sheely is fine. She is with Miriam."

Sarah sat up again, spearing him with a look of uncertainty. "Sheely's... a-alive?"

Lisa stood and crossed over to the door. "I'll send for Miriam," she said.

"How can Sheely be alive?" Sarah asked.

"Shh, sweetheart. You and I both missed a lot while we were gone," Mikhail explained.

Lisa returned and reclaimed her seat beside Baphomet. She smiled over at Sarah, the sisterly affection she felt toward the older woman clearly showing through her glowing eyes, and she said, "We're so glad you made it back. You gave us quite a fright, you know?"

Sarah blinked in confusion. She couldn't understand what had happened. Mikhail had been dead. Sheely had been dead. She had been stuck in that awful blue dimension for so long, cold and alone. Now it was as if none of it had even happened, except somehow Sarah had missed giving birth to Sheely.

All of a sudden, her psychic connection with Mikhail was restored and everything he had experienced since last they had been connected came rushing into her mind. The images and emotions were overwhelming and she tightly wrapped her hair and arms around him as scene after scene played out before her mind's eye.

Mikhail squeezed back, as all she had experienced played itself out simultaneously within *his* mind. He held her as close as he could as he felt her sorrow at Sheely's loss. Then, however, his entire body became consumed with rage that Djibril would dare to suggest Sarah should become *his* mate.

"Don't," Sarah said against his neck. "He thought you were dead. We both did."

Mikhail could feel her compassion toward his sibling and he understood the logic of it all. After all, Israfil had said he believed the one who had found Djibril's body was Djibril's mate. If that was the case, then Mikhail knew it was possible his brother could have confused the energies he had felt coming from his mate with Sarah's.

Logic. It made sense. Unfortunately, Mikhail had not been able to depend much on logic to rule his mind since he had met Sarah. She was his mate – *his* – and right now he bloody well felt like ripping Djibril's head off!

"Shall I hold him down for you?" Baphomet asked

through his chuckles. Lisa turned and smacked him on the arm, but she wasn't having much more success hiding her own smile.

Israfil was fighting a smile and Suri, who was completely confused by now, asked, "What is so funny?"

Sarah sighed in frustration, fighting back a grin of her own. "Gabriel hit on me after we thought Mikhail was dead," she explained.

Understanding hit Suriyah and she looked over at Mikhail, finding it difficult now herself to hide a smile.

After a moment, Sarah felt a slight chuckle escape Mikhail's chest. Then he growled as he pulled her closer and kissed her hard and deep on the mouth. Soon, Sarah could only think of him. She became so involved in the kiss that it was a shock to her senses when the door suddenly opened to allow the old Kurr, Miriam, to enter with a very brightly-glowing Sheely in her arms.

Everyone gasped at the waves of energy coming off the tiny bundle in pulses, like the beating of her tiny heart. Sarah accepted her daughter from Miriam and then sat staring down into the most beautiful bright blue eyes she had ever seen. Sheely just stared right back up at her. Sarah realized she could no longer hear Sheely's interminable chatter, now that she had been born, and a part of her felt bereft, as if she had lost a close, personal friend.

I think everything is just so confusing to her, love, that she has chosen to hide her thoughts, as Cabal did with Lisa and Baphomet, Mikhail's gentle voice said silently within her mind. *But Hantsushept has given her a perfect bill of health, so there is no need to worry.*

Sarah looked up at him, hope burning in her eyes. He smiled at her and then they both looked back down onto Sheely's beautiful little face. She yawned all of a sudden and nearly everyone in the room softly crowed, "Aww."

Nearly everyone.

For some reason, Azra'il stared not at the baby but at the old Kurr, Miriam. After a moment, however, he pulled himself up off his lounging position against the wall, choosing to ignore whatever it was about the old Kurr that was bothering him just on the outskirts of his consciousness. Instead, he approached the happy couple with the baby. Hesitantly, he asked, "M-May I… hold her?"

Baphomet, Israfil, Lisa, *and* Suriyah were all four immediately on their feet, moving to position themselves in a defensive position in front of the trio they held so dear.

No, Sarah, Mikhail's voice hissed through her mind. But as Sarah stared up at the daunting and distrusting Lori before her, she heard what she quickly realized was a plea from Sheely, asking to be allowed to go to him. Sarah frowned down at her daughter's bright blue eyes and Sheely blinked up at her. *We cannot trust him yet*, Mikhail's voice whispered urgently in her mind.

As Sarah stared down at the baby, she had the strangest feeling inside, as if she was playing a part in something much bigger than she or Mikhail or any of them could ever comprehend. Although most everyone else in the room looked at her like she had gone completely mad when she did it, Sarah turned slightly and carefully handed Sheely's bundled form up to Azra'il's waiting arms.

And that's when all hell broke loose.

***

Azra'il cackled inwardly with glee as the female lifted her arms out toward him. The fool was actually going to just hand over the infant, just like that! He couldn't believe how simple it had been. There had been that moment when all of his siblings around the room had gathered protectively around the babe and Azra'il had thought they might stop him from gaining possession of the thing. And that old Kurr – Azra'il didn't know what it was about her that had caught his senses and he didn't like it. But now, Sarah was going to simply hand over her defenseless daughter to him.

What luck! It appeared his plan would work after all.

As Azra'il reached for the tiny bundle, a faint alarm sounded from somewhere in the deepest recesses of his mind. Then he had the child in his arms and it was too late as everything in his existence broke. He staggered back against the gurney behind him as flashes of image after image suddenly crowded through his mind. Every place the babe touched his body was immediately on fire as the child's energies raced into his cells, spreading like wildfire in a drought, and he thought he was going to explode.

Azra'il couldn't keep up with the images and he grabbed hold of the gurney to keep from falling. A tremendous pain raced across his scalp and his eyeballs felt as if they were being scraped by sand. He screamed in terror as he looked down onto the infant's form and then, like the crack of lightning, there was peace.

In his arms, the silent being was silent no more. She spoke to him, not in words at all, but in feeling. He could hear her thoughts, the way her mind worked in that strange language that was not a language. He understood what she understood and he felt what she felt. He knew she belonged with him and he with her. They were one and no force in the heavens or on Earth could ever separate them again.

He was amazed to see that her eyes glowed a brilliant white now instead of being the ice blue color they had been mere seconds before. The child's hair, which before had been a short, baby-fine light brown color, now stretched from her scalp all the way around his upper torso and was a glimmering iridescent white.

"Brother!" Mikhail called suddenly.

Azra'il tore his gaze from the angelic child he held in his right arm to look upon the brother who was standing directly before him. He couldn't catch his breath, could barely hear Mikhail's voice. So much was going through his mind. His eyes were suddenly burning again, his scalp felt as if someone was peeling it off his skull, and the rest of his body was simply on fire from the inside out. He looked back down at the babe and tried to hand her over to his brother.

Sheely would have none of that. She screamed suddenly and the sound pierced the air, causing everyone save Azra'il to cover their ears. The majority of her new hair tightened around his torso, while a small portion of it lashed out, slicing through Mikhail's outstretched hands.

Mikhail immediately retreated, protecting his injured hands and staring in complete shock at the scene before him.

"T-Take her!" Azra'il stammered as he attempted to hand the child over to his brother.

No one moved.

Azra'il stared mutely at those facing him. They merely stared right back. No one stepped forward to retrieve the child from him. No one called for assistance. He looked down upon the child once more and realized his pain was now gone. His eyes felt quite fine and, although he could still feel Sheely's energies racing through his body, it was having an altogether different effect on him now. He felt a wave of tenderness so pure and sweet he thought he would weep.

She was perfect. Her tones sang the purest song in his mind and he saw her with a clarity he had never before experienced. Her energy glow was brilliant, but beautiful. He was drawn to her and his face softened as he bent to rub his nose along the side of her cheek. Inhaling her scent had his senses reeling and he suddenly realized this was where he belonged. Wherever Sheely was, that was where he would be, forever more.

"Azra'il?" Israfil asked quietly from just behind Mikhail and Sarah, reminding Azra'il that there were others still in the room.

He looked up at his siblings, his face a mask of astonishment. They each still stared at him, merely stared, as if there was something wrong with him. None of them, save for Sarah, was looking at Sheely. Why? She was the one who had just transformed before their very eyes. Why wouldn't they be staring at her?

"Azra'il?" Suriyah suddenly asked, coming to stand just a few feet in front of him. At his questioning look, she asked, "A-Are you all right?"

He frowned. "I am fine," he said. "I-I think there is something wrong with Sheely, though." He turned to lay her onto the gurney, but her hair wouldn't loosen its grip around his torso. Turning a helpless look upon Mikhail and Sarah, he asked, "How…?"

The two remained where they were, transfixed.

Azra'il started as a group of white hair strands from

behind him suddenly crept along his right arm and then caressed Sheely's cheek, as if it was showing affection to the child. This hair was not iridescent. It was merely snow white and very long. Azra'il looked to his right and was shocked to find that the hair strands were coming from somewhere behind him and up. He reached behind himself, turning to try to find its source.

He came to a halt facing Mikhail and Sarah and the rest of the assemblage as realization dawned. This was *his* hair! The strands slowly wrapped around his hand and fingers and then went back to smoothing down the sides of Sheely's cheeks.

"Oh, my blessed Designers," he suddenly said, breathless. "What have you done to me?"

Sarah stared one more second before suddenly stepping forward and reaching out for Sheely. Azra'il immediately handed the child over to its mother and Sheely made no protest. Her hair dropped its hold on his torso and Sarah took her back into her arms, moving to stand behind Mikhail where Azra'il could no longer see Sheely.

Azra'il looked around at the multiple pairs of eyes staring at him in mute amazement. He blinked a few times to make sure he was really seeing what he thought he was seeing. The auras of his brothers and their mates gleamed, multicolored mirages shimmering around their bodies, and a radiance beamed from the center of each one's skull. Suriyah had a different kind of glow, lesser than that of his other siblings. She still glowed, but it was as if she was only half lit, as if part of her was missing or hadn't yet been ignited.

Israfil had a strange glow as well. His appeared as if it was floundering, doing its best to shine as brightly as it could, but having difficulty. His stretched the farthest, reaching very far out into the room, but there was something about the coloring that made Azra'il feel pain when he looked at it too long.

Those scattered throughout the large room were more than amazed at the physical transformations they had witnessed, but none of them realized how much was going on inside. Azra'il had barely noticed his own physical transformation as he had concentrated on the most beautiful Loric creature he had ever before beheld in his life. Mikhail moved slightly and he saw that she now lay quietly staring up at her mother where Sarah stood with her.

Sheely's transformation and energies were not all to capture Azra'il's attention, however, as he suddenly found himself staring into the dark abyss of space. At first, he thought he had somehow physically traveled from the room at the Medical Facility at the Complex to the dark reaches of emptiness, and his heart rate increased in fear for Sheely's well-being.

Her strange language in his mind assured him he had no reason to fear for her and he forced himself to calm down and concentrate on what was around him. That was when he realized he, himself, had not gone anywhere. Instead, what he was witnessing were things he saw only with his mind's eye. The rest of him, his physical self, he believed was most likely still standing in the room at the Complex with the others.

The scene before him was not of the far reaches of space either, as he had at first thought. Earth could now clearly be seen far below and Azra'il's mind settled in to watch.

It was odd. The area of the scene appeared to be located just a few miles up from the planet, barely even out of Earth's atmosphere, and yet it was remarkably quiet and clutter-free. Azra'il had traveled this far out before in his mind in attempts to discover the location humans' tether lines were connected to throughout their lives. The only things he had ever encountered had been noises, or chatter, from man-made satellite contraptions humans had stationed in orbit around the planet – but they had *been* there. Now, it was as if all of that had gone away. Azra'il heard nothing, saw nothing.

But some suspicious instinct cautioned him against this belief and he refocused his attention on his surroundings.

Off in the distance, a tiny pin-prick of light suddenly appeared. It was an indistinct object of some sort. The longer Azra'il remained focused on the thing emitting the light, the larger it appeared to grow. The object did not slow in its approach and Azra'il soon found himself staring at a massive machine that appeared to be in stasis around the planet. As it neared, however, he heard several sounds escape from within its metallic-like walls and there were multiple lights that flared to life.

That was when Azra'il noticed the tethers. There were literally hundreds of thousands of human tether lines running through the massive contraption. He concentrated on the portion of the tethers above the machine, but discovered everything was as he had seen it before... the lines merely disappeared into the surrounding darkness. As he returned his attention to the machine, he noticed that a few thousand, give or take, of the tethers seemed a bit thinner than the majority of the others. Each one of these appeared to be paired with very thick tethers. Every now and then there was one thick one by itself or one thin one, but these were few and far between.

Then the machine emitted a beastly growl of a sound as even more lights blinked to life and Azra'il noticed something very odd happening to the tether lines. The thick ones glowed very brightly. The thin ones were exceedingly dim, some to the point of near invisibility. Every now and then, a thick tether would intertwine with its thin one and there would be a brilliant momentary flash of light. Afterward, the two would move up through the machine, actually coming out of the top of it and disappearing somewhere up to where Azra'il could not see. On the horizon, he spotted another similar contraption with hundreds of thousands of tether lines attached as it approached. Not far beyond this one was another and then another. Now that he knew what to look for, Azra'il could see a whole horde of the devices ringing the entire planet.

It angered him that he still could not see where the tether lines ended, and he realized that he wanted to leave this place. As he attempted to return to his body, he found himself powerless to move from the location where he was currently stationed. No matter what he tried, he merely continued floating in the earliest reaches of space, just beyond the earth's atmosphere, stuck for all intents and purposes. It was Sheely's thoughts, or impressions really, coming through to him in his mind that finally brought his attention back to the room where they all still stood.

She commanded his attention and Azra'il gave it willingly. Sheely loved her mother very much and Azra'il found himself for the first time feeling an emotion toward Sarah he had never believed possible for him to feel – affection. Then he realized he was wrong. It wasn't that *he* was feeling this emotion, it was Sheely feeling it *through* him.

He suddenly had an impression of Mikhail's hands being sliced open earlier when he had reached for Sheely and Azra'il looked down to see his brother's hands now hanging limply by his sides.

"Sheely wants to know if your hands are all right," he announced to Mikhail.

Gasps were heard all around.

"You can hear her?" Mikhail quietly asked in an odd tone.

"Yes," Azra'il said softly. "I-I hear her; I *feel* her. I…" He could manage no more. Sheely was inside him. She was an integral part of his soul. She was part of his cellular make-up, part of his genes, part of everything. Without her, there was nothing and Azra'il could understand neither what made this so nor how it had happened.

Mikhail turned and stared deep into Sarah's eyes, their thoughts whizzing between the two of them. Baphomet and Lisa did the same, though their thoughts were more out of concern for Mikhail and Sarah – and Sheely, of course.

Azra'il heaved a deep sigh. He didn't know what to say or do. How could he express to them what he was feeling when he didn't even understand it himself? He could not leave Sheely, not now. He needed to be here to protect her. She was his life, after all. He could not even *think* of returning to Lorim City without her.

Mikhail and Sarah returned their gazes to Azra'il and Mikhail said, "Brother, I cannot stand here and tell you I am pleased by what has apparently transpired. You hold to a different philosophy than that which governs those of us whom you have banished from our former home. But it appears my daughter has discovered in you something none of us could see."

Mikhail came closer to Azra'il and asked, "Can you feel and hear Sheely now?"

Azra'il nodded without hesitation, for he most certainly could.

Mikhail looked back at Sarah. After a moment, he turned back to Azra'il, nodded once and said, "Then I guess that settles it. You will have to stay here with us."

Azra'il stared at his brother in astonishment. What was he saying? Stay at the Complex? In the Badlands?

Sarah suddenly stepped around Mikhail and pushed a very fussy Sheely toward Azra'il, announcing brusquely, "She wants you again."

Azra'il's eyes widened, but he immediately held out his arms and accepted the babe once more. It felt like coming home. She was where she belonged and he was doing what he had been created to do – protecting Sheely. He looked into Sarah's eyes and whispered, "Thank you."

Sarah hesitated a moment and then said curtly, "You're welcome." She turned and went back to stand beside Mikhail, taking his hand in hers.

Sheely yawned and slowly closed her eyes, drifting off to sleep as if nothing had happened.

Mikhail heaved a deep sigh and, looking down at Sarah, stated in a soft, concerned voice, "Well, I guess we need to work out some sleeping arrangements then."

Sarah looked around then and, spotting Miriam still sitting on a chair by the wall, said, "Wait. Miriam? Where's Thom…?" She didn't finish her statement as the memory of Mikhail finding out about Thomas' disappearance suddenly rushed through her mind. She began to tremble. But then Mikhail grabbed her chin and forced her to look into his eyes.

This we can deal with after Sheely is taken care of, his voice said in her mind.

Sarah stared into his eyes as every instinct inside her screamed in agony. But then she caught Mikhail's thoughts as he relayed his theory about Nera having taken Thomas for some reason and she realized he was right. They had to hold onto the hope that *that* was what had happened and that Thomas would be okay. Besides, there was nothing they could do other than to try to contact Nera. Sarah didn't like not knowing where Thomas was or if he was all right, but she really didn't have a choice. The only path to holding onto her sanity after everything she had been through was to hold to this Nera theory.

As soon as her mind settled, Mikhail wrapped an arm around her and looked back around at the crowd. "So," he said. "To the Main House?"

A soft noise at the back of the room suddenly had the entire assemblage whipping around to see what was going on.

***

Djibril was severely exhausted by the time the buildings at the Complex came into view. He just wanted to crawl into bed with Chris and sleep for a week, and seeing the Main House directly in front of them made him all the more tired.

But he couldn't just show up and install two humans in the Main House without so much as a by your leave. He knew sleep would have to wait and paused mid-air to see if he could locate anyone so he could obtain permission to have Chris and Lyss there.

Oddly enough, he didn't find anyone's energies where he had expected to find them. They were all at the Medical facility, not the Main House. Concern immediately replaced Djibril's exhaustion as he forced his way through the building's façade and into the room where apparently every Lori in the world was gathered.

He dropped his shields the moment his feet touched down and just stood there exhausted, staring at the group before him as he held the two unconscious twin humans in his arms.

Mikhail and Sarah stood right there in front of him – alive! And, on top of that shocker, there was Azra'il.

What was Azra'il doing here and *how* had he

changed?

Djibril's jaw hung open as he stared in amazement, first at Azra'il and then at Baphomet and *his* mate. What was going on? Was there an epidemic? Suriyah and Israfil still looked the same, but no one else did and Djibril was too stunned to speak.

"Gabriel?" Sarah suddenly said, breaking the silence as she came toward him, a half smile on her face.

Djibril noticed the look he got from Mikhail was not quite as welcoming. In fact, he imagined he could almost feel hatred emitting from his brother. But he nodded to Sarah and finally found his tongue. "I, ah, apparently missed something, did I not?" His gravelly voice sounded too loud to his ears in the quiet room.

Sarah smiled and said, "You have no idea." She noticed the two sleeping humans in his arms and raised a brow in question.

Djibril looked down at Chris' face and then back toward Sarah, saying, "Ah, I am... at a loss." He didn't know what to say to her. The last time he had seen her, he had tried to convince her that Mikhail was dead, which he obviously was not. What could he say to her now?

Sarah held up a hand and said, "No. Don't worry 'bout it. It's been a very long day and we all just need some rest." She turned and headed for the door, catching up with Mikhail, who also had turned toward the door. "Come on," Sarah called to Djibril. "You can tell us all about it after everybody's gotten some sleep. We'll get those two a room, unless...?" She paused and turned to look up at him.

Djibril immediately said, "Chris stays with me."

Sarah stared long and hard at him a moment, then she nodded and turned back to Mikhail. And for the first time since the little group had come to live in the Badlands, all of the Lorim were together.

Chapter 10

Thomas came slowly to consciousness. His mind felt extremely sluggish, as if it had been almost dead asleep for a long, long time. He sucked in a deep breath and then nearly doubled over on his side coughing. His lungs hurt as if they were filled with fluid. He hacked and hacked, finally subsiding as he managed at last to get a good enough breath into his lungs to supply him with the oxygen his body needed.

He opened his eyes to mere slits and found that everything was blurry. The light was much too bright for him and he quickly closed his eyes again.

What had happened?

There was an odd humming noise all around that felt like it was vibrating even up through the bed where he lay and he stretched his arm out to grab hold of the edge of the mattress. He touched something, or some*one*, and a shaft of electricity shot up his arm.

His eyes sprang open and he was momentarily blinded by the brightness of the room. He sucked in another breath, just managing not to go into another coughing fit, and then his vision cleared enough for him to recognize that Nera was sitting next to the bed holding his hand.

She looked different, he noticed. He closed his eyes and opened his mouth to say her name. An odd, scratchy noise was all his throat would produce.

"Do not speak," Nera whispered in some different language. "Your vocal cords will not be able to properly function for a short time due to lack of use."

Thomas didn't know how he understood the words she said and he opened his eyes again to look at her. That's when he noticed she wasn't alone. Just behind her stood a very tall, very brightly glowing alien with whiter-than-white glowing eyes and the long white hair similar to that of his mother and Mikhail.

He recognized the alien without really knowing who he was, kind of like déjà vu. The alien smiled down at him and said in that same strangely-familiar language, "Welcome back." Thomas frowned at the alien, wondering who he was. It was obvious the alien knew him, but Thomas just couldn't think clearly at the moment.

He closed his eyes again and squeezed Nera's hand.

"Sleep," she said next to his ear.

The suggestion was all Thomas needed and he sighed as a wave of unconsciousness swamped his senses.

As Nera sat next to the bed holding Talis' hand, she looked up at Lokai and softly asked, "He can sleep for a little while more, right?"

Lokai looked down upon his brother's sleeping form and frowned. "There is not much time, Nera" he said. "It will take him some time to get back up to speed and then we will have to act, or all will be lost." He stepped around her for a moment and reached forward to place a hand on his brother's forehead. Sighing resignedly, he said, "I shall allow him just a bit more sleep, but then he will have to be brought to the bridge."

Nera sighed and nodded her acceptance of his terms. She just hoped it would be enough time for Talis to recover from being off ship. She knew their time was running short, but she didn't want Talis to have to confront what was coming without having the opportunity to fully recover. She just hoped she hadn't waited too long to pull him back from his assignment. She closed her eyes as she brought the hand she held up to her lips.

So much was riding on this, their last chance.

***

Azra'il walked along with his siblings toward the main building on the Complex grounds. He still didn't fully understand what was going on, but he knew he had no choice but to follow along because there was no way he was leaving Sheely. The fact that his brothers were allowing him to stay overwhelmed him, especially after one considered the fact that it was he who had banished *them* from Lorim City.

Just the thought of his home brought the memory of why he had come to the Complex in the first place roaring back into his mind and he suddenly remembered the small elite Guard unit he had left waiting on the other side of the grounds.

"Mikhail, hold," he said, stopping in his tracks.

Everyone stopped and turned to see what the matter was.

He didn't want to admit what he had to tell them, but there was nothing for it but to say it outright. "I, ah, did not come here alone," he said.

Mikhail frowned as he noticed his other siblings immediately taking defensive stances as they looked around for hidden threats. "How many came with you and where are they?" Mikhail asked angrily.

Azra'il blinked a couple of times at his brother's instant condemnation of him, but then he nodded. "This way," he said as he started off in the direction of the location where his Guard awaited his return. His brother was right to blame him, he realized.

"Hold, Azra'il," Mikhail ordered. Azra'il obediently stopped, turning to wait for him. Mikhail instructed Sarah, "Take Sheely to the house. Get everything arranged for our guests. For the now, I think it would be best if Azra'il stayed with us in our suite, seeing as how Sheely is so attached to him."

Sarah nodded.

"I shall return as soon as possible," he said, as he leaned forward and kissed her tenderly on the forehead.

Be careful and remember that I love you, her voice whispered in his mind as she nodded once more.

He softly ran his index finger down the side of her cheek. *You are my love*, his voice said in her mind. Then, after Sarah retrieved Sheely's sleeping form from Azra'il, Mikhail turned and walked off with him. Israfil, Baphomet, and Lisa followed their two brothers, just in case there was trouble.

Djibril, Suriyah, and the two sleeping humans they carried followed the old Kurr, Miriam, and Sarah, who still carried the sleeping Sheely, to the main house. All the medical staff had already departed to their separate living quarters elsewhere around the Complex.

Mikhail had not been pleased to discover that his brother had not come to the Complex alone, but he supposed it was to be expected. After all, Azra'il and the council had already sent several stages of attacks by the City's elite Guardsmen. Mikhail supposed he should have expected this visit by his brother, especially in light of the result of the last Guard attack.

The group came upon a make-shift campsite where a small contingency of elite Guardsmen waited.

"Lord Azra'il," the captain of the unit called upon catching sight of his master's approach. He immediately stood and made to approach the newcomers. When he was close enough to see Azra'il's countenance clearly, however, he stopped in his tracks and exclaimed, "My Lord! What have they done to you?"

All the other Guardsmen quickly gathered in formation behind their captain, each clearly confused and a bit unhinged by the sight confronting them. Each one of them recalled the grisly nature of the bodies of the last group of Guardsmen who had confronted these evil outland Lorim. Now they were facing four of them, and it looked as if the creatures had possibly turned their Lord Azra'il into one of *them*.

"I have come to inform you that your mission here has been cancelled," Azra'il said. "The humans we sought in this place are no longer. I bid you return to Lorim City and inform the council that I have decreed that our Realm is no longer in danger of encroachment by humans."

The captain of the Guard blinked a couple of times and then, completely surprising everyone, took a step forward into a ready fighting stance and said, "I am afraid I cannot do that, my Lord."

Azra'il frowned. He was unaccustomed to having any order disobeyed and his ire rose to the fore as he asked sibilantly, "And just exactly why not?"

The captain pulled out his sword and, licking his lips and readying to strike should he need to, he said, "Our mission was to kill any Lorim we encountered as well as any humans. We were also instructed that if you interfered with that mission in any way, we were to dispatch you as well." The captain slowly started forward toward Azra'il, a little shakily, but with deadly and determined intent in his eyes.

Immediately, the entire assemblage of Guardsmen collapsed to their knees as both Israfil and Baphomet took possession of each Kurr's mind and either twisted it so far into a sense of helplessness that the Kurr could no longer remain sane, as was the case with those affected by Baphomet's powerful mind, or each Kurr's thoughts became so muddled he could not even think clearly enough to remain standing, which was the effect Israfil had on each mind he touched.

Azra'il stared in amazement as his own innate abilities kicked in and he checked on each of his team's well-being. His brothers were not harming the Kurr in the least. They were merely confusing them and twisting reality for them to the point that logic and reason no longer existed.

Mikhail stepped forward and closed his eyes in concentration. Within seconds, each Kurr lying on the ground was in a deep state of unconsciousness. Baphomet and Israfil blinked a couple of times as the Kurr minds slipped away. Realization dawned and each turned to regard Mikhail. He sighed heavily and then opened his eyes to gaze upon his handiwork.

Azra'il was stunned. Why hadn't they killed the Guardsmen as they had the ones before?

"That was not the work of these, your brothers," Lisa suddenly said to him. "Your sister and Sarah, and the two young ones, were defending *me* from those attackers that day," she explained. "They were there to kill all of us and there was no time to do anything *but* kill or be killed."

A chill ran down Azra'il's spine at the thought that Sarah and Suriyah could have done what had been done to the squadron that had been slaughtered. He didn't know who these two young ones were that Lisa was referring to, but he knew anyone with that kind of fighting ability was a foe not to be reckoned with lightly and he intended to find out exactly how much training, and what type, these creatures really had so that his own Guard could better learn to fight them, should the need ever arise.

"So, what do we do with them now?" he asked.

"Bundle them up, throw them in the ocean," Baphomet said. Lisa punched him in the arm. "Ow! What?" he asked, rubbing his arm where she had hit him.

Mikhail scowled at his recalcitrant brother and then turned to Azra'il, saying, "If we send them back to Lorim City, they will only return with reinforcements."

"I agree," Israfil stated.

"I think it would be best to keep them here, for the time being at least, under house arrest," Mikhail continued. "Hopefully, in time they will come to understand we mean no one in the Loric Realm any harm. At that point, they should be allowed to return to their homes." He asked Azra'il, "Did you give our location to the council?"

"I-I informed a small number of them of this location for the last mission that was sent," Azra'il said. "The group here was the only one informed of the location this time."

Mikhail nodded once and sighed. "Hopefully the council members who were told before will have forgotten the location then," he said. "But I would not count on it." He turned to Israfil and Baphomet. "We shall have to post guards along the outskirts of the Complex for the now."

His brothers each nodded once.

"Lisa and Baphomet," Mikhail instructed, "please return to the Complex and then bring reinforcements to come here and take these Kurr to one of the storage units along the south side of the Complex. Sleeping and living accommodations will have to be arranged within the unit, and a round-the-clock guard will have to be established as well, both inside and out."

The two merely nodded once before setting off back toward the Complex.

Azra'il watched as the two departed. He wondered if *he* would end up being placed under house arrest. Mikhail had said earlier that he was to stay with Sheely and Sarah and him within *their* suite. But that had been before those he had brought with him had turned on everyone.

"You worry too much, my brother," Mikhail stated as

he placed a hand on Azra'il's shoulder.

Azra'il turned to face Mikhail. "So you will not arrest me as well?" he asked.

Mikhail dropped his hand and his gaze and swallowed a huge lump in his throat, as if struggling with some internal demon. Then he said simply, "I cannot." With that, he turned and walked to the far side of the camp site.

Azra'il watched him go, wondering what on earth his brother had meant.

***

Suriyah stopped at a bedroom door along the corridor of the Main House's second floor and adjusted her hold on the twin she carried as she asked Sarah, "Will this one do for the humans?"

Sarah started to respond, but halted as Djibril said in his new deep, gravelly voice, "Chris stays with me."

"Well, do you not think it will be strange for one of them to wake up with no one in the room with her?" Suriyah asked him in frustration.

"We can assign a Kurr to attend Lyss for whatever needs she may have," he informed her, "but Chris stays with me."

Suriyah turned suddenly pleading eyes on Sarah, and Sarah sighed before stating, "This room will be fine for, uh, Lyss. You go ahead and put her in there an' if you'll stay with her for a spell, I'll see what I can do about sendin' somebody over to stay with her for the next few hours, at least. Your room is still vacant, so you can sleep there if you want."

Although Suriyah didn't like this plan, she sighed and nodded her acceptance and then entered the bedroom without further comment.

Djibril, Sarah, and Miriam continued along the corridor to another suite of rooms where Sarah thought her brother and his new mate would be more comfortable. The old Kurr stayed in the corridor with Sheely while Sarah followed Djibril in and waited while he placed Chris onto the bed.

Once he had Chris safely tucked under the covers, he turned and walked her to the door, clearly ready to be alone with the girl. "Thank you," he said softly, "for welcoming me back."

She slanted a smile up at him and said, "Israfil explained everything to Mikhail an' I got everything from him." At Djibril's look of confusion, she explained, "You were simply feelin' the effects of Chris' energies on you. That's what made you think you and I were…" She gave a shrug and left the rest unsaid as understanding finally dawned on him. She then reached up and patted him on the arm, saying, "Get some sleep. You're probably gonna need it for all the explanations you're gonna have to provide when they wake up."

Djibril's eyebrows rose and he nodded as he held the door open for her.

Sarah took Sheely back into her arms from the old Kurr and they returned to the suite of rooms Sarah shared with Mikhail. She wasn't ready yet to have the newborn sleeping in the nursery Mikhail had built onto the house, so she took Sheely to their bedroom instead and placed her on the middle of the bed.

Sarah was exhausted. She would like nothing more than to crawl onto the bed with Sheely and fall sound asleep for the next however many hours she would be allowed to rest. So far, Sheely hadn't started protesting about being hungry or needing to be changed, but Sarah had played this role before and she knew what the coming months were going to be like. She also still felt the loss of Thomas so difficult to take that she didn't know if she would be able to sleep anytime soon.

"Shall I send for tea?" Miriam asked as she placed a few cloth diapers and towels for changing the baby on a nearby table.

Sarah had forgotten the old Kurr was even there, she was so tired. But she was glad for the woman's presence. "That would be wonderful," she said as she took a seat on the side of the bed.

"I shall make sleeping arrangements for Lord Azra'il

and for myself, if that will be all right?" the Kurr suggested.

Sarah just nodded. She was too exhausted to even think clearly. She had to stay awake until Mikhail returned and any offer of help at this point was welcomed. She looked up at the old Kurr with a wan smile, yawning and saying, "Thank you, Miriam. I can't tell you how much I appreciate all you've done for us."

Miriam smiled serenely down at Sarah and said, "You are quite welcome, my Lady." Then the old Kurr turned and made her way out the door in search of others who could help with the arrangements.

Sarah lay down on the edge of the bed and reached over to tuck a little part of Sheely's swaddling blanket under her tiny chin. She was such a beautiful little girl, but Sarah could feel the energy pumping through her, just beneath the surface. *How could such a tiny thing hold so much energy within itself?* she wondered.

She touched the blanket in the area where Sheely's feet were and then rubbed her hand on the area above Sheely's belly. She yawned again and thought she might just close her eyes for a few minutes. But then a thought pierced her brain and her eyes flew open as a frown creased her face.

Azra'il would be returning with Mikhail when he came back. Sheely might possibly want to be with him more than she would want to be with Mikhail and her. She knew this because she had seen what had happened in the medical center. She had witnessed the coming together of two souls that belonged to each other.

She knew her daughter no longer belonged to her but to Azra'il, and the thought was almost more than she could stand. She had only just gotten her. How could she have lost her already? And now that she had lost Thomas, too... how could she deal with all of this?

Sheely's eyes opened all of a sudden and she looked directly up into her mother's. With that one look, a sense of peace washed over Sarah as she stared down into her daughter's brighter than bright eyes. Everything would be okay. Thomas was most likely with Nera somewhere and they would be contacted when the strange alien that was Nera chose to involve them in whatever she was doing.

And as for Sheely, she loved Sarah and Mikhail. Sarah could feel it. The child would always want to be with Azra'il, for he was the other half of her soul. But she somehow understood that it was her mother who would best be able to look after her for the time being. All this information Sheely conveyed silently to Sarah as they gazed upon each other and Sarah was finally able to relax.

She was completely calm by the time Mikhail and Azra'il returned to the house and she welcomed her mate's brother with an open mind and heart. Miriam had done her job well, as there were now two cots arranged for sleeping, one for her in Sheely's nursery and one for Azra'il in the study. Miriam, it appeared, had assigned herself the role of Sheely's new nanny and she went off to set up her personal belongings in the nursery.

Azra'il, of course, immediately asked to see Sheely and the three of them spent the next couple of hours in the master bedroom, simply looking at Sheely and remarking on this or that aspect about her. It was close to lunch time when Azra'il finally yawned and announced that he was in need of sleep.

He paused at the door of their bedroom before leaving and turned to face the two, saying hesitantly, "Thank you for... everything. I did not expect this."

"Today has been full of surprises for everyone," Mikhail announced as he joined his brother at the door. "But you are right. We all need sleep."

Azra'il nodded and then threw one last glance at Sheely to make sure she was still okay before he turned and left.

Mikhail silently closed the door behind his brother and whispered, "I thought he would never *leave*."

Sarah quietly chuckled as he returned to the bed where she and Sheely were laying. He carefully climbed up opposite Sarah, doing his best to move the mattress as little as possible as he gazed down upon their beautiful daughter. She was once again sleeping soundly. Her little bottom lip moved every now and then in what Sarah said was a sucking motion, indicating that she was either dreaming or she was hungry. Mikhail smiled. It was so strange, but he found that he was quite content just lying there watching his daughter sleep.

Sarah stretched out and laid her head down onto her arm. "I used to do this with Thomas when he was a baby," she whispered.

Mikhail saw a shadow of sadness gloss over her brilliant eyes and he reached over to caress her cheek. She smiled up at him and reached her hand up to cover his.

"I guess we'll have to make some sort of arrangements for Thomas... for his...," Sarah's words trailed off. She simply could not bring herself to say the word "body" for fear it would mean Thomas was dead.

Mikhail softly shushed her, tucking a lock of her hair behind her ear as he informed her, "Hantsushept already had his staff take care of things, just in case."

This explanation appeared to ease her troubled mind, but still she frowned. He touched her gently again and she closed her eyes. "Tomorrow," he whispered, "we will go there and you will see for yourself that everything has been done that can be done." Sarah gave him a grateful little smile and then snuggled a little closer to Sheely and him. Mikhail laid his head down onto his own arm and within minutes, like the little one between them, the two were sound asleep.

I stopped speaking, my gaze narrowing on some obscure, imaginary point as I listened. Ana was very far away now and I could sense the aches in her every joint and muscle. How I wanted to demand that she return. I should not have allowed her to go.

It's fine, *she laughed.* I think I'm just getting old.

My mouth twitched as I did my best to hide the grin I felt coming on. At least she was still safe.

"Joss Tobin?" *Jarba asked, bringing my attention back to my current location.*

I blinked a few times, my mind leaving the scene where my beloved Jess *was and returning to the great round chamber lined with Samarean people. "Forgive me," I pleaded. "Where was I?"*

Jarba reminded me that I had ended on Mikhail and Sarah finally getting a chance to rest with the newborn Sheely. A spear of sadness shot through my heart for a moment, but I shook it off. I put the emotions flirting around my heart out of my mind and continued with my tale...

Chapter 11

Chris' brain slowly began functioning properly again. She didn't move. It was odd. When she had been a little girl, she had always greeted every morning with excitement and enthusiasm. But ever since that fateful day when she had lost her parents, it seemed as if she just couldn't find the will to drag herself out of bed each morning. She left that to Lyss. Chris always wanted to sleep just a little bit longer. She would happily take the night watch so Lyss could go to bed early, which was how Lyss liked it. For now, Chris just wanted a few more minutes. That was all. Just a few more minutes.

She curled up even tighter under the clean-smelling blanket of warmth surrounding her. Shock rocketed through her brain, however, as she realized it was an uber-warm body heating her frame all over, not a blanket. She tensed as her mind quick-flashed through memories of last night in attempts to discover why she was waking to find someone else in her bed.

Opening her eyes, Chris discovered she was not in her bed. In fact, she had no idea where she was. This was not her room at the house on Long Island. She needed to figure this thing out because no memories from last night appeared to be forthcoming as yet. Moving as slowly and carefully as possible, Chris first tried to inch her way forward toward the edge of the bed. But the heavy weight of the person's right arm and leg wrapped securely about her body prevented that. Next she tried turning very slowly, while lifting up the imprisoning limbs and scooching simultaneously away. Things were going pretty well with this plan until she suddenly caught sight of the body's face. That's when her memory of the previous evening's events came slamming back to mind and she stilled her escape efforts.

The man looked absolutely beautiful in his peaceful slumber. The mark surrounding the majority of his neck was barely even noticeable now, Chris noted, and he looked almost completely recovered from her attack on him in the stairwell of the parking garage in London. Chris wondered how he had managed to heal so fast.

As she gazed upon his features, his eyes opened and he lay there in silence staring right back into her eyes. Chris marveled at the beautiful ice-blue color of his irises and she wondered how she could have missed such a striking feature in her inventory of him after he had first awakened last night. Of course, it had been very dark by the time he had taken Lyss and her with him to wherever they were now and she had been completely freaked out. Still, she had to admit, his eyes, and the rest of him, were very beautiful.

The memory of last night's events were oddly fuzzy in her mind and she quickly looked around the strange room, asking, "Where are we? And where's Lyss?" Chris did not recall arriving at their destination last night. All she remembered was holding onto both Lyss and the man before her as his... wings, she guessed they were, had wrapped tightly around all three of them. Next, their little trio had lifted off the ground and passed right through the ceiling of the beach house! Chris recalled being amazed at the sight of individual wood grain particles as they had passed through the building's structure. After that, there had been only the night passing, both above and below them. Then... nothing. There was nothing more until she had awakened here a few minutes ago.

"Relax," the man's gravelly-deep voice said around a yawn. "We are safe now."

He rolled onto his back and raised both arms above his head in a full-bodied stretch.

Chris hated to admit it, even to herself, but she felt a bit bereft the moment he broke physical contact with her skin. Instead, she asked, "And my sister? Where is she?"

The man relaxed from his stretching and yawned again. "She is just down the hall in a room of her own," he calmly explained, lazily watching her with interest now.

As she looked right back at him, Chris didn't know what to do. She searched her fuzzy memory again and again for something that would reveal more clues as to the man's identity. Had he said at one point that he was an Angel? The man could fly. Here she was, lying on a bed with what might be an actual, honest-to-goodness Angel. Up until last night, Chris hadn't really even believed Angels existed, let alone that she would ever be involved in an Angelic encounter of any kind! Was there some sort of protocol she should follow? Were there certain words she should use to address him? She had been raised as a Catholic, but she recalled nothing detailing how one was to behave when/if one ever found oneself face-to-face with a true servant of God.

Hell, over the past few years, Chris had even begun to doubt the very existence of God Himself!

She quickly looked up at the Angel's face to check to make sure he hadn't caught that last thought from her mind. She didn't know much about Angels, but she would bet they could easily read the minds of all mankind. Those beautiful ice-blue eyes merely stared right back at her, unblinking.

After a moment of each one staring silently at the other, Chris asked, "Wh-what do we do now?"

A slight lifting of one corner of his beautiful mouth gave a boyish charm to his features and he softly said, "Well, I am a bit hungry, and you will probably want to check in on your sister, but there are some things we shall need to discuss."

Chris frowned a little in confusion at his blasé attitude.

He shrugged. "Other than that, we can do whatever we wish."

Chris blinked. This was too bizarre! What did he mean?

The mattress rocked heavily as he suddenly rolled his massive frame over and off the bed on the other side from her. Chris quickly looked away, though not before she had taken in his near-perfect form. He was clothed only in a skin-tight pair of knickers, so she had gotten to see an eyeful. There had been a rather large tell-tale bulge protruding from the front of his form as well, suggesting someone somewhere had gotten things woefully wrong when they had suggested that Angels were all androgynous!

Chris quickly peeked under the covers to check on her own state of dress. A sigh of relief nearly escaped her as she discovered herself safely covered by her usual plain white t-shirt and boys' boxer briefs, a skin-tight but stretchy red pair she remembered dressing in the day before. Quickly throwing the sheet and blanket aside, she scooted off the bed and looked around for the rest of her clothes.

"Um, I did not think to grab shoes for you before we left last night," the Angel said. "I shall have to see about getting some for you from somewhere in the Complex today. I am sure someone will have a pair your size."

Chris turned to face him. He was dressed by now in a pair of hip-hugging blue jeans topped by a skin-tight long-sleeved cream Henley. His long black hair hung in a loose, gleaming curtain all the way down to the small of his back. He was all man, even with the long hair, and Chris could only stare in mute admiration at the beautiful figure he cut.

An Angel – absolutely mesmerizing!

A slight chill shook her small frame and the Angel turned and quickly pulled bits and pieces of clothing from a nearby wardrobe. He then handed the bundle of clothes to her and said, "You can wear these, I think, until we can get some new things for you. They will not fit, of course, but you should at least be comfortable enough, I should think." He escorted her over to a large restroom. "There should be a new toothbrush in the top drawer by the sink, assuming things were set up in here the way they were throughout the rest of the house." He turned then and headed back into the bedroom. "I shall go check on Lyss and arrange for some food while you freshen up, hmm?"

The door closed quietly behind him.

Chris was glad in a way that he had gone. She was still desperately searching through her memories of last night's events. She couldn't for the life of her recall the Angel's name. Had he given it to her? She honestly couldn't remember. She had been so freaked out by all that had happened that she simply could not recall.

Her shoulders slumped as she realized there was nothing she could do but introduce herself "formally" to him and hope he responded in kind. If he didn't, there would be nothing left but to ask out-right.

Sighing, she stepped over to the shower and turned on the flow of steaming hot water.

***

The young guard kept watch as the others huddled together toward the back of the small room where they had been stashed. He was the newest member of the team, so he got all the stupid duties. He didn't mind. He knew the lieutenants and the captain had more experience than he and he would do whatever it took to allow them time to plan the escape.

He had only been commissioned as a fully-fledged elite Guardsman a short time ago and knew it would take years for him to learn the strategies and techniques he would need for fighting their enemies. Until the start of this mission, he had never even seen a Lori in person. And now, he wished he could un-see the things Loris become when they associate with humans. Lord Azra'il had been fearsome enough as a Lori. But after the humans had changed him into whatever he was now, the young guard found him terrifying!

A sound on the other side of the door caught the young Kurr's attention and he signaled his company to disperse. The group quickly broke up and spread around the small room, lounging casually on their bunks as the door opened. A couple of serving Kurr entered with a couple of carts laden with steaming food. Drinks were brought in next and then the serving Kurr left, the door closing and locking it behind them.

The food smelled delicious and every one of the guardsmen was starving, but not a soul moved to eat or drink anything that had been left for them. Instead, a lieutenant motioned for the young guard to return to the door and the rest of the group reassembled at the back of the room to continue planning their next move.

***

Azra'il stared at his new self reflected in the mirror. It had been a long, sleepless night, if that was what one could call the past few hours they had all spent lying in bed since everything that had happened. Sheely's voice sounded in his head again.

She liked the way he looked, or so she said. The language she used was one that had never before been uttered by human tongues, but Azra'il still understood her. She said she liked his hair and eyes the best, but that the rest of him was pretty okay, too.

He chuckled aloud and turned away from the mirror. The rest of the household was not yet up, other than the serving Kurr, and Azra'il wondered how long he was going to have to wait around before everyone else awoke and he would be able to go to Sheely.

An ear-piercing scream cut the silence of the suite as Sheely silently told him to hold on a second.

Azra'il frowned and thought, *Brat!*

Sheely's loud wailing simply increased in volume.

By the time Azra'il reached Sarah's and Mikhail's room, a whole army of serving Kurr was up and each one of them looked ready to take flight to escape the infant's fierce crying. Sarah sat back against the bed's headboard holding Sheely's struggling little form, rocking and shushing the child simultaneously while a very concerned Mikhail bent over them both with the most helpless expression on his face. It was almost comical.

That one old serving Kurr, the one named Miriam, was standing off to the far side of the bed, but Azra'il paid her no mind as he strode directly over to the side closest to him and held out his arms. Sarah looked at him, then at Mikhail, and then she made a decision.

Sheely's wailing ceased the very second she was passed into Azra'il's safekeeping.

Mikhail frowned, but said nothing as he took one of Sarah's hands in his.

Sarah frowned and sighed heavily. "She hasn't eaten yet," was all she said, though her frustration at the situation was clearly evident.

Sheely's long white tresses wrapped securely around Azra'il's arms and waist the moment he took her in his arms and she lay there, quietly staring up at him. Of course, her constant chatter inside his mind continued, but none of the others heard any of this. It was for him and him alone.

"She is not hungry, just now," Azra'il informed Sarah.

Sarah and Mikhail both frowned at him again, but neither said anything more on the subject. A chair was moved close to the bed so Azra'il could sit, which he did. Breakfast was served to the adults in the room and then cleared away.

Mikhail went to take Sheely back, thinking his daughter must surely be ready for some food or at least a nap by now. The moment Azra'il went to pass her over to his sibling, however, Sheely let out another ear-piercing scream. Mikhail and Sarah both looked accusingly at Azra'il, as if he had something to do with their daughter not allowing anyone else to hold her.

"What?" Azra'il asked, frustrated. Sheely's chatter increased tenfold for a moment and then she went completely silent. Azra'il understood what she had meant, but a part of him was actually considering the alternative now that there was complete silence on her end. Another ear-piercing scream suddenly had Azra'il frowning and passing on his tiny soul-mate's message. "Sheely says her father should go do what he normally does, instead of hanging out here worrying about how she is doing."

Mikhail and Sarah both frowned.

"And just what are *you* going to be doing while I am out?" Mikhail asked his brother suspiciously. A part of him couldn't help still thinking of his dark brother as a foe instead of the loving sibling he had once known and Mikhail simply didn't trust him.

After throwing a doubtful glance Sarah's way, Azra'il turned to face his brother head-on and said, "Sarah, Sheely and I will spend some time getting to know each other better, per the request of your daughter."

Mikhail wasn't sure how he felt about that.

Don't worry, Sarah's voice softly sounded in his mind. *I don't think he'll do anything with Sheely bein' here.*

She smiled over at him and Mikhail leaned in to give

her a quick kiss before saying, "Well, in that case, I think I shall get out to the practice clearing to work with Samuel. I believe he will have many questions after he learns about everything that has happened." He silently instructed Sarah, *Alert me instantly should you feel he might be planning any kind of move, either against you or Sheely, you understand?*

Sarah pushed away and crawled off the bed, heading for the bathroom as she silently ordered, *Quit your monitoring! We'll be fine.*

Mikhail threw a dubious look in Azra'il's direction but then decided to go ahead and give his brother the benefit of the doubt. He quickly dressed and left the suite, headed for the practice clearing. In the main hallway at the top of the stairs, he came across one of the humans Djibril had brought back from that dimension last night. This was the twin of Djibril's human mate. Mikhail noticed her wary and confused expression as she took in his strange countenance.

"Hello there," he said in English. "I am Mikhail, brother of Djibril." He extended a hand toward her in the human way so as to make her feel more comfortable.

The twin hesitantly reached forward to take the offered hand. "I-I'm Alyssana, um, Lyss," she stammered. She narrowed her eyes a bit at his appearance, but didn't comment on it.

"You look a bit lost," Mikhail noted.

"I, uh, am a bit confused as to where I am," she admitted slowly.

Mikhail appreciated the courage she showed in talking with him and actually doing it without displaying much of a reaction to his looks. He had noted how strong her handshake was and an idea occurred to him. "Why not come with me for a bit and we can discuss that and a few other matters?" he asked, as he held a hand out, silently inviting her to precede him down the main staircase.

After a brief hesitation, Lyss nodded, then turned and quickly made her way downstairs. Mikhail was right there with her every step of the way and the two of them soon reached the practice clearing in the wood on the outskirts of the Complex grounds.

Sure enough, Samuel was already there waiting for Mikhail and Thomas to show up for their regular afternoon workout session. They had already missed their pre-dawn one. Suriyah was waiting with him today and Mikhail gave her a grateful nod as Lyss and he entered the clearing. He knew Samuel would need someone to talk with after he found out about Thomas' sudden disappearance and Suri's shoulders were better than any for soothing one's fears. Mikhail himself knew this from his own personal experience.

He was also glad Suriyah had shown up because he knew the human twin, Lyss, would be sure to feel more comfortable around creatures that at least resembled humans. Mikhail and Sarah had each noticed more and more changes in their outward appearances lately, not to mention a plethora of new extrasensory abilities they had each gained, and he knew he was the *last* creature to put into a room with a frightened human.

Although, as he took a good hard look at this Lyss, he noticed she didn't appear so much frightened as she did confused – or perhaps she was more bemused by all she was discovering?

Introductions were made and Lyss waited with Suriyah while Mikhail got straight to the task of telling Samuel about Thomas. The young Kurr was immediately filled with sadness for the loss of his best friend, but Mikhail was quick to assure him that not all hope was lost. He explained the situation and made sure Samuel understood that all that could be done was being done already and that Samuel would be the first to be informed of any new developments in the case. In the meantime, Mikhail and Samuel both agreed it would be much better for all concerned to continue with their normal routine.

Mikhail and Samuel returned to the clearing from the short walk they had taken for their talk, and Mikhail invited Lyss and Suriyah to participate in today's workout so that Samuel wouldn't be forced to perform solo. They both agreed to the plan and soon all three were punching, jabbing, somersaulting, and doing all manner of unbelievable feats using psycho-kinetics, a thing which Lyss hadn't even known humans were capable of doing. Mikhail barked out orders for one or more of them to move this object or to cause the wind to blow this direction at this particular speed at just the right moment. It was very involved and each of the three taking the orders from him was soon showing signs of terrific improvement.

***

Djibril figured it must be mid-afternoon, judging by the sun's current placement in the sky. He had stopped by the room Suriyah had installed Lyss in last night, but there had been no one there, so he had gone in search of others. One of the Kurr he encountered in the hallway informed him there were at least two Lorim currently out at the practice clearing. After making arrangements for a food tray and some ladies' clothing and shoes in what he hoped would be the right sizes to be delivered to his room for Chris, Djibril went on out to the clearing. He hoped that was where Chris' sister was, as he planned to check on Lyss and then return to Chris.

He'd had to force himself to let go of her earlier. It had felt so good waking up holding her and he had wanted nothing more than to take her in every imaginable manner right then and there. She wasn't ready, though, and he knew it.

After seeing how both she and her sister had reacted toward him last night after his impromptu reveal, he knew Chris would need some time before she would be ready for them to take their relationship to the next level. Djibril had waited this long and he knew it would only help Chris to accept him more easily if he was patient with her. So he was willing to wait until she was ready for him. He only hoped she wouldn't require a lot of time before being able to accept him. She was so sweet-feeling and his body already yearned physically for hers.

***

Sarah watched with a practiced eye as her infant daughter lay in the arms of her future mate. Sheely's bright eyes stared lovingly up at Azra'il as he fed her the mid-afternoon bottle containing a special formula Hantsushept had created for her. Azra'il stared back at the baby just as adoringly, and Sarah could almost feel the pool of compassion and love welled within each of the beings before her. She was sad *she* hadn't had the opportunity to bond with Sheely prior to the bonding between Sheely and Azra'il occurring, but that bonding was such a cause for celebration that she truly couldn't regret it. But it still rankled.

Now, if only Sarah could figure out how to get Nera and Thomas bonded. Not that she even knew for certain that Thomas was alive and with Nera. If she were being honest with herself, she would admit that she needed to face reality and prepare for the possibility that Thomas might actually be gone. A trickle of fear raced through her at this thought.

That's when Sarah realized Azra'il was staring at her.

"You are worried about your son?" Azra'il asked.

"Among other things – yes," she reluctantly agreed.

The Lori nodded. Then he confessed, "I, too, worry about things. For instance, I worry about how I shall convince the council members of both houses to accept my family back into the City, especially now that most of us have transformed, if that is how one describes what has occurred. I shall also need to find a way of convincing them to accept Sheely and Lisa… and now Chris… and you, as well, of course."

"Oh, of course," Sarah said. She took no offense. The two of them had been on opposite sides of the fence for so long that it was natural for him to still think of her as an outsider. Sarah knew this. However, the time for that kind of thinking was gone as they were all in the same proverbial boat now, so to speak, and they were all going to have to learn to live together if there was going to be any getting through this.

They had all changed – well, nearly all of them – and it would take everyone's collective cooperation to convince both houses of the Sanhedrin and the elite Sanhedrin Guard to not only allow the Lorim and their new mates back into Lorim City, but to also return control of the people's government back over to the higher-ranking Lorim, whether they were ready to do so or not. Sarah knew that would not be a simple task, now that the council members had been given the opportunity to taste a bit of power. And, with a traitor still in their midst, she would bet the councilmembers of the Great Sanhedrin at least were most likely not going to want to relinquish their newfound powers so easily.

As if he had read her mind, Azra'il said, "It truly is a pity we cannot show the Kurr the things we have learned thus far about where all humans and Kurr come from and what awaits them when they expire – should they ever do so."

Sarah stared at him in surprise.

He knew! She realized it in an instant. The damned Lori knew – at least, he knew of the tether machines to which the humans were all linked. "You've seen the machines?" she asked. He narrowed his gaze upon her, but then his expression cleared and he nodded, saying, "Yes. There were quite a few. Although I noticed there was only one machine to which the Kurr were attached."

"Only the Kurr?" Sarah asked. "What about those of us who have...?"

Azra'il shook his head. "None of the transformed humans are linked now," he explained. "And, of course, I saw no Lori as being linked, at least to my recollection."

"So, there's a separate machine for Kurr?"

He nodded.

That kind of fit with what Sarah had seen in her visions, though she had seen the souls of the Lorim pulled through one machine as well.

A thought suddenly occurred to her and she turned eager, brightly-glowing eyes on the Lori, asking, "Can you detect where Thomas is? I mean, you can detect his tether, right? Then, you can find where he is, right?"

Azra'il shook his head. "Trust me," he said, looking down upon the tiny face of his future mate. "Sheely has already had me looking for the one she knows as her brother and I can find no trace of him. It is as if he simply ceased to exist, leaving no trace behind."

"But how can that be?" a deflated and frustrated Sarah asked.

He shook his head again, murmuring, "I do not know. I simply do not know."

***

It annoyed Mikhail a bit when Djibril showed up, but a silent word or two from Sarah's ever-present mind reminded him that Djibril had confused the energies he was feeling from his actual human counterpart with energies he thought were coming from Sarah, and that there had been no possible way he could have known of his mistake prior to waking in the human realm. Even Sarah herself had believed Mikhail to have died when she could no longer see the glow from his energies in her ring in the blue dimension. So Mikhail figured he would have to treat Djibril as civilly as possible.

Sarah also informed him of a celebratory supper she and Azra'il, of all Lorim, were planning for the evening in order to celebrate Sheely's birth. Apparently, Sheely was all for it and Azra'il was bending over backward in his attempts to do for her whatever she wanted done. Even had there not been the physical changes within each of them to indicate that they were a bonded pair meant to be together, Azra'il's constant attempts at pleasing Sheely would have been enough to convince even the blindest idiot of the truth and validity of their condition.

Mikhail and Sarah had both come to that conclusion as well, after the time Sarah had spent already with the two of them. There was nothing for it but to accept the truth. Their daughter, whom they had so looked forward to spending a good measure of their lives with, raising her, watching her grow, getting all the parental experiences available – no longer belonged to them. Sheely and Azra'il were to be mated.

Azra'il had assured Sarah this afternoon he would never take Sheely prior to the point at which she was mature enough, both mentally and physically, and although this seemed of little comfort now, Mikhail knew his sibling would forever honor his word. He simply hoped he, as a father, could find a way to eventually come to believe there would *ever* come a day when he would think of his daughter as being mature enough for Azra'il to take her!

* * *

As Djibril came to the clearing, thoughts of his and Chris' first union suddenly fled his mind as he came face-to-face with a very tense, yet restrained, Mikhail. When he had arrived earlier at the Medical Facility, he had felt his more powerful sibling's anger toward Djibril for his behavior with Sarah in the other dimension. He had hoped for the possibility that Mikhail would not have known about Djibril's suggestion that Sarah allow him to kiss her, but one look at his brother's fierce expression and he had known *that* possibility was dead.

There was nothing for it but to face the music head on and Djibril marched directly up to Mikhail without an ounce of hesitation. "Mikhail," he stated in greeting, nodding once at his tightly-strung sibling. He then turned his attention to those in the clearing. Suriyah, Samuel, and Lyss were all three practicing punching and kicking maneuvers in the clearing's center.

After a moment, Djibril felt Mikhail's attention shift back to the goings on in the clearing. "Brother," Mikhail finally greeted tightly. "How are you?"

Djibril thought for a moment before saying, "Well, I think my voice is stuck this way for good, but other than that I believe I shall be fine."

Mikhail finally threw a crooked grin his way and asked, "Is she worth it?"

Djibril clapped a hand on his brother's shoulder. "Every bit," he answered solemnly.

Chapter 12

Chris walked along the worn pathway the serving Kurr had shown her. Once she had emerged from her shower, she had gotten dressed and brushed her teeth. When she had finished up in the restroom, she had discovered a slightly smelly serving Kurr waiting for her in the bedroom with a table full of delicious foods and instructions for her to eat.

When Chris asked who had ordered the food to be delivered, the Kurr had merely said it had been her Lord, and Chris had still been unable to recall the Angel's name. She knew he had told her his name when he had revealed himself back in the bedroom of her house, but for some reason her mind was blocking that information from her and, as luck would have it, she couldn't remember to save her life and was becoming very frustrated because of it. The Kurr didn't mention the Angel's name when Chris had asked where she could find him, either.

She had eaten as much of the food as she could on such a nervous stomach and then had followed the serving Kurr out to the pathway where she had listened to instructions on how to reach the clearing. Now Chris wondered if Lyss would be at the clearing or if she was still back at the house. She had been too wrapped up in thoughts of the Angel who had been in bed with her to think about going down the hallway to check on her sister before leaving.

Sounds from up ahead on the path had her quickening her step. After a moment, she came to an opening in the wood where she noticed several things going on all at once. First of all, there were several people in the clearing, including Lyss and the handsome Angel who had shared a bed with her earlier. Second, Lyss was involved in a sparring match with what appeared to be two other Angels, one a young male and the other an unbelievably beautiful female Angel.

The fact that they were all three sparring was not what captured Chris' attention so. The fact that Lyss and the other two were using telekinesis as part of their sparring techniques was what astonished her. There were rocks and all manner of other objects flying all over the place and the three fighters were flying through the air as if they thought nothing of it. Objects were either avoided or knocked out of the way by thrusts or jabs and the other players in the game had to watch out!

From the sidelines, a deep voice called out instructions to the players, critiquing their moves or suggesting methods of improvement, and Chris turned to check out this paragon of fighting techniques. That's when she truly freaked out!

The male figure calling out to the three fighters stood next to the Angel Chris had come to find, but she had no idea what that other creature was. He had long, white hair that appeared to be alive, for the ends of it would lift randomly from time to time, though there was no breeze evident that she could detect within the little clearing. As if that wasn't enough to make the creature appear completely alien, its eyes glowed a brilliant white that shed light on the entirety of everyone and everything within the clearing. The creature's skin even glowed, making it appear as if there was some inner energy emitting from within it. Either that, or the thing was some type of advanced Japanese robot that ran on light energy!

Chris cautiously made her way over to where the creature and her Angel were standing, all the while keeping a watchful eye on the thing. She didn't trust the odd-looking creature and she wished her Angel would just get away from it. She didn't know the Angel all that well, but she suddenly felt a streak of protectiveness shoot through her for the beautiful male.

Her dark-haired Angel finally noticed her approach and turned to smile at her as he watched and waited. He held out a hand to her and Chris placed her much smaller hand into his large one as soon as she reached him, enjoying the quick zing of electricity that raced up her arm at his touch.

"Here she is," the dark Angel rasped with a smile. He turned to the creature beside him and said, "Mikhail, may I present Christiana Harrington, or Chris for short." Turning back to her, he said softly, "Chris, this is my brother, Mikhail."

Chris' eyes widened a moment as she darted a quick look of utter disbelief up at her Angel. Then she realized she was being very rude and blinked away her astonishment. The thing was her Angel's *brother*? What was wrong with him, she wanted to know. She was glad the thing merely nodded toward her in greeting. She was glad it hadn't reached out to shake hands with her, for she was more than a little afraid of touching him. Turning to watch the trio sparring in the clearing, she quietly said, "Thank you for the wonderful meal. It hit the spot."

Her Angel merely turned to her and, after a slight frowning hesitation, threw a lop-sided smile her way, squeezing her hand ever so slightly.

The sparring continued.

Chris was amazed at the maneuvers the three participants in the clearing used. She had never seen her sister move in such a manner and it struck her that each one of the three warriors within the clearing was somehow able to anticipate the others' moves before they were made, as if each was clairvoyant. This became Chris' main theory about what she was watching, as time and again the two Angels sparring with Lyss would suddenly lunge toward her, but Lyss would gyrate or perform a mid-air somersault, perfectly executed, at just the right moment to escape both parties untouched.

Chris knew there had to be something more than just normal sparring going on when the creature, Mikhail, suddenly encouraged, "That is it, Lyss! Anticipate the moves of your opponents and then simply avoid them. You are getting the hang of this!" The creature turned then to face Chris and asked, "Lyss informs me you are her normal sparring partner. Would you like to give it a try?"

Chris immediately sidled up closer to her Angel's big body for protection and shook her head. "No," she said, looking back toward the clearing. She didn't like what she was seeing here one bit. "As a matter of fact," she continued, "I'd actually like to take a quick walk with my sister, if that's all right?"

The creature and her Angel exchanged a quick look, but neither denied her request. Chris quickly called out to Lyss, interrupting the sparring match and motioning silently to her sister before stealing off into the nearby wood as fast as she could.

"Hey, slow down," Lyss complained, as she hurried to catch up with her twin. "What's the big deal?"

The sparring match had continued in the nearby clearing and the noise from the melee could still be heard off in the distance. But the twins were deep enough into the wood now that they could talk in private without worrying someone would overhear their conversation. Chris stopped walking and whipped around. "What the hell was *that* all about?" she demanded of Lyss.

Lyss' eyes widened and she grinned. "I know. It was great, huh?" she exclaimed. She had an excited glow about her and she almost bounced as she walked around the wooded area. "I mean, I never would've thought such ability would be possible. But I was able to pick it up fairly quickly. I just had to be shown that it was possible and then how to do it!"

She was grinning ear-to-ear and Chris frowned back at her. Did Lyss just not *get* it? For her entire life, she and Lyss had shared everything, from facial expressions to thoughts to religious beliefs to emotions. Now it was as if Lyss was a completely different person, utterly detached from Chris.

"Mikhail and Suriyah said they were very impressed with how quickly I was able to grasp the concept of telekinesis and let go of my pre-conceived human laws of nature," Lyss continued. "They said most humans only need to *believe* in a thing for it to be reality for them. I guess that makes sense, huh?"

Chris stood there staring at her mirror image in utter confusion while Lyss continued with her excited, yet oblivious chatter.

"Wasn't it great? I mean, learning to manipulate the very air around my enemy will prove worth more than a thousand katanas! Just think how freaked out anyone would be to suddenly have things come flying at them from all around during a fight. Hell, I wouldn't even *have* to fight!"

Chris had had enough. "Wait a minute!" she suddenly shouted. "Just – Just wait a minute!"

Lyss started and stared with concern at her sister.

"Did you even notice that Mikhail creature?" Chris demanded.

Again, Lyss' eyes widened and she grinned broadly as she gushed, "I know. Isn't he awesome? I mean, don't get me wrong. Your Djibril is stunning, as far as Arch Angels go, and Suriyah is off-the-charts beautiful and wicked good at fighting techniques, but Mikhail rocks just to look at! Even *I* would turn tail and run if I came across *him* in the middle of the night... or day, for that matter!"

Of everything her obviously enthralled and brainwashed twin had said, Chris' mind had focused in on the fact that she had finally learned her Angel's name: Djibril. It wasn't a very attractive name, she reflected, but it was interesting. Chris rolled it around in her mind a bit while Lyss continued with her raving over that Mikhail creature.

Djibril...

Djibril...

Why had Lyss said he was Chris' Djibril? Frowning, Chris concentrated again on the jibber-jabber still streaming from her excited twin's unusually talkative self. Apparently, the creature named Mikhail had once been normal-looking, like all the others, but then he had mated with his soul-mate, who had been human at the time, and they had both become the glowing monster things. There was another brother who had done the same, with another human and with the same results, but Lyss hadn't found out much more than that about that one.

A sudden snap of a twig underfoot had Lyss immediately silenced and the two startled twins turned identical green gazes upon the dark intruder.

Djibril slowly approached, clearing his throat and cautiously eyeing the two women. "I was wondering where you two had gotten off to," he said in his now-ruined voice, though he had known precisely where his other half had gone, as he had followed them mere seconds after they had left the clearing. "Although we are near the Complex, we must take heed while in wooded areas. There is still danger lurking about, unfortunately."

Lyss shot a conspiratorial glance in Chris' direction and gave a wink before smiling beautifully at the Angel and saying, "That's okay. I was just about ready to get back for a little more training before we lose the daylight." With that, she quickly left her twin in the Angel's company.

Djibril slowly approached where Chris stood, his hands clasped behind his back. She watched in mute appreciation as his lithe body moved toward her. It was like watching one of the big cats move. You knew there was raw power hidden just beneath the surface and that it could burst out at any second, but you could also sense the indomitable will holding that power in check – but only just.

Chris leaned her back against the thick trunk of the tree behind her as she looked up at Djibril's dark features. He was quite tall, but she liked that about him. It made her feel more feminine, somehow, just standing next to him... protected.

Djibril...

The name echoed through her mind again and again as she studied his features.

He stopped just next to her and looked her over from head to feet and back. "You did not wish to participate?" he asked, an eyebrow hitched along his broad forehead.

"I don't have my katana," she immediately responded, then wished she had said anything but that as Djibril absently touched the remaining thin strip of scar tissue encircling the majority of his neck.

"Hmm...," was his only response and each looked away from the other for the moment.

Lyss' voice echoed through Chris' mind again calling him "your Djibril" and Chris frowned as she puzzled over the phrasing. What had Lyss meant?

Djibril turned back to her and ran his hand slowly along her forearm, back and forth, as he considered his next words. The tingling feeling of electricity shot repeatedly up through each one's body. Chris enjoyed the sensation, but a part of her mind sounded warning signals. She was a human. He was an Arch Angel. This could not happen!

She licked suddenly parched lips and asked, "Why did you bring us here?"

Djibril stared at her mouth. He had become momentarily fascinated by the sight of her pink tongue as it had darted out between her lips to wet them and now he couldn't stop wondering what it would be like to taste her. Reaching up with his other hand, he ran his fingers back behind her ear into her glorious red hair, lightly cupping the back of her head as he absently said in his now-gravelly voice, "Because you belong here with me."

Chris frowned again, but she was semi-mesmerized by the contrasting colors of his ice-blue irises next to his blacker-than-night lashes. His face moved closer and the tips of their noses rubbed against each other. Their mouths were mere centimeters away from each other, but this was erotic in itself, this almost-kissing.

Breathing became an afterthought and in some dim recess of her mind, Chris realized her toes were curling and uncurling in her borrowed shoes again and again, as she took in his clean scent. She watched in amazed fascination as her hands and fingers chose of their own volition to run lightly along his muscled arms and shoulders and chest before circling around to his back and exerting just the slightest pressure to pull him closer.

Djibril needed no further encouragement and he quickly dipped his head the rest of the way down to her luscious little mouth. His eyes rolled back into his head as his eyelids slid closed and sensation took over. He was suddenly beyond all rational thought. One hand held her head captive while his other banded around her back, plastering her small frame against his entire front. He forced her lips apart with his heated tongue and the world slipped away.

The sound of someone's throat clearing off to her right startled Chris from her daze and she jerked her head around to frown fiercely at the intruder. It was Lyss, looking quite contrite for having interrupted them, but very pleased by the scene she had just witnessed.

Lyss cleared her throat once more as Djibril finally turned to regard her, though he kept his protective hold on her sister, she noticed. "Um... we're done for the day," she quickly informed them. "Mikhail wanted me to tell you there's to be a birthday celebration dinner in their suite tonight. It starts in about an hour, he said, and we're all invited."

Djibril looked back down at his soon-to-be mate. "Thank you, Lyss," he said as softly as he could with his ruined voice. "We shall be along shortly."

Lyss winked once more at Chris, gave her a thumbs-up and flashed a quick grin before silently turning and heading back in the direction of the main Complex center.

Chris very loudly swallowed a lump in her throat, wondering what on earth she was doing. She didn't belong here with this Angel, no matter what he said. She swallowed again, still trying to get her bearings, even as she realized Djibril was not moving, but was watching *her*. She broke away from him and took a few steps, anything to help regain her mental balance.

Djibril remained still by the tree, watching her in silence.

"We should get going," she finally said without looking at him. "We'll go to this thing tonight, since Lyss obviously wants to go, but then she and I will have to return to our home."

That brought Djibril up short. He stepped toward her, his face a mask of confusion. "You wish to return to the human realm – even after...?" He didn't understand. It was all too new to him, the sensations he had experienced simply by touching her. Words utterly failed to adequately describe what he had just shared with her. And now she wanted to go home?

"What?" Chris asked, finally facing him again. "A kiss?" She shook her head and shrugged. "That's all it was. Look you're an Angel. I'm a human. Up until last night, things like Angels didn't even exist for me." She swallowed again – hard. "You were just fairy-tale creatures parents told their kids about to make them feel safe at night."

Djibril frowned, but didn't interrupt. It was important for him to understand the cultural differences that would have to be overcome in order for the two of them to survive becoming a mated pair.

Chris looked away again, whispering almost to herself, "I wish things were different." Images from when her parents had died suddenly crowded her mind and she was overwhelmed with questions as to why there had been no Angels there that day, why they couldn't have done something to at least save her parents, if not the others. *Why?*

The sunlight was fading and a shadowy darkness was pervading their little wooded corner of the world. Chris felt no fear, however, for he was there with her. She could feel him, could almost feel his blood pulsing through his veins. It was an odd sensation, since she had never been that close to anyone before. It felt to her as if she was even closer to this Angel than she was with Lyss, which should have been impossible. She had only just met him!

Djibril's massive frame finally moved toward her and she mistook his meaning as she too turned to start making the trek back toward the Main House. A large hand on her shoulder had her pulling up short to look back and up at him in inquiry.

"We shall attend the birthday celebration," he quietly said, "but there is still much to be discussed between us before there is any further discussion about the human realm." With that, he placed his hand at the small of her back and silently, but firmly, led her back to the Main House and the small suite of rooms where she had awakened with him earlier.

When they reached the suite, he closed the door behind them and went directly to his chest-of-drawers to remove some clean clothing. "If you do not mind," he said, "I shall freshen up first."

"Actually," Chris said, attempting to establish some ground rules since he was determined to keep her here for at least a little while longer, "I think it would be best if I were to move in with Lyss until we leave here."

Djibril stopped in the doorway of the restroom and turned to regard her. His eyes were narrowed and a corner of his mouth twitched as if he was doing his best to keep his anger in check in order to keep from saying the wrong thing. Chris got the distinct impression she had just ticked him off, big time. He confirmed this as he finally said in a soft but still-gravelly voice filled with steel, "Over my dead body."

Without another word, he turned and entered the restroom, closing the door behind himself with a definite click.

Chris stood staring at the closed door, even after the sound of the shower pervaded the room. What was going on here? She had stated logical reasons why they couldn't be together. Surely, he understood the sense of it? They were of two different species! They came from different worlds... or realms, or whatever! Everybody could see that! What was wrong with him?

The sound of the shower stopped and still she stood staring at the door.

He was an Angel, an actual Angel! What did he want with her? She hadn't attended church since the day of her parents' funeral all those years ago and the last one-sided conversation she had had with God had consisted of her calling Him every bad thing her then-young, naïve mind could come up with.

She had even thought she had come to *dis*believe in the very existence of God until last night. It had taken Djibril revealing himself as an Angel to prove to her that at least some of what she had been taught growing up had been true. She wasn't yet sure how she felt about that, especially considering her chosen profession and the events that had led up to that particular career choice, but she would figure out all of *that* once she and Lyss returned home. For now, she just needed to somehow get it through to Djibril that they simply could *not* be together.

Lyss' voice calling him "your Djibril" echoed once more through her mind and Chris frowned. Something about that gnawed at her.

She shook her head. This was crazy! She sighed heavily and walked over to the wardrobe Djibril had gotten things out of for her earlier, hoping he had *some*thing she could wear to this thing tonight. She gasped as she opened the door to discover half of the closet was packed with attractive women's clothing – most of it exactly her size!

How had he arranged that?

The door to the restroom opened and he stepped out, beautiful and gleaming clean, as steam from the little room billowed out from behind him. Chris couldn't help but stare as he approached. He wore a fine-tailored pair of charcoal slacks and another long-sleeved Henley, burgundy this time. His midnight hair hung in a straight curtain down his back, sleek and shining with health. She had no idea how he had managed to get it dry so fast. She hadn't heard a blow dryer. Her own thick hair took forever to dry, even with mechanical assistance!

He stopped next to her and she was momentarily dazed by his clean scent. Hell, if she was honest with herself, she would admit that everything about him was absolutely perfect. The only problem was that he was an Angel and she was a human.

"You found the clothing," he said in his gruff voice, finally breaking the silence.

"Yes – th-thank you," she stammered. "You're – I mean, they're beautiful."

One corner of his mouth lifted at her slip of the tongue and he reached up and ran his index finger down the side of her arm. "I am glad you like them," he softly said.

Chris' entire complexion turned beet-red and she turned to regard the clothes – anything to get her mind off the sensations his touch was causing. "Um, I'm not sure which of these to choose for this thing tonight," she confessed.

Djibril reached across her front to grab a silken emerald dress and handed it to her without a word. It was gorgeous, but still casual enough to be comfortable in any setting.

She looked sheepishly up at him. "Thanks."

He touched her cheek and then just under her chin. "You are very welcome," he whispered. A second later, his lips brushed across hers in the most fleeting touch and Chris suddenly found herself aching for more as she watched him then turn and walk toward the door to the hallway.

"I shall return in twenty minutes," he simply stated. Then he was gone and she was left standing alone in a room that suddenly seemed dull and lifeless.

***

Sarah watched as Mikhail dressed for the celebration. Sheely was with Azra'il, of course, and Sarah's parents had finally returned to their place. Liz was still uncomfortable around Sarah and Mikhail, so both seniors had begged off tonight's supper. That wasn't the reason they had given for turning down the invitation, but Sarah knew it was the real reason. Her mom was pretty easy for her to read. After all, they had been so close for so long that Sarah knew her every twitch and tell.

Do not worry so, my love, Mikhail's beautifully masculine voice floated through her mind.

Sarah offered him a soft little smile of appreciation, but said nothing. It wasn't as easy as she had thought – having all these new abilities and being so different from everyone else. Her mom had often remarked, "Life's not always what it's cracked up to be." Sarah had wondered for years what the hell Liz had meant by that, but the meaning was blatantly clear to her now.

Mikhail caught the bent her thoughts had taken and he cocked a brow toward her, asking for clarification. "You have to learn to appreciate the cracks, sometimes," was all Sarah said as she stood and left the room to go in search of her daughter and Azra'il.

Some part of her felt a need for solitude and she quickly threw up a buffer between Mikhail and herself without waiting for a response from him. She was suddenly feeling quite antsy, as if sensing something was going to happen. Sarah didn't think anyone at the Complex had anything to do with whatever was bugging her, but there was definitely something knocking at the door of her mind and she couldn't figure it out. Mikhail's thoughts and his constant monitoring of *her* thoughts would only serve to hamper her from discovering whatever it was her senses were picking up on and she wanted to know.

The sudden silence and feeling of solitude was a bit daunting, as Sarah was immediately taken back for a moment to those last few hours/days/weeks she had spent alone in the blue dimension. The urge to drop the buffer and re-establish her connection with Mikhail was almost overwhelming, but she resisted it.

After Mikhail had returned from the workout session with the others this afternoon, he and Sarah had visited the Medical Facility to see Thomas – or what was left of him.

Sarah had nearly collapsed upon sight of her son's lifeless body. It had been so still and she had felt nothing but death from it. She had remarked on this, but Mikhail had reassured her that Nera had taken Thomas and that he would return as soon as he could. It was the only spark of hope Sarah had left and she had reminded herself that Thomas would not want her to spend her life worrying about him. He had trusted Nera, and the creature had helped with Baphomet and Lisa. Sarah believed she had no other option but to trust that the strange creature that was Nera would keep Thomas safe and eventually return him to the Complex.

She suddenly realized the bent her thoughts had taken and decided she needed some other distraction to get her head back on other matters. She went back upstairs, but turned left instead of heading back toward the bedroom she shared with Mikhail. She was not sure of where she was heading, but knew she had to find someplace where she could shake off thoughts of Thomas and Nera and everything else that was going on. She came to a door and paused, a seed of something she couldn't identify tugging at her mind, pulling at her and she reached for the door handle.

As she entered the study, she pushed aside all the wayward and fearful thoughts of earlier and concentrated on the scene confronting her. Azra'il was sitting on one of the comfortable settees in the spacious, book-lined room. He held an open book in one hand and Sheely's tiny form within the crook of his other arm. She appeared to be sound asleep against her protector and Sarah quietly approached to take a seat on a chair just next to the settee.

She had spent the first part of the day in her suite of rooms entertaining her parents, along with Azra'il and Sheely, all the while keeping lines of communication open for Mikhail so that he would know what was going on with their daughter. She hadn't shared any of her thoughts regarding his brother with Mikhail and now she studied the powerful Lori more closely.

Azra'il flipped over the book he had been reading and placed it on the arm of the settee. "You seem distressed," he said, looking her over with narrowed eyes.

Sarah watched Sheely as she slept within the crook of Azra'il's arm. A feeling of utter loneliness unexpectedly engulfed her and she decided to go ahead and give in to Mikhail's pull on her mind as she dropped the buffer between her lover and herself. She felt his presence immediately. As she watched the couple on the settee, Sarah realized she missed the constant chatter Sheely had always kept going in her mind before she'd been born. She told Azra'il so.

After rolling his eyes, Azra'il softly said, "I wish I could learn to shut it *off* sometimes. Is there no way to break the connection once it begins?" He gave her a pleading look.

Sarah cracked a half-smile at him, asking, "Not everything you thought it would be, huh?"

"I never thought about it at all," he said, appearing just as surprised by the admission as she.

"You were content to continue with things the way they were?" she asked, sobering.

Azra'il thought about it for a moment. There had never been any time. Even while he slept, Azra'il was usually hard at work dealing with those human souls that needed assistance following their tether-lines back up to that other place. His siblings did not deal with things like that, not that Azra'il had never held that against any of them. They each had their jobs to do and he happily did his.

But now there was Sheely.

Azra'il had never been jealous of his time before. The blessed Great Designers had assigned him his duties prior to their departure those many thousands of years ago and Azra'il had felt happy to spend the life they had given him in their service. Now, however, there was this creature the Designers had created specifically to be with him. Why would they have put this wonderful being in his life, which he absolutely did believe, if they didn't intend for him to be preparing for their return? The only way Azra'il could justify the effect Sheely had on him was to say that he was about to have nothing to do and Sheely was his reward for having done the job he had been given to do before they had left.

Azra'il wasn't sure what all of this meant as far as the humans were concerned. If he was no longer required to assist human souls along their tether-lines, then who was going to do it? Sheely obviously had nothing to do with humans or their souls or tether-lines, judging by the feelings and thoughts she had expressed to him. So, what did it all mean?

Azra'il could feel her, even now, as she slept soundly within the cradle of his strong arms, could *feel* what she was feeling. Her thoughts, as usual, were more emotions and images than actual thoughts, but he could sense contentment coming from her tiny mind. As long as she was content, he was fine. When he thought of the possibility of her ever having to be alone in this world, or of her not being safe and secure at any point in time, his skin crawled and his blood boiled within his veins.

Sheely belonged with him! The Designers had created her to be with him.

A niggling little doubt crept in at this thought and Azra'il threw a quick glance toward Sarah. Had she implanted that doubt inside him? Even if the Designers were found to *not* be responsible for the creation of such as Sheely, as he believed Mikhail and Sarah thought, Azra'il knew he would do whatever it took to keep Sheely safe and with him.

Sarah stared at him without blinking. Azra'il felt as if she was somehow monitoring his thoughts and he wasn't so sure he felt comfortable with the idea that one such as she would have access to his mind without his consent. He stared right back at her, his own mind throwing up wall after wall while simultaneously searching for any signs of an attempt by her to intrude.

This afternoon, as he had studied himself in the mirror of the restroom he was using for the time being, he had been startled by the changes he saw in his own reflection. All indications were that he and Sheely both were becoming more like Sarah and the others. He wasn't sure if that was a good thing or not. But Sheely was with him and Azra'il was not going to do anything to jeopardize his ability to remain with her. From all indications, Sheely was happy with the way things were turning out, so far.

Getting back to Sarah's question, Azra'il said, "The Designers declared it taboo for Lorim to mate with humans, so I did not." Looking down at Sheely's peacefully slumbering form, he came to the same conclusion Sarah did, at the same time.

Sarah stated the obvious, "She wouldn't be here if Mikhail and I hadn't broken that particular rule."

Just the thought of not having Sheely in his life was painful to Azra'il and he gently raised her tiny form up to place a soft kiss upon her forehead. Sheely slept on, the knowledge and confidence of complete safety within his arms enough to assure her she was in no danger.

"I cannot explain all that I am feeling now that she is in my life," he said simply.

Sarah regarded him curiously. This was not the Azra'il she had come to expect. From their one previous meeting, other than the time they had spent in this same room this afternoon with her parents, Azra'il had seemed so much like a true warrior – filled with anger and energy and only able to rid himself of that rage by going out and destroying something. Now, as she watched him holding her daughter with the greatest of care, she realized Mikhail had been right about Azra'il. The waters definitely ran deep with this one, and yet he kept the rest of himself very closed off from others' scrutiny.

Sheely's hair tightened slightly as she yawned all of a

sudden and then opened her beautiful white-glowing eyes only to frown up at the male holding her. Sarah smiled a little as within her mind she caught a slightly sardonic remark from her daughter that basically translated into, "He might have still waters running deep, but his thoughts sure are *loud*!"

Azra'il could sense some form of communication occurring between mother and daughter, but he didn't press to discover what was being said. He felt guilty enough at having waltzed into the Complex and laid claim to his brother's newborn daughter. If she chose to keep separate a small piece of herself for just her parents, Azra'il would understand. He would be jealous, but he would understand.

So much had changed since she had entered his life. Just thinking about it stymied him. The very idea that his need of her could be wrong, the thought that she might not have been created specifically for him, the idea that the Designers had had no part of any plan for Sheely and Azra'il to be together for all time – these were things he would not acknowledge at this time. He still worshipped and felt a deep fealty toward his creators, the blessed Great Designers, and he would continue functioning as their loyal servant. He was unsure *how* he would accomplish this feat, since he was adamant in his refusal to leave Sheely even in Sarah and Mikhail's care.

As these feelings of uncertainty preyed upon his mind, he turned to Sarah for understanding. "Since our blessed Designers chose to reveal themselves to us, I have attempted to live my life according to their rule and I have been rewarded in kind. If Sheely is an example of such reward, then I happily accept her as such. I do admit that I am unable to understand completely the inner workings of the minds of our gods, so it would be logical for me to be unable to have expectations of anything in the future other than the expectation that I actually have one. As far as me feeling content or not, there is no argument against following the word of our Designers. They are our creators and must therefore, be obeyed. It would be foolish not to do so."

"And if you are wrong?" Sarah asked quietly.

"Wrong about what?" Azra'il immediately countered. "Wrong to obey those who created me and my entire race? Wrong to trust they know what is best for us?"

"Wrong to trust complete strangers who show up and declare they were the ones who created you," she clarified.

He frowned. "You are saying our beloved Designers, whom we have worshiped for tens of thousands of years here in the Loric Realm, were deceivers?" At her solemn nod, Azra'il shook his head and said incredulously, "I am still amazed by how disturbed the human brain can be. You know, I feel sorry for the entire human race."

His ire was obviously rising as he warmed to his subject and he scooted forward on the settee for more emphasis, continuing to press his point. "You all are so intent on finding anything to explain away your miserable little lives. Yet each time we have presented you with a suitable solution, you have rejected it because one group demands more power or some other explanation. Why can you not just accept the truth for what it is?" He huffed in frustration and Sheely started, her little chin wobbling as she sensed the tension in both her intended mate and her mother.

Sarah remained calm on the outside, but she was determined to get through to him – if not for the sake of the entire Kurric race, then at least for Sheely's sake.

Tread carefully, my heart, came Mikhail's voice in her mind. *I know you can feel his disquiet on this subject. Let him have time to adjust.*

Sarah was not to be silenced. *He would appreciate being respected enough for us to be as open and clear on the subject as possible, wouldn't you agree, and for us not to hide things from him, even if we do so in order to protect him?* she silently asked her mate.

Throughout this silent exchange, Sheely and Azra'il were having one of their own, it appeared, as Sarah noticed Azra'il suddenly frowning down at the glowing babe he held in his arms.

My love, I wish you would not push him – at least not while I am not present. We truly still do not know if we can trust him or not. He is far more powerful than I believe you give him credit for being. Sarah could almost feel her lover sighing in frustration. When she still did not change the set of her mind, he softly begged, *Please?*

Wait! she suddenly said.

Azra'il had continued ruminating throughout Sarah and Mikhail's silent conversation and was now considering the possibility of assigning a temporary leader of the Great Sanhedrin, when Sarah interrupted his thoughts.

"You know you cannot govern from outside the City walls," she baldly stated.

Azra'il tensed at her statement. So his thoughts *were* open to her! He would have to watch that. But he had to admit she was right. There was no way he could preside over either house without actually being present within the City's walls – especially not while there was still the possibility of a traitor being in their midst. Azra'il may have banished every other Lori from Lorim City's borders, but he still felt there was a traitor hiding somewhere within and presumably posing as a member of one of the houses of the Sanhedrin!

The lack of activity of late on the traitor's part was yet another worry, and Azra'il knew his people needed him to return soon to resolve the issue before any further incidents occurred. As Azra'il's mind churned away on this problem, the beginnings of an idea formed within. It had to do with Sarah going willingly into the City as his prisoner.

A sharp cry immediately split the room's silence as Sheely chimed in *her* two cents' worth on that idea.

Azra'il hugged her close and gently soothed her, but the worm was there in his mind. Whoever was orchestrating things must be stopped. Mikhail and the others might very well have to be allowed back into the City, but Azra'il knew any such move on his part prior to ferreting out the traitor would lead only to rebellion, and then flat out civil war between those Kurr who were for human integration and those who were against it. He could not be responsible for that.

The Captain of the Guard had mentioned the fact that someone else had issued the order for him and the rest of the Guard to destroy all those residing at the Complex, even the

Lorim. No Kurr would be mad enough to go up against the Complex Lorim without at least one Lori on his side – not after having witnessed the state of those Kurr who had previously fallen in battle with those very same beings.

Sheely's cries eventually quieted, but the damage was done.

Sarah merely sat there, silent as the grave, as they awaited the arrival of the other guests for the night's celebrations.

Chapter 13

Iblis and Satariel snuck along the quiet streets of Lorim City. They had left their Dalbits in a nearby glade before entering the City on foot. It was still dark out and there was little chance anyone would see them, but they could ill afford to get caught within City walls. As Iblis had expected, the moment he awakened from the stupor caused by crossing the rift into the Loric Realm, he had been summoned into the City – the One already eager to exact vengeance for Iblis' failure to carry out the previous plan. But Iblis felt no fear this evening. He had Satariel with him and two Shaitans were sure to be more than a match for a single Kurr, no matter what gifts it had.

A movement up ahead in the darkened alleyway had both Shaitans immediately pressing up close to the nearest wall. They were as still and silent as the grave.

Waiting.

Suddenly, a dark, hooded figure appeared from out of nowhere, just behind them on the street. The only signal the Shaitans got that someone was there was a soft puff of wind.

They whipped around, focusing on the newcomer. There were no lights nearby, so the Kurr's features were completely hidden from view. But the raw energy pulsing out of the creature was daunting enough to have Satariel taking a good step or two back away from the thing. Not Iblis, though. He stood there with his chest puffed out and his chin up. He was done playing the whimpering fool.

What he thought might be a chuckle flitted through his mind and he had the strange sensation that the One was laughing at him. *Too afraid to come on your own?* Iblis thought he heard the thing say in his mind and his eyes narrowed in defiance.

Without warning, Satariel crumpled to the ground, his limbs seizing and his breathing shallow around grunts of uncontrollable spasms. A shiver shimmied down Iblis' spine as he realized his nemesis knew exactly what to do to exhibit just how vulnerable the two Shaitans were.

In the next instance, Satariel's quaking stopped and

the One backed off slightly, giving the two outlanders some breathing room. When both Shaitans were steady again and focused on the creature before them, a slightly tanned hand held out an envelope which Iblis took. He quickly opened the envelope, read the instructions on the piece of paper it contained and then dug two tiny capsules out from within the envelope.

Iblis shot a shocked look toward the hooded figure, but received only a nod from the caped head and then the two Shaitans found themselves once again standing alone on the dark and quiet streets of the City. Iblis understood what had to be done, and the consequences he and Satariel would face if they should fail. He held up one of the little pills.

A quiver shook his form, but he knew they had no choice. His brilliant plan to prove himself against the powerful Kurr had failed miserably and now he just wanted all of this to be over. He handed one pill to Satariel, making sure he understood what they had to do, and then he pocketed the other in the waistcoat he wore. The two looked at the map on the back of the paper with the instructions and Iblis softly said, "This will be some journey even with Dalbits. We had best get a move on."

Satariel shakily nodded his agreement and they both turned and made their way back out of the City.

The sun was setting on the third day of their journey when they finally caught a glimpse of the Complex. According to the information the One had given him, he knew the Kurr here were intermingling with humans. Iblis believed it as he recalled how upset Baphomet had become in the human realm, first over that extraordinary half-breed they had found in the middle of the Outback, and then over the trusting sister on the seedy side of London. Those other Lorim had shown up to protect the Shaitan King from Iblis and his followers and Iblis now wondered if perhaps the Lorim had brought their ailing brother here to recuperate.

He hoped not. He and Satariel already had enough to contend with, what with that one glowing-eyed Lori that supposedly ran this joint. That one had nearly destroyed Iblis' entire group of Shaitans in London and it was an experience Iblis would prefer never to repeat. Add to that a very pissed-off Shaitan King who had most assuredly healed by now and Iblis and Satariel would definitely be screwed – if Baphomet was at the Complex and discovered what they were about to do.

Honestly though, Iblis knew he would rather take his chances with Lord Baphomet than to fail the one who had sent Satariel and him on this mission. The Lorim were just, especially when there were more than one present. The punishments they doled out could almost always be sure to fit the crime and only that. The one who had sent Satariel and Iblis on this mission, however, could not be counted on for such leniency. A swift and most assuredly brutal castigation would be the best one could hope for if one did not live up to *that* Master's expectations.

Another shiver ran down Iblis' spine as he recalled some of the terrifying images the One had put into his mind after his last failure. He quickly urged Satariel on toward the area marked on the map. There were only a few Kurr out and about, but still they had to be cautious. The light was fading and most of the Complex inhabitants should be either returning to their own homes for the night or getting ready for the evening meal at the main building of the Complex. The layout of the Complex appeared to be quite similar to the Shaitan city of Knor – at least the center of it – and Iblis was easily able to discover the main Complex building.

He and Satariel had to quickly tuck themselves into a nearby copse of brush to avoid being seen by a group headed from the wood toward the main house. It was a mixed group, it appeared, but it did confirm that the Lorim at the Complex were definitely keeping company with humans. A fiery red-headed female human walked among the group, conversing and interacting with them as if she had always walked with such as they. It made Iblis sick to watch and he wanted to kill the thing right then and there.

Patience. It was not his strong suit. But he was no fool and he certainly had no death wish. He and Satariel would first scout out the Complex. Then they would scour the surrounding area for any wayward Shaitan groups. This time of year there were usually small bands of country Shaitans who would jump at an opportunity to fatten their human slave stocks. They wouldn't take much convincing at all to attack the Complex.

Within 20 minutes, Iblis had seen enough and he and Satariel headed back into the surrounding woods to gather their team. As nearly every Shaitan they encountered fell in line, Iblis became more aware of the importance of this night. The whole point of this mission boiled down to the fight against human encroachment upon the Loric Realm. It was why the One had sent first one team, and now Satariel and Iblis. This war, although still in its infancy, was already going full-swing and every Kurr had better hurry up and pick a side, because as far as Iblis could see, things were about to get hairy.

Just do as the One ordered and then come back to take care of the rubble, he thought to himself. Yes. Satariel and he would ensure *all* of those remaining at the Complex were dealt with – and then they would finally be welcomed back into Lorim City to be recognized for their patriotism and service to all Kurr-kind.

***

Lisa paused again. Once more, Baphomet and Israfil came to a halt, both of them now more than just a little concerned. This was the third time Lisa had stopped in her tracks as their little group made its way from Israfil's home on the outskirts of the Complex to Mikhail's and Sarah's home, which was situated at the very center of the Complex. Both males regarded the pregnant Lori with concern.

Lisa listened. There were whispers on the winds. Every Ngarinyin knew that. She had not grown up completely cut off from her people and she remembered the old ways her mother had taught her. She knew how important it was to pay attention to the songs of the animals and the whispers they sent out on the winds. She had been hearing them all day and now they sounded almost urgent, alarming.

Something coming, they said.

A strong shiver shook her frame and she could feel baby Cabal quickly moving, curling himself up into a tight ball. He did that whenever he was afraid. Before he had grown too big, he had often hidden himself away inside his mother's womb whenever he had become frightened. Now, however, he was much too big to hide away, so he merely curled himself up into a tight ball formation.

Baphomet sensed both individuals' fears and he pulled Lisa securely into his strong arms, whispering to her that everything would be just fine. "We do not have to go to this celebration tonight," he told her. "Mikhail and Sarah would understand."

"No-no," Lisa said. She smiled up at him. "We'll be fine."

Baphomet exchanged a nervous glance with his brother but didn't press the issue further.

***

Chris stood nervously beside Djibril. Lyss stood on his other side. Introductions to Djibril's other siblings and their mates were being made. Fortunately, it appeared Lorim, as Djibril had explained they were called, were not in the habit of shaking hands or hugging when greeting someone for the first time. Chris was glad, for just the *idea* of being touched by one of the strange, glowy-eyed creatures made her skin crawl. She edged a little closer to Djibril, clasping his hand a little tighter as the one named Lisa spoke politely with Lyss.

The walk through the corridors of the giant mansion had been an experience. Djibril had informed Chris that this place, which he called the Badlands Complex, had only just recently been built, but it seemed to be fully-equipped with electricity. When Lyss asked about how the place had electricity when it was in another dimension, separate from the human realm, Djibril explained that it was powered by hydroelectricity. The Lorim, it appeared, were quite the engineers and had cleverly designed a hydro-electric system that functioned by generating power using the energy created by the rise and fall of the tide in the nearby Nameless Bay.

A serving Kurr appeared then to lead the trio to their seats along the long dining table, forcing Chris' mind back to the situation at hand. Never once did Djibril release his hold on her hand, as if he could sense how nervous she felt just being in the same room with all those strange, white-eyed and glowing creatures. It was odd, but she could handle being in a room full of terrorists who wanted to kill her without feeling the least bit nervous. But when faced with a room full of strange alien creatures with glowing eyes and skin that almost seemed to vibrate with energy, she felt completely out of her element.

Even the infant, whose birth was apparently the reason for the dinner party, sported a pair of brightly-glowing eyes. It appeared, though, that the child only had eyes for the male holding it. That one had been introduced to her as Azra'il. He was very quiet and fierce-looking and Chris hoped she never had the misfortune of getting on his bad side.

He sat next to Djibril's brother Mikhail, who sat next to his own mate, a fierce-looking female named Sarah. There was something odd about that Sarah, something almost familiar, and Chris made a mental note to ask Djibril about this female Lori before Lyss and she returned home.

To Chris' immediate right sat a very quiet, but normal-looking Lori named Israfil. He was another of Djibril's brothers, but he didn't frighten her. He had the same beautiful ice-blue eyes as Djibril. His hair was uncharacteristically short for an Arch Angel, as if she had so much historical knowledge to go by, and it was just plain sandy-brown. His skin even sported a healthy light tan. Chris was glad he had been placed next to her instead of her ending up having to sit next to one of the glowy-eyed creatures.

Israfil sat next to Azra'il. Azra'il held the baby, of course, and her name was Sheely. He watched over her as if she was the most precious thing in the world. His eyes darted here and there while his strange white hair slowly comforted the child, constantly rubbing her body and encircling it in a protective manner.

Chris was glad he and the one named Sarah were both more concerned with caring for Sheely than with actually participating in the party.

The powerful male Chris had met earlier, Mikhail, sat on Sarah's left at the end of the table. His glowing eyes seemed to see everything, though for the most part he only had eyes for Sarah and Sheely. That was fine by Chris as well. After hearing in the practice clearing how knowledgeable he was about fighting techniques, Chris figured she was better off avoiding him altogether.

Directly across from Chris sat Lyss, while Djibril occupied the end of the long table nearest her. Next to Lyss sat Suriyah, whom they had met earlier in the practice clearing. She had long white hair, but it was just normal hair. Suriyah proved to be extremely friendly. Her quick smile and pleasant demeanor was the only thing other than Djibril's touch keeping Chris from darting from the room in order to put as much distance as possible between these strange creatures and herself.

To Suriyah's left were the last of the strange creatures, another brother of Djibril's named Baphomet and his mate, who was named Lisa. Lisa was quite a bit darker than the others in the room and Chris wondered why that was. Like Djibril, Baphomet never released his hold on Lisa, Chris noted, and he could often be observed reaching over to lightly rub a lighted spot on Lisa's abdomen. Chris decided the couple must be expecting and she determined to add that to the growing list of things to ask Djibril about before she returned home tonight.

One thing Chris had to admit about the creatures was that they truly appeared dedicated to family. It was a large and varied group, but the "normal" Lorim and the glowing creatures alike all appeared accepting of each other. The only problem was that they all appeared to think there was something going on between Djibril and her, judging from the smiling looks Chris kept intercepting from the majority of those seated around the table. Djibril was the consummate gentleman, however, and she could not blame him for his siblings' faulty assumptions.

The talk around the table remained light and cheerful throughout the meal and Chris was pleased by the fact that Lyss was treated just as well as she by all in attendance. It appeared there was even a Medical Facility at the Complex and Suriyah spoke at some length with Lyss about some of the goings on within it. Apparently, in addition to being absolutely beautiful and an excellent fighter, Suriyah was also very skilled as some sort of health practitioner. Chris thought she heard the female Lori refer to herself as a Jinn, though Chris herself knew very little about the healthcare field. Lyss didn't appear to know much about any kind of Jinn either, though, so Chris figured it might be a Loric term.

Toward the end of the meal, a liveried servant Kurr entered the room and delivered some news to the one named Mikhail. Once the Kurr left, Mikhail announced, "We have a guest."

All eyes turned toward the entrance to the room as the door there swung open to reveal a very dark-skinned woman who looked as if she might be some sort of Aborigine. The creature named Lisa suddenly stood and blurted out, "Mum?"

The older woman appeared to relax as she took in her surroundings and then quickly came farther into the room toward Lisa. She stopped about four yards away from the female Lori who awaited her and looked her over, up and down. "You've changed," the newcomer said to Lisa.

Lisa blinked a few times. "Wh-what are you doing here, Mum?" Lisa stammered. Baphomet stood and moved to stand beside his mate and he placed a protective hand at the small of her back.

The older woman's eyes narrowed upon the tall creature standing next to her daughter. "So, you're the one who come and took my daughter," she simply stated.

Baphomet merely stared mutely at the woman, still guarding Lisa.

Chris was amazed. So Lisa had been *human*? How could that be?

"Mum," Lisa repeated, "What are you doing here?"

The older woman sighed and nodded before saying, "I needed to see for meself that you was okay and to warn you and your new people that there's danger comin' to the Ngarinyin world."

"What do you mean?" Lisa asked, completely rounding the table now as she headed toward her mother, her face drawn in instant concern.

"The elders have been told of grave danger comin' soon from the sky people," the older woman said. "I told them I would come see if there was anythin' you an' your new people could do to help." Tears had formed in the woman's eyes by now and Lisa hugged her mother, soothing her with a calming voice while she looked pleadingly up at Baphomet for help.

"Here," Baphomet said, "let us move this to somewhere where we can talk, shall we?" He turned toward the other end of the table without relinquishing his hold on Lisa. "Mikhail?"

Mikhail, along with Suriyah and Israfil, rose and moved to follow the others from the room.

Djibril rose and helped Chris to stand as he politely thanked Sarah for the meal and made a quick apology for needing to leave early. It was obvious to everyone that the party was over, so his polite gesture was merely the proper protocol that he performed without difficulty. Chris frowned as Djibril escorted her from the suite of rooms and back out into the main hallway. Lyss had remained within the suite and Djibril was still leading Chris farther away from it.

"If we're going to return home tonight," she said. "Shouldn't Lyss come with us as well?"

Djibril halted in his tracks. As he stood there staring down at her, all tense, he frowned and quietly asked, "You still wish to leave the Complex?"

Chris frowned up at him. "Well, I-I thought that was the plan," she stammered.

A muscle worked in his jaw and Djibril turned suddenly and punched his fist against the hallway wall. A blood stain immediately marked the dark slate lining the wall and Chris reached for his injured hand, her eyes wide as she wondered why on earth he would have done such a thing. As she stood there cradling his injured appendage within her two smaller hands, Djibril reached up with his other hand to cup the back of her head, gently forcing her to look him in the eyes. He stared intently at her for a moment before quietly asking, "Is there some *reason* you need to hurry back to the human realm?"

She looked back down at his blood-stained knuckles. The wounds that had spilled the blood were all but healed already and she frowned. "W-Well, no. I-I don't guess so," she slowly said, looking back up at him.

The fingers he had enmeshed in her hair gently massaged her scalp and little sparks of electricity jolted along her nerve endings all over the back of her head and down her neck. Chris gasped at the sensation as he lowered his lips to hers.

She was going to stop this, she really was. After all, they were standing in the middle of the main hallway where anyone could see them. She had to stop this. But each time she made up her mind to pull away, he changed the angle of his head to a new position, creating new sensations along previously unaffected nerve endings and Chris quickly forgot about everything except the feeling of tiny jolts of electricity darting all over her body.

Djibril moaned in that gravelly voice and once again sought a better angle with which to taste her, settling now for nibbling a trail down the side of her neck as he used his body to maneuver hers around and backward until she was flush up against the cold slate wall. Still, he continued tasting her, touching her, lightly scraping his teeth across her skin and then opening his mouth wide upon her flesh to suck gently on it and to brush it with his tongue. She tasted so good, he felt as if he could die a happy Lori just devouring her.

Electricity shot through each one's entire being and the rest of the world had nearly disappeared when suddenly, the sound of a surprised gasp echoed in the hallway, breaking the momentary thrall the two had been under. Djibril raised his head and stepped more fully in front of Chris to protect her from whatever unseen danger had interrupted their tryst. Looking around, he spotted a very red-faced serving Kurr who quickly apologized for having interrupted the couple and excused himself, scurrying off down the hallway as quickly as he could.

Djibril sighed in frustration as he turned to lead Chris back to their suite. Neither spoke as they traversed the corridors – each wrapped in his or her own thoughts. As soon as they were behind the closed doors of their suite of rooms, Djibril reached to pull her back into his arms so that they could continue where they had left off. But Chris stepped back, blinking up at him as she moved away from the Lori. She wanted nothing more than to go to him and finish what they had started back there in the hallway, but it was wrong.

Djibril swallowed his frustration, taking a mental step back as he argued with himself about how he should handle this situation. She was only human, he silently argued. But his Loric body felt as if it was on the verge of a complete meltdown if he didn't find some form of release soon. The energies flowing into him from her body whenever they touched were accumulating at an alarming rate and Djibril had yet to do anything substantial to relieve the mounting pressure. He knew he would either have to take her soon or take care of matters on his own. If he didn't, he was liable to go insane. The problem, however, was Chris.

She was more important than his primal physical needs. But the baser side of himself appeared to be gaining the upper hand as far as who got to call the shots where his physical body's well-being was concerned, and Djibril was afraid he might soon snap the way Baphomet had done after he and Lisa had been separated too long. Granted, that had been an entirely different situation and Djibril had since learned that they had eventually discovered that the two of them always had to be touching or bad things would happen. But it still worried Djibril, never-the-less. If something was to happen and Djibril didn't find a way of relieving the pressure, he knew even Chris could possibly be in danger.

Still, she needed time. He would give her as much as he could. But he hoped she wouldn't take too long.

Chris stared at him, her mind racing as she argued

back and forth with herself. Okay, so he was a Lori and she was a human. From what she had learned at the dinner party, Lisa at least had been born to a human, so there might possibly be a way to get around the problem of each of them being of different species – that was, *if* Lisa had been completely human in the first place, and not some hybrid Lori-human mix.

A part of her desperately hoped this was the case because she didn't know if she could stand being around Djibril much longer without taking things to the next level. Even more of a problem was that the more time she spent with him, the less she was beginning to care about their physical differences.

She wanted him... and he wanted her. What more was there to think about?

The realization shook her to her core. She had been raised Catholic. Granted, it had been almost two decades since she had last attended mass or even entered a church. But she still retained the memories of everything she had been taught about Angels as she had grown up. They were the right hand of the Lord! She was just a lowly human – a sinner. The two of them were not created to be equal. They weren't meant to be together, period.

Still, she wanted him and she knew he wanted her.

Chris was no child. Neither was she some whimpering virgin. She suspected Djibril wasn't either, for that matter. They were both mature enough to either choose to take things to the next level or to ignore the attraction each felt for the other. It was obvious which path Djibril had chosen, but she still didn't know what to do.

He was obviously willing to give her time to make up her mind. Otherwise, he would already be across the room to force her to continue what had been going on earlier in the hallway. Perhaps he would be willing to allow her enough time to get to know him a bit more, to become more accustomed to the idea of him being an honest-to-goodness Angel.

"Look," she said. "If I'm going to be here for any length of time, I think I should probably move into Lyss' room with her." She had tried this tack earlier, but she thought she might give it one more go.

That muscle worked again in his jaw and he softly said, "I repeat, over my dead Loric corpse."

Chris rolled her eyes and sighed in frustration. There was no way she would be able to hold out if she was sleeping with him! She was already finding it damned near impossible to resist throwing caution and a lifetime of religious belief out the window in order to just jump him and do as she wanted with his gorgeous body.

"Djibril, we're too different," she said, hoping logic would help convince him – and possibly herself – that this was crazy. "You're an Arch Angel. I'm a human."

"Yes, as you have pointed out before," he interrupted. "What of it? Sarah was human. Lisa was human. My brothers are Lorim. Apparently, our two species are physically compatible."

Chris digested this information, not without some difficulty. Sarah and Lisa looked nothing like humans now. Of course, their mates looked nothing like Arch Angels, either. A small part of her brain wondered what they each had looked like before they had mutated into the freaky-looking alien creatures they were now. A larger part of her brain wondered how and why they had mutated in the first place.

She was scared. It was obvious.

"Look," Djibril said. "I shall happily explain to you everything I know on the subject." He approached her cautiously, reaching to lightly rub her arms – up and down, up and down. "They were like us," he explained. "They mated and then they changed."

Chris frowned and tensed up, pulling back a step.

Djibril knew her fear. He felt it as a palpable thing. But he had started this, and he needed to finish it. "I do not know if you and I will change after we mate, but I certainly would not rule it out." He paused, letting that sink in. Then he hit her with the big cannon, confessing, "I do not care, though. I want you and I mean to mate with you eventually."

Chris took another step back, shaking her head. "I-I

can't become like them," she said. "I can't – no." She shook her head more firmly now and with greater determination. "I won't." Then she said, "I want to go home."

Without another word, she stepped around him and walked out.

Djibril stood still, with her words still hanging in the air, still echoing in the hollows of his mind. The two of them had been specifically created for each other, yet she could not – or would not – see it.

***

"Mum, how did you even get here?" Lisa asked after their small group reached Mikhail's private study and everyone was comfortably seated throughout.

The older Aborigine regarded the creature before her. She saw traces of the daughter she had known for years in the thing sitting directly across from her. But the changes her child would have had to endure to end up looking like this were inconceivable.

"The elders wanted me to ask if you and your people could help the Ngarinyin before the sky people come down an' it's too late," the older woman said evenly. Her directness was deeply at odds with the emotions clearly displayed in her eyes. Each and every Lori in the room could feel how frightened the woman was of the idea that her request might be denied. "They used a bit o' the old magicks to get me through to your world," she continued. "The rest was just listening to the spirits to discover which way to go to find you."

Lisa tightened her grip on Baphomet's hand.

"You mentioned some threat from the sky?" Mikhail asked.

The old woman turned to regard him, her eyes narrowing. It was admittedly quite a testament to the old woman's strength of character that she was willing to face one such as Mikhail, looking the way he did. But, face him she did. She bravely answered his questions, describing an attack on her people by some*one* or some*thing* from above.

She informed Mikhail and the others gathered in the

room that the spirits of both the Ngarinyin ancestors and the animals had been warning the elders of the coming danger for a while now. And because Lisa had been born "special," it was the hope of the Ngarinyin that the guardians of this Realm would choose to help her original people.

Again, Lisa's grip on Baphomet's hand tightened.

Baphomet experienced a flash of anger emanating from within his mate. Her feelings about her former people were mixed, he sensed. He could feel the love she felt for her mother, but he also felt anger in her toward the elders who had ostracized her throughout her entire human lifetime. He himself felt a certain degree of anger toward these elders. But then he recalled the old Koradji who had assisted him in his quest to have access to Lisa's mind. He believed the Koradji may have known what was coming for them even when Baphomet had been dealing with him, and Baphomet felt as if that must have meant something.

Mikhail's voice asking the old woman if she would please wait outside the study interrupted Baphomet's thoughts and he slowly rubbed his thumb across Lisa's hand in a comforting gesture. Whatever was happening here was meant to be, Baphomet was certain of it, and he felt it very important that at least Lisa, if not the others, understand that.

He could sense Lisa monitoring his thoughts and the range of emotions welling within her ran the gamut. All Baphomet could do was to hold on tight and hope she would find the best answer to this problem without too much distress. As it was, Cabal had already pulled back and clammed up. Baphomet threw a quick glance at the lighted spot on Lisa's abdomen. Sure enough, the light appeared smaller and dimmer now than it had just a few hours ago. Baphomet *had* to find a way to get Lisa to relax.

"Have any of you had indications of anything like what she described?" Mikhail suddenly asked. It appeared he had startled everyone out of deep thoughts, for it took a moment before anyone answered.

"I-I have heard the same warnings my mum spoke of," Lisa hesitantly stated, throwing a pleading look toward Baphomet. "All day today," she continued. "I've been hearing the warnings from the animals that something's coming."

Suriyah cleared her throat and softly said, "This is precisely what happened in my visions."

Everyone knew of Suriyah's visions. She had had them so long ago, but they had ruled all of their lives since she had experienced them. No one was about to question what she said.

"What are we to do?" Mikhail asked solemnly.

Suriyah merely stared at them for a moment. She couldn't believe it had actually come to this. "This is insane," she whispered harshly as she launched herself up out of her seat and stalked over to stare out one of the darkened windows. The visions had affected each and every member of her life – and how she despised them for it! But so far, everything had happened the way she had seen. Who was she then to question the validity of what she had been shown was to happen next? Closing her eyes and announcing on a heavy sigh, she said, "We bring them here to live."

"The Ngarinyin?" Mikhail asked.

"All of the Aboriginal people," Suri answered softly, as if she was in the middle of some other vision and was not quite aware of what was going on around her at the moment.

Everyone else in the room was stunned!

How could anyone even conceive of such a thing? The entire Loric Realm had already been turned upside down by the introduction of just a handful of humans into its society. What would the addition of such a huge number of them do?

"My heart," Baphomet stated with concern as he turned toward his mate. Lisa was suddenly very pale and there appeared to be a fine sheen of sweat beading along her forehead. Suriyah was instantly by her side as Mikhail ordered a Kurr to fetch Hantsushept immediately. It appeared everyone was upset by Suriyah's announcement, but what could they do? It seemed the whole world was going crazy and here they were, mere Lorim, struggling through as best they could without anyone to guide them – regardless of the fact that they were Lorim.

Hantsushept arrived shortly thereafter and performed a cursory examination on Lisa. His prognosis, as everyone had suspected, was that she was suffering from an anxiety attack. When told *why* the young Lori was so distressed, the good physician merely raised his brows and said, "I see."

Mikhail was a bit stunned. "Is that all you have to say?" he asked incredulously.

Hantsushept thought for a moment and then said, "No. You are probably going to need to quarantine them when they first arrive." He bent and packed up his bag. Straightening again, he said, "I would recommend at least two weeks in quarantine, if not four. We do not know, after all, what kinds of illnesses or communicable diseases they will be carrying and which ones here will affect them." He patted Lisa's hand a couple of times. "Do try and rest, m' dear," he said in a kindly voice. "If not for yourself, then do it for young Cabal, hmm?"

He smiled and turned back to Mikhail. "It is my understanding you have a human here now who has medical training?" he asked.

Mikhail, who was still stymied by the old Kurr's nonchalant reaction to the news about the coming horde of humans, merely nodded and said, "One of the twins, I believe."

Hantsushept nodded. "I would like to invite her to help out at the clinic, if you would not mind," he stated. "I shall need someone with her human health expertise, especially if we are to have such a huge influx of them here."

Mikhail barely even nodded and the old Kurr left, black bag in hand.

Suriyah came to stand beside him. "I guess I should gather a team together to go to the human realm, huh?" she asked.

Mikhail gave her a look that clearly said she was crazy.

"What?" she asked. "You heard Hantsushept." She paused a moment, but then said simply, "It has to be, Mikhail."

That was all there was to it.

Israfil, who had remained silent and uninvolved throughout everything that had transpired, merely stood and tended to Lisa, helping her along. He remained quiet as Lisa, Baphomet and he exited the room. Neither Mikhail nor Suriyah bothered him. Mikhail, at least, knew Israfil suffered from his own demons still.

"I shall take the old woman," Suriyah announced. "She and I will cross over into the human realm, gather her people, and then return." After a moment's pause, she continued, "I shall have my Jinn construct a temporary encampment area for them on the South side of the Complex. That way, they will be far enough away from the Kurr living here to cause too much of a stir, but close enough to be cared for by the medical staff."

Mikhail stood rooted to the spot. Finally, he found his voice and softly asked, "Suri, where is all this headed?"

Suriyah raked a hand through her long blond tresses in frustration, uncaring that it messed up her perfect coif. Sighing heavily, she reminded him, "I told you when I first had the visions where it was headed. I simply do not know if my interpretations of the visions were correct."

And therein lay the problem. Everything hinged on how she had chosen to interpret what she had seen and they all had so much to lose if it turned out she had chosen the wrong interpretation. Long ago, Mikhail had listened to what Azra'il, Israfil and the council members of both Sanhedrin houses had decided on this matter and it had cost so many so much.

However, there was infinitely more at stake this time around.

Suriyah didn't even realize she was holding her breath as she waited for Mikhail's decision. Long ago, she had stood before him, asking for his trust in a similar situation. Her disbelief, anger, and heartache at his decision then had nearly been her undoing. The same mixture of fear and hope that had filled her then consumed her now.

Her breath came gushing out on a huge sigh of relief as he said, "Take the old woman. Gather your Jinn. Go fetch as many of their people as will come. We shall do for them whatever we can to protect them from whatever this threat is." After giving him a teary nod, Suriyah turned and left.

As the door to his study softly closed behind Suriyah's rapidly departing form, Mikhail practically fell back into his chair behind his desk. He was now alone in the room, but he knew Sarah was there in his mind. He had sensed her presence tagging along the moment he had left the party earlier and now he was grateful for her presence.

I'm here, her soft thoughts confirmed as they floated through the whirling river of his mind. He swallowed a lump in his throat. There was so much at stake now. Part of him was confident that he had made the right decision. But a larger part was now scared half to death at the decision he had made. *If it's any consolation*, Sarah's beautiful voice echoed through his mind, *I agree with your decision.*

Another voice suddenly sounded in his mind, though it came across more as conceptual than as one using an actual language. The message it conveyed was simple. *You did the right thing, Daddy*, it said.

Mikhail buried his face in his hands and broke down sitting right there at his desk.

Chapter 14

Nera cringed as she heard Talis cough again. It sounded as if the entirety of everything he had inside his body, which at this point could not be much since he had not actually eaten anything in years, would come gushing out with the next cough he expelled. She held his hand, but the very idea of being anywhere near someone so ill repelled her.

It wasn't as if she had planned on being this way. She had been extremely sheltered during her time on the physical plane of her planet and she had never encountered sickness. As a member of the Royal Family, she had always been kept from such things. Now, however, those who had sheltered her before were long gone. She was left to deal with this issue all on her own.

A part of her blamed Talis for her predicament, not to mention what he was experiencing at the moment. He had continued sheltering her even after they had come aboard the ship with his brother and the others. There had been times when she had truly wished to help, but Talis had forbidden it. Nera hadn't wished to go against his wishes, but now she felt impotent, unable to assist him in any way, shape or form.

The door to the room smoothly slid open, admitting a very disgruntled-looking Lokai.

Just as he prepared to let loose what she figured was a series of expletives and admonitions at the fact that Talis and she had yet to return to the bridge, Nera asked, "Has Lalia recovered?"

Her brother-by-association paused, frowning down at her slight form. An image of his mate flashed suddenly before his mind's eye and his hardened heart melted just a bit toward his naïve young sister. "My Lalia is recovering nicely," he informed her. He frowned, however, as his gaze fell to his brother. "He is faring well?" he suddenly asked.

Nera shook her head, looking back at Talis' pale face. "The medical staff have informed me that his temperature is elevated and his body is engaged in battle with some foreign menace he may have brought back somehow from that physical plane," she softly explained, all the while gripping her Talis' hand as tightly as she dared.

"Nera," Lokai said, "we need him."

She looked up at him with pleading eyes. He had to give Talis more time! Just a little, at least.

With a heavy sigh, Lokai shook his head and covered his eyes. This was his brother, after all. Nera could understand the conflict that had to be raging through him, but this was her mate!

Finally, Lokai looked at her, sighing heavily once more, as he said, "I expect you to do whatever is necessary to assist him with his recovery. After all, we are all in this because of one person and I expect that one to participate, as well."

Nera's eyes were wide as saucers as she realized what he was asking of her.

She had never had anything to do with situations like this! She had been sheltered her entire life, even in the after-time. Now he expected her to just step up, as if she had done this a million times before?

"No!" he exclaimed in heated disbelief. "I expect you to do whatever is necessary to save this batch! And if that is not enough, then I expect you to do whatever it takes to save your mate!" With that, he turned and exited the room in a rush.

Nera stared at the door to the room for several minutes after he had left, her mouth hanging open in astonishment. Lokai expected her to give of herself in order to save someone else. He expected her to give so that another – indeed, many others – would be able to continue. No one had ever charged her with such responsibility and Nera was not certain she liked it. As she turned back to look upon her mate's pale features, however, her own heart melted and she knew, now more than ever before, she was ready to do whatever it took to help him back to health so that they could once again concentrate on saving this batch of children. After all, they had been the only Sephor team in all known history to have successfully cultivated each and every batch they had attempted and she had no desire to besmirch that record.

She stood, wondering what she should do. Talis' big body took up most of the space on the thin medical bed and Nera was unsure of herself in this area. After a moment of thought, she decided it would probably benefit Talis most if she were to lie directly next to his body, lengthwise, so that her own energies could infuse into his body, thereby helping him to heal more quickly than he would otherwise be able to do on his own.

Carefully, she climbed upon the thin Medical bed, taking care not to lie upon any part of his anatomy for fear of harming him in some way. She placed an arm about his chest and one leg over both of his, hoping to share as much of her energies as possible.

Immediately, she felt a repellant energy from somewhere inside his body. She had sensed this energy before, when she had used the comm device to transmit through to the physical plane down onto the surface of the planet where Talis had been. Of course, that had been before it had been damaged when they had brought him back from the physical body he had occupied there. But she still felt the energy, even now.

As bile rose in her throat, she forced her body to calm itself and she settled back alongside Talis' form, forcing herself to calm down so that his body could draw whatever energy it needed from hers.

As her eyes closed, she prayed to the ancient gods her original people had worshipped, pleading, "Let this strengthen him so that we may save our children."

***

Azra'il leaned back against the soft chair back. He wasn't sure *what* he felt inside at this point. Millennia ago, Mikhail had approached him to ask his opinion about the visions Suriyah had claimed she had experienced regarding the blessed Great Designers. Azra'il had offered his honest opinion at the time, and as a result Mikhail had chosen to banish Suriyah, Baphomet and any and all Kurr loyal to them to the Badlands of the Loric Realm, which at that time had been a wild, uninhabited part of their land.

His siblings had obviously survived, and even thrived, outside the walls of Lorim City. But now, Azra'il wondered if perhaps there wasn't more to things than he had previously considered. Mikhail had made a momentous decision just now, as far as Azra'il was concerned. He had felt every emotion raging through his brother's mind as Suriyah had pleaded her case to Mikhail, and he knew his brother struggled still with the idea that the Lorim and all those within the Loric Realm had possibly chosen to place their trust in false gods. Mikhail still felt the yoke of responsibility for all those on the planet, and Azra'il's mind was overwhelmed by the magnitude and depth of Mikhail's well of emotional strength.

After Sarah had caused so much chaos within Lorim City, when the members of the Great Sanhedrin had chosen him to lead the Kurr there, Azra'il had suddenly been overwhelmed by such a huge responsibility – taking care of all the Kurr within the civilized borders of their land *was* a huge responsibility, especially when one considered the duties Azra'il had been assigned by the blessed Great Designers, which he was still performing.

However, the number of Kurr housed within the borders of Lorim City was nothing compared to the entire planet's Kurric *and human* population and that was apparently the body for which Mikhail still felt responsible, even though he had been banished from Lorim City and technically relieved of his responsibilities. Azra'il frowned as Sheely's hair tightened slightly around his mid-section. She obviously agreed with Mikhail's decision to go ahead and trust Suriyah's interpretations of the visions she had experienced all those years ago, and why wouldn't she? He was her father.

Look deeper, Azra'il suddenly heard her tiny voice say in his mind.

Again, he frowned, his mind furiously working to understand the concepts she was trying to explain to him. She had never met nor interacted with the Designers. How could she form any kind of opinion about them without having stood within their presence and felt the energies they emitted? How could she know of their greatness? How could she imagine the incredibly humbling experience of standing before such ancient, benevolent creatures as they?

Azra'il understood her youth and inexperience as being the primary reason for her naïveté. What he absolutely could *not* understand was why *he*, Lori Azra'il, elected and accepted Lord of the Kurr of Lorim City, was now wondering about something that had happened well over ten thousand years ago.

His infant future mate resting comfortably within his arms let out a soft mew of a sound, drawing his attention to her. As he stared at her tiny glowing eyes, she stared right back up at him, as if trying to see through to his very soul.

***

Sarah watched the tableau before her with a mixture of pride and sadness. She could actually "feel" what Sheely was thinking, so she knew her daughter's understanding of the situation went far beyond even the level Mikhail and Sarah had achieved. This made her extremely proud of her young chatterbox. Unfortunately, it also meant Sheely was now maturing well past the point when she actually needed her mother for anything more than just the mundane physical needs of a normal infant and Sarah knew she could, and most likely would, get *those* needs taken care of by Azra'il and the house and medical staff.

Sarah, it seemed, had already become obsolete, if you will, in her infant daughter's life!

It didn't matter. Sarah's mind switched focus to the idea she had discovered earlier hidden deep within the depths of Azra'il's mind. If Sheely was ever going to have a chance at a normal life, the Kurr of Lorim City would have to accept her. Until the people could somehow feel safe from Sarah and all other humans, they would never accept Sheely as Azra'il's mate and Sarah knew her daughter and Azra'il could never truly be happy until they were both welcome in his chosen home. She just hoped this plan of his would do the trick before the Loric Realm was filled with aborigines and a full-out war started.

But that wasn't even the real problem. Convincing Mikhail of the plan's worth was going to be a monumental task – one which Sarah knew she could not do alone. She needed reinforcements and she needed them now!

***

Chris ground her teeth as she closed the door to Lyss' room and continued on down the hallway in search of her sister. *Where the bloody hell can she be? Surely, Lyss wouldn't still be at the main suite?*, Chris thought as she continued down this hallway and that, not truly realizing that she was concentrating on Lyss' current location.

Instead, she did this on a sub-conscious level as a replay of the past half-hour with Djibril occupied the conscious part of her brain. Therefore, it was a complete surprise to her when she found herself standing outside the door to a suite of rooms – not in the Main House of the Complex, but in another building entirely. She wondered briefly why she had chosen *this* as the place to search for Lyss, but she could find no logical explanation.

It was as good a place as any to look for her sister, though, and so she knocked.

A Kurr, of course, answered the door after only a short time. He was older than most of the Kurr she had met so far, though it seemed to her they must age differently than humans, for the Lorim, themselves, appeared to be immortal. The Kurr tilted his head and asked, "May I help you, m' dear?"

"I-I'm looking for my sister, Lyss," she stammered. "She looks like me." She felt completely foolish now, and she finished with an embarrassed smirk, asking, "You wouldn't happen to have seen her, by any chance?"

The Kurr turned, motioning for her to enter the room. "Indeed," he said curiously.

Chris frowned in confusion, but she entered, as he'd bade, and then followed the old Kurr into another room. There, seated comfortably on a long leather sofa, was Lyss. Her sister's eyes widened as she spotted Chris and she immediately stood.

"I'm sorry to interrupt," Chris said, "but Lyss and I must go now."

"Of course," the Kurr said.

Lyss hesitated, but then said, "I'm so sorry, Hantsushept. I'll contact you later to continue our discussion."

"That will be fine, m' dear," the Kurr said, smiling kindly at Lyss.

Chris watched the exchange with interest. She almost said something about how Lyss wouldn't be coming back to continue any conversation, but then she thought better of it. She followed the two to the door and then she and Lyss left.

Walking along the path between buildings, Chris chose to veer off to the right, away from the Main House, and Lyss followed. After a few moments, the two came to the practice clearing. It appeared Chris was intending to just continue on walking through the woods and Lyss finally stopped and demanded, "What's going on?"

Chris stopped and turned to face her sister. For a moment, she simply stood there. After a moment, she said, "I want to go home."

"Why?" Lyss asked, approaching her twin with concern. She ran her hands down the sides of Chris' upper arms, frowning. "Has someone done something to you or said something?"

"No, no," Chris shook her head. "I just – I want to go home, now." She looked pleadingly at her twin.

Lyss stared at her for a bit. After a moment, she said, "I think you should stay here a little longer."

Blinking in confusion, Chris shook her head and said, "You don't understand." When Lyss didn't immediately respond, Chris asked, "Don't *you* want to go home?"

"No," Lyss responded honestly. "I don't." She turned and walked over to a wooden bench at the perimeter of the clearing where she proceeded to sit down and consider Chris for another moment before continuing, asking, "What has happened that has made you so desperate to return home? Or is it something that's just made you desperate to leave here?"

Chris shook her head and joined Lyss on the bench. "You don't understand," she repeated. "Djibril – he wants..." She frowned. Finally, she sighed and said, "He wants the two of us to... to... to m-mate."

Lyss lifted an eyebrow and gave her a little smile of encouragement, but said nothing.

Frustration swelled within Chris and she jumped up to begin pacing back and forth, finally coming to stand in front of Lyss to demand, "Do you *know* what happens when one of them mates with one of us?"

A surge of anger swelled within Lyss as she stared up at her twin. "How nice for you," she finally spat.

Chris took a step back, frowning in confusion.

"It must be so thrilling to be even too good for a Lori," Lyss continued.

"Lyss, I'm not too good for him," Chris explained angrily. "He's of a different species, for Christ's sake!"

"One that's clearly compatible with humans!" Lyss yelled back. When Chris merely stood there staring at her as if she'd lost her mind, Lyss said, "I don't know what it's like to have an Arch Angel want me the way Djibril obviously wants you. In fact, I don't really know what it's like to have any man want me, to be honest."

Lyss was no virgin and Chris knew it. She opened her mouth to protest this obvious falsehood but then remained silent as Lyss held up a silencing hand to her before she continued.

"I've always gotten a guy when I wanted him or felt a physical need or desire for one, as I suspect have you. But, Chris, neither one of us has ever really had anyone chase after us – not since high school, I mean. Before, we were too busy with our studies and all the activities Mum and Dad kept us doing when we weren't in school. Then, after... well, you know, it was like we had to keep everyone out of our lives so we could concentrate on taking out as many Muslim bastards as possible."

Chris looked away suddenly. Lyss had painted a fairly accurate picture of things.

Lyss suddenly grabbed Chris' hand and waited for her

to face her. "It's not the worst place to be, you know? And it's not as if our lives were so-o interesting over the past decade or so that hob-knobbing with a group of Lorim is a chore. I *like* it here. I like the people *and* the place. I feel safe for the first time in my adult life and I've been offered a position working at the Medical Facility here at the Complex."

Chris frowned.

"That's what Hantsushept and I were discussing when you came for me earlier," Lyss explained. She gave Chris a pleading look. "I'd like to stay for a while," she continued. "And I think it might behoove you to stick around, as well." When Chris frowned at her, Lyss shrugged and said, "I've never seen two peop-... two individuals more suited for each other than Djibril and you."

Chris thought about this. She liked Djibril. He always found a way to make her feel like a woman, dainty and special, as if she might break if he didn't protect her. And, he was gorgeous! He was patient, yet firm. He seemed incredibly intelligent and observant. He was strong, both physically and emotionally. But most importantly of all, even though she had almost killed him, he seemed completely taken with her.

What more could a girl ask for?

"But, Lyss," Chris finally said in a small voice, as a thought occurred to her and she revealed her true fear. "I might become like that Sarah if Djibril and I...," she left the rest unsaid as she stared fearfully at her twin.

Lyss shrugged, suggesting, "I think you'd look great as an uber-blond."

Chris frowned. "I'm serious, Lyss."

Lyss rolled her eyes and then said, "Look, I know you're scared and that the idea of going through some kind of physiological change freaks you out. If I could take your place, I would, *believe me*. If for no other reason than to obtain all the abilities they seem to have once they change."

Chris frowned again. She hadn't heard anything about any special abilities.

"I haven't been offered that chance, though," Lyss

continued. "You have, and you now have an obligation - if not to yourself, then to me because I need to know that, should the fit hit the shan, I have someone out there who will be able to protect me and mine."

As Chris stood staring in shock down at her twin, a noise like the snapping of a twig sounded off to her left and she and Lyss immediately went into fight mode as they each whipped their heads around to look in the direction of the noise. They could see very little in the surrounding darkness, but Chris imagined she could almost *feel* what seemed like a whole *group* of people nearby. She quickly crouched down low to the ground and out of habit, reached up and behind herself for her katana. Only then did she remember that it was still at the beach house on Long Island.

Lyss slowly sidled up next to her, catching her attention with a quick wave and then, using a system of hand signals and gestures they had perfected over the past decade or so, conveyed a plan of attack on the unseen intruders.

Chris nodded her understanding and each set off in her planned direction.

***

The elite Guardsmen stopped in their tracks. Their newest member looked shamefully down at the offending foot. The broken twig beneath it appeared to be grinning up at him, as if laughing at his stupidity. If the two females in the little clearing caught sight of them, it would be over and he knew it.

No one moved a muscle as the two women cautiously made their way to the edge of the clearing, one toward the South side and the other toward the North. The one on the North side came so close the Guardsmen all held their breath, fearing it might be seen in the cool night air.

All of a sudden there was another noise, this time from the southern side of the woods. The Guardsmen didn't waste time waiting around to see what newcomer had made the sound. Without waiting for the female at the North end to reach the southern end of the clearing, they all took off running northward, only changing back toward the southeast once they had made it a full kilometer away from the Complex.

It would take days for them to reach Lorim City, and that was assuming nothing untoward occurred between here and there. But at least they were free of the diseased Lorim and were now headed home.

The group traveled silently through the night, only stopping when they found a good spot high upon a ridge that afforded both cover from the sun and a good vantage point for spotting intruders. After establishing a watch, everyone else sacked out for the few hours remaining until dawn.

***

Baphomet stilled. He had been assisting Lisa as she had attempted to explain to her mother everything that had happened between herself and Baphomet, including the fact that they were now the proud expectant parents of the very shy Cabal. But he had suddenly detected thoughts from someone else nearby, their energy disrupting the normal flow around the Complex.

Baphomet knew this energy pattern. In fact, the last time he had felt it, he had pretty much figured his time on this planet was over.

When he jumped up from his seat and whipped out his shields, taking off from the room without explanation, the two remaining Lorim and one human in the room stared uncomprehending at the now-empty spot where Baphomet had been standing. It took a moment, but Lisa soon tracked him down. She tried connecting with him by re-establishing the mind-link he and she normally shared. It had strangely been interrupted just before he had taken off and for some reason it wasn't working so well now. It was almost as if Baphomet was consciously blocking Lisa from his thoughts, a thing she hadn't even known he was capable of doing.

Why would he block her? As she maneuvered around the psychic buffer protecting his thoughts, searching for any opening, she swore she could almost taste *fear* in him.

Baphomet afraid?

Lisa pulled back and looked suddenly toward Israfil.

She knew he had already seen what she had seen. With a slight nod of his head, he indicated he was ready to go. Lisa quickly handled her mother, seeing to it that the older woman understood she was to stay at the house unless there was some type of emergency. There were no serving Kurr, nor anyone else, in the house. Cabal still shied away from others too much and Lisa and Baphomet had found it simpler merely to continue on with their solitary lifestyle for the baby's sake – at least until he was born. Israfil had agreed that their decision was simpler and easier, and so now Lisa's mom was going to have to be left alone.

Out of the blue, Sarah appeared carrying a very sleepy Sheely. Without even bothering with a greeting, she said, "Go ahead. I'll stay here with your mom."

Lisa didn't even hesitate. She and Israfil immediately whipped out their own shields and disappeared.

***

A group of little more than a dozen large figures moved slowly, cautiously into the clearing, apparently intent on heading toward the Complex. They had come from the direction of the Southern end of it, though one couldn't really be sure.

Without warning, two small figures attacked the group from both sides of the clearing and the entire group quickly dispersed. Within seconds, only two remained to fight off the two attackers. As one of the remaining dark figures caught hold of one of the attackers, a surprised deep voice announced, "They're using the humans as guards!"

"Humans?" the other dark figure demanded as he fought off his own crafty attacker. A second later, however, this one had nothing more to worry about from his human attacker as, with a simple twist of her arm and wrist, the dark figure within her grasp crumpled to the ground in a dead heap, his neck snapped in two.

The other dark figure still had his hands full dealing with his own human attacker when he heard his partner's neck snap. He whipped around in time to see the Shaitan fall to the ground. The one who had just killed his partner wasted no time gloating over her kill as a Shaitan would have done. Instead, she immediately turned and started his way with a dangerous look of intent in her eyes. The dark figure yanked up on the assailant he currently held in his hands and hissed at the figure as she approached, warning her with his primal hiss that he would happily kill his captive if she didn't stop right where she was.

To both the left and the right of the dark figure there suddenly appeared three Lorim out of thin air. The dark figure jerked his captive up so she acted as a shield, keeping him from the new arrivals' direct line of sight. There was a slight scuffle among the new arrivals as Djibril caught sight of Chris, but then the arrival of three more bright beings caught the dark figure's attention and Mikhail's razor-sharp hair immediately lashed out at the assailant's arms. In a split second, Chris was freed. Djibril grabbed hold of her and pulled her out of harm's way, shuffling her off to the edge of the clearing before looking back to see the outcome of the unexpected battle.

Lyss rushed forward and captured the lacerated hands of the dark figure, taking him in a hold from behind that was nearly impossible to escape.

Mikhail caught Djibril's attention as soon as the Shaitan was secured and he hitched his head in a quick jerk in the direction of the Complex. Djibril needed no further urging and he quickly whipped out his shields again and whisked Chris away from the scene and back to the safety of their suite of rooms at the Main House. It happened so quickly that Chris could only stand there blinking in stunned disbelief when Djibril's shields dropped to reveal that they now stood in the middle of the bedroom they had shared the previous evening.

Djibril squeezed his eyes shut and hugged Chris tightly before loosening his grip to look down at her, asking softly, "Were you harmed?"

"I-I'm fine," Chris whispered shakily. She was unaccustomed to anyone other than Lyss caring whether she was okay or not and she didn't know how to deal with his display of affection.

Djibril's eyes squeezed shut again and he sighed in anguished relief as he held her close. After a moment of reliving what had to be the longest two minutes of his life, he whispered, "Do not ever do that to me again."

Chris pulled back, frowning up at him in confusion.

"When I discovered you were directly in the path of the Shaitans, I did not know what I might find by the time I reached you," he explained, shaking his head. He then pulled her close again and sighed, saying, "I am just glad we were able to get there when we did."

Chris stood within the circle of his arms, still reeling from the fact that she had been so powerless during the attack. She felt certain she would have died had Djibril and the others not arrived when they did. The feel of Djibril's hands as they rubbed up and down her back and sides brought her mind back to the situation at hand. He was warm and strong, yet infinitely gentle with her. She reluctantly admitted she was glad he was holding her and she did not want to face the fact that she had been so afraid earlier when the creature Djibril had called a Shaitan had taken her captive.

She had been outmaneuvered and over-powered as she had struggled against the creature, and it had been a bloody revelation to see Lyss standing her ground against such a foe. Chris had simultaneously felt proud of her twin and disgusted with herself for her own weakness. Again, she marveled at how relieved she had been when Djibril and his brothers arrived. Now, as she stood within the security of her savior's arms, she experienced an odd sensation. She felt like... like crying – a thing she never did!

Djibril finally loosened his hold on her, pulling back a bit and tilting her face upward to look him in the eyes. "Come lie with me?" he softly requested, motioning toward the king-sized bed in the far corner of the room. "I would like to hold you a while," he said.

Chris looked to the bed and then back up at him shyly. She wasn't sure what to do. If all he wanted to do was to hold her, she should be okay with that, even though the idea of being that close to him on a bed again scared the living daylights out of her. As he took her hand in his and moved toward the bed, she followed along without protest. She was still shaken by the earlier incident and the thought of having his big, strong arms around her as she slept was somehow comforting. Having never before been in this kind of situation, she thought it might be exactly what she needed.

Djibril waited as she removed her shoes and climbed onto the massive bed, situating herself a little more than half-way across. Then he sat down and removed his shoes, never once removing his eyes from her. He then scooched himself over right up next to her and lay down, taking her securely in his arms again. Finally, he closed his eyes and tried to relax. He felt as if he was exactly where he was meant to be for the first time in his long life.

After a few minutes of lying there listening to her Lori's heartbeat, a thought occurred to Chris and she quietly asked, "Djibril, how did you find Lyss and me tonight?" She hadn't told him where she had been headed. She hadn't even realized where she was going, herself. So, how had he found her?

"That is one of my abilities as a Lori," he simply stated. "I am able to sense the energies of others quite easily. I believe you would refer to me as a tracker."

Chris thought about this. She, herself, was an excellent tracker and one of the reasons was because she believed she could almost "feel" people. She had always had that ability. A curious sensation raced down her spine suddenly as she thought there just might be something to what Lyss had said about how well-suited Djibril and Chris were for each other.

His hand continued rubbing up and down her back, soothing her and keeping her from feeling the need to jump up and run off on her own. She closed her eyes. He smelled so good. He felt so warm. But there were questions she needed to ask, and now was as good a time as any.

"Is it really true that Lisa and Sarah were human before they came to live here?" she asked.

"Yes," he simply said.

Chris was silent for a few more minutes. "I don't

want to change like them," she announced.

Djibril's hand stopped moving along her back. "That may not be up to you – or to me, for that matter," he said.

"What do you mean?" she asked, pulling up to look him directly in the eyes.

"I mean, you and I have had physical contact with each other. From what I have observed, that might be all it takes for the two of us to start the transformation process."

"I thought you said we would have to mate in order for us to change," she challenged.

"That completes the process, as far as we can tell," he explained.

"So, I may already be transforming, even as we speak?"

He looked her face over, noticing no changes. "You may be changing on the inside, though I cannot yet see any obvious changes on the outside," he explained. "Of course, the same thing is probably happening to me as well."

Chris frowned. She didn't want to change! She didn't want to transform! Hell! She didn't want *him* to change, either.

Djibril ran a hand up into her beautiful red hair, reassuring her by saying, "We need not worry about it tonight, love. Let us rest for the now, hmm?" His hand applied a slight pressure on her head to urge her to relax against him and she decided that would be best. She would discuss things with him tomorrow. Yawning a huge yawn, the events of this evening finally caught up with her and she realized she felt more exhausted than she could remember feeling in a long time, so she allowed her head to lay comfortably against his strong chest. Her body moved of its own volition to snuggle up closer to his warmth as her eyelids slid closed and darkness overcame her mind.

Djibril squeezed shut his eyes, turning to place a soft, slow kiss onto her forehead as she slept soundly within his arms. He disliked controlling her like that, forcing her into a sleep state to keep her from worrying about the inevitable transformation. It *was* inevitable, for Djibril could already feel her energies working on *his* body. What worried him was the fact that his own energies did not appear to be having the same effect on her body, for she seemed almost weaker than she had been before she had come to the Loric Realm. Just tonight, although Lyss had displayed incredible agility and masterful ability where the Shaitans were concerned, Chris had appeared small, weak and completely helpless.

Because of her energies' work on his body, Djibril had experienced no difficulty locating both Chris and Lyss as soon as Baphomet had informed Mikhail that he had sensed Shaitan energies nearby. Although the particular Shaitan Baphomet had thought was closing in on the Complex had not been found, Djibril had easily picked up the energies of the other Shaitans nearing the Complex.

As he lay in bed now holding his soon-to-be mate, he allowed his mind to extend out, seeking the Shaitan energies from the bastard creature Mikhail and the others had taken prisoner before Djibril had swept Chris from the area. Djibril would happily kill this Shaitan for daring to lay a finger on Chris. Oddly enough, he no longer sensed the thing's energies. Surely, Mikhail and the others would not have released the foul creature back into the wooded area surrounding the Complex?

The skill and ferocity with which Lyss had dispatched the Shaitans she had fought during the short attack had left Djibril with the impression that she would be the one to kill the filthy thing that had taken Chris captive as help had arrived. But Djibril sensed her energies back in her room at the Main House of the Complex.

He searched the entirety of the house for his brethren, finally discovering the group in what he believed was Mikhail's upstairs study. The discovery of the Shaitans' attack on the Complex was something for which none of them had been prepared, and he was certain his brethren were now working on a plan to stop any further Shaitan attacks on the Complex. Had it not been for Lyss, the night may well have ended very differently and Djibril decided he would have to do something special for the human to ensure she was awarded for her bravery. Then his mind returned to that awful moment earlier in the night.

Djibril's heart had nearly slammed out of his chest when he had landed in the wood to discover Chris held captive within the bastard Shaitan's grip. A rage so violent had overcome him to such a degree that Mikhail had actually had to use force against Djibril to keep him from rushing forward to attack and annihilate the creature. But now Djibril lay holding his sweet soul mate within his arms, her energies rushing through his body in the most wonderfully delicious sensation he had ever experienced.

He wondered at the fact that, of all the times he had slept with Kurr back in Lorim City, he had never once experienced delight in simply holding one of them without going any farther with matters. Now the very idea that he had the rest of the night to hold Chris thrilled him through to his core and Djibril sighed contentedly as he allowed his eyes to finally close on a slow wave of elation. Sleep came swiftly and his mind's nighttime theatre consisted of sweet little scenarios of Chris and him coming together again and again.

Chapter 15

Suriyah moved through the dark night on autopilot, her mind consumed by a maelstrom of thoughts. Mikhail had chosen *her* over his Designers! What did that mean? Suriyah and Baphomet had both been banished from Lorim City thousands of years ago because Mikhail had done just the opposite at that time. Suriyah had always believed he had done it more out of a sense of duty than out of personal anger and that he still cared for them both, but still, entire peoples had been forced from their homes, forced to traverse wild, uncharted terrain, all because one Lori chose one way over another. What had happened to make him change his mind now?

Was it Sarah?

Was it the birth of little Sheely?

Suriyah simply did not know. Truthfully, she didn't really care. Her brother had finally chosen to put his faith in her and she would not fail him. She had already traveled to Jinn Territory, alerting everyone there of the monumental task before them. She had set her ladies in waiting into a frenzy of scurrying to and fro as they attempted to pack a suitable and adequate wardrobe for her for her upcoming trip to and possible stay within the human realm.

This would be one of the most massive migrations of humans ever before orchestrated by the Jinn and it truly was comical for Suriyah to see how some of her Jinn were handling it.

A brilliant flash of light suddenly flashed across the landscape of her mind and Suriyah halted in the crisp night air, hanging suspended and still above the tree line as the new vision's scenes played out before her mind's eye. Within seconds, it was over.

What could this mean?

Suriyah heard the call of a distant Labi, one of the elusive sea creatures of this region, and snapped out of her thoughts. That haunting call whipped her attention back to her mission and she focused on her intended destination. If she was near the sea, she was near the Complex. Once there, she would be able to find whatever answers she sought before taking Lisa's mother back to the human realm to see to the Aborigine migration. Mikhail would surely explain why she had just had a vision of a group of Shaitans causing mischief at the Badlands Complex.

* * *

Mikhail straightened and turned from the fireplace as he sensed his sister's arrival. Sarah, he noticed, sat in her chair staring directly at the spot where Suriyah finally appeared and dropped her shields, looking around to all within the assemblage. Azra'il was seated in a chair next to Sarah with Sheely resting comfortably within the crook of his arm, and he nodded his acknowledgement of his sister's sudden appearance in the room. Israfil and Lisa both nodded their greetings as well, but with welcoming half-smiles each. Baphomet rushed up and gave her a big bear hug, demanding, "Where have you been? We have a major crisis going on here, or do you simply not care?"

Suriyah frowned and then punched him in the chest. "I have only just returned from making preparations for your Mother-in-law and the rest of her people to migrate from the human realm to the Loric Realm, so I am afraid you will have to catch me up to speed, you dolt," she practically spat at him. Her thoughts turned immediately from her brat brother to the vision of the Shaitan horde and she turned toward Mikhail, asking, "Why would I be seeing visions of Shaitans here at the Complex?"

"There were only a few," he cryptically answered.

"Were?"

Israfil chimed in, explaining, "They created such a commotion that the elite Guard escaped. The Shaitans attempted to escape, but Chris and her twin stopped them."

Wide-eyed with concern, Suriyah gushed, "Is everyone all right?"

Lisa answered, softly saying, "Lyss was able to fend off the majority of them, but the only losses were Shaitans. The last one took his own life before he could be interrogated."

Suriyah's eyes were the size of saucers as she wondered what on Earth could cause an immortal to take his own life! She simply could not fathom such a thing.

The room lapsed back into silence.

Finally, Azra'il quietly said, "You know this is the only logical solution, Mikhail."

Mikhail whipped around, his white eyes hotly glowing and his sharp white hair whipping around in a frenzy all around him as if gale-force winds buffeted it. "You are asking me to rip the beating heart from my chest and entrust it to *your* safe-keeping for an indefinite period of time!" he bellowed.

Sarah jumped up and went to him, grabbing hold of his upper arm with her two tiny hands. She looked up at him with sad, softly-glowing eyes and said, "Mikhail, I can't think of any other way to do this." He turned a pain-filled face toward her and she continued, explaining, "This way, the council will be satisfied and Azra'il will have some time to sniff out the traitor."

Mikhail made to protest, but Sarah cut him off. "It will also guarantee that the attacks against the Complex are over with – at least from anyone from Lorim City. If we're gonna have a bunch of humans millin' around here, the last thing we need are more attacks from either the Guard or anti-human Kurr, don't you think? Besides," and here she moved a little closer and lowered her voice almost to a whisper, her jaw trembling as she said, "I need you to find out what's happened to Thomas." Mikhail's pained frown deepened and he lowered his forehead to rest upon hers. "I still haven't heard from either him or Nera and I'm gettin' worried."

Suriyah threw a quick inquisitive look over at Baphomet, whispering, "What is going on here?"

Baphomet leaned in closer to her and, without taking his eyes off the scene playing out before them, whispered back, "Azra'il wants to take Sarah back to Lorim City as his captive. That way the council will be satisfied and Azra'il can discover who the traitor is on the council. He figures whoever it is will try something in an attempt to kill Sarah and he will then be able to catch the traitor in the act, so to speak."

Suriyah's brows shot up. She understood Mikhail's trepidation. It sounded like a risky plan, for certain. As she turned the idea over in her head a few times, however, she realized this was probably the best plan available to them.

Azra'il *needed* to return. Lorim City would not survive long without its leader. And with him gone, if there *was* an actual traitor sitting on the council, who knew what kind of lies and deceptions he was poisoning the other council members with while Azra'il was away? The entire City government was at risk.

Of course, Suriyah supposed there was always the option of all of the Lorim storming the City and taking it back by force. But that would lead to several difficulties. First, the Kurr of Lorim City, who were innocents as far as Suriyah was concerned, would suffer – some would possibly even die defending their stronghold, and the rest would become a conquered people. That meant there would remain the possibility of rebel groups springing up continuously and the Lorim would forever have a Kurric enemy.

Second was the problem of the humans – those who were already living within the Loric Realm and the large numbers she was about to bring over to this dimension from the human one. The Kurr of Lorim City were already conflicted over their feelings toward humans encroaching upon the Loric Realm, but to have the Lorim simply dictate to them, forcing their acceptance of the lower creatures within their society, would only lead to more heated resentment and rebellion against authority.

Lastly were the Lorim, themselves.

Suriyah didn't know about the others, but she knew she would have a difficult time leaving her current home to return to Lorim City. She was no longer the naïve Lori she had been before. She and her Jinn had lived apart from the other Kurr of Lorim City for so long that she was unsure if they even *could* live alongside them again. After all, each group had developed vastly different viewpoints on life and the Kurric role within it over the millennia and it might not be feasible for them to live side-by-side.

There would be similar issues with Baphomet and the Shaitans. And, although it had only been a short time since they had been banished – relatively speaking – Israfil and Djibril were sure to have at least *some* reservations about returning to a community that had previously voted to evict them. And now, Djibril had a human mate who also came along with a human twin.

Mikhail and Sarah looked so different, as did Baphomet, Lisa, and now Azra'il. And then there was Sheely.

She contradicted the word of the very gods the Kurr of Lorim City worshipped. Her very existence disproved the age-old belief that Lorim could not reproduce. It created the question of why the blessed Great Designers would have forbidden the Lorim from mating with humans in the first place. Was there something bad that would happen to the Lorim in addition to the transformations they went through after mating, something that had caused the Designers to set that one rule upon them? Was there some danger to the world simply because Sheely's conception and birth had been successful?

The answers to those questions would have an earth-shattering effect on the entirety of Kurric society, regardless of community.

Mikhail must have considered each and every one of these points, if not more she was missing, because he now hugged Sarah close to himself and whispered, "I could not continue on without you, should anything happen while you were there."

Azra'il rose with Sheely's tiny slumbering form and approached the two glowing creatures. He handed the babe off to Mikhail as he softly said, "I shall guard her with my life, my brother, as I expect you will do with Sheely."

Mikhail cocked his head, hitching a sardonic brow at his powerful brother. "She was my daughter before becoming your... whatever," Mikhail spat quietly at his sibling as he took his daughter's tiny form into his big, strong arms. "And I have not yet agreed to this farce of a plan!"

Azra'il frowned as he thought over his brother's

statement. When he made to contradict it, Mikhail snapped, "Oh, just shut up, will you?"

Israfil interrupted the tense scene, asking, "How exactly are you planning to quote-unquote capture Sarah or to transport her to the City?"

"We'll use those binder things we put on Baphomet," Sarah said.

A strong chill stole down Baphomet's spine as recollection of his time spent in the painful binders suddenly flooded his mind.

Mikhail and Lisa caught the emotion emanating from Baphomet and they both immediately barked out, "No!" Their raised voices woke the sleeping child who set to squalling in a very loud wail.

Lisa could feel her mate's revulsion of the dreaded binders at the mere mention of them and, as she had developed strong feelings of kinship for Sarah over the past weeks, she felt truly distressed at the thought of Sarah suffering such ill-effects.

Mikhail remembered how difficult it had been for his brothers to endure the pain from the binders and he didn't want his other half suffering like that. The three male Lorim had each suffered tremendous neurological pain while imprisoned in the binders. Mikhail could not imagine a female, even one as strong as Sarah, enduring that without some pretty ill-effects.

Sarah knew his thoughts, but she also believed there was no other way. Closing her eyes on a soft, but deep sigh, she reached up and hugged Mikhail as close as she could around Sheely. She was exhausted, but this had to be done.

"Listen," she said. "I need you to stay here."

Mikhail made to protest and she pulled back to look up at him.

Placing a hand on each side of his face, she softly said, "Sheely needs you and I need you to look for Thomas. Like I told you, I still haven't had even a hint from Nera that she has Thomas with her, so I need to know you'll still be lookin' for him while I'm gone."

Sheely started whimpering and Azra'il closed his eyes

in concentration as he worked to soothe her psychically.

"But...," Mikhail began.

"No buts," Sarah interrupted. "Listen to me." He made to protest once more and she said more firmly, "Listen to me!" He finally calmed down and she said, "We're gonna leave the binders undone so they won't be workin' while I'm wearin' 'em. I'll pretend like they're workin' an' Azra'il will keep everybody away from me. That way, everybody there is satisfied and so there won't be any more attacks here. You can keep lookin' for Thomas an' in the meantime, everybody else can work on figurin' out a way to end this so I can come home."

Mikhail appeared somewhat mollified by the fact that the binders wouldn't actually be activated while she wore them, but he was still nervous about the whole thing. In his mind, Sarah's soft voice begged, *Please, Mikhail? Please do this for me?*

He grabbed her and squeezed her slender body in a fierce hug. "I cannot endure the thought of you suffering so. I simply cannot."

Sarah pulled back, looking up at him. "But this is what we have to do so that Sheely and everybody else will be safe again."

Mikhail could sense that her mind was made up. She had decided this was the only course of action available to them and nothing he said would change her mind. He steeled himself for a fight and said, "I will not agree to this plan."

Both Azra'il and Sarah made to protest and Mikhail held up a staying hand. "Until I have a clear understanding of every minute, step-by-step of how you plan to do this. Only then will I even *think* about allowing it."

Sarah hugged him back, nodding and assuring him, "We'll think it through and get you the information you need."

Azra'il said nothing.

They all agreed to meet again in the coming days to discuss the overall plan and what details they needed to work out and everyone left.

***

Chris sighed as she finally caught sight of the Main House. She had been walking for the last half hour to try to cool down. She had awakened early this morning, long before dawn, to find Djibril staring down at her and it had freaked her out. She had quickly dressed in her borrowed clothes and excused herself so she could think through her next steps. Apparently, she had slept so soundly last night that she hadn't had a single dream. She couldn't recall ever having slept that well – not since her parents had died, at least – and she wondered if it had been due to the fact that Djibril had held her all night. A part of her worried that that was precisely the reason and that she would never sleep so well again if she left him.

The only thing her morning walk had done was to confuse her even more. She wanted to go home. She wanted to get back to what she did best – ridding the world of terrorists. She definitely did *not* want to turn into one of those glowy-eyed freaks! But the problem with everything she did not want was that it all boiled down to one thing – she would have to leave Djibril.

Of course, after the workout session she had just come from with Lyss and the other two who had been in the clearing working out with Lyss yesterday, Chris wondered if perhaps the decision was being made for her. At the end of her morning walk, she had come upon Djibril and Lyss and they had invited her to the workout they had planned in the practice circle in the clearing by the wood. Chris hadn't wanted to go. But after her failure during the last night's battle with the Shaitans, she had decided she could probably use some practice and possibly some new moves.

Never had she been proven more wrong!

The workout had exhausted her, yet she had barely hit any of the targets. Each time she had moved to strike whatever target Mikhail had proposed, someone else had either beaten her to it or blocked her so successfully that she had failed to reach her goal. She could not for the life of her get the hang of telekinesis and she had absolutely no telepathic ability, judging by how easily fooled she had been by each of her workout mates. As far as she was concerned, she was now nothing more than a sitting duck with bright neon signs flashing all around her that said, "Attack me!"

She turned the corner that brought her to the back of the main building where she had slept for the past couple of nights and pulled up short. That glowing-eyed Sarah woman was sitting in the garden behind the enormous house. Her white hair moved gracefully in the slight breeze, as if it enjoyed the movement. There really wasn't even that much of a breeze, but the hair's own movement made it appear as if it was quite windy out.

Chris immediately turned to leave. The last thing she wanted was to get caught alone by one of the freaks.

With that thought still in her mind, Chris felt a chill steal down her spine. It felt as if someone was standing directly behind her and in her mind she heard the voice of that Sarah woman. *Surely, we're not all that strange?* it softly asked, a little lilting laughter coloring the question.

Chris turned, feeling awkward as Hell, but ready to face the music.

The white-haired witch was nowhere near her! In fact, she was exactly where she had been when Chris had rounded the building's corner. Her back still faced Chris as she continued working diligently in the good-sized garden. Chris had to hand it to her – this Sarah had quite the green thumb, for there were flowers blooming everywhere. Some of the plants and vines were so heavy with blooming flowers that they lay flat on the ground. Although Chris was no expert, it was obvious from the straining stalks that this was not plants' natural state.

Various types of honey bees busied themselves with the process of pollination as they collected that which they could carry to take back to their hives – wherever those might be. In fact, Chris noticed there appeared to be an inordinate amount of the fat bees softly buzzing about the densely-packed garden, and she wondered if perhaps it might be unsafe for anyone to inhabit the area while so many bees were present.

Soft laughter sounded in her mind and Chris wondered for a moment if she had simply imagined it, for the white-haired Sarah still diligently worked on her garden, seemingly oblivious to Chris' presence. But the deception was shattered as Sarah turned toward Chris as she moved to stand up, all the while smiling directly at her and her voice sounding in Chris' mind, saying, *Oh, I don't think anybody in this dimension ever has to worry about bein' attacked by any bees – especially not the honey bees. They have long memories.*

Sarah wiped the soil from her hands and finally spoke aloud. "I think they'll be grateful to the Kurr for a long time for givin' 'em a pesticide- and chemical-free land to live in," she said, looking around the blooming garden with satisfaction. "Don't you?"

Chris looked around the place. Sure, it was beautiful and fragrant, but Chris didn't like bugs.

She shrugged and said, "Sure."

Sarah gave her an odd, quizzical look, as if she was trying to figure out the human standing before her. Chris stood tall and proud – well, as much as was possible next to such an awesome creature. Sarah smiled again and turned, saying, "Let's have a seat over here in the shade where we can talk."

Chris didn't want to, but it wasn't as if she was fool enough to say that to this creature. She instinctively knew old White-Eyes could tear her to pieces in a heart-beat. She sighed silently and followed along the stone path to a bench that was situated in the shade of a giant Willow tree of some sort. Sarah politely waited for Chris to sit and become comfortably situated before taking her place on the incredibly soft wooden bench. It smelled of cedar and Chris wondered if that was what it was made of.

"Cedar is my favorite," Sarah said, nodding. "Mikhail made it – and several others out here – for me when we first moved here. Of course, I was pregnant at that time and I think he thought I might get so big I'd have to sit down all the time, which might explain how deep the seats all are on the benches and swings throughout the garden."

Chris raised her eyebrows and smiled politely. What else was she supposed to do? Who cared about some stupid benches in a stupid garden? In fact, who cared about *any* of this? Chris just wanted to get out of here before she turned into one of these white-eyed, white-haired freaks of nature. She needed to leave, but the longer she stayed the less likely it was that anyone would help her to find her way back home.

"So, Djibril *has* discussed matters with you," Sarah stated.

"He, um…, he told me I would change to look like you and that other woman, if I stayed here," Chris stated hesitantly.

Sarah frowned slightly. "But you don't want that?" she asked.

"Well, no," Chris replied derisively, swallowing a huge lump in her throat. "I mean, who would?"

Sarah raised a brow and gave a half-smile, saying, "Oh, I don't know. The looks are only one part of the change. And they can actually be quite useful."

Chris frowned.

"For instance," Sarah continued, "Mikhail informed me your sister and you enjoy learning fightin' techniques."

"So?" Chris was immediately on the defensive. She had every right to be good at her job and that job just so happened to include fighting.

Sarah laughed softly aloud, interrupting Chris' silent tantrum. "It's okay, Chris," she said. "But if you think about how other people see those of us who have already transformed, you might just realize how frightenin' we can seem to everybody. And, it's not as if we don't develop all kinds of special abilities, too!"

Chris frowned again, asking, "What? Like being able to fly and all?"

"Well, yes, there is that," Sarah said, nodding. "But there's more, too."

"Like what?"

Sarah had a secret little smile on her face as she leaned in closer to the young human, saying, "Well, for instance, I can read the mind of most anyone I encounter, so I usually have a heads-up on what someone's gonna do before they do it."

Chris frowned. Well, that didn't freak her out even more than she had already felt! Now she would have to find a way to avoid each of the six white-haired freaks at all costs just to keep them from constantly reading her mind. Of course, she probably didn't have to worry much about the baby, Sheely. Chris doubted that one would be inclined to do anything to her simply because of something she thought.

Because those of us who have already transformed into "white-haired freaks" certainly wouldn't have anything else to think about other than what you're up to, right? Sarah's voice asked sardonically in Chris' mind.

Chris at least had the sense to feel remorse for her self-centered thoughts. "Sorry," she said uncomfortably, blushing a deep shade of red. Then a thought occurred to her and she halted, staring at the woman. There was something almost familiar about the creature sitting beside her. *Sarah... Sarah...* she wondered. *Sarah Baker?*

Chris focused on the woman's face, studying it closer. Could this be the Sarah Baker who had caused all the controversy all those months ago?

Sarah merely lifted a brow, a sly smile tugging at her lips.

***

Djibril returned to the suite of rooms he now shared with Chris at the Main House. She was still on her walk and he had decided to give her some alone time. He knew her exact location, so he felt comfortable allowing her to go off without him. If she strayed too far, he would sense it and would then go to her. After last night, he was determined to keep an eye on her, so to speak, at all times to ensure her safety. The workout session they had had earlier had only served to reinforce his decision. It certainly hadn't turned out the way he had expected.

After this morning's breakfast, she had gone on a walk and it had taken everything in him to allow her to go without him along to keep a watchful eye on her. But instead of just sitting in their suite worrying about her, Djibril had gone in search of Mikhail to ask his advice. When he had finally located his brother, he was surprised to discover that all of his siblings had been in attendance at some type of meeting in Mikhail's study. The meeting ended just as Djibril appeared and he had watched in confusion as everyone save for Mikhail left the room.

Even before Mikhail could close the door, Djibril asked what was going on.

Mikhail hesitated at first, but then he told him everything about Azra'il's and Sarah's plan.

"So now," Mikhail said in frustration, "Azra'il has convinced her that this is the only way to get both houses of the Sanhedrin to accept all of us back into Lorim City. And nothing I say can convince her – or our brother – otherwise."

Mikhail covered his face with both hands, rubbing hard at both eyes. Djibril could feel his frustration, his sense of utter helplessness and he thought he understood. He, himself, felt a similar sense of frustration and helplessness where Chris was concerned.

He was unaccustomed to her particular culture and, although he felt a sense of urgency when it came to the two of them mating, he knew she was not ready for the changes their union would bring. She was an assassin and she enjoyed it. She probably felt she would not suffer a bit if she returned to her home in her dimension. After all, she could go back to killing those whom she blamed for her parents' deaths and she would be quite satisfied just doing that for the remainder of her days.

But that wasn't really a possibility now, was it? As Mikhail sat wrapped in his own torturous thoughts, Djibril took a mental moment to check on Chris. She was with Sarah in the garden at the back of the Main House and he knew she would be safe.

As if sensing his brother's discomfort, Mikhail said, "I am sorry, brother. I have been selfish. You had something you wished to discuss with me?"

Djibril immediately waved off his brother's apology. "Think nothing of it. You have your hands full. But, if I can add my own thoughts on the matter…?"

At Mikhail's go-ahead nod, Djibril confessed, "I believe Azra'il is correct. They, like him before he came here, believe Sarah to be at the root of all the problems in our realm and they will not be satisfied until they have her in their custody."

"But that is the difficulty," Mikhail said, interrupting him. "They will have her in their custody. Who knows what they could do to her? And I would be powerless to help, should they intend her harm."

"Azra'il will be there," Djibril reminded him. "And she would not be completely powerless. If the binders are not activated, she should be more than capable of defending herself against any attack."

Again, Mikhail buried his face in his hands, rubbing at his forehead and eyes as his mind was again wracked with gruesome images of his mate being tortured and then murdered by the Kurr of Lorim City. He could see the sense of Djibril's argument, but there was still a feeling like a lead weight lodged in the pit of his core and it filled him with dread at the thought of allowing Sarah to go along with this hair-brained idea Azra'il had concocted.

His sense of self-preservation roared to life at the idea of ever losing Sarah and he sought her out within his mind, needing to feel her essence, to know she was safe. He found her in the garden just behind the house where he sat. She was safe, talking with the human, Chris.

Relief flashed through him and then he remembered that Djibril had come to him for an altogether different reason and he immediately switched the subject. "I will take your words into consideration. Thank you," he said. "Now, how can I help you, brother?"

Djibril hesitantly stated his concerns. "I-I would ask your advice… about Chris." He paused as he considered how to broach this subject. "I feel her energies working on me – even now, here in this very room. I know without a doubt that, of all the humans and Kurr on this planet, she is the one for whom I was created and who was created for me. But we… we have not yet… I mean, technically speaking…

we..."

Mikhail understood. "You have not yet consummated the relationship," he offered.

"Technically, no," Djibril said. "W-We have lain together and-and I want to. But I do not believe Chris is ready for such a giant leap. After all, it has only been a few days since she came to be here."

Mikhail thought on the matter. He had learned from the other human, Lyss, that the two of them had been hired assassins in the human realm. That fully explained the abilities Lyss had displayed in the practice ring. But Mikhail had been in attendance at the workout this morning and he had noticed how poorly Chris had fared, as if she suffered from a lack of athletic ability. If anything, she had appeared a novice at best. Even young Samuel had bested her at each opportunity.

"I fear for her safety, brother," Djibril softly confessed.

Mikhail knew his brother had reason to fear for her safety. The Shaitan attack last night had proven that. "Are you certain she had more ability before coming here?" he respectfully asked.

Djibril absently touched the thick scar still rimming his neck. "She bested me in the human realm – nearly killed me, remember?"

Mikhail shrugged and said simply, "So then you bed her. Your energies pour into her, strengthening her and bringing on the transformation and your problem is solved."

"But she still wishes to return to her old life," Djibril said.

A half-smile claimed Mikhail's face as he said, "If history is any indicator, once she has conceived, she will no longer have any thoughts of the human realm."

Djibril rubbed at his own eyes as he considered his brother's words. It made sense. That was how it had worked for both Sarah and Lisa. Why should it be any different for Chris? Finally, he nodded, saying, "Thank you, brother. I am certain you are correct." He stood and left the study without another word.

As the door closed behind Djibril, Mikhail's mind returned to the coming days. He was certain that once Djibril and Chris consummated their relationship, she would strengthen and that her transformation would commence. There would be no worry there. But the idea of Sarah being in the custody of the Lorim City Kurr while wearing the dreaded binders – albeit deactivated – was more than he could imagine. If anything went wrong with their plan, if she was harmed in any way, Mikhail would not and could not imagine how he could continue.

Just then, Azra'il burst unannounced through the study door carrying a wailing Sheely, shouting, "Whatever it is you are obsessing over, will you please stop!"

Chapter 16

Chris returned to the suite she shared with Djibril. He emerged from the bathroom, having obviously just showered, as Chris stopped just inside the suite's door.

The Lori stood staring at her a moment and then said, "I have ordered food. It should be here momentarily."

Chris nodded. Her head was still spinning from all she had learned from Sarah earlier and she knew she needed to let Djibril know of the decision she had made. She just wasn't sure she was ready yet. "I think I'll go clean up real quick before eating…, if that's okay."

Djibril merely nodded and made his way over to the small lounge located through an archway just on the other side of the room. Chris watched silently as the Lori picked out a book from the shelves there and took a seat on a comfortable-looking sofa. Then she turned and went to shower.

Thirty minutes later, she and Djibril finished up a delicious late afternoon lunch that had only missed being perfect due to a lack of conversation. Djibril had attempted several times to engage her, but Chris' one-word answers had finally gotten to him and he had stopped trying. Now, as they rose from the small table in the corner of the room, Chris searched for a way to break the silence.

A Kurr entered to clear away the meal as Chris' mind worked furiously at a solution to her problem. She needed to tell the Lori of her decision, but she had thus far been unable to think of a way to even start the conversation. As the Kurr finished up and left, Chris heard the door click shut and then the key turning in the lock, effectively trapping her inside with Djibril. Instantly, she was swamped with nervousness.

Her back was turned to the room as she gazed out upon the distant sea, and she heard a strange sound coming from the bay just below the cliff where the house was situated. Some type of creature must lurk in the waters off the coast and she wondered what kind of animal made such a hauntingly beautiful noise. Then she felt Djibril's touch on her back and shoulder and all thoughts of the sound's owner fled her mind as sensation took over. She didn't turn to face him, but instead leaned back against the warm wall of his chest, her eyes closing and her head falling back to rest against his breast as his strong arms circled around her front. One hand came up to cup her breast and Chris softly moaned aloud.

Djibril leaned down and nuzzled his way through her long red hair to her neck, where he lavished her with soft kisses and whispers of how very beautiful he thought she was. Chris felt as if she could have stood there a thousand years, just as long as he kept touching her. The Lori suddenly turned her around and kissed her, gently seeking entry into her mouth. Chris tentatively opened up to him and then marveled at how hot his tongue felt inside her.

Djibril kept his touch light, though Chris could feel how tense he was as she ran her fingers lightly along his biceps and shoulders. Pulling back from the kiss, she looked up at him with wide eyes. She had never before actually been attracted to anyone she had slept with. She had merely done it because she had needed something, either information or a way to get into a place or some other reason. Never had she had sex simply because she liked the guy or was attracted to him.

Djibril looked down and gently grabbed her hand, before turning to lead her silently back into the other room and over to the bed. When she made to protest, the Lori placed a finger across her lips, shushing her and whispering, "Do not fear. We are only going to lay with one another, to touch and get to know each other."

It took all of two seconds for Chris to agree to this, as her body demanded at least that much, and she went ahead and climbed onto the bed, moving over toward the other side so he would have room to lie down. At first Chris lay on her back, not knowing what to do. But that seemed silly, especially since she was no virgin, and she quickly turned to her side to face him.

Djibril pushed his long black hair back behind him as he moved to lie on his side so they would be facing each other. He traced a finger up her arm and then her neck, finally allowing it to move up onto her face and along the curve of her lower lip.

"You are so beautiful," he whispered in his ruined, gravelly voice.

Chris stared at his ice-blue eyes, wondering how someone as handsome as he, who had lived among such perfectly beautiful creatures as even the serving Kurr of this place were, could actually believe her to be beautiful. All thoughts fled her mind, however, as he leaned forward and kissed her in what was the softest, sweetest kiss she had ever experienced in her life.

He took his time with the kiss, lingering over her lips before he softly urged her lips to part. Then, as before, the heat coming from him overwhelmed her and Chris found she could no longer think a single lucid thought. All she could do was feel.

Sensation was all-encompassing and her hands began their own exploration as they lifted and touched and felt as much of his anatomy as they could reach. Every now and then, Djibril would groan in that gravelly voice of his against her neck as he kissed her there and little shivers of excitement would trace throughout Chris' body, delighting her and spurring her onward to even more exploration. Djibril stopped her hand when her fingers sought to dip below the waistline of the slacks he wore and Chris pulled back a little to see his face, wondering why he had stopped her.

"I promised we would take things slowly at first and that is what we are going to do," he whispered in response to her look of confusion. "So you can touch anywhere above the waist, okay?"

Chris nodded, grateful that he would consider her wishes. The problem was that she didn't know how to do this. As she lay there softly running her palms up and down his shirt front, wondering what he expected of her, he sighed and pulled her over to him and then half onto him as he turned onto his back, leaving her lying half on top of his full length, her head resting against his chest.

Chris' first reaction was to pull away, but then his

hand at her back started moving up and down in the most wonderful pattern and she simply rested there against him, listening to his heartbeat. As she lay there, her brain's wheels ticked up their endless spinning and she wondered if this was what her life would be like with him forever. This thought brought another to mind, one that had been nagging her since she had had her conversation with Sarah. As Djibril's hand on her back continued its slow rubbing rhythm – up and down, up and down – Chris finally asked in a soft little voice, "D-Does it hurt when you transform?"

Djibril's hand halted momentarily, half-way down her back, but after only a second it resumed its slow rhythm again. What was no longer slow, however, was his heartbeat. It had increased its pace exponentially, it seemed, and it didn't appear it would slow down anytime soon.

Djibril cleared his throat. A part of him couldn't believe Chris had asked such a question. Another part of him wanted to immediately deny it so he could convince her to consummate their relationship right then and there. However, his ever-sensible mind chose yet a third option. He chose honesty and patience, hoping it was what she needed.

"It is my understanding," he softly replied, "that the process can be quite painful for the human involved. I believe this would be because of the greater physiological and anatomical changes necessary for her."

"So it would hurt me, but not you?" she asked in a shy voice.

"I have not heard any mention of my brothers having suffered any physical pain during their transformations. Although, I doubt they would mention it even if it did hurt," he clarified. After a moment, he said, "I believe there should be a way to get around either party having to suffer due to the process."

Chris rose up onto an elbow and hitched an inquiring brow.

Djibril explained, saying, "We have an excellent Medical Facility here."

"Yes," Chris interrupted. "Lyss introduced me to the

head physician there and said he's offered her a position on his staff."

Djibril's eyebrows rose and he said, "She must be very good at what she does, then. Hantsushept is not an easy Kurr to impress."

Chris absorbed this in silence.

"Anyway," Djibril continued, "Hantsushept would most likely be able to concoct some sort of elixir to make the entire process completely painless, I am sure."

Chris lay back down, her head resting again on his chest, as she contemplated what it would be like to go through with everything. Lyss had already told her Djibril and she belonged together. Chris just didn't know.

"Would I change immediately after we…," she asked, her words simply trailing away as her cowardly fear kept her from actually saying it aloud.

Still, Djibril's hand maintained its slow and steady course, up and down her back, soothing her, helping her maintain her calm, and Chris was grateful for that as he answered, saying, "It is my understanding that both parties transform fairly quickly following consummation."

"W-Would I become p-pregnant immediately?" she stammered.

Djibril closed his eyes for a second and then tilted his head so he could place a small kiss on her forehead before telling her honestly, "That is what has happened with my two new sisters." After a moment of simply staring up at the ceiling, wondering what it would truly be like, he said, "I have lived upon this earth for what you would call a million years… and yet, I have never been afforded the opportunity to reproduce."

Chris frowned, concern lacing her voice as she asked simply, "Why?"

"It was forbidden."

Her frown deepened, but she didn't say anything else.

Djibril hesitated before saying, "I cannot tell you the idea of my offspring growing within your womb does not thrill me, and the idea of producing them with you thrills me more than I can even express. However, I also understand that I am not the only one involved here, that all of this must be very difficult for you, and that you may not feel the same about certain things as I. Again, I believe Hantsushept should be able to make it so that we only have to consider the possibility of reproducing if and when you choose."

A mental image of a young Djibril suddenly flashed through her mind and Chris knew what her heart wanted. Even if their child turned out to look like the glowing-eyed Sheely creature, Chris didn't care. She could argue with herself all she wanted, but she suddenly knew – Djibril belonged with her and she belonged with him.

She rose up onto her elbow again and then reached up with her free hand to grab a lock of his dark hair. "I like your hair this color," she softly said. "And you have the most beautiful blue eyes."

Djibril stared at her, his big hand continuing its ministrations. He was glad for the compliments, but he wished she felt more.

His hand stopped dead in its tracks, however, as Chris suddenly announced, "But I think you'll be just as good-looking with razor-sharp white hair and glowing eyes."

It took a moment for Djibril to fully comprehend the meaning of her words. Once it was clear, however, he suddenly rolled over, pushing her onto her back as he covered her mouth with his. His kiss was deep and powerful, conveying as much emotion as he contained, yet he made sure not to hurt her.

Chris broke the kiss for the simple reason that she needed *air*! She looked up at him and gave a small smile as she whispered, "How soon do you think that Hantsushept guy would be able…?"

She never got to finish her question. In a flash, Djibril had whipped out his shields, wrapped the two of them securely within them and transported them to the Complex's Medical Facility where they both now stood in a hallway outside Hantsushept's living quarters. Djibril was already banging on the familiar door before Chris even realized what had happened. "To…," she finished. After realization kicked in, she gave a slightly frustrated sigh and hissed, "You have to warn me before doing things like that!"

Djibril threw a half-grin down at her, then bent to place a chaste kiss upon her lips, whispering, "Sorry." He then proved the lie of his impatience as he banged again on the door with his fist and frowned as he waited for an answer from within.

Chris hugged him a little more tightly around the waist as she hid a secret little smile up against his chest. He was anxious to get things settled. It felt good to know he wanted her that desperately. It was odd, though. She never would have considered herself the kind of girl who needed that kind of validation, but here she was and it felt good, especially knowing he was an Arch Angel, to boot.

The door opened and Hantsushept blinked in surprise, exclaiming, "Lord Djibril!"

"Hantsushept," was Djibril's only response as he nodded once to the Kurric physician.

Hantsushept stepped back, opening the door wide and waving an inviting hand inward. "Come in, my Lord, come in," he invited. "Yes, and you, too, m' dear. Please."

The next half-hour was a bit awkward for Chris, what with Djibril explaining to Hantsushept, sometimes in great detail, what they needed of him. She wasn't embarrassed enough, however, to interrupt him and call a halt to the whole thing. So she sat there, quiet as a mouse, holding tightly to her Lori's hand as he discussed everything with the old Kurric physician.

Finally, Hantsushept turned to her and said, "M' dear, you have actually come at a good time. I have had an entire room set up for just this purpose in the hope that at least one of the Lorim would allow us to observe a full transformation. Every angle of the room can be observed and recorded by our imaging tools, tracking all changes in the Lori and human respectively – physiological and otherwise – throughout the entire process. The readings from the observations will provide invaluable information regarding the transformation process. We have had only three, you see, and two of the three have occurred without any witness other than those involved. The third, I am afraid, was quite an unusual one, involving an infant and an adult, so you see we are quite in need of volunteers for our research."

Chris gave him a shaky half-smile. She wasn't all that keen on having a bunch of Kurric strangers, be they trained medical professionals or no, watching videos, or heaven forbid live footage, of her being intimate with Djibril. But what could she say? "No thanks, I've completely changed my mind, now that you've explained everything to me?"

As if he'd heard her very thoughts, Hantsushept said, "I assure you, m' dear, the only one observing any of the actual footage from within the observation room will be your sister, as we have discussed here today. All other information will be in the form of numbers and colors and scales and charts. Your privacy will be quite well protected."

Chris blinked several times. It was suddenly a bit overwhelming to realize how much these complete strangers were willing to do to accommodate her into their culture. After over a decade of keeping herself closed off from all but Lyss, from trusting no one but Lyss, from being completely alone except for the presence of Lyss, this entire race of beings had suddenly opened their hearts and minds and homes to her sister and her without question, without expecting anything in return.

Djibril did not expect anything of her. He wanted her, yes, but nothing was expected. Now, Hantsushept was basically bending over backward to help ensure there would be no difficulty with the transformation that was sure to follow in the wake of Djibril's and her consummation of their relationship. Chris was simply blown away.

Djibril stood then and they were on their way. A Kurr was sent to fetch Lyss and Chris and Djibril were soon firmly installed in the special room that had been set up for the transformation observation. Inside, there was a king-sized bed along the center of one wall and a washroom off to the side. All four walls of the bedroom were made of darkened glass which gave off a perfect reflection of the entire room at all times while allowing the imaging machines' components to record everything within the space. The restroom was the only location within the area without a single recording or imaging device, making it the only place where one could find a bit of privacy.

Lyss soon entered and asked if they had any questions or requests for anything before getting started. She had obviously been briefed on the situation and was ready to get to work.

"Y-You'll be watching us?" Chris gulped, realization suddenly hitting her hard.

Lyss gave a short chuckle, saying, "My dear sister, I realize you think my life revolves around you, but I'm interested only in the information I'll be getting from the imaging machines here and nothing else, I assure you." She set a tray upon the one small bedside table in the room and said, "Whenever you're done, this should help you sleep without pain for a few hours." She turned back to Chris and put a hand on her shoulder. "I'll be just in the next room, if you need anything."

Without another word, she turned and left the room, quietly closing the door behind herself.

Djibril and Chris were suddenly alone in the bedroom. Chris, who was standing by the bottom of the bed, turned to look at Djibril, who had earlier situated himself on the bed. He appeared pretty relaxed already as he lounged back against the massive headboard, his long legs stretched out before him, crossed casually at the ankles. He was still fully dressed and he sat atop the bed's covers and pillows, but he was ahead of the game by already being *on* the bed.

Chris felt a sudden surge of nerves and didn't know if she could do this. She audibly swallowed a lump in her throat as she searched for something to say. Nothing immediately came to mind and she found she was extremely embarrassed by this whole situation.

"Come sit beside me," Djibril's deep, gravelly voice invited, as he patted the space beside him on the mattress. Slowly, Chris moved to sit beside him. He smiled at her then. "It is all right, Chris," he said, reaching up to cup her cheek. "You and I are under no obligation to perform here at all. We can just lie here getting comfortable, if you like. Or we could return to the suite at the Main House. Whatever you want." He leaned his head back against the headboard, closing his eyes and sighing a great sigh. "Just by us laying here touching each other, our energies are working on each cell in our bodies and the machines will be able to gather the information Hantsushept needs. It simply will not be as fast as it would otherwise be," he said finally.

"Y-You mean we don't technically have to do anything but lay here for Hantsushept's machines to gather the information he wants and for us to transform?" she asked haltingly.

"Apparently," Djibril lazily stated, shrugging. "It will just take longer and there will be no chance of conception." Djibril hoped he had not conveyed to her how nervous he was about this whole thing, especially the last part. He wanted her so much, and he wanted his seed inside her, but he would not rush her.

Oddly enough, it was the last bit of what Djibril said that made a difference with Chris and she found herself turning to look upon her Lori's countenance. His eyes remained closed and he appeared completely at ease as he rested his large frame back against the beautiful carved wooden headboard. But Chris felt an entirely different energy coming from him. The waves of heat she caught coming off him made her believe he was anything but calm on the inside and she felt all the more grateful to him for being so patient with her.

She swallowed hard once more and then tentatively reached over to touch his hand. When he finally looked down at her, she softly asked, "Will you lie down with me?"

Chris could feel his body instantly tightening, but his expression remained calm and gentle as he quietly moved to lie next to her on top of the covers. They both lay there facing each other, neither one willing to break the peaceful calm surrounding them.

As she stared at him, Chris wondered what she had done to have deserved this chance. He was an Arch Angel. She was a killer. Of course, there had been an extraordinary set of circumstances that had led to her chosen profession, but the fact was that she was a paid assassin. Not only did she take jobs professionally, but she used *that* job to finance her one hobby in life – killing as many Muslim males as she could. She didn't care if they were terrorists or not. If they were Muslim, that put them on her radar. Sure, she felt better about it if they turned out to be terrorists. But those were few and far between and the majority of the ones she ended up killing, she knew, were simple men who had lives and families. And if she were honest with herself, she knew the majority of those men would never even think of killing another person.

She didn't care. It had been Muslim males who had killed her parents, *both* of her parents, along with thousands of others since 9/11. They hadn't discriminated on that day or any other, other than in their choice of venues, so she didn't discriminate in her revenge.

Now, however, she wondered why this being – this holier-than-holy being – had chosen her as his mate. She didn't think there was any way she could continue with him without revealing everything about her life to him. It wouldn't be fair. But she didn't know how she could tell him. She felt uncomfortable now and she rolled over and stood, stepping a few paces away from the bed to put a bit of distance between the Lori and herself. To her surprise, however, it took only a second before she sensed him standing directly behind her.

She turned to look up at him.

Djibril reached out and ran the backs of his fingers down the side of her cheek. His eyes were kind and his touch incredibly gentle. A shiver ran down Chris' spine. Her life had been without kindness and gentility for so long, she didn't know how to handle it. But she had never been one to run from a challenge, so she did the only thing she could. She reached up, trailing her fingers up his thick chest and then circling around his neck. A slight pull downward brought his lips close enough for her to take his mouth with her own in a kiss that she owned, that she could control, that she made into so much more than just a kiss.

Pulling back, Djibril gasped. His entire body was on

fire, but something wasn't quite right. He frowned down at her, wondering what was wrong. He got the sense that Chris was content with her foreplay, but Djibril couldn't continue – he simply couldn't. "Stop," he said, stepping back from her. Chris reached in order to continue touching him. "Stop," he said again, a little more forcefully this time.

Chris came up short. His deep, gravelly voice had sounded almost angry. She thought over the past few minutes quickly in her mind. She could find no reasons for him to be angry with her and as she continued standing there turning it over in her mind and wondering what the hell this strange creature that affected her so was thinking, her own ire rose.

"What?" she finally demanded, irked and feeling like striking out at something or at someone... maybe even at him.

Djibril shook his head, backing another step away from her, as he said, "I-I cannot."

All of the trouble they had endured, the trouble they had put others to, the arrangements they had made, and now he didn't want to go through with the whole thing?

Chris cocked a hip to one side and crossed her arms in front of her, asking, "Why?"

Djibril shook his head again. He wanted her. Hantsushept had gone to great lengths to set up this space for them. And now she was angry. Even *he* didn't get it. But something about the whole situation felt repellent and it created a feeling of disgust within him to the point that he simply wanted to walk out. One look at Chris' face, though, and he knew that would be a major mistake.

He wondered how his brothers had handled this situation. After all, neither of them had known their humans before they had fully mated with them. Perhaps his feelings of discomfort were there simply because in his mind one should get to know another prior to mating with her? He knew he would have to get over that, if for no other reason than to keep her safe. After all, he hadn't always known every Kurr he had ever bedded and yet he had felt no discomfort while having intercourse with any of them. But some instinct told him he was running out of time with Chris.

Djibril pursed his lips as he came to a decision. There was no doubt in his mind that Chris was his intended mate. How could there be? Each time they touched, her energies raced through him and he could feel those energies working on his body. He already felt stronger than he had ever felt in his long life and had already noticed the development of several new abilities, along with tremendous enhancements of his other natural ones.

Chris cleared her throat loudly in an attempt to direct his attention back to the issue at hand.

After a slight hesitation, Djibril nodded once and stepped forward to hesitantly take her into his arms.

The switch in mood was so abrupt that Chris didn't have time to react before she found herself engaged in another passionate embrace. This time, however, there was no holding back by either one of them. Chris gasped as Djibril's big hand cupped her breast through the flimsy t-shirt she wore. Tingles shot from the tip of her nipple straight through to that most sensitive area between her legs and she knew she had never experienced anything like this with any of the human males she'd had sex with before. As Djibril moved to trace a row of kisses down the side of her throat, Chris' knees gave out and she fell. Luckily, Djibril's strong arms caught her mid-fall and he gathered her up close to him and picked her up before taking her over to the big bed.

He was so gentle with his handling of her that a part of Chris, the feminine side of her, wanted to cry. *This* was what she had needed all these years. *This* was the very thing that most secret part of her heart had looked for in every man she had met, yet none had possessed it. How could they have done? Such serene gentility could surely only come from one from the Loric Realm, she was certain.

As her Lori lover moved back up to reclaim her mouth in a searing kiss, Chris could think no more and she gave herself over to pure sensation.

Djibril felt the moment she surrendered to him. Instead of her whole body being tense and unyielding, certain parts of her were now soft and welcoming, while other parts of her felt taught in anticipation of his touch. His mind was thrilled with this discovery and little shivers ran down his spine to pool hotly in his groin each time he touched her in a new way, just as he felt her body responding.

He laid her down onto the bed, uncaring of the fact that Lyss was watching, and then slowly undressed her, taking his time. Chris was momentarily embarrassed when he revealed her breasts, but she quickly got over it as his fevered exploration of her body continued.

Djibril nipped at her skin, tasting every last inch revealed. And when he finally removed the last stitch of her clothing, there was the most perfect triangle of curly red hair at the apex of her legs, just waiting for him. He quickly obliged, nuzzling down into the center of it with his mouth and nose as he kneeled on the floor beside the bed. She smelled wonderful and her taste, when he darted out his tongue, was the sweetest, purest nectar he had ever experienced in all his long years on Earth.

He wanted more!

His touch was driving her wild and Chris didn't know what to do. Her own breath was coming in short little gasps, but then she would hear Djibril's deep growls as he sought and found better angles for his skillful mouth and tongue and she couldn't breathe at all! She was just lying there, legs spread wide open, head thrown back, panting – and it was sheer Heaven!

Is this Heaven? she wondered somewhere in the dim recesses of her mind. Had she died and suddenly gone to Heaven with her Loric lover?

His tongue moved across her most sensitive bud and that was it. She reared up off the mattress, a deep-throated call bursting forth from some secret place within, and yet her Lori merely tightened his arms around her thighs as he widened his mouth on her most secret part and drank every bit of her special fluids that gushed forth in her release. Chris fell back against the covers, her body completely spent.

Djibril licked up the last of the cool liquid honey that had just moments ago burst from within her core. He hadn't realized he had been starved for her taste until the blast of liquid had suddenly poured out for him and he had taken his first swallow. Then there had been nothing else! It had tasted better than any substance he had ever had and he had known, then and there, that this was his! No one else would ever drink from Chris' well! Already Djibril could feel the liquid spreading so much more of her energies throughout his body than that which he normally got from just touching her. This was part of *her* flowing inside him, and he could feel it working on his body, changing it, heightening his senses and making him stronger.

Chris had gone still and silent beneath him and he knew he should give her at least a few moments to recover. But Djibril wanted her! He wanted her to experience the same thrill of his special juices flowing throughout her body so she would know how special this was. He moved up her body, worshipping it as he went. Her eyes were open, watching him intently as he approached, and he moved to whisper in her ear, "I shall endeavor to be gentle with you, my dearest Christiana, but I fear I shall not prove up to the task."

With that somewhat apology, Djibril maneuvered into place and pushed forward.

Chris felt as if the world she knew no longer existed. Surely, she had left the Earth behind entirely! No one alive could have ever felt such earth-shattering fulfillment and lived to tell the tale. Not such as this. Not such as this.

The few times Chris had deigned to grace someone's bed with her presence, she had left without feeling anything more than satisfaction that she had achieved whatever goal she'd had in mind when she had agreed to sleep with whatever man-child it had happened to be. But Djibril was a million years old. He could no more be thought of as a boy than Chris and his aptitude with her body proved that. But there was something more. He loved with the skill of the consummate lothario, yes, but he took things one step further. At some point, Chris felt as if her Loric lover's very soul had reached out and linked with hers, making it so that theirs was a single, shared unit that ran in an unbreakable thick energy stream between them. There was no him. There was no her. There was only them.

"What?" Djibril gasped, halting his movements a moment as he frowned down at her, his voice and face full of concern.

Chris blinked a couple of times, frowning herself now. "What, what?" she asked, completely confused.

"You are crying. Was I hurting you?"

Chris slowly reached a hand up to touch her cheek. There were tears there. She *had* been crying.

"Christiana?"

She started, her focus returning suddenly to the present. "I'm sorry," she said. "No, you didn't hurt me."

"Then why were you crying?" he asked.

Chris reached up, running her hands smoothly along his skin until she had clasped them together at the back of his neck, just above some odd-feeling patch of skin on his back, which she assumed was some type of scar. "I was merely caught up in the moment," she explained. "That's all."

The look on his face made her feel so special, and yet, so very scared. Chris suddenly realized just how perfectly wonderful he was... and how completely wrong for him she was.

It had been nearly a decade since Chris had made her first kill. She had killed over 100 since that first night. What was worse was that she had also dragged her twin, Lyss, into her chosen lifestyle. Chris had been the one to convince Lyss to join her in her quest to avenge their parents' deaths. Up to that point, Lyss had been well on her way to becoming a surgeon. That hadn't fit too well with Chris' plans, however, so she had convinced Lyss to go for a less time-consuming degree program so she would be able to help Chris. She had switched her major from pre-med to nursing the next day and that had been that.

The two had graduated – with honors – and had then simply disappeared from public life. The social lifestyle of two young female college grads would have interfered too much with Chris' plans. So, she had led and Lyss had followed. Each kill had made it just a little simpler to do and before long, thanks to Chris' acumen with numbers and predictions of market trends, the two were getting regular contract offers, had made a name for themselves within the cleaning business world and had amassed a small fortune.

Chris, however, had only felt the slightest taste of satisfaction after she made her first kill of a cell of Saudi terrorists she had discovered living in New York. That had been the major turning point for Lyss as well. Up to that point, she had seemed less and less enthused about accepting money for taking out complete strangers. As soon as Chris had told her about the terrorist cell, though, Lyss had been fully on board with the mission and the two of them had focused on their training with the intensity of Olympic athletes.

They had become legend within the Arabic world. Recalcitrant children were told that the white twins would come to get them in the night if they didn't behave, and even grown men feared the night because of what Chris and Lyss had done to the Muslim world. Lyss had never uttered a word of protest, even when they had both learned of their legends spreading throughout the Arabic nations of the world.

And, now they were here in the Loric Realm, and there was no way Chris would ever be good enough for an Angel – especially not a Lori!

As Djibril picked up his movements and rhythm again, Chris had to keep herself from crying more. She would give him this night. He deserved that much, even though he had erred so very much in his absolute conviction that she was his true soul mate. He had done his best to convince her and he had been incredibly nice to her all along.

She wished she had some other choice. He deserved better. But the best she had to offer was this night and then to leave him sometime during the night after the elixir that Hantsushept guy had supplied took effect.

All of a sudden, Djibril's rhythm changed and something within her body responded to it in the most undeniable way. All lucid thought fled her mind and sensation became all. Djibril had apparently felt the change within her, because he picked up the intensity even more. Within seconds, Chris found herself clinging to the Lori simply to assure herself she still shared space on the planet with him.

She felt an intense pressure welling deep within her core and then, out of nowhere, there was a supernova that happened just behind her eyelids. Chris saw a vision of each and every single Kurr in existence on the planet – in both dimensions. She was amazed at how many were in the human realm... and no one knew! She saw the humans near some of the Kurr and not one of the humans was aware of being watched or influenced by anyone.

This was no vision. Chris realized she must be seeing these things because of Djibril's energies and the fact that he had suddenly just taken over her life. She wondered with her last shred of lucidity if this was what Sarah had meant when she had spoken of the new abilities Chris would develop after having mated with Djibril. Then she could think no more as both Djibril *and* she gave themselves over to sensation.

Stars collided and everything in existence reached a point where it was balanced precariously along a razor's edge of continuation and complete oblivion. Throughout it all, Chris felt no fear. Djibril was there with her and she knew he would never abandon her. He would never leave her.

As if on a soft breeze, the jarring and jolting of their journey through space and time eased and they gently floated down in their return to the room at the Medical Facility. They still clung tightly to each other and Chris purposely cleared her mind of all thought. She wanted just a little more time with this – with him. Then the world could intrude and she would go back to reality. But for now, she just wanted a few minutes more.

Without even realizing it, Djibril broke the spell by giving her temple a kiss and then leaning across her to retrieve the tiny medicine cup containing the bright green-colored elixir that was to help the two of them sleep through whatever supposed transformation they each were expected to experience now that they had fully mated with one another. He gazed deeply into her eyes as he held the tiny cup to her lips. Chris returned his gaze as she took approximately half the contents into her mouth, but didn't swallow. She watched as Djibril then moved the little cup to his own lips and drank the remainder of the elixir, swallowing every last drop.

True to Hantsushept's word, even without having swallowed the potent elixir, Chris felt her eyelids getting heavy. The elixir was working on Djibril as well. He yawned, sucking in a deep breath as he put the cup back onto the nightstand and then made sure Chris was comfortable before he fell into oblivion. Before the elixir knocked her out entirely simply by absorbing into the thin epithelial cells of her mouth, Chris grabbed the tiny cup and spat out everything left in her mouth. Then, her eyes closing and her muscles weak, she laid down her fuzz-filled head and allowed the drug to take her.

Chapter 17

Chris awoke slowly. One of Djibril's big, thick arms was wrapped securely around her waist, while her head rested comfortably upon his other. One of his heavy legs was thrown across both of hers, effectively trapping her on the bed.

She felt incredibly groggy and had no clue how much time had elapsed since she had blacked out, but her mind was quickly clearing and she remembered that she had things to do. Moving slowly and as carefully as possible, she extricated herself from beneath her Lori and stood.

Oddly enough, she didn't feel any different as she moved over to the mirrored observation wall covering one whole side of the room. She had on not one stitch of clothing and she knew there could be just about anyone on the other side of the mirror, but still Chris stood there... staring, wondering for a moment if she would actually be able to detect changes within her body.

She felt nothing as she stared into the mirror at the same reflection she had seen day after day her entire life. She hadn't changed one bit that she could detect.

Of course.

Hair still looked as red and curly as ever. Eyes were still the same green they had been since before she could remember. She still looked exactly like Lyss.

Lyss...

Chris stared at her reflection, but it was her sister she saw. Chris knew Lyss wouldn't want to leave the Loric Realm. She had even said so before. But they hadn't ever been apart for any great length of time or distance since birth and Chris felt a stab of fear at just the thought of being so separated from the one person in her life who knew her through and through. Would Lyss suffer from being separated from Chris as well? Would the fact that they would each be living in a different dimension make it so that they no longer shared their "twin sense" as they liked to call the special mental bond they had with one another?

Would Chris be able to sense her sister at all once she

crossed back over to the human realm?

She looked down suddenly to the reflection of her lower abdomen. The creamy-white skin covering it looked the way it always did. There was no bright patch of light showing through it.

Tears suddenly pooled in her eyes. As she continued staring, Chris realized some small part of her had actually come to believe something would happen once she and Djibril mated. Even Lyss had believed. But now Chris was being confronted with the hard, undeniable proof that they had all been wrong.

Chris was not Djibril's true soul mate. She was just a ruthless killer, a murderer who took money for her services, a whore to sin and other sinners. How could anyone such as she ever be accepted into the life Djibril and all the others believed she had been designed for?

No.

As one teardrop finally crested her eyelid and fell down her cheek, Chris returned her gaze to the reflection of her *own* eyes and her decision solidified within her mind. She was not fit to live here among these beautiful creatures. Lyss was, but not Chris. So she would go. She would return to the world of humans, where sin was always the order of the day, and she would continue taking out those who sought only to cause chaos, death and destruction. And maybe, just maybe, she would be able to do the world a small favor by sacrificing her already-tarnished and damned soul in order to make the world a safer place for the innocent.

Her mind made up, she turned and found her clothes. The sooner she left and crossed that barrier thing at the rift between the two dimensions, the sooner she would be able to get on with the long, lonely life that awaited her. Completely avoiding looking at the sleeping Lori for fear she would chicken out and not go, Chris finished dressing and quietly slipped out the door and down the hallway.

Lyss stood on the opposite side of the mirrored observation wall watching her twin. She felt no embarrassment at staring at her sister's nude form. It was just like staring into a mirror at her own unclothed body. As Chris continued her own visual examination of herself reflected in the mirror on her side of the wall, Lyss concentrated just that little bit necessary so she would know what her twin was thinking.

It was part of what Chris and she thought of as their "twin sense" and it had always existed between them. One could pick up on what the other was thinking and feeling simply by concentrating in a special way they had each instinctively known how to do since birth. But from what she could see at the moment, it appeared Chris either hadn't a clue that Lyss stood opposite her on the other side of the glass or she simply did not care, as she continued staring at her reflection.

Lyss had seen her twin spit the elixir back into the tiny paper cup a couple of hours ago, though that had not been the plan the last Lyss had heard. Now, as she continued watching Chris, she realized exactly what was going on in her twin's head and she didn't like it one bit! As Chris dressed hurriedly in the other room, Lyss became more and more ticked off.

When she looked back on her life up to this point, she realized what complete monsters she and her sister had become. They had both strayed into a life of sin, losing both their way in life and their faith. Death, money and revenge had come to be all either one of them had cared about and Lyss wished with every fiber of her being that she could simply erase the past decade and start over. But she couldn't and she knew it.

Fortunately, however, a miracle had happened. God had stepped in to give her twin and her a second chance!

Here they were, in some alternate dimension very few humans even knew about, living with actual Angels and being accepted by them – even though Lyss had told them about the type of lifestyle she and her sister had been living prior to having been brought to this realm. Lyss knew this was God's way of offering her sister and her His forgiveness for their sins. And now, Chris was thinking of throwing all of that back at God, of saying, "No, thanks," to Him and walking away to return to her former life of sin – even though God had offered her one of His highest-ranked Angels in return for her giving up that sinful lifestyle.

Lyss simply could not let her sister do such a thing! Chris must be convinced to stay – not for Lyss' sake, but for Chris' own sake, for Lyss loved her twin and wanted only the best future possible for her. She knew sin was like a drug and that people could become addicted to the thrill and instant gratification it offered. But also like drugs, Lyss knew nothing good could ever truly come from sin and the sinner must stop "using" in order to reclaim her life. Lyss was determined to save her sister and would do whatever she had to do to stop Chris from making the biggest mistake of her life.

Her mind set, Lyss returned her attention to the scene before her, and that was when she realized Chris was no longer even in the room!

Lyss burst through the door connecting both rooms, uncaring of the loud "bang" it made as it crashed against the glass wall. Chris wasn't in the attached bathroom, either.

As Lyss passed by the foot of the giant bed, her leg happened to knock against the mattress, shaking the bed quite jarringly, and she heard Djibril grunt as he woke.

"Wh-What…?" he asked groggily as his gaze landed on her form standing at the foot of the bed. It took but a second before he turned to see the empty space on the bed beside him. He immediately turned back to Lyss, his deep, gravelly voice quite clear and controlled as he demanded, "Where is Christiana?"

A dart of fear suddenly raced through Lyss. She had no clue how Djibril had known she wasn't Chris, but the dark aura that had suddenly "appeared" around his form had her backing up a step or two, for certain. She shook her head and said simply, "I-I don't know. She was here just a moment ago, but then she must have left."

Djibril's brilliant light-blue eyes lowered in thought and Lyss used his sudden shift of attention as her opportunity to escape the now-overwhelmingly frightening-looking Lori. She had almost made it to the door leading to the hallway when his steely voice stopped her.

"Wait!"

Djibril tried his best to control his excitement, but he was still suffering from the mind-numbing effects of the elixir. He hadn't expected to awaken to Lyss standing at the bottom of the bed and no sign of Chris in the room. Lyss might look exactly like Chris, but the energy waves and frequencies coming off her were radically different from Chris' and Djibril had known the difference immediately.

Where was Chris? If Lyss hadn't seen her leave the room, did that mean Chris had simply disappeared using her new shields? Could they have formed that quickly? He needed to find her.

"Check the video footage, will you?" he asked. He needed to get dressed and, although she had observed them making love, he didn't want to embarrass Chris' twin with his lack of clothing. Lyss quickly crossed back over to the observation room and Djibril dressed with record speed. If Chris' shields had already developed, would that mean her hair and eyes would have changed already? His own had not, he noticed, and questions plagued Djibril as he finished up dressing and headed for the door to the tiny observation room in the corner. "Have you queued it up, yet?" he asked.

Lyss nodded and hit a key on the tiny keyboard. Video footage of Chris appeared on a computer monitor stationed on a desktop directly before Djibril. She had been nude and Djibril saw no evidence of any physical changes in her form. In the video, Chris just stood there staring at herself for a time before finally turning and dressing hurriedly before walking out the door of the room. Djibril stared at the tiny monitor, even after the video footage had ended. Chris hadn't looked at his sleeping form once during the footage. She had simply left. And there had been no changes in her appearance. More importantly, there had been no bright light showing through the skin covering her abdomen.

What did this mean?

A movement to his left suddenly caught Djibril's

attention and he turned to stare at Lyss. He realized she was quite afraid of him, although he certainly had no designs on harming her. But it was more than that. She revered him, thought of him as something close to divinity.

Djibril frowned.

Was this the reason why Chris had run? Did she think like Lyss? Was she frightened now that they had mated, afraid that she would be punished for having committed such an act with a Lori, what she thought of as an Angel?

Djibril had to find her and explain.

Like a flash of lightning in his mind, he suddenly knew exactly where his lover was. He could clearly sense the location of her energies and, without hesitation, his shields smoothly stole out and took him off, leaving a befuddled Lyss standing alone in the tiny observation room.

Chris halted in her race to escape the Loric Realm. In her haste to get this part of her life over with, she had simply run. She hadn't truly known where to go or how she was supposed to get back to the human realm, but she had known travel between the two dimensions to be possible and she had trusted that she would somehow manage it – assuming she could find one of those rift things Djibril had told her about. The moment she had left and put her mind to finding a rift, however, she had realized her mind knew exactly where to go. Amazingly, her sense of rifts all around had grown stronger and stronger the closer she had come to them.

Now she stood before one and a part of her rebelled at the idea of actually crossing over back into the human realm. She hadn't been awake for the initial crossing when Djibril had brought her and Lyss over, so she didn't know what to expect. And if she were honest with herself, she would admit she was more than just a little afraid of what might await her.

An image of Djibril's smiling face flashed within her mind and she knew she couldn't put it off another minute. She had to return. She had to let him go. Taking a deep breath for courage, she steeled herself for whatever was going to happen and stepped forward through the invisible rift.

Tiny pinpricks of pain hit her entire body. It felt like a swarm of coals from giant sparklers hitting her from every direction and she gasped at the pain. As she looked around for the source of the painful little lights, she saw a riot of colors surrounding her. It was as if she travelled through a tunnel of light with red, pink and purple hues amid a bright swirl of gold. It was everywhere and Chris marveled at the sight.

The next thing she knew, she was through the rift and into a world filled with the stench of chemicals. The very air burned her eyes and with each breath she took, the air singed the insides of her nostrils and burned like acid all the way down into her lungs. She squinted as she sought the source of the terrible smell, but found she was deep in a forest.

There appeared to be nothing around that produced the filthy, toxic air and Chris wondered what on Earth she had gotten herself into. Without thinking, she turned and raced back toward the rift she still sensed. The tiny burns she felt from the little lights all around were just as painful. She raced through the rift, not bothering to marvel at the light show. Then she was on the other side, back in the Loric Realm, and was finally able to breathe again.

She stood there, stunned. She had no idea what could have happened to have made the air within the human realm be filled with such an acrid stench, but she knew she could not be there anymore. But that meant she now had nowhere to go.

Just then, she sensed a presence there in the woods with her. Without realizing it, she recognized the energy she felt as Djibril. He was there, she was certain of it. As she continued standing there in the dark woods, she sensed only him, as if he was standing directly behind her, arms crossed, waiting for her to turn and acknowledge him.

She wouldn't. She simply couldn't. Her reasons for having left were good ones and he just needed to accept the fact that they were not made for one another. They were not made to be together as he believed and he should simply let her go – though she had no clue as to where she could go.

Tears formed in her eyes again and Chris wished this part would just get over and done with.

"I do not even warrant a 'good-bye'?" he finally asked quietly.

Chris hung her head in shame. What could she say? None of the clichés she would normally use in a situation like this would work because…because, she suddenly realized, she truly didn't want to leave. She didn't *want* to leave her sister. She didn't want to leave Djibril and his welcoming family. Most of all, however, she didn't want to return to the lonesome lifestyle she had been leading since the day her parents had died, even if she could find a way to survive in the filth on the other side of the rift.

The tears overflowed as she thought of her parents and how much she wished they were here to guide her. She felt so lost and alone for the first time in her life and she just wished her dad was here to hold her and offer some words of wisdom. But he wasn't ever going to do that again, was he? He couldn't. He and her mother, along with thousands of other people had been robbed of their lives thanks to Islamic terrorists. And now Chris had a decision to make.

Djibril was standing right behind her. Yes, he was probably wicked angry that she had left – but he had come after her. Somewhere inside Chris' mind, a tiny glimmer of hope sprang to life.

"Chris?" Djibril asked softly, as she merely continued standing with her back to him, not moving, not speaking. Was she hurt? She appeared to be unharmed, from what he could see.

Finally, she turned and looked up at him.

Djibril's heart melted inside as he took in her tears and the hope of forgiveness shining up at him in her light-green eyes. He wiped away one trail of tears from her face and wrapped her in a protective hug.

Chris broke down at the first sign of his kindness. She hugged him tightly and let go of all her anger and pain. Djibril simply held her, allowing her to let it all out, to come to terms with everything.

They stood there for what felt like hours to Chris.

When finally she calmed enough that she could speak, he jokingly asked, "Was it *that* bad?"

Chris' sense of humor was still intact and she chuckled. The very fact that he could still want her after all of this was incredible and some part of Chris' mind realized that Lyss had been right. Chris did need to explore this… whatever it was that Djibril was offering her before she made any decisions about returning to the human realm. Her hold on the tall Lori tightened. But then she wondered if he might not want her to stay once he realized that nothing had happened to her – even though they had fully mated.

Would he make her leave when he realized his mistake in believing her to be his true soul mate? She couldn't bear the thought of that happening and her arms tightened their hold on him just a bit more in an attempt to somehow keep them together. Desperate now to make him understand that she wanted to try to be what he was looking for, she reached out and brought his lips down to hers, pouring every bit of emotion into her kiss.

She didn't stop with merely showing him how much she now cared for him and how eager she was to make things work between them. Instead, she showed him everything, laying her heart completely open for him to know. She felt somehow that just by wanting him to know that part of herself, he would experience it and learn what made her the way she was. So she gave everything she had to offer, hoping against all hope that it would be enough to convince him to give her one more chance.

Djibril was at first shocked and a trifle fearful when she suddenly demanded the kiss. However, as she deepened their kiss, a well-spring of emotion poured into Djibril's mind. It was all coming from her! She was giving him access to her soul, whether she knew it or not, and he now understood precisely why she had run from their bed earlier. She had been woefully mistaken, of course, but he now understood her thinking.

So lonely! From the thoughts and feelings he had received from her mind, Djibril was nearly overwhelmed by the utter loneliness she had endured for years. And the only source of love she had had during that long stretch of time since her parents' deaths had been her twin, Lyss. But with both girls struggling with their own individual emotional crises, neither one had learned to truly express themselves in a healthy manner, either physically or emotionally.

They had each tried to help the other, but their paths and dangerous lifestyle had made any hope of a normal sisterly relationship impossible. In his mind's eye, Djibril realized how starved for affection and approval his mate was, even though it seemed she needed to take things much more slowly than even he had realized before because of her trust issues.

Djibril pulled back from the kiss, taking a deep calming breath and returning to just hugging his young lover. He would have to take care from now on not to allow himself to go beyond a certain point in his arousal for Chris until such time as she was ready for more. She needed patience and understanding. He realized that.

She had a horrible sense of self-worth and it would take some work to change her self-loathing to inner happiness, but Djibril was willing to do it. After witnessing how completely devoted to their mates his brothers had become, he knew that was what he wanted as well, and he was determined to do anything necessary to help Chris through so that they could finally become a transformed pair.

The one remaining problem with that whole scenario, however, was the fact that Chris appeared not to have experienced any physical changes as yet stemming from their union. Djibril was not sure how long it had been since they had fallen asleep, but he thought something should surely have occurred by now, if it was going to as a result of their mating.

Djibril, himself, felt incredibly stronger inside and he could actually feel the locations of his siblings and everyone else throughout the Complex as he stood in the woods with his mate, even though he still showed no physical changes on the outside. Perhaps Chris and he would change all of a sudden, like Azra'il and Sheely had purportedly done?

As he stood there holding Chris, Djibril realized he didn't care how long it took. Even if they never changed on the outside, he would not care. The way he felt about Chris – it already consumed him!

He could not imagine feeling more for her than he already felt, simply because everything he had inside already belonged to her. If nothing ever happened – either with their appearances or her abilities – it simply would not make a difference to him. In his mind, she and he belonged to one another. They always had and always would, no matter what. If she needed more information, as he sensed she would eventually seek if things between them did not progress as soon as expected, then he would enlist either Hantsushept's aid or that of his siblings.

Djibril would do whatever it took to appease Chris, but to him there was no doubt. Chris and he belonged together. It was that simple.

In a flash, he had them whizzing through the air back to the room at the Medical Facility. As their feet touched down and he lowered his shields, Chris stepped back from him and looked toward the giant bed, a frown suddenly crinkling the little patch of skin between her brows.

"Would you prefer the suite at the Main House?" he quietly asked.

She immediately shook her head, but continued staring at the big bed. It was still mussed from their earlier use of it and each of them was reminded of what had happened there.

"Christiana," Djibril softly said. "I wish only for sleep, for *I* actually ingested the elixir Hantsushept provided."

Immediately, Chris was flooded with guilt for having caused him to have to deal with matters while he was so exhausted. "I'm so sorry," she said, her voice hushed as she struggled to deal with the situation without bursting into tears again.

He held out a hand and asked, "Will you lie down with me?"

His request was so simple, so plain. Chris nodded,

placing her hand into his much larger one as they rounded the bed. She climbed upon the high mattress and then moved over to make room for him. Djibril swiftly removed his clothing, except the underwear he had thrown on earlier, and then lifted the covers and crawled onto the giant bed, putting himself directly behind where she had situated herself.

He did not pretend with her. Instead, he took her in his strong arms and brought the entire length of her up against his frame. She was tense at first, but within seconds she heard his natural breathing as exhaustion overcame his consciousness and she relaxed against him, thrilling to the natural heat of his body. It was still hours later, however, before her busy mind calmed enough to allow her to finally fall asleep.

***

"I'm glad you decided to stay," Lyss said. She and Chris were sitting on one of the benches bordering the practice circle while the others continued with their training. Lyss took another sip of water and turned back to watch as Sarah performed a particularly spectacular feat involving bending tree branches via telekinesis to deliver a walloping blow to Baphomet before he could attack *her*.

Chris was silent. She didn't know what to say to her twin. She knew Lyss had figured out Chris had left last night without her – without even telling her "good-bye". When Chris had lain with Djibril the second time last night, at some point during the night she had realized it was probably Lyss who had either alerted him that Chris had gone or she had at least helped him to find her in that special way the twins had always had of knowing where the other was at all times.

Chris didn't blame Lyss. Indeed, she was actually glad Lyss had helped Djibril to find her. As she had lain in bed last night listening to him breathe, she had come to understand that this was an opportunity for both Lyss and her to start over. There were no Muslim terrorists here. They could both live here in peace without ever having to worry about being attacked again. And Djibril truly appeared to want her to stay. Perhaps Lyss would be able to find

227

someone to love in the Loric Realm as well. Of course, that was until Djibril realized he had made an egregious mistake believing Chris to be his true soul mate!

This was the one thing keeping Chris from the belief that a happy-ever-after was a possibility for her.

Why hadn't she changed? Sarah and Lisa and Sheely had all changed, so then why hadn't Chris changed yet? Even in the practice circle this morning, Chris still couldn't keep up with Lyss as she had attempted again to learn the Loric way of fighting. It almost felt like Chris was even weaker now than she had been before and that only reinforced her feeling that it should have been Lyss who had been chosen as Djibril's soul mate.

Of course, just the thought of any other – even Lyss – touching Djibril had Chris seeing red.

"Hey," Lyss said, bringing Chris' mind back to the present. "You okay?"

Because of the scenario Chris had just been imagining, she turned not-so-friendly eyes on her sister and Lyss' expression clearly displayed how hurt she was by her twin's anger, unintended though it had been. By the time Chris realized what had happened, however, it was too late and Lyss had stomped off. Chris hung her head in defeat.

This really just wasn't her week!

At the moment, however, Lyss was the least of Chris' worries. If she was honest with herself, Chris would realize just how selfish she was being by not going after her sister to comfort her. After all, Chris had Djibril to comfort her, should she need it. Whom did Lyss have? This thought was just taking hold when Chris caught sight of Djibril's powerful form suddenly storming the practice clearing. Apparently, he had decided to take on everyone in the large circle all at once, and attack they did! All thoughts of her twin fled from her mind as her heart jumped into her throat as the scene played out before her. Sarah attacked from the left, Baphomet from the right and Samuel from behind, while Mikhail, the most intimidating of them all, came directly at him from the front.

Chris was not pleased to watch her blue-eyed Lori taking on his more-evolved siblings in a head-on fight, but there had been no talking him out of the practice today. He had apparently decided that because Chris had not yet changed, she needed further protection.

Chris didn't understand what made him think he would be able to protect her from anyone any better than she would be able to protect herself – especially since he, himself, had yet to show any signs of changing as a result of their mating, either. She merely needed to find some way of retrieving her katana from her home back in the human realm and she was sure she would then be fine.

She nearly lost it the next moment as all four attackers converged at once, with murder clearly evident in their eyes, onto the center of the clearing where Djibril stood. And Djibril... Djibril simply stood still, waiting, with his eyes closed!

Baphomet lunged at Djibril, missing by less than an inch as Chris' lover twisted at the last second. Djibril also moved just in time to avoid Sarah's strike, leaving the two of them to hit only each other in a head-on collision as Djibril moved smoothly out of their range. Both Sarah and Baphomet went down after their bang. That still left the young Kurr named Samuel and, worse yet, Mikhail.

Djibril still had his eyes closed as he moved to the left of where Chris sat and, for a moment, Chris thought she could hear his ruined voice softly speaking to her in her mind, telling her everything would be all right, that he had everything under control. In the next second, however, Samuel went in for the kill, with Mikhail quickly closing in for his own strike from the other side. Djibril stopped and cocked his head, as if he was listening to something.

Suddenly, there was a breeze. It rushed down into the clearing and then circled around the space, tightening in on the group there. Leaves and other woodland debris was picked up by the brusque wind and flew into the air where it became a flurry of dangerous airborne projectiles.

In a flash, Djibril's shields deployed and he zoomed up and around, executing a perfect back somersault before deftly touching down behind Mikhail. Meanwhile, all the debris picked up by the powerful winds struck the three of the contenders within the circle. Samuel was hit so hard he fell to the ground, nearly losing consciousness as more and more of the flying projectiles struck him blow after blow. Mikhail, on the other hand, remained completely untouched as his own shields shot out to protect him. He wasn't still, though.

Even as Samuel went down, Mikhail's glowing eyes trained directly onto his brother's waiting form. Without hesitation, Mikhail shot through the air and then Djibril turned, throwing up his arms with his palms facing outward and – bam! Mikhail appeared to hit some sort of invisible wall. His body hit the ground nearly as hard as it had hit the invisible wall.

Djibril finally opened his eyes and took a look around at his handiwork, surveying the damage he had inflicted with an air of pride beaming from his confident stance. He turned toward Chris, a huge grin on his face. The next second, however, found him lying flat on his back, as Samuel suddenly recovered enough to slam his palms flat onto the ground, directing a line of energy directly toward Djibril's legs, knocking his feet out from beneath him.

Chris was on her feet, immediately concerned for her lover. She reached him in two seconds as Djibril's brother, Baphomet, cackled at the sight of Djibril lying flat on his back. A second later, everyone else in the circle was laughing at Baphomet, however, because Sarah had apparently found his laughter inappropriate and had used her telekinetic abilities to have a branch from a nearby Zaljia Willow quickly slap him across his bum. Baphomet immediately stopped laughing and rubbed his smarting behind.

With their training session at an end and Baphomet properly chastised, everyone simply drifted off laughing with his or her companion to clean up and prepare for the rest of the day.

A quarter of an hour later, Djibril was still in a good mood from his win in the practice circle and it spread to Chris, as well, for she was humming as she entered the shower in the small suite she shared with Djibril at the Medical Facility. She still had no idea what was going to happen to her when he figured out he had chosen the wrong human, but she was in too good a mood to dwell on it.

She couldn't even bring herself to worry much about Lyss. Chris knew her sister was safe and that was all that mattered. In fact, Chris knew precisely where Lyss was at that very moment – on a different floor of the Medical Facility having some sort of lesson on what looked to Chris' untrained mind like Kurric first aid. Lyss was all wrapped up in the lesson from what she could see and a smile crept across Chris' face as she rinsed her long, red hair. Her twin was going to be just fine here at the Complex.

Her shower done, Chris dried herself and then did her best to dry her thick hair. They really would have to do something about getting a blow dryer, if Chris was going to be staying here much longer. After all, she couldn't very well walk around in wet clothing all the time because her hair took so long to dry! But for now, Chris did the best she could with the towel and then wrapped the thick, curly mass up in a smaller towel, wrapping herself up in one of the thick, luxurious robes she had discovered folded on a shelf next to the towels.

Djibril was just finishing up a plate of food when Chris entered the room after her shower. He quickly showed her where an entire buffet of food had been laid out for their enjoyment, much of which Chris couldn't even identify.

Djibril placed his now-empty plate on a nearby table and stepped in to nuzzle her neck with his nose and lips. She smelled so good, he simply couldn't resist touching her, even though he had promised himself they were going to take things slow for a while so she could adjust. After all, he had waited this long for her, and he wanted her to enjoy their intimacy as much as he, so he was willing to wait just a little while longer before they went at it again. Just so long as it *was* just a little while longer.

This morning's practice session had been more than just goofing off for him, as Chris had probably thought. Djibril realized this morning when he had awakened to find that neither of them had yet changed that he would have to protect Chris. Until she evolved, she would be incredibly vulnerable and unable to defend herself against the many dangers present within the Badlands.

Her sister, Lyss, was being trained by Mikhail so there would be no worries about *her* vulnerability and Djibril had been pleased to see how very well she had taken to the training so far. It had been Mikhail's idea to train her and everything appeared to be working out quite well.

Chris rasped out a moan on a ragged breath and Djibril suddenly realized what he was doing. She stood in his arms, completely undressed now, her glorious red hair hanging limp and damp all around her as he finally broke away from her neck where he had simply taken hold of her as he had breathed in her overwhelmingly irresistible scent. Now, there was a mark where his mouth had been latched onto her skin.

Djibril smiled softly at her as he forced himself to step away from her slender body. Instead, he turned back toward the buffet and said, "The kitchen staff have truly outdone themselves today."

Chris stood there staring at her Lori's back, wondering what had happened. They had been experiencing a wonderful moment of closeness in which she had completely lost herself – and then he had just stopped! She didn't understand. Had he found her response to his touch dissatisfying? As she continued standing there, silently staring and puzzling over what had gone wrong, Djibril turned.

The look of hurt and confusion covering her face had him by her side immediately.

"Sweetheart, what is it?" he asked, reaching to touch her face.

Chris frowned in complete confusion. He was being so nice, so gentle and concerned. She didn't understand. Did he want her or not?

She looked over at the bed.

"Christiana?" he asked, suddenly very concerned, for she still had not explained what was wrong.

Chris looked back up at his beautiful face. "I thought...," she started. Then, she shook her head and said,

"Nothing. It-It's nothing." She disengaged from his hold on her and, re-donning her robe, made her way over to the small buffet table. If she was honest with herself, she would admit that she was starving and one always thought better on a full stomach.

She piled a plate high with food and then went to sit on the edge of the bed to eat.

After a tense moment of silence, Djibril climbed onto the bed just behind where she sat and arranged himself around her, his legs spread out on either side of her. There, he started rubbing her back and shoulders while she ate. "I was very impressed with your skills this morning during the practice session with the others," he told her.

"Why?" she asked around a mouthful of some tasty green leafy food she couldn't identify, yet which she absolutely loved. "I was the slowest one out there!"

He made a sound of agreement, but then said, "But I know enough about sparring to know it is not always how quick one is, but how intelligently one fights."

After a moment of digesting his words, Chris shrugged. She still didn't feel very confident of her abilities when she compared them to Lyss', let alone to any of the Lorim's, but she knew she would continue training if they let her, and that she would therefore improve over time. She just had to discover the one thing holding her back and she knew once that was done, she would be able to advance much more quickly.

The difficulty was, that one thing that was holding her back frightened her a bit. Since her parents' death, Chris had always felt this great emptiness inside that had separated her from everyone else, including Lyss. She had tried talking with herself, reasoning it out, but to no avail. As the years had gone by, that feeling of emptiness had increased until it had become a great gaping chasm surrounding her on a tiny little island in her mind. And now Djibril, who was so patient and caring, was sitting behind her, touching her with the greatest tenderness she had ever experienced, and she wanted more than anything for him to understand her.

She stood, her hunger suddenly eclipsed by her loneliness. After setting her plate back on the edge of the buffet table, Chris returned to the bed, climbing up to sit directly before Djibril, wrapping her legs around his waist.

Djibril reached a hand up to gently stroke her brow, and somehow the words just started flowing. She told him her entire life's history, including the wonderful times she had spent with her parents, and even the lowest points when she had taken such pleasure in killing innocent men simply because of their professed religious beliefs.

Djibril listened without interrupting as she spoke of the morning her parents had last gone into the city to the jobs they had so loved. She recalled her mother having to threaten to kick Lyss and her out of the car as they drove toward the twins' college because of their incessant bickering. Barely an hour later, Lyss and Chris had watched in horror as the events of that day unfolded. There had been no escape, neither for their parents nor for the twins, as every media outlet had displayed everything in stark detail.

When her story was done, with the whole ugly truth having been revealed, Chris knew he would now change his mind about her. She could not blame him. This, she decided, was why she had been chosen – to pay for her sins by ultimately being rejected by an Angel.

Instead of rejecting her, however, Djibril confused her by saying, "It was all my fault, you know." When she merely continued frowning at him in complete and utter confusion, he elaborated by explaining, "I told you before, I was the one who taught the ways of Islam to the human known as Mohammad. I created that whole belief system and tutored him in the cave. Afterward, I made sure his battle campaigns were successful."

"But I thought Israfil…," she haltingly offered. She had only studied a little of the Qur'an in an attempt to understand her enemy better, but she had thought it had been Israfil who had taught Mohammad the ways of Islam in the cave.

Djibril shook his head. "Iz helped me out a little. But I was the main reason for the birth and success of Islam within the human realm."

Djibril then went on to explain about the Lesser and Greater Sanhedrin houses within Lorim City and of how it had traditionally been the custom to try to steer humans with too much soul-energy in a direction more suitable for all whenever they were detected, and of how one of the methods the Lorim used to do this was to create a new system of religion and to have the humans live with that for a while until another human with too much soul-energy was detected somewhere down the line.

"You mean like Jesus?" Chris asked.

"I was not directly involved in that one," Djibril said. "I think Iz was the one who dealt with that case, but it was the same type of deal, I am certain."

Chris chewed over everything for a moment. Then she asked in a small voice, "Why?"

It was a simple question and the answer, Djibril knew, was just as simple. He didn't sugar-coat anything. He simply stated, "Because that was what humans needed at that time." He explained how the Lorim had first discovered humans by accident and then of how the blessed Great Designers had been discovered.

He told her of the One Law and of how Mikhail and Sarah had defied that Law only to discover that the entire belief system that had sustained the earth's Kurric population for close to one hundred thousand years might possibly have been built upon a complete falsehood, and that because of that possibility, they were all at a loss as to what to believe anymore. The human realm was a mess, to be certain, but so was the Loric Realm, and things appeared only to be getting worse.

"All we do know for certain," he finally said, "is that Mikhail and Sarah each transformed after mating with one another and Sarah conceived and then gave birth to Sheely, something the Designers had led the Lorim to believe was impossible for us to do. Now, Baphomet and Lisa appear to have accomplished the impossible as well."

Djibril rubbed her brow again.

"I do not know what to believe anymore," he whispered. "All I do know is that you are the only creature on this planet in one million years to have affected me the way you do. I cannot and will not live without you, if I have anything to do with it. I do not care that you chose a lifestyle that, under the circumstances, is completely understandable, although morally wrong. I do not apologize for having been the one to have created the very belief system which led to the circumstances that so affected your life and the life of your sister.

"I will not apologize for wanting to make violent and passionate love to you at all hours of the day and night, either. However, I will not force you to do anything you are not ready to do, even if that means I must stand by and watch you age for years to come without being able to make love with you again in hopes that we can finally evolve into whatever it is we are supposed to become." He reached his other hand up and framed her face between his palms. "I belong with you, Christiana Harrington," he stated firmly, "and you belong with me. We were created specifically one for the other and that is how it must be."

With that said, there seemed to be no more that could be said and Djibril leaned forward and planted a firm kiss upon her shocked lips. In seconds, however, her shock had faded to pleasure and she no longer thought about or even cared that her sister, whom she could feel, now sat in the next room monitoring everything going on in this one. Touching him and being touched by him was all that mattered.

The two were soon completely absorbed in each other. The temperature within the room was warm, so they didn't bother covering themselves as they slowly made love, nor even later, as exhausted, they quickly took the liquid in the little cup someone had replenished that would make them sleep and then, their bodies fully-entwined, they slept without dreaming.

Lyss stood in the observation room, watching the monitor for any changes. Hantsushept had appeared concerned earlier this afternoon that there had thus far been nothing of any great significance to take place and Lyss wanted to see something happening. She could feel the connection her sister had with the Angel Djibril and she wondered at the fact that there had yet to be any physical changes in either of them.

What could it mean? she wondered.

If the others were anything to go by – and why wouldn't she use them as the standard – then why was Chris not changing yet? Judging by the readings the monitors were picking up, there was definitely something going on. But there were still no outward, visible changes in either of them.

Chapter 18

Iblis sat in front of the group of Shaitans from Knor, waiting for his words to sink in. The stunned audience absorbed the incredible news with shock, disbelief and anger – much as Iblis had believed they would. In fact, he was counting on it. After watching the "country" Shaitans fall at the slaughter just outside the new Lorim base, Iblis had realized it would take more than just a couple dozen Shaitans to accomplish the task the One had set before him and Satariel. He knew also that it would take learned Shaitans, not a bunch of country bumpkins, to take down the Lorim.

Not only were there the entire group of Lorim to contend with, but the damned Lords had gone and enlisted the assistance of humans! And judging by the moves Iblis had witnessed, the Lorim were training the humans in combat techniques. Satariel's capture and death had proven that and it had been a heavy blow to watch as his long-time friend took his own life using the capsule the One had given each of them at the outset of the mission for their use should they fail. But that wasn't what had angered Iblis so.

The thing that had captured Iblis' attention was that during the battle he had seen the impossible. Lord Baphomet had arrived, which had confirmed that the Shaitan King had indeed switched sides. Iblis knew only skilled Shaitans – and a lot of them – would stand a chance against that creature in battle. But even that was not what now drove Iblis.

The image of the one who had arrived shortly after Lord Baphomet was what was now seared into Iblis' mind. That was the human female Iblis and his team had previously handed over to Lord Baphomet. But she wasn't human now. Instead, Iblis had felt her power and he knew… that one human was now a Lori! He didn't know how it had been accomplished, but his senses had not deceived him. His eyes, maybe. But not the rest of his senses.

The one thing that had kept running through his mind since he first laid eyes on the creature was that if a human could be transformed into a Lori, then Iblis sure as Hell believed a Shaitan could be transformed into one. And he would not rest until he discovered a way to transform himself!

***

She was traveling through the stars. There were multiple strings stretched both below and above her. She was moving along the strings, going fast upward toward the spot where they disappeared into the great empty black chasm. She needed to reach the end of the strings, but she couldn't for the life of her remember why. For that matter, she had no clue what the strings were, nor what they were connected to, nor how she had come to be traveling along them in outer space. She simply knew she had to reach the other end. She pushed herself harder, using every ounce of energy she had to go faster.

Something touching her face caught the edges of Chris' consciousness, interrupting her progress and dragging her mind to full lucidity. She dragged her eyelids open and discovered Djibril softly smiling down at her. Although it took a moment for her to realize she had only been dreaming, she finally did so and then she was overcome with annoyance. Was he going to wake her every morning this way?

He rubbed one of his long fingers down the length of her cheek as he leaned in to gently touch his lips to hers. Pulling back, he whispered, "Good morning, my dear Christiana."

His ice-blue eyes were still the brightest blue color Chris had ever seen and for a moment she merely marveled at the fact that such a beautiful creature would be so taken with her. Then she remembered where they were and why and an agonizing depression sank in as she realized that he had not changed. She frowned as she took in his long dark hair. Reaching up, she caught hold of a lock of her own fiery red hair and brought it up to study it. It was still the same unruly tangled mess it had been since time immemorial and she guessed she was still the same as well.

Djibril softly rubbed his thumb into the crease between her brows, easing it away as he asked, "What nightmare plagues you this morning?"

Chris hesitantly confessed, "Well, I-I thought we would have changed. I mean, after last night…"

Djibril kissed the spot between her brows and said, "We are changing, just not as fast as we had thought. Can you not feel it?"

"Feel what?"

He studied her intently. Admittedly, he had been surprised to wake this morning to discover that still no outward physical changes had taken place in either of them. But he recalled how long it had taken Mikhail and Sarah to reach transformation. He had not been present for Baphomet's and Lisa's transformations, so he did not know how long theirs had taken.

He knew his own body had been changing ever since he had brought Chris to the Loric Realm, if not since the first moment they had made contact. But Chris was another matter. He felt changes within her energies and he thought that was signaling changes within her. But her physical strength, which by all rights should be increasing exponentially, instead appeared to ebb with each passing day.

He rubbed her skin and thought it felt smoother today than it had last night. That had to be a good sign and he decided he would take it as such. He pushed up and off the bed, turning toward the bathroom. "Come on, sleepyhead," he said. "We are going to the practice ring again."

Chris groaned in dismay and asked, "Do we have to?" She didn't want to go through the humiliation of being bested by each and every person out there again. Surely, they could find some other occupation for the day?

Instead of giving in to her plea for clemency, Djibril paused at the door to the restroom, saying, "If we have learned anything from the Shaitan attack, it is that we need to be better prepared. Shaitans are not the only dangerous creatures out there, nor are they the only ones who wish us ill. We must be ready for attack from both Shaitans and the elite Guard, for both will attack the Complex again."

Chris frowned. She had not known of Shaitans until the attack. Now there was some elite Guard they had to worry about? How many other dangers were out there that she didn't know about? She realized that, whether she was able to deal with it or not, just by being here with Djibril was putting her sister and her in danger and she had better do whatever she could to ensure nothing happened to either of them.

***

Chris was so sore she felt like crying every time she moved a muscle. That, of course, only served to piss her off and she snapped at anyone who dared speak to her. She felt bad about doing it, but she was exhausted and had just come from another grueling workout session during which she had been bested by each and every participant – including the kid named Samuel, who was a black belt compared to her!

It didn't matter how hard she tried, she had not gotten in a single punch or strike against anyone throughout the entire session. Now she could barely keep her eyes open, she was so tired. And all of this put together was proving too much for her to handle. Back in the human realm, she had been quite fit and spry, able to take out grown men with little effort. But here, she had weakened to the point that even a kid could beat her.

She was fuming over her continued failure at the practice sessions as she walked in silence alongside Djibril back to the Medical Facility. Fortunately for him, he appeared to have picked up on her bad mood because he, too, walked in silence. As they entered the building and then climbed the stairs up to the floor containing the room Hantsushept had arranged for them, Chris felt a growing sense of dread. She didn't want to be around anyone right now – not even him.

As they entered the room, Chris realized someone had been to leave a sumptuous feast for their late afternoon lunch. But she couldn't even think about eating, she was so disgusted! She went for a shower, hoping the hot water beating down upon her aching shoulders would ease her mood.

She was so tired. All she really wanted to do was to

sleep.

The shower felt good, easing her exhaustion somewhat, but she was still in a foul mood upon her return to the main room. She was glad Djibril excused himself for his own shower and, although she still was not hungry, she forced herself to eat. Unfortunately, his shower didn't last anywhere near as long as she had wished it would. Within minutes, he was back in the room, invading the silence and grating on her already frayed nerves.

The moment he touched her, she snapped at him.

"Look!" she barked. "I need some space!"

Djibril immediately backed off, both hands up in supplication. "My dear, I meant no disrespect," he softly remarked. "Shall I leave you here – is that what you wish?" he asked.

Chris wanted to say "yes". She wanted him to leave. But in her core, she really just wanted him to hold her, to hear him telling her everything would be okay and to know that she was safe, that he would always be there to protect her sister and her. It hurt to know she had become so weak that she would be the type of female who would need a man to protect her. It was kind of laughable, judging by Lyss' recent successes in the practice ring.

Finally, she hung her head and whispered, "No."

Immediately, Djibril's arms were around her, hugging her close to his freshly-showered skin, as he whispered, "It is all right, my dear heart. Everything will be all right."

Chris hugged him close. His heat felt so good to her suddenly frigid skin and she pressed as close to him as she physically could. The cold of the room and, indeed, of the world itself, felt like it was crushing in on her and she couldn't bear it. She clung to him for dear life, begging with her body and mind for him to save her. Djibril gave of himself without hesitation and she was soon embroiled in a rapid, no-holds-barred embrace with him on the nearby bed.

Before she even realized it was happening, she was once again in outer space, travelling up and along the strings. Her whole life had been lived for this – to discover where the strings led. She was moving upward, ever upward, speeding along the strings' path, searching for the source – but the source of what?

The next thing she knew, Djibril was there, calling to her, beckoning her back to the little room at the Medical Facility where he held the tiny cup to her lips. She drank without reservation. She would happily black out this day for the opportunity to simply sleep away the night. She was so tired.

***

Lyss stood in the observation room in awe, watching both the colorful images on the monitor hooked up to the sleek advanced imaging system Hantsushept had instructed her on and the live show of her sister and the Lori. Even before the readings indicated the two within the heated room in front of her had lost consciousness, Lyss could see changes happening. For instance, Chris' hair was already growing noticeably longer as she closed her eyes for sleep and Lyss caught two flashes of bright white light just before Djibril's eyes slid closed for the night.

Now, as she stood next to the floor-to-ceiling mirrored tempered glass separating the two rooms, Lyss wondered how much her twin would change and how different all their lives would become because of it.

Once again, she wished she could find someone she could feel so linked with, as Chris had done. But until she did, she would help her sister.

She watched as the changes took effect on the two within the room, occasionally checking to ensure everything was being recorded properly. Hopefully, Hantsushept would be able to gain enough data to be able to help any others who were meant to go through such changes and to discover why these few individuals were meant to endure them.

***

Chris heard someone talking in the dim recesses of her mind. She couldn't quite make out what was being said. Her brain, as usual, awoke by stages, so when something tiny and feather-light started touching her body in many different areas all at once, she didn't immediately realize what she was doing until she found herself standing on the side of the room, alone and nude in front of the mirrored surface of glass separating this room from the monitoring one.

She didn't even think about being monitored. She merely stood there staring at the reflection staring back at her. It was *not* the same one she had gone to bed with earlier. This one had wide glowing eyes whose irises were completely devoid of color. There was long white hair sprouting forth from the reflection's head and the moment Chris thought this, the ends of the hair moved of their own volition, reaching to touch different parts of her body, along with the reflection of it, itself, shown in the giant mirror of a wall, where tiny little tinkling sounds issued forth as the razor-sharp, metal-like ends of the hair touched the glass.

The creature's skin in the reflection appeared incredibly smooth and blemish-free. The underlying muscles appeared tight and firm and Chris experimentally flexed here and there, narrowing her newly-glowing eyes as she took in the fine movements. She felt almost half her age and a gleeful, excited energy rushed through her.

That's when she spotted two small glowing patches in the mirror emitting from deep within her reflection's core in the area of the abdomen. With shaking fingers, she lightly touched her own abdomen where the two little glowing dots resided. They were very warm and the moment her fingers passed over them, she heard what sounded like two soft tiny voices whispering back and forth with each other. Chris couldn't make out what they were saying, but she could definitely detect two distinct and separate voices. Although she couldn't be certain she was actually hearing the voices, she didn't believe they were occurring solely in her mind.

"C-Chris?" Djibril's gravelly, groggy voice suddenly echoed toward her and Chris immediately found herself standing directly next to the bed, facing her slowly-waking lover. She hadn't even thought about what she was doing. Djibril had called to her and she'd felt an odd tightening down the sides of her spine. The next thing she had known, she was standing on the side of the bed looking down upon what she realized was the newly-transformed figure of her dark Lori.

That term didn't fit him now, to be certain.

Even as she stood there staring at his countenance in amazement, long strands of his white hair moved to gently stroke her hand and arm and to entwine with the long strands connected to her own scalp. Djibril's eyelids finally opened to reveal two bright, glowing orbs staring up at her. After a momentary shock, a smile of prideful happiness suddenly spread across his face and he reached for her.

That's when he spotted the two glowing dots upon her abdomen.

His movements halted as he stared at the twin dots, although the long strands of hair from his head still carried on their exploration of her body. He appeared transfixed by the two tiny dots of light and Chris didn't know quite what to do or where to focus her own attention as he simply lay there staring at her abdomen. He was just as nude as she, and her eyes naturally strayed to the private area of his anatomy.

Even the pubic hair at the juncture between his legs was snow white now, though it appeared to be just regular old hair. The golden rod springing forth from within the white patch of hair was impressively large and semi-hard, even in Djibril's relaxed state and Chris, herself, became a bit transfixed.

Djibril's hand suddenly moved to touch deep within her at the juncture between her own legs, bringing Chris' attention once more to him and he smiled up at her, asking, "Twins?"

She didn't need to ask what he meant. The sounds of their twins' whispering voices echoed again through her mind, but this time Chris realized she wasn't the only one hearing the tiny voices.

What was that? asked Djibril's voice, though his mouth never once opened. Chris realized she was hearing his thoughts! What on earth?

I-It was the twins, she thought to him. The only indication she had that she had gotten through to him was that he immediately looked down at the two glowing dots and leaned forward to kiss them each softly. He closed his eyes and hugged her waist. Chris didn't know what else to do, so she slowly rubbed his shoulders and back. Djibril's hand between her legs continued its ministrations and Chris sighed heavily as sensation took over. She craved to touch him as well, and reached for him.

One of her hands strayed upon the little flap of skin on his back near the top of his spine.

What's this? she silently asked him.

It is called a "cutapi", he thought to her. *Yours should already have formed.*

Chris frowned, but then reached back behind herself to feel the spot directly between her shoulder blades near the top of her spine where a paper-thin flap of skin now resided. She reached under it and gently touched the spinal nodules there. Six tiny bumps were there, extremely sensitive to the touch, and she wondered how it all had gotten there.

It happened while we slept, Djibril's voice softly echoed within her mind. *See the blood on the bed?* When she frowned at the large stain on the lovely bed, he silently continued, *It appears the potion Hantsushept gave us worked its magic on both of us, after all. I felt nothing after falling asleep.*

Nothing? she thought, hiking a brow as he raised his glowing eyes to hers.

A slow smile plastered itself across his mouth as he suddenly reached to pull her face down to his.

Lyss watched the accumulating data with wonder. There was so much going on beneath the surface between her twin and the Lord Lori Djibril, yet they each looked as calm as could be on the outside. It was clear from the fMRI scans that the two were communicating telepathically.

Lyss felt a pang of both jealousy and guilt as she watched the couple. The jealousy she felt because she wished *she* could find someone who at least wanted her as much as Djibril obviously wanted Chris. The guilt Lyss felt because she had secretly thought of ways to kill Djibril before he had brought Chris and her to the Loric Realm.

After she had discovered who and what he was, the Christian part of her had kicked in and she had no longer felt the need to kill him. After all, he had turned out not to be one of those scum-sucking Arabs, like she had believed him to be originally.

Now, as Lyss watched her sister and Djibril becoming intimate again, she wondered if there would ever be anyone who would look at her like that. It was quite clear to Lyss that Chris would no longer wish to return to the human realm. Chris would never again accompany Lyss on any missions to destroy the true human infidels of the world. Lyss would be all alone. Lyss wondered how long she would have to continue with the missions before enough had been killed to avenge her parents' deaths. Would one more mission do it? Ten more? What was the magic number? It wasn't as if any number would ever bring her parents back. But then what? Never mind the fact that Lyss didn't want to return to the human realm anyway. She liked it here.

Lyss suddenly saw a spike on the data showing on the screen and realized there must also be some form of communication going on between the two in the next room, and then saw what appeared to be twin orbs of energy housed deep within the core of Chris' body. As Lyss' concentration shifted from what she saw on the color monitor to the live show going on in the room before her, it was obvious neither Djibril nor her sister understood anything coming from the energy orbs. It was also obvious, however, that the two before Lyss clearly were aware of the twin energy orbs and that they *were* being heard, if not understood.

The data continued to compile and Lyss continued her silent vigil as the sun arose on a new day.

***

Mikhail stood staring out the long open window in his office. The sun had barely risen on the nameless bay below, but already he could hear the soft sounds of the Labi younglings frolicking in the bay's shallow waters.

Just after they had come to live in this part of the world, Mikhail and Sarah had often made their way down to the bay, attempting to catch sight of the elusive mer creatures who inhabited the waters off this stretch of the Western coast. The songs the strange creatures sang each morning and night had enraptured Sarah just after they had come to live here, and Mikhail had enjoyed visiting the small cove just at the bottom of the high cliff walls above which they had built the Complex. They had never actually caught sight of the creatures, but they still heard their hauntingly beautiful songs each evening. Mikhail wondered if tonight would be the last night he and Sarah had together in this wonderful place they had each come to think of as home.

A knock at the door brought his mind back inside and he called, "Come."

Azra'il entered with a bright-eyed Sheely tucked in her usual spot in the crook of his arm. He closed the door and came to stand just on the other side of Mikhail's great Mahogany desk, where he simply stood staring at his brother.

Mikhail didn't really feel like talking with Azra'il. In fact, he didn't really feel like acknowledging this particular brother's very existence, at the moment.

Azra'il harrumphed and shook his head as he seated himself in one of the high-backed chairs stationed directly before the large desk.

Mikhail turned back to the window, a muscle working at his jaw as he contemplated tossing his brother out the window so that Sarah, Sheely and he could simply get back to living their lives the way they had envisioned before Azra'il had so unexpectedly insinuated himself into their small part of the world.

"And I wonder how Sheely would have fared had I not been there on the morning of her birth," Azra'il softly speculated.

"What do you mean?" Mikhail demanded, as anger slammed into him and he turned to regard his brother once more.

"I mean," he said, "Sheely would never have survived being born so early had my energies not assisted her body to grow as quickly as it needed to just to breathe."

Mikhail plopped down into his chair, his mind reviewing everything that had happened that terrible morning at the Medical Facility. Hantsushept had been working on Sheely the moment Mikhail had come to and, from what he had learned from his mind-link with Baphomet that day, Mikhail knew the good doctor had been working on her for quite some time before that. It was true, Sheely had been born quite prematurely and Mikhail knew an infant's lung function was one of the last obstacles to overcome when facing a premature birth.

As his brother sat before him, staring confidently back at him, Mikhail suddenly knew Azra'il was right. Somehow, he knew his brother's energies had helped Sheely's body to live when she otherwise most assuredly would have died. Mikhail knew they didn't have the necessary equipment here at the Complex for such complications and, although Hantsushept was practically a miracle worker in the Health Sciences field, Mikhail knew the old Kurr could not have influenced the growth of his daughter's lungs. It appeared he owed his daughter's very existence to Azra'il.

Azra'il frowned, adjusting his position in the chair and then said, "I cannot claim intentional responsibility, Mikhail. I did not know my energies helped, merely that she instinctively took them from me as soon as I first approached her."

Sheely made a faint noise and the two males each heard and understood her to mean, *I knew what I was doing!*

The two males frowned in irritation.

"Okay," Mikhail said on a heavy sigh. "So it was fate. You were obviously meant to be together and I will not toss you off the cliff wall. So what? I still am not happy with this situation and I am not happy with the plan you and Sarah have concocted. She is my mate and I do not wish her to come to any harm – which she most definitely will should she return to Lorim City!"

Azra'il held up a staying hand, effectively halting Mikhail's tirade. "I understand your concerns," he said. "Sarah is mother to the one creature on this planet to whom I am bound and she is an essential part of her life. Whether

Sarah and you realize it or not, Sheely still draws energy from the two of you and I would never do anything to jeopardize her livelihood. She needs both of you, as well as me, in her life to sustain her until her own body is strong enough to sustain itself."

Mikhail quietly absorbed this information. A sense of hope sprang back to life within his chest. He had thought Sheely no longer needed Sarah or him, now that she had transformed with Azra'il. However, if what his brother said was true, then Mikhail and Sarah still had a role to play in their infant daughter's life and Mikhail might actually get to experience the thrills of fatherhood.

"*Of course*, she is still your daughter," Azra'il said. "And she needs you now more than ever before." He leaned in closer to Mikhail. "Sheely will never be safe until we convince both houses of the Sanhedrin that our Realm is not in danger from the humans, that indeed it depends on humans being allowed into it. But before we can convince them of that, we must first allay their fears where Sarah is concerned and then we must expose the traitor. Surely you understand that?"

Mikhail closed his eyes. He hadn't yet made love to Sarah since they had come back from the blue dimension. He was trying to give her time to heal, yet Sarah and Azra'il wished to leave for Lorim City as soon as possible in attempts to beat the Guard who had stolen away into the night when the Shaitan scum had attacked and inadvertently allowed them opportunity to escape. As he had lain in bed with her last night and this morning, he had held onto her so tightly, fearing those might be their last moments together for a very long time. Now that fear exploded within his heart and he felt momentarily overwhelmed.

Suddenly, Sheely was there in his mind with him. His eyes flew open and he watched as she raised her two small brightly-glowing eyes to his, staring deep into his soul, her voice sounding in his mind. *Mommy can help. She wants to help. She wants to keep us safe. She is afraid, but she loves us very much and she knows this is what has to be done so that everything gets back to where it needs to be. Please help her not feel so afraid, Daddy. She is so afraid, but she knows this is the right thing to do. Please, Daddy?*

Tears overflowed and Mikhail was immediately on his feet, rounding the desk and reaching for his daughter. *Of course Daddy will help her, sweetheart,* he silently told her. *You are safe. Mommy and Daddy will make everything safe for you.*

Sheely's hair wrapped tightly around his arms and torso. *I love you, Daddy.*

Mikhail buried his face in the small juncture between her neck and shoulder, crying openly, and whispered, "I love you, Sheely."

***

Djibril came awake slowly, feeling for the first time in his life as if waking was a chore that he definitely did not like. Every single day of his life that he could remember he had awakened quite easily, brushing off the night without any difficulty. Today, however, he felt himself struggling just to drag open his eyes. But he was glad when he finally did because that's when he saw Chris' eyes open.

A slow smile curved her lips and he moved in to softly kiss her for the first time today. Her glowing eyes slid closed on the kiss and she eagerly responded, touching her tongue to his lips to request entry into his mouth. Djibril was only too happy to oblige.

Suddenly, however, Chris pulled back and lay staring directly into his eyes, a slight frown marring her perfect little features.

What is wrong, my love? Djibril silently asked, concern filling him as he watched her closely. She didn't respond, didn't even move or blink. She merely continued staring directly into his eyes. Djibril rose onto an elbow and reached over to cup the back of her head, gently massaging her there as he asked aloud, "Chris? Sweetheart, are you okay?"

Her eyes still stared forward, as if she was in a daze and she couldn't see anything around herself. Djibril's heart rate increased and a wealth of fear for his mate streaked down his spine. He sat up, climbing onto his knees, and forced her over onto her back, loudly calling in his gravelly voice, "Christiana! Chris! Sweetheart, wake up!"

The door from the observation room swung open and Hantsushept rushed in.

"Do not disturb her, my Lord," the Kurr instructed.

"What?" Djibril demanded, sick with fear. "Why? What is happening?" His eyes raked over her, searching for any signs of injury.

"Her Alpha waves are off the chart, sir," Lyss said excitedly as she entered the room carrying some type of electronic tablet. She thrust it into Hantsushept's hands. "She's seeing something, for certain."

Djibril returned his gaze to his lover. "You mean like a vision?"

"We cannot tell from these simple instruments," Hantsushept explained. "However, there is massive neural activity going on." He turned to the human, instructing, "Take her vitals."

Djibril moved to allow his mate's sister access to take the readings, swallowing a huge lump of fear. "Should we not attempt to bring her back from wherever it is she has gone?" he asked.

Hantsushept shook his head. "My Lord, I do not believe that would benefit the Lady at all. In fact, I fear it may do substantial harm to her psyche were she to be interrupted in such an abrupt manner, for we have no idea what she is experiencing, wherever she is."

Djibril looked Chris up and down, frantically searching for anything he could think of to bring her back. "What if I attempt to mind-link with her?" he feverishly asked.

That got the good doctor's attention. His brows shot up into his hairline and he shrugged, indicating the Lori should give it a try.

Djibril laid back down onto the bed beside Chris, reaching over to place his hand upon her brow as he closed his eyes and tried to relax. Concentrating on reaching her mind with his, Djibril reached out to her. He could feel her energies and he rushed toward them, melding his own with hers. He felt that her energies were stretched very far and he traveled up along what he guessed was her tether line. It kept going and going. At one point, Djibril looked down and realized he was already far outside the earth's atmosphere and still he could not see where her energies had stopped.

He continued moving up along the line, determined to get her back.

The human and the Kurr standing by the giant bed started all of a sudden as the room was unexpectedly filled with a host of Lorim, four white-haired and glowy-eyed and one normal.

"What happens here?" Mikhail immediately demanded.

The unflappable Hantsushept explained what had happened to the best of his knowledge and the newcomers stared in fearful amazement at the two unmoving figures lying prone upon the bed.

"Tell me exactly what Djibril said before he attempted the mind-link," Mikhail instructed.

Israfil stepped around the bed and leaned in to place his hand upon his brother's forehead, closing his eyes in concentration. A second later, his eyes whipped open and he turned to the gathering announcing, "We need Azra'il for this."

Almost before the words were out of his mouth, the Lori appeared, dropping his shields to reveal Sheely and himself. He handed Sheely over to Sarah without a word and made his way over to stand beside Israfil. His eyes narrowed first upon Djibril's form, but then quickly switched over to Chris' form, a deep frown marring his features. "How the...?" he asked distractedly.

Sarah grabbed hold of Mikhail's arm and Lisa moved even closer to Baphomet as they all fixed their gazes on their newest sister.

Azra'il slowly sat down onto the bed, tilting his head as he digested the information he had received upon his initial examination of the female. She had a tether, except it wasn't a tether. He had never seen anything like it, but it looked like she had stretched her energies so high away from her body that it had thinned out to the mere width of a normal tether line. Azra'il could not tell how high up her stretched energy line went, but he believed somewhere up there would be where Djibril would be located.

As he studied those before him, Mikhail finally caught sight of the energy line stretching up from the newly-turned Lori female and through his mind-link with her, Sarah soon had her eye on it as well. Soon, every transformed Lori in the room could clearly see it and all five of them stared not at the two lying on the bed, but upward, as they tried to discern how far up the lines reached.

"Wait," Israfil suddenly said. "There are two distinct energy lines. See?" He pointed to the second one, not stretched quite as thin as the first one. The shock everyone felt at learning that Israfil was also able to detect the energy lines shook everyone to the core, but all remained silent as they continued wondering what could be done to save the two newly-transformed Lorim on the bed.

The human and the Kurric doctor stood wondering what on earth the Lord had meant, for they had seen nothing where Lord Israfil had pointed.

Azra'il followed the second line back to its origin. "That comes from Djibril," he announced as he climbed farther up onto the bed, moving to settle on his knees between the two Lorim lying there. "Mikhail?" he asked.

Mikhail immediately stepped forward, coming to stand directly across from Azra'il on the side of the bed closest to where Chris lay. "What do you need of me?"

"See if you can mind-link with Djibril," Azra'il instructed. He did not look at Mikhail. Instead, he raised his hands and cupped them around the entwined energy lines before him, ringing the bundle with his fingers, but not touching it.

Mikhail closed his eyes in concentration, directing his energies toward Djibril's energy signature, reaching out in a desperate search for his brother. Only a minute later, however, he opened his eyes. "I cannot locate him," he announced.

Azra'il slowly nodded, still monitoring the energy bundle within his hands. "Israfil," he said. "Help Mikhail establish a mind-link with Djibril. Baphomet, you may need to assist as well, for he is very far from this room, from what I can tell."

Baphomet gave Lisa a quick glance and then moved to stand behind Mikhail, with Israfil rounding the bed to come to stand beside Baphomet. All three closed their eyes in concentration. A second later, Azra'il's eyes closed.

Sarah stared in wonder at the energy lines that were now clearly visible to her. There were not just the two extending upward from Chris and Djibril as they lay upon the bed. Now, there were four more, as the energies of the four Lorim brothers had also traveled up and out of their bodies only to disappear into some unseen region of the Universe.

The room was deathly quiet as the remaining members of their small group waited. As the minutes ticked by, though, Sarah felt the first stirrings of some unwanted disturbance invading the silence. She checked Sheely, wondering what on earth the odd feeling could be. Then, as she looked around for the source of the disturbance, her gaze fell upon Lisa and she knew exactly what was happening. The problem was that Sarah did not know how to stop it from happening. She needed either Baphomet or Israfil for that.

"Lyss," she said, getting the human's attention. "Here, take Sheely." The human woman immediately moved to comply, but was bleeding in a heartbeat as soon as she reached for the babe.

"Sheely!" Sarah yelled, horrified that her daughter would do such a thing. Then she heard Sheely's voice in her mind.

Lisa was shaking by now and Sarah didn't know what to do other than to just put Sheely in front of herself while Sarah tightly hugged Lisa face-to-face. As soon as she was close up against the woman, Sheely placed her tiny palms against Lisa's chest by her shoulders and laid her tiny cheek against the bare throat below Lisa's chin. Sarah could feel the wave of voices now headed out to sea, leaving her sister's mind, but Lisa could still sense them waiting in the background, searching for any opportunity to encroach on her vulnerable mind, along with that of her silent child Cabal still housed within her womb.

Concentrate, mommy, Sheely's soft voice urged and Sarah took a deep breath, sending her thoughts out to Lisa, assuring the Lori that Sheely and she would not leave until their mates returned. Lisa's form relaxed just the slightest bit and Sarah knew she had gotten the message.

Hantsushept, who had immediately assisted Lyss in the small observation room with the gaping wound on her forearm courtesy of Sheely's hair, now studied the readings coming from each group of Lorim in the suite before him. There was so much activity going on all over the place it was difficult to keep up. A part of him was very distressed and fearful that his Lords or Ladies would suffer from whatever was occurring in there, but there was another part of him that was very excited by all the data being collected. "Fascinating!" he whispered.

That's when he remembered how deadly the evolved Loric hair strands could be and he immediately turned toward his new human assistant. Luckily, he was able to catch her just as she collapsed. He gently laid her down onto the floor, hoping beyond hope the Lorim in the other room would quickly finish their tasks so that at least one of them would be able to help revive the suffering human girl.

Mikhail moved forever upward, sticking as close to the energy line as he could without touching it. There was something about it that kept him at a safe distance away, as if he feared that to touch it might pull him off to whatever place it was that had so enraptured his brother and new sister that they had simply forgotten their bodies back on the physical plane on Earth.

Keep moving, Mikhail, Baphomet's straining voice echoed in his mind. *They cannot be too far ahead.*

Mikhail doubled his concentration, hoping his brother was right as he stretched his own energy so thin it hurt. He was determined to retrieve his relatives from their captor, whatever the cost.

Suddenly, Azra'il was there, pushing all three of his brothers even farther up and up along the two energy lines they followed. His well of strength felt endless as it pulled them so far upward the other three could no longer feel their physical selves back in the room at the Medical Facility. They were all moving at such an incredible speed that only streaks of light could be observed and the three became dizzy from the experience. Up ahead in the distance, a dim light appeared. It grew the closer they got to it, and then, in a flash, Azra'il was everywhere, enveloping everyone, including Djibril and Chris, and the entire assemblage returned in lightning speed to their waiting bodies back at the Complex, each slamming back into his or her respective physical encasement.

Pain was engulfing, as hearts began beating again and blood coursed through veins. Each standing Lori fell to his hands and knees, breathing hard and trying to keep from vomiting. Djibril and Chris both gasped for breath as their eyes opened upon the simple scene of their room at the Medical Facility.

Azra'il blinked and then looked at the two, searching for any signs of a tether line on either of them. Complete souls resided within each of them as far as he could tell, and he nodded. He then turned to find Sheely.

"Baphomet," he called, catching his brother's attention as he climbed off the bed and made his way over to the three females near the other end of the room.

Baphomet crawled to get turned around and then haltingly picked himself up off the floor to get to Lisa. He lost his battle with his stomach and vomited all over the floor before finally reaching the trio of female Lorim, at which point he reached in to extricate Lisa from the hugging group. Lisa didn't hesitate. Instead, she immediately grabbed hold of him and hugged him in close to her, plastering her body all the way up against his.

"Leece," he whispered, cradling the back of her head with his big hand. He squeezed his eyes shut as he whispered, "It is done, sweet Lisa. You need not fear them any longer. I am here, my heart. I am here."

Sarah's eyes opened and Azra'il immediately reached for Sheely. Sarah surrendered her daughter and then turned to find Mikhail. He was still doubled over on the floor next to the bed and Sarah went to him, helping him to stand and then to recover. He held onto her as he fought wave after wave of nausea.

Israfil lost his control and vomited.

Mikhail and Sarah both bent to help their lone brother. Then they heard Sheely calling out to them to tell them Lyss needed their help. They both entered the observation room and bent to the task of withdrawing as much of the milky-white venom from within her veins as possible. Within minutes, the wounds looked much better and the human was even conscious again as she joked with Hantsushept about never having thought she would have to worry about being killed by deadly hair!

It took about fifteen minutes until everyone in the bedroom fully recovered. In the meantime, a couple of Kurr came in to clear away any mess. When the servants were finished and gone and the others finally recovered, they all turned toward the two still on the bed. Haltingly, Chris and Djibril recounted what had happened.

"I had just awakened and Djibril was awake, too," Chris explained. "Then before I even knew what was happening, I was rising up from this room, going up and up. I saw Djibril lying on the bed with my body and Lyss and Hantsushept in the monitoring room. Then I went up through the roof and out into the air above the trees. I didn't even think about what was happening. I just kept going up. Next thing I knew, I was up above the whole planet and…" She stopped and frowned as she thought about what she had seen. "Next," she continued, "I saw all these machines surrounding the planet, hundreds, if not thousands of them. Some were even stationed far away from the planet, simply moving in orbit with it around the sun. It was so strange because it looked like all these little glowing strings were attached to each one of the machines. The strings stretched from something down on the planet up through the machines and then farther up to some point I couldn't see.

"I remember wondering where they all went and then I was zooming through space, passing planets and stars and all manner of other things. I saw comets and asteroids and other… things."

"What kind of other things?" Israfil asked.

Chris looked up at him, frowning in confusion. Then she turned to Djibril and softly said, "I think they were creatures, aliens inside alien ships."

The group digested this information, each marveling at the scope of what this meant.

"That's when I felt Djibril there, catching up with me."

Her eyes narrowed and she suddenly turned more fully toward him, astounded, saying, "You knew!"

He looked away for a second, the whole journey playing out again in his own mind.

"You knew about them!" she softly accused.

"Y-Yes," he haltingly said. "Although, I do not recall *how* I knew about them."

"Knew about what?" Lyss asked, as she finally recovered enough to return to the bedroom where the others were gathered.

"The machines surrounding the planet," Sarah explained.

Chris shot Sarah a look of astonishment. "You knew, too?"

Sarah moved to sit on the bed alongside Chris' legs. "I saw visions while I was human. I didn't understand what I saw at that time, but once I came here and transformed, I finally understood."

"What are the strings?" Chris asked.

"Those are soul-strings, or tether lines," Azra'il answered from the seat he occupied in the corner of the room. He still held Sheely's now-sleeping form in the crook of his arm as his body steadily replenished her energies.

"You all knew?" Chris demanded, feeling somewhat like the last to know this big secret as she looked around at the other Lorim crowding the room.

Djibril took her hand, drawing her attention back to him. "It is not something humans, or even regular Kurr, can see," he explained. "In fact, up to this point in my life, I have not been able to see them myself. It is only since transforming that I have apparently developed the ability to see them."

"But you knew," she accused, sad that he had not shared that with her.

"I-I think it was somewhere in my memory from…," he paused, thinking, searching for the root of the memory. Suddenly, his gaze darted to Mikhail's face and he said, "I had vague impressions of it from the mind-link with Mikhail that first time when Sarah and her human family were missing."

"And how did you find out?" Chris asked Mikhail.

Mikhail wrapped an arm around the bedpost directly behind Sarah and smiled his usual lop-sided smile, saying, "I first learned of them when Sarah and I began our transformations. Up until then, I had not been able to see tether lines or any such thing."

Chris swung her gaze toward Baphomet and Lisa, who immediately nodded, saying, "Not until we transformed did we know of them."

When she looked to Azra'il, he merely lifted a brow as he looked at Djibril.

"Azra'il has always known of them, sweetheart," Djibril said. "It is one of the gifts with which he was born."

Chris looked around. Her gaze fell finally onto Israfil and she opened her mouth to ask him, but he suddenly wrapped himself in his shields and was instantly gone. Turning back to Djibril, she asked, "Why did he leave?"

Djibril raised her hand to his lips, brushing the backs of her fingers with a light kiss and saying, "We shall discuss Israfil later, sweetheart." He smiled at her to soften his words.

A thought suddenly occurred to Djibril and he turned back to Azra'il, asking, "What would have happened had you not found us and brought us back?"

Azra'il adjusted his position in the chair and frowned

slightly. "I can only speculate, as I have never encountered such a thing," he explained. "I believe your soul energies would most likely have thinned to the point that eventually they simply abandoned your physical shells, if you will, on this plane as they caught up with the rest of themselves wherever you went. That would effectively strand them to float without direction or control forever wherever you had gone."

Djibril and Chris shivered simultaneously, for each recalled their last position before being found by Azra'il and the others. They had been very far out in the far reaches of some distant galaxy.

"Wait," Chris said. "The tether lines we followed were still going, far past where we were when you found us."

"Yes," Azra'il said tightly. It was still a sore point with him that he had always been unable to see the place to which the tether lines were linked.

Sweetheart, please do not continue with this discussion, Djibril's voice in her mind requested. It was clear the subject had upset her new brooding brother holding the infant Lori and Chris nodded without looking at Djibril.

"Djibril?" Mikhail suddenly asked. "Did you experience the same type of vision... quest?"

He thought for a moment, frowning. Then, he said, "N-No. At first, I went to find Chris in order to help her back home. But then I realized I could see things, soul energies. I saw everything as if it was on a grid and I knew the exact location of each of the things. The farther out we went, the more I came to know – the locations of things, that is."

"What kinds of things?" Sarah asked.

"Soul energies, mostly," Djibril explained. "I saw the distinct energies of each and every soul surrounding this planet. Then, when I got farther out, I saw soul energies surrounding other planets, or just moving through space in both large and small groups. Sometimes there would be singular ones just floating along on some unseen current, but they were usually in groups when I encountered them."

"And the farther away from the planet you went?" Sarah asked.

He frowned. "Outside our own system of planets, there were other planetary systems where what appeared to be sentient creatures inhabited the physical realm. Each of those had a tether line that ran through similar machines that surrounded the inhabitable planets."

Sarah turned to look up into Mikhail's face.

Mikhail immediately asked Chris, "You said you saw ships?"

She nodded, recalling the memory. "I thought they were ships."

"Were there any near our planet?" he asked.

She shook her head. "Not that I recall."

Mikhail reached out to Sarah, placing his large hand onto her shoulder where he massaged the muscle there. Sarah's gaze fell to her hands in her lap. He had the sense that she was sad about something and Djibril's voice sounded again in Chris' mind, urging her to change the subject.

Chris realized she was in way over her head here. This group of Lorim, even though she was now one of them, had far too many secrets for her to know what she should and should not discuss around them and she felt instantly out of her depth. Just then, a huge yawn escaped her and she turned to curl into Djibril's waiting arms. Her eyes fell closed as she heard her lover tell everyone else she needed some rest now. The others immediately apologized for keeping her so long and left without further ado.

Djibril moved to a more comfortable position next to her, his arm still holding her tight to his side and Chris succumbed to the exhaustion suddenly swamping her mind and body. Djibril felt just the slightest sensation of guilt that he had induced a deep exhaustion within his lover. However, she had started feeling uncomfortable around the others and, if he was honest with himself, so had he. He hadn't realized his brothers and sisters had developed such incredible abilities, and a part of him wondered if there were not somehow a danger inherent in the development of such astounding power.

He squeezed Chris' form closer to his body, a deep-rooted flash of fear pulsing through him as he recalled how quickly she had just left. He had had to push really hard to catch up with her, but he had known somehow that her journey had not been taxing on her energies in the least. She had simply gone, without even a thought to caution. She was so powerful and yet so naïve about her power, and Djibril felt even more keenly a sense of responsibility to protect her than he had previously.

His last lucid thought before exhaustion from the day's events claimed his own consciousness was that she would have to be made to understand that she could *never again* go *up!*

Hantsushept and Lyss. sat in the small monitoring room connected to the suite where the mated Lori couple slumbered, each involved in interpreting the data that had been and continued to be collected by the monitoring machines lining the walls of the suite. Every now and then, the old Kurr would reverently whisper, "Fascinating!"

Lyss simply searched for anything she could discover that might help her sister progress beyond what was obviously a dangerous period of her transformation from a human being into a Lori.

Chapter 19

Mikhail walked silently along with the others as their group left the Medical Facility. This new development had everyone's head spinning and they all needed time to adjust to what they had learned with today's activities. Mikhail, however, was more concerned with the plan Azra'il and, more importantly, Sarah had of returning to Lorim City, and he did not look forward to the meeting he believed the two would attempt to convene with him this very evening.

He wished the two of them would simply forget this idea and leave things alone. The Lorim were now more powerful than ever and should have no difficulty defeating anyone who was foolish enough to lay siege to the Complex, be that Kurr or human, no matter their number. Of course the humans living at the Complex, which would soon expand exponentially in number, would still require the protection of the Lorim, but Mikhail believed they could figure out some solution, if only they would all work together.

A wealth of frustration filled him as he thought of all the possibilities facing Sarah if she returned to his old home.

Sarah walked along with the others with thoughts of her own occupying her mind. She had erected a buffer between Mikhail and herself the very second he had begun thinking about the plan she and Azra'il had devised for their return to Lorim City. He had known she had done it and she refused to feel ashamed for having done so. She had been through each and every one of his arguments and she still believed she was following the right plan.

What troubled her more at the moment was the fact that she had still been unable to contact or even locate Thomas or Nera. Well, actually that and the knowledge that there was something seriously bothering Israfil. When he had taken off unexpectedly earlier, she had almost gone after him. Everyone had been stunned when he had left so suddenly, not to mention by the fact that he had been able to see the tether lines. But Sarah understood a bit better than most of the others and she believed she could possibly help him. The difficulty was that Israfil was not someone who easily opened himself up when others offered their help.

She glanced up suddenly and, for just a moment, thought she had seen a flash of someone she recognized moving in her garden. An urgent need to go there sprang to life within her chest and she quietly excused herself from the group, extricating her hand from within Mikhail's grasp and walking off alone.

Mikhail, who had stopped the minute she had made to pull away, stood and stared after her until Azra'il placed a hand upon his shoulder, saying, "Let her go, brother. She will be fine."

Mikhail turned to regard his daughter's future mate, frowning as he wondered why Sarah had left. With the buffer up between them, however, he could only guess at the reason. He finally resumed his slow walk toward the Main House of the Complex

In the garden behind the Main House, Sarah discovered the person she thought she had seen in the garden was not who was actually there, for it was Israfil who walked slowly along the gravel path. Sarah's approach was marked by the sound of the tiny pieces of gravel crunching together beneath her feet and the blue-eyed Lori stopped and turned to watch her approach.

"Well, hello stranger," she said, a broad smile lighting up her glowing face in the twilight pervading the garden.

Israfil did not return her smile, merely nodding once to her instead. He turned to continue his walk and Sarah fell into step beside him. She turned to watch his face every now and then, searching for some conversation starter she could use to get him to open up a little.

"Please, do not," he suddenly said, his voice filled with exhaustion and sadness.

There was no point in asking what he meant, but an errant thought he had not hidden suddenly reached her powerful mind and she gasped, stopping dead in her tracks as she looked at him. Israfil glanced at her, but then did a double take as he caught the drift of her thoughts. A deep frown marred his perfect features momentarily as he reached out with his own powerful mind, but he was soon shaking his head, saying, "I am sorry, Sarah. There is something blocking me. I cannot detect him anywhere."

Sarah sighed, suddenly deflated. "Well, thank you for tryin' at least," she said. She had hoped he could help her discover Thomas' whereabouts, since she had caught him thinking about her son for some reason. It was just one more thing for her to file away to take out at a later date to examine. She, herself was now exhausted and she asked if they could sit for a while, motioning to one of the comfortable benches Mikhail had built into the garden for her.

As they sat, Israfil said, "He is worried about you, you know."

Sarah sighed. She knew her mate was nervous about this plan she and Azra'il had hatched. "I know," she said.

Israfil looked out over the beautiful blooms crowding the little garden. The night creatures were softly calling to one another and then the hauntingly beautiful lowing of the Labi started up. The two Lorim sat listening for a while, wondering what the elusive creatures were like – and wondering about other things neither one felt like discussing with the other.

As the moon moved high in the cloudless sky, Sarah softly asked, "Do you think I should go with Azra'il back to the City?"

He frowned, considering his answer. After a moment, he said, "I cannot objectively answer the question."

"What do you mean?" Sarah asked.

He turned to regard her in the bright moonlight shining directly down onto their little spot in the garden. "I have come to care too much for you and Mikhail to be able to view the situation objectively and without emotion," he explained. "I feel my brother's fear for your safety and so it becomes my own."

Sarah swallowed a lump of her own emotion and looked away. She had come to care for Israfil a great deal since coming to the Loric Realm, but it was a surprise to hear that he had come to care for her as well. She had thought of him as an emotional nomad due to the things she had learned of his past experiences. But now it seemed she had grossly misjudged him and she was glad. She turned and smiled up at him, *genuinely* smiled this time.

He reached and took her hand in his, giving her a small smile in return as he gently squeezed her hand.

A rush of energy suddenly caught their attention and they turned to watch as Mikhail dropped his shields just off to their right, a muscle working in his jaw.

Israfil immediately released Sarah's hand and stood, nodding once to his brother and then politely excusing himself. He was gone in an instant and a part of Sarah felt sorrowful that they hadn't had a little more time alone. She could feel Mikhail's jealous energy shooting out toward her like tiny stinging sparks and she quickly dropped the buffer between them so he could discover that nothing had actually happened between his brother and her.

He immediately looked contrite, but Sarah knew this was only the first battle of the night. She heaved a heavy sigh in preparation for the coming fight.

Mikhail reached her in two strides, pulling her up and into his arms. "I do not wish to fight with you," he said.

Sarah now felt an overwhelming sadness, and something else, coming from him. What was it? As she silently hugged him back, she realized it was resignation. Pulling back, she sought his eyes, looking deep into their subdued glowing depths.

"I ask only that you give me a few more hours," he said in an anguished voice. "I just want to hold you to me for a few hours more."

Sarah melted inside. She had never felt so loved or so trapped. She could see no other solution to their problem, although she had spent almost every waking hour since she and Azra'il had concocted their plan searching for any other solution, but none had been forthcoming. Either they all lived life on the run from the elite Guard while allowing the human realm to fall into utter chaos, or she allowed Azra'il to take her prisoner and return her to Lorim City.

As she embraced her lover again, wrapping her arms and legs tightly about his warm, lithe body, she silently told him how much he meant to her, all the while taking whatever energy he could offer in the hopes of discovering some way to get a part of him inside her so that she could carry it with her when she left.

Mikhail transported them both to their bedroom back in the house without even thinking about it. He just wanted to be lying in their bed with her, holding her naked body up against his own, making love to her however she would allow. As his shields fell away, revealing they had actually landed on the bed, he didn't even hesitate or wait until they had sat down on the mattress. He simply pulled at her clothing, ripping the fine silk blouse she wore, caring not one whit that he destroyed the rich fabric. The pants she wore came next, the buttons on the fly popping off to go scattering across the room unheeded.

Mikhail was suddenly in a race against time, against the world – both Kurric and human – and he couldn't get inside her waiting cool depths quickly enough! He forced her slower body quickly down onto the mattress, spreading her legs with one powerful hand, immediately parting her folds and entering her with his fingers as he cupped her soft feminine mound. She was ready for him and he was all too ready to oblige. He moved above her, not even bothering to remove his clothing all the way. He merely pulled his slacks down just enough so that his hardened staff was freed from its bondage and then he entered her, ramming into her cool body all the way up to the hilt.

"Ah!" each one shouted, as if this was the first time they had been together in years and their bodies had been starved and only by joining could they finally be fulfilled once more. Their lovemaking was fierce and intense. Thankfully, her Loric healing abilities had kicked in after Sheely's birth and Sarah was more than able to withstand the onslaught.

Mikhail was too urgent to be gentle with her and Sarah loved him all the more for it, for she felt a sense of desperation as she clung to his sweat-drenched back, pulling him in as deep as her body would allow and then using her legs and feet to push him just a little deeper inside herself. He was jutting up into her body so fast and hard it hurt, but Sarah didn't care. She wanted to feel every inch of him inside her and she would have pushed him even farther if she had been able.

A scream ripped from deep within as she climaxed and she shuddered, her muscles clenching and unclenching in rapid succession as Mikhail suddenly jerked uncontrollably, pounding into her as he lost all control. His booming voice sounded then, loud enough to wake the entire Complex, and his body tensed. When he finished, he collapsed onto her, still inside her and too weak even to pull out and move over to her side.

Sarah lay beneath his heavy form, completely covered in sweat and more exhausted than she could ever recall being. She didn't even have enough energy to lift her hand to touch her lover. And she felt completely sated.

Mikhail slowly tucked his face down into the juncture between her neck and shoulder and very lightly brushed his lips across her skin. The memory of what had driven him to take her so recklessly suddenly came crashing back into his mind and he painfully squeezed his eyes shut, wishing only to block it out until it was no longer true.

I love you, Sarah, he silently told her, which was all he could do since he hadn't even the energy to speak.

A single tear rolled from the corner of Sarah's eye, slowly trickling down to rest in the thin shell of her little ear.

***

Azra'il released a heavy sigh. He didn't want to do this. He didn't want to leave Sheely – not after he had only just found her. As he sensed his brother and new sister approaching the study, he smiled tremulously down at the glowing babe he cradled within his arms. Her chin wobbled a little and he felt a stab of heartache coming from her. She was not yet adept at controlling emotions. She was trying to be brave for him, for he knew she believed this to be the right thing for Sarah and him to do. However, Azra'il knew she could feel what this was doing to him. She simply could not hide her emotions from him as her psyche picked up on his feelings while having to deal with her own as well.

The door opened as a very subdued and solemn Mikhail and Sarah entered.

A sob tore unchecked from Sheely's chest before she could stop it and he quickly held her closer to his chest, bending down to whisper to her, once again assuring her everything would be over soon and they would be back together, even though he had no idea when or even if he and Sarah would make it out of this game alive. The brave front she presented when he finally pulled back enough to look down into her face again was nearly his undoing and he quickly turned to Mikhail to hand her off. Those gathered around the room merely continued silently watching.

Sarah looked around and then frowned as she moved off toward another. "Suriyah," she said in surprise. "What happened to you?"

Suriyah stood and sighed heavily, explaining, "I was tracking the elite Guardsmen who escaped. You and Azra'il should have enough time to beat them to the City if you leave within the hour."

Sarah turned her gaze back to Mikhail and, although this was not the news he had hoped for, he held a hand out for her while he said, "Thank you, Suri."

Sarah gripped his hand like it was a lifeline and she edged right up against him, suddenly needing his warmth more than ever before.

Just then, a serving Kurr entered the room. He brought with him a box which he placed onto Mikhail's desk and then left. Without a word, Azra'il moved over to the desk. Nobody else moved. No one else even breathed as Azra'il reached in and pulled out a pair of the dreaded binders. As soon as the dull gray metal binders came into view, several gasps issued forth around the room.

The things appeared innocuous enough, but each and every transformed member of the group could suddenly *feel* vibrations coming off the binders, almost like the feeling one would experience when someone's fingernails scratched down a chalkboard. The very air itself seemed to crackle with vile energy.

Azra'il cringed just carrying the things over to Sarah. He checked quickly to make sure they hadn't accidentally been activated as a strong metallic taste invaded his mouth, but they were switched off. Sarah disengaged from Mikhail's hold and held out both hands. As soon as Azra'il touched the binders to the skin of Sarah's outstretched wrists, he could feel her tense up and he knew the things were already affecting her.

Sarah was suddenly wracked with pain in her wrists and hands, like tiny paper cuts that ran deep. She immediately threw up a buffer so that Mikhail wouldn't notice. Next, she threw a cautious glance Israfil's way to see if he had noticed. His poker face was in place, as usual, but she got the impression he knew exactly what was going on. To his credit, however, he remained quiet and watchful.

Mikhail felt as if something was wrong. Everyone was so still. He carefully studied Sarah's face, searching for any signs of distress.

He could sense nothing from her mind and from what he could see, she appeared to be as yet unaffected by the evil binders.

"Come," Azra'il said, keeping his face neutral as he placed a hand on Sarah's shoulder to help guide her from the room. Fortunately, no one else attempted to touch her and Sarah and Azra'il were soon on their way to Lorim City. They tried flying with Sarah wearing the deactivated binders, using only Azra'il's shields for transportation, but the vibrations and painful shocks from the binders caused too much interference and soon they had to land at a bald spot in the forest, where they removed the binders from her wrists.

The plan was to wrap the binders well enough so that they no longer interfered with their flight and then they would fly separately until they were just outside the city. Then they would land, replace the binders – without activating them, of course – and Azra'il would then fly her the short distance to the council chamber of the Great Sanhedrin, where he would make a spectacular entrance, announcing that he had captured the evil human, Sarah Baker, and that all was now well.

If any of the council members dared ask about Azra'il's appearance, he would claim that he had had to sacrifice himself and pretend to allow the outlanders to indoctrinate him into their clan by allowing them to change his physical appearance. This, he figured, would also work well as a cover story should any of the elite Sanhedrin Guardsmen who had escaped during the night of the Shaitans' prison bust confront him as having switched sides.

Azra'il and Sarah landed just outside the City hours later. Before unwrapping the binders and putting them on, Sarah psychically contacted Mikhail to assure him everything was going swimmingly and that he shouldn't worry because she was intentionally erecting a buffer for the next few hours. She wanted none of the gifted Kurr on the council to be able to detect the link she shared with him, and therefore discover the lie that the binders had been activated or that she was not truly Azra'il's prisoner. That would not help anyone involved and Mikhail soon saw the sense of the plan, so he agreed, though he didn't like it.

Erecting the strongest buffer she could manage, Sarah sighed in deep dreaded anticipation and held out her wrists, palm side up. "We may as well get goin'," she said.

Azra'il frowned at the thought of hurting her. He hadn't spent much time with her during his time at the Complex, but that which he had had shown her to be a very nice, open, caring and intelligent being. He knew she had had reservations about him due to their past interactions because of his past actions, but she had accepted him in her daughter's life without protest as soon as Sheely had made it known that Sheely and he belonged together.

Most parents would have fought tooth and nail to keep him from their daughter. Azra'il even recalled several female Kurr within the walls of Lorim City who had caught his eye and then had not been able to accommodate him due to the fact that their parents had not wished their daughters to be associated with him. Azra'il could not blame them. When he thought of Sheely, he could imagine no one ever being good enough for her – not even himself.

He was going to do his best to *be* the best for her, though. And that was all he could do.

Sarah had somehow seen past all of the pre-conceived notions the Kurr had told her about him and she had outright accepted him, had even allowed him to move into her home – her own suite of rooms within the Main House, even – all so that Sheely and he could spend valuable time together.

Azra'il would not soon forget that.

He did his best to keep the contact between the binders and her skin to a minimum, but he felt her tense up again even before the evil little things touched her. Because he was also touching her when he wrapped his shields around both of them, the painful vibrations from the binders extended out to him and he cringed as he flew. It was one of the worst flights of his long life.

Seconds later, Azra'il allowed his shields to completely drop and both he *and* Sarah breathed an audible anguished sigh of relief as they each appeared out of thin air and took their first step onto the raised platform at the very center of the council chamber, where it appeared a full session of the Great Sanhedrin was in full swing.

Council members swooned to the left and right. All around, everyone was in a tizzy, wondering aloud to his or her neighboring council members about what had just happened before their very eyes. "I just cannot believe it," and "Do you see that? What *is* that?" could be heard echoing clearly from multiple council members seated around the room.

Finally, Azra'il recovered enough from the short but difficult flight to raise his arm for their attention, speaking very loudly, "My people!"

More gasps followed by even louder exclamations from the audience came as the identity of the male glowing-eyed creature was just confirmed. This had even the most staid and level-headed of council members pricking up their ears and edging closer in their seats for a better look.

Azra'il turned full-circle on the round raised platform at the very center of the room. His arm was still raised for their attention and he said again, even louder, "My people!" He looked around. Council members were finally clamming up and reclaiming their seats around the chamber in anticipation of Azra'il's coming speech.

Sarah put on her best performance as the neutered captive, Azra'il noted. She gasped for breath every few seconds. Her entire frame shook uncontrollably and every now and then, she would jerk as if suffering from painful muscle spasms. She appeared to all around as if she was barely able to remain standing. Azra'il was proud of her.

As soon as the council had quieted enough that he could be heard by all, Azra'il lowered his arm and said, "My people. I have finally returned from the settlement where the outlaws have made their base. As you see, I was able to capture their leader, the once-human Sarah Baker!"

Several gasps could be heard around the room. Very few Kurr within Lorim City's walls had ever actually seen Sarah before she had transformed, so they had no prior image to which they could compare her current looks. However, one Kurr approached and attempted to touch the odd hair that hung low from Sarah's head and the strands there immediately struck out, slicing off two of the man's fingers before Sarah screamed in mock pain and fell to her knees, bowing her head and continuing with her act.

There were more gasps, more swooning, and medical assistance had to be called for the now-dismembered councilman who simply lay there bleeding. It looked as if he might have gone into shock. The medical team immediately confirmed this when they arrived.

Suddenly, a councilwoman sitting nearest where her fallen comrade lay screamed as it was discovered the wounds the male Kurr had sustained were worsening. Not only that, but they were spreading up the councilman's hand and it appeared the flesh inside the skin was being dissolved from within. A thick, milky substance oozed slowly out of the open wounds and a horrible stench pervaded the room.

Council members covered their noses and scurried away from the area near the fallen Kurr and watched in horror as the medical team cleaned up the male's hand and prepared him for evacuation to the medical center. It took five of them to move the large councilman.

When he was gone and the milky mess had finally been cleared away, one of the oldest council members stood and cautiously stepped forward a couple of paces toward Azra'il. She was a radiantly beautiful Kurr who looked nowhere near her 700 thousand years of age. But she had the knowledge and wisdom of one her age and she gestured toward Sarah, asking, "My L-Lord, why would you bring this thing here? Why not kill it and all remaining ones like it?"

Azra'il slowly took one step toward her, saying, "My dear councilwoman Razzia..."

The Kurr immediately took a step back from him.

Azra'il stopped and his hair chose *that* moment to begin moving again. It was only at the ends and it wasn't even moving very much, but it was apparently enough to upset much of the council chamber. Azra'il held up his hand once more for silence.

The crowd's volume increased again as all present now regarded Azra'il as one of the evil creatures. The Kurr Razzia studied him intently for a moment, frowning as she looked him up and down. Then she turned toward the crowd and raised her own hand, having to shout for the crowd's attention, "My fellow council members!" It took only a few seconds before nearly the entire assemblage once again focused on her, which spoke to how very well respected she was within the Great Sanhedrin. When all was quiet again, she said, "I believe he should be allowed to speak, to explain why he has done this terrible thing." She turned back toward Azra'il and looked up at him expectantly.

There was something in her eyes – not accusation exactly, but hurt and confusion and... fear. Azra'il saw it. When he finally spoke, it was directly to the Kurr Razzia. "My dear, I would never bring harm upon any within the hallowed walls of Lorim City. Why, I helped build these walls with my own two hands! Why would I do such a thing if I later would plan to destroy it? And I love each and every Kurr within the walls of the City. Why would I ever turn against any of them? I was witness to the birth of so many of you, down almost to one. Again, why would I seek to destroy you? You are my people. You elected me your leader. I am your *servant*, not your executioner."

Razzia's eyes filled with tears and she shook her head, saying softly, "You have served the Kurr of Lorim City well. You stepped in at a time of much confusion and disorder, largely thanks to this poor creature." She approached Sarah's still-kneeling form, though she kept her distance to avoid Sarah's deadly hair. "I am told she was a very pretty human," she continued, looking down at Sarah with a pitying, sorrowful countenance. "It is too bad Lord Mikhail and the other Lorim chose to surrender to her charms the way they did. Then again, perhaps they did not consciously surrender after all?"

Razzia turned back toward Azra'il, her eyes showing the dawning of understanding. "My Lord," she said. "I know you *seem* as if you still care for your people here, but I believe there is something much more sinister going on here than even *you* can see."

She turned toward the audience and raised her voice, explaining, "I believe, through no fault of his own, that Lord Azra'il has become the victim of infection." Again, multiple gasps sounded around the chamber. "This poor creature was patient zero, if you will," she continued. "She brought the disease with her when she entered our Realm from the human dimension, most likely unknowingly as we have seen so many human explorers and missionaries do, and now it has begun to spread. First, Lord Mikhail contracted it. That would explain rumors of his strange appearance. I know those of us who had gathered in this very chamber for the trial of Lords Djibril and Israfil can still recall precious little from that day, but it is my belief that the two of them were taken somehow, and infected as well, and that is why we have not seen them since in this, their home City."

There were nods of agreement all around. Everyone knew the Kurr Razzia to be very wise and knowledgeable and she was certainly proving that now.

"I believe Lord Azra'il chose to give of himself in service to his people in the noblest and most honorable way possible," she said solemnly. "By going to the Outlander settlement and allowing himself to become infected, he was obviously able to gain the trust of the Outlanders – enough so that he could capture and bring back the very creature who started everything. I mean, look at her." Razzia approached Sarah's form again, though not close enough that the sharp white hair could reach her. "This poor creature suffers agonizing pain from the binders that are not even fully fastened or activated."

Many of those sitting near where Sarah kneeled immediately jumped up in fear of her suddenly freeing herself and attacking. Razzia quickly calmed them, however, and they returned to their seats.

"As soon as we are able to restrain her enough to get close to them," Razzia assured the council, "we shall secure the binders and activate them. This we must do, if for no other reason than to protect anyone else from being struck by the thing's venomous hair!" At that very moment the evil hair strands moved and a multitude of those sitting near the kneeling creature gasped with horror and ran for some other part of the round room.

Sarah's hair moved slowly to cover her face and she squeezed her eyes shut. She was truly in a lot of pain here, and yet the Kurr Razzia did not lie. The binders were not fully-clasped, nor had they been activated. Sarah didn't understand why then she should be in so much pain. She did know one thing, however. She knew she would never survive wearing fully-activated binders.

The Kurr Razzia continued with her speech, but Sarah was past the point of caring anymore. She cautiously tried lowering the buffer she had erected earlier between Mikhail and herself. Nothing untoward happened. There were still the same strong painful vibrations emitting from the binders.

The pain had actually been slowly increasing the longer she wore the dreadful things, but what could Sarah do? She had been weakened so by the pain that she was now finding it a chore merely to continue breathing. She had lost her ability to stand earlier and now she felt almost on the verge of complete collapse. She knew there would be no way for her to fight her way out of this one. Her only hope, she believed, was to contact Mikhail telepathically to let him know what was going on. Then he and the others would hopefully be able to think of a plan to rescue Azra'il and her, if they hadn't already worked one out during the time it had taken the two of them to reach the City.

Sarah hoped they had and that that was how it would work.

She concentrated on dropping the buffer entirely. No great influx of pain occurred, so she decided to try opening the line of communication between Mikhail's mind and her own. Immediately, a blinding sea of pain surrounded her and she screamed out in utter agony, falling to the floor on her side and jerking in several full-bodied pain-induced seizure spasms.

"See," the Kurr Razzia pointed to the unfortunate creature lying on the raised platform in the center of the chamber. "The poor thing is suffering and that, my fellow council members, is what each and every one of us may well have to look forward to if we have already been infected, as I have explained to you just now."

Quiet astonishment gripped each council member as they all stared at the two infected creatures upon the platform. What was to become of them all?

The bell alerting the council that someone was about to enter the chamber sounded and the Kurr Razzia yelled, "No! Block the entrance! No one goes in or out of these chambers until we can be certain none is infected."

Azra'il stepped forward again, raising both hands, along with his voice, imploring, "Listen to me! Listen to me!" But the council members would not listen to him now. He had performed a heroic feat, which was for certain. By allowing himself to become infected, he had accomplished the task of bringing the host carrier of the disease to Lorim City. At least this way, the City's medical team would be able to develop an anti-serum from Sarah Baker's blood after she had either become overcome by the disease or died. They all believed, however, that it was most likely too late for poor Lord Azra'il.

It was determined that the entirety of the council, or at least those present at today's proceedings, were to be quarantined until an anti-serum could be developed. It was the only way to be safe. The medical team was to send over an anesthetic in aerosol form so Sarah Baker's binders could finally be properly fastened and activated. Because of his heroism and bravery, not to mention his self-sacrifice, the council decided not to punish dear Lord Azra'il by placing binders onto him, but to make him as comfortable as possible until his unfortunate demise. However, since no one knew what someone infected with the disease was capable of, and especially since he was an infected Lori, it was decided that he, too, would be anesthetized – just enough to put him into a light, drug-induced coma until something could be worked out.

Sarah lay on the platform, her breathing laborious, every part of her body feeling as if someone was taking just one corner of a razor blade and making a quick, tiny incision and then pouring lemon juice onto it. Her chest was beginning to feel as if a thousand pounds of bricks rested atop it and she knew she didn't have long before she would no longer be capable of breathing on her own. She tried listening to what was going on in the chamber room, but she could barely hear anything over the pounding of blood rushing through her veins.

Azra'il, she saw, still stood to her side, though he looked bad. Apparently, he had been unsuccessful with his plan of convincing the council that Sarah posed no threat to anyone in Lorim City. From her vantage point, it looked to Sarah's weakening eyesight as if Azra'il was attempting communication with those at the Complex. Sarah hoped that was what he was up to and that he was successful at it because there was absolutely no way she would live past another attempt to contact Mikhail again while she wore the dreaded binders. She knew it wasn't long before sweet oblivion claimed her consciousness anyway, so she did her best to relax as she waited for the darkness to set in.

It felt as if the pain lessened whenever she relaxed and stopped fighting against the binders. They still hurt as their vibrations resonated throughout her body, but it was less painful if they were met with no resistance as they traveled along her synapses. Time became a surreal concept to her and she had no idea how much had passed. Her eyelids worked to open successfully only half the time and her field of vision narrowed more and more each time she did manage to get them open.

Once, she thought she could feel herself coughing violently and then she felt the binders being removed. For just a moment, everything cleared – her mind, her vision, the pain – everything. She could finally take a full breath, completely filling her lungs. In that one moment of clarity, Sarah saw Azra'il's unconscious form lying prone on the platform. The council members were all milling about as if they were just taking a quick break before their session resumed.

There were two Kurr in white lab coats sitting next to her. One held what looked like some sort of aerosol can in one hand while his other hand was busy working to secure her hair, which had gone strangely still, she noticed. The other white-coated Kurr was holding the binders Sarah had previously worn. He appeared to be checking them for damage and to ensure they would still clasp and activate.

She didn't know what possessed her mind in that one moment of clarity, but as the white coat with the binders moved to return them to her wrists, Sarah put as much energy as she could muster into a psychic push. Then there was a slight click and a beep and everything went blank.

***

Mikhail walked along the hallway of the main house, bouncing Sheely's wailing form in his arms lightly, rocking her just a bit back and forth, gently singing an ancient lullaby he had somehow recalled hearing Suri sing on many occasions to sick infants she had been helping in the human realm. Earlier, when Sheely had just started wailing out of the blue, his first instinct had been to call for Miriam. After all, he was busy trying to keep his mind off what was happening with Sarah and his brother while he did his best to contact Nera. The idea of doing normal parenthood chores seemed utterly ridiculous amid everything else that was going on.

However, he had decided against having the old Kurr come in to take charge of things just because Sheely had finally started acting like a normal, healthy baby. Mikhail truly had no idea what he was doing, but this was what he had missed out on his entire life. He wasn't about to turn tail and run at the first sign of trouble! So he had picked her up from her cradle where she had been napping moments before and he had started walking. Since then, he had walked and walked as her wails had become louder and louder. It had been almost two hours now without stop and Mikhail was starting to worry.

Was this normal infant behavior? He had felt her head for signs of fever, but there had been none. She had felt cool to his touch. He had tried burping her, feeding her, changing her, everything he could think of and yet still she cried. He wondered if perhaps she was in pain and was on the verge of heading over to the Medical Facility when, all of a sudden, a vision knocked him to the floor!

It was only quick thinking on his part that stopped him from crushing Sheely's little body beneath his giant self by twisting so that he landed on his back with her plopping down onto his chest. His head hit the stone floor hard and he laid there for a moment, dazed and a little confused. He had no idea how he had even thought to twist around because his mind was consumed with the image and sound the vision had shown him. He had seen Sarah's face as she had screamed his name, her arms desperately reaching out toward him. He had felt an overwhelming sense of pain coming from everywhere around her and it had looked as if there were people on either side of her, though their images had been blurred in his mind.

Mikhail!

Her voice from the vision kept echoing through his head and his mind focused on the pain he had felt with the vision. Sheely's wailing was now much louder than before as the two of them lay in the deserted hallway. Mikhail was helpless, for certain, as the vision played over and over in his mind. He just hoped someone would come along soon so Sheely could be rescued. His body jerked time and again as the vision repeated before his mind's eye.

Suddenly, in some dim recess of his mind, he thought he heard someone coming toward him down the corridor. It was Israfil's voice yelling, "They are here!" that finally captured his attention away from the short scene in the vision. "Mikhail!" Israfil yelled much closer to where Mikhail lay. Mikhail jerked again, then he felt a warm hand on his chest and there was no more pain. The vision replayed in his mind only a couple more times and then all was calm.

As Mikhail's vision cleared, he realized there were now concerned Kurr standing all around the hallway, each awaiting orders as to how to help. Sheely was still crying and Mikhail moved to fetch her from the floor where she had rolled after he had become senseless with the pain from the vision. Israfil beat him to her and Mikhail watched as his brother cautiously lifted the babe. "She has been crying non-stop like that for the past couple of hours," he told Israfil. "I was thinking of taking her to see Hantsushept when I collapsed."

Israfil held up his hand for silence and tilted his head as if listening to something. "She is deathly afraid," Israfil said as if in a daze. "She can no longer establish a link with Azra'il and he had not sounded good when last they communicated." Israfil's vision appeared to clear and he looked over at Mikhail. "From what I gathered from her mind, things have not gone well with the council," he told him.

Mikhail swallowed hard. He could understand the council not wanting to accept Sarah because she was an actual outsider, a different species. But for them to reject Azra'il, as well... Mikhail could not fathom it. Granted, Azra'il now looked very different from the way he had looked when last they had seen him, but the idea that the council would reject its Lori leader...?

An idea occurred to him and he asked, "Do you think I could mind-link with either of them through Sheely?"

Israfil was shaking his head even before Mikhail's question was completed. "Her mind is not like ours, brother. Her brain, although it seems completely formed, still has a lot of mapping to do. We can have no idea of what effects just linking *with* her is having, let alone if one were to attempt linking *through* her to another. She is also still using more of a conceptual language with us. Every now and then I have caught her using one of the ancient tongues from the human realm, but it was a dead language and, for the most part, inadequate for use in our world and time. It is doubtful we would be able to glean much more than emotional content from linking through her, and even that would be limited to whatever her brain has thus far managed to experience. I would imagine it would be more beneficial for us to have Djibril track Sarah and Azra'il so that we can get a fix on their locations and just go and retrieve them both before further harm is done to anyone."

Mikhail stood with the help of one of the lower Kurr still standing around. Sheely was still wailing and he raised his voice as he asked, "What about the escaped elite Guardsmen?"

"With luck, they would not yet have had time to reach the City," Israfil informed him.

The two brothers with the wailing infant hurried along the corridors of the main house on their way to fetch Djibril so he could track down the exact location of their loved ones. When they reached Djibril's suite of rooms, they found it empty. "I thought they had said they intended to move back over to the Main House this morning," Israfil barked at Mikhail in frustration. When his brother merely shrugged, Israfil quickly handed the still-disgruntled Sheely over to him and then sat on one of the chairs in Djibril's living room, closing his eyes in concentration. A few moments later, he re-opened his eyes and sighed in frustration. "Do you think perhaps you could take her outside into the hallway while I do this?" he asked Mikhail.

Mikhail immediately agreed and left the room.

Five minutes later, Israfil emerged from the suite. He nodded once toward his sibling as he said, "I have found him." They started down the hallway and Israfil explained, "He and Chris appear to still be inhabiting that observation room at the Medical Facility." Mikhail threw him a concerned look, but Israfil shook his head and explained to him, "It appears Djibril and his mate believed Hantsushept might be able to assist them as they dealt with the issue they experienced last night, brother."

Mikhail frowned, but then his thoughts returned to his own present predicament as Sheely's wails unbelievably increased in volume even more. If he hadn't been so concerned for his own mate's safety, Mikhail would have been only too happy to offer his assistance to his brother and new sister, for he knew anyone who could accomplish what she had done last night without even trying would someday make a formidable ally. Not to mention the fact that another Lori being opened up to the transformation was definitely cause for celebration, and Mikhail suddenly wondered at what stage of the transformation they would find Djibril and his mate when they finally arrived.

Chapter 20

Hantsushept patiently moved aside the infant's leg and placed the flat side of the stethoscope to one side of her tiny lower abdomen and then to the other side. "Yes, I know, sweetheart," he soothed in a quiet, altered voice in an attempt to calm the babe.

"Do you think she was hurt when I fell in the hallway?" Mikhail asked, concerned that he may have inadvertently injured her internally when he had collapsed.

"She does not appear to have been injured, My Lord," the old physician said, "and everything sounds normal internally." He moved out of the way of the Kurr Miriam, who had been brought over to assist. The old maid picked up the babe and then took her over to a wooden rocking chair where she sat down and started singing softly as she rocked. Within seconds, the wailing had stopped altogether.

Mikhail nodded and followed Hantsushept down the hall to where Djibril and Chris were still firmly installed in the observation room at the Facility. Israfil was waiting there for them. "Any luck?" Mikhail asked as he and the good doctor entered.

"We can get no reading whatsoever on Sarah," Djibril said. Mikhail looked away. After a second, Djibril cleared his throat, saying, "Yes, well, Chris was able to locate Azra'il. But there is a problem." Everyone frowned as they looked expectantly toward him. "It is a *very* weak signal," he explained. "I missed it entirely." As the others puzzled over this, he continued. "I cannot tell if Azra'il is deep underground, or if he has been encased in some type of thick structure or… if he is dead and this is just the residual energy left over with the body."

As everyone absorbed this information, Chris reached up to touch Djibril's sleeve. He turned his head and looked down at her. "Oh, yes," he said, as an afterthought. "Chris has an alternate theory."

All eyes turned to her as she sat next to Djibril. "I-I don't think he's dead," she haltingly announced. Everyone tensed as they watched her expectantly and finally she continued nervously. "I don't have any difficulty getting to him in my mind, but there's some sort of void next to him, wherever he is, that's kicking me away each time I hone in on him."

"Some kind of void?" Mikhail asked. "What do you mean?"

"I can't explain it," she said, shaking her head. "I tried to see it, whatever it is, but it's repulsive. It's like there's some sort of a blank reading coming from just next to Azra'il, but each time I focus on that spot, the void figures out that I'm looking at it and I'm pushed away."

"A cloaking or shielding device?" Israfil suggested to Mikhail.

"Some type of psychic barrier the council has installed since we left?" Mikhail wondered.

"Why would Azra'il not have known of it?" Djibril asked.

"My Lords," Hantsushept interrupted them. "Might you consider the use of magnetics, as the Designers did with the binders they gave for your use?"

"The magnets, depending on what type they are, could be used to repel a certain type of energy," Israfil offered.

"Yes," Hantsushept agreed. "And I believe the binders have been shown to learn and adjust the longer they are used, correct?"

Most of the males present had worn the dreaded binders at one time or another and they each recalled how the binders would adjust to their host, tightening and lying in wait for the captive to attempt the use of his innate energies. The things certainly had seemed to get to the point of being able almost to anticipate moves.

Mikhail sighed heavily. "Iz," he asked, "do you think either you or Djibril would be able to mind-link with Azra'il if I got you there through Chris? It would not be the exact same as when we did it with Thomas and Sarah, but it is worth a try, right?"

Israfil frowned, thinking over this plan.

Djibril frowned and then he and Chris looked at each

other. A second later, she reached down to where two bright twin spots of light showed through on her abdomen. After only a second, she nodded to her mate.

Djibril frowned, but then turned to Mikhail and said, "You can count on our cooperation."

"My Lords," Hantsushept politely interrupted again. "If I may be so bold – I do not believe that would be a wise plan." When he had everyone's attention, he explained. "My latest data report shows Lady Christiana has received telepathic transmissions already from the twins. Is that correct, m' dear?"

"W-Well, I've heard *them* talking, if that's what you mean?" Chris said with a frown.

"Precisely," the physician continued. "If the twins have already linked with her..."

Realization was dawning all over the room.

Mikhail nodded, crestfallen. "I see your point." He sighed heavily. He just wanted to find Sarah and Azra'il and then to go get them out of the City. He didn't care how it was done. He just wanted his family to be safe and with him.

Israfil suddenly spoke up, asking Chris, "Would you mind if I *alone* mind-linked with you?" At the shake of her head, he explained. "If I can get a quick fix on their location, I can go and retrieve them."

"But Chris has only managed to locate Azra'il, thus far," Djibril reminded him.

"Then I shall remain hidden inside my shields as I look around for Sarah."

"Yes," Mikhail and the others agreed enthusiastically.

"Except," Mikhail said, "Djibril and I shall accompany you when you actually go to get them." Everyone nodded agreement with this plan. It was certainly better to have three working together than just one.

They all waited as Israfil seated himself before Chris. The two of them stared quietly into each other's eyes, concentrating on completing the mind-link. It took only a moment before their eyes slid closed and both slumped in relaxation as their minds forgot about their bodies temporarily. The tracker did her job, moving her mind in lightning-fast succession along pathways she had found earlier in her quest to locate her new family members.

The mind tagging along with hers slowed her only the slightest fraction, and for this she was grateful. She was still learning this method of tracking, but she had already learned enough from her time doing it with Djibril to know she could do it much easier and faster on her own, without having to wait for someone else. A small part of her mind rejoiced at the fact that Israfil's mind was apparently far more advanced than that of her lover and she allowed herself the freedom to stretch harder, dashing along the nearly invisible grid she could now detect, thrilling at how wonderful it felt to use her newly-developed abilities. The mind tagging along with hers stayed right beside her as the miles simply melted away.

Minutes later, Chris located her target. He was weak, much weaker than when she had found him earlier and it felt like he was fading fast. Chris didn't waste any time. She made sure her tag-along knew where to go and then she pulled back into her body in a flash. Opening her eyes, she was shocked to realize Israfil was already back from their joint mind-link and he and the other two, including her mate, were preparing to leave.

"I have a very bad feeling about this," she quietly told them.

"It is all right, sweetheart," Djibril assured her as he bent to brush a quick kiss across her lips. "This should not take long."

The three brothers stood in a close circle near the bed, concentrating to establish a mind-link with each other. As soon as each one had a clear picture of their intended destination, they slowly separated in order to have enough room to release their shields, so they could then fly to the City.

Suddenly, Suriyah appeared in the very center of the room. She was preceded by her voice, yelling, "Wait! Wait!"

She was out of breath and Hantsushept immediately offered her a place to sit and rest while another nurse was sent to fetch refreshment for her.

As she worked to catch her breath, she brokenly said, "You must... wait. It is n-not safe. A vision... I had a vision showing danger."

Mikhail stepped forward. "Suri, we at least know where Azra'il is at this moment. If we do not rescue him now, there is no telling when, or even if, we shall get another opportunity!"

"No," she said, shaking her head vigorously. "It is not safe for you or for Djibril."

It took only a second for Mikhail to demand, "So are you saying it is safe for Israfil, then?"

Suriyah frowned. Only Mikhail and Djibril had been shown being captured in her vision. There had been nothing shown to her regarding Israfil. She sighed and explained, "I do not know. I can only tell you that if Djibril goes or if you go, it is most certain you will each be captured."

This put a new spin on things and they all sat to think through this new problem.

A moment later, Israfil stood and adamantly declared, "I do not care. I am going. We have Azra'il on our radar and we may never have an opportunity like this again." The emotions displayed in the eyes of those around him ranged from gratitude to pride to awe – all laced with fear and concern for him. "I shall grab Azra'il and search as long as I can for Sarah before departing. I am certain there will be some clue as to where she is being held. If I can but locate her, I should be able to get to her to bring her back."

When there were no objections, Israfil looked around and, giving a brief nod, released all six of his shields and took off. Those he left behind were now forced to endure the waiting. None of them was happy with that, but neither were they willing to leave the Medical Facility as they waited.

***

Israfil cautiously approached the council chamber. This was where Chris had shown him Azra'il was being held. The void she had described had been there when she and Israfil had made their tracking journey and Israfil had to admit he was more than just a little concerned about it. What could it be? Was it a cloaking device of some kind? If so, what was it cloaking and why? Could it be some new form of weaponry the Kurr of Lorim City had developed since last he had lived there? Would such a weapon work on Lorim? Then another thought invaded his consciousness. Why would Suriyah's vision show danger for Mikhail and Djibril if they made this journey, but not for Israfil?

None of it made sense to him and he decided it would probably be best to just push aside all of those questions so he could concentrate on the task at hand. In seconds, he had gained access to the main council chamber without any of the Kurr inside being any the wiser. What he saw once he arrived only served to confuse him more.

Nearly every member of the Great Sanhedrin was in attendance, but there was no meeting actually in session. Everyone was just standing around, talking quietly with one another, or they were sitting in small groups talking. Some had even made themselves as comfortable as possible in their seats and were trying to sleep right there in the chamber, uncomfortable as it was. There were only five figures on the raised platform in the center of the room, however, and this was what had Israfil suddenly reeling.

Three of the individuals upon the platform were obviously medical personnel who were busy working on someone. Off to the side, almost on the edge of the platform, lay Azra'il – still breathing, but completely unconscious. Israfil took just a moment to check his brother for any signs of injury. He found none, but he did detect a large amount of some sort of chemical in Azra'il's bloodstream which appeared to be maintaining Azra'il's current comatose state of being.

No one else in the room was paying any attention to Azra'il, however, and Israfil slowly edged closer to where he lay.

That's when he felt it – the void.

He turned back to where the three medical Kurr still worked and realized they were in the very spot where the void was. But they were not alone. There, lying on the floor, surrounded by the three Kurr whom Israfil now recognized as

"The Three", lay Sarah. For some reason, "The Three" were dressed in medical personnel garb as they tended to Sara's prone form.

Suddenly, it dawned on Israfil *why* she had appeared as a void when Chris and he had looked in on this room. Looking at Sarah's body as it lay there, Israfil could *feel* that the binders had been securely fastened around her wrists and activated. Her hands and lower arms appeared to be completely devoid of flowing blood and had turned an unhealthy shade of blue as the effects of the wretched binders spread insidiously up each arm. The rest of Sarah was ashen and Israfil wondered if some type of powder hadn't been rubbed all over her body. Even her usually active hair lay limp and lifeless as an impotent crown of white.

"The Three" guarded over her, as was their function. Israfil wondered why they were in disguise, for no one else appeared to recognize them for who they were.

He didn't have time for puzzling out such mysteries, however. Israfil could feel the effects of the binders on *himself* growing stronger and he knew he must do his duty. He would save Azra'il and then work with the others to solve the issue of how to rescue Sarah. One last look in her direction gave proof the binders were still activated, which hopefully meant she still lived. She certainly looked like death was upon her, though.

Israfil couldn't help that right now. He couldn't help *her* right now. But he could help Azra'il, and that was precisely what he did. Swooping in as fast as his shields would allow under the influence of the wicked binders with their disruptive vibrations and without hesitation, Israfil dropped his shields in a flash to gather up Azra'il's body and then "Poof!", he and Azra'il were safely covered by all six of Israfil's shields and were already on their way up and out of the building before anyone could even react.

Apparently, someone in the chamber had been watching Azra'il, for Israfil heard several gasps as he and his sibling rushed through the ceiling's fabric.

Israfil flew faster than he had ever flown before while carrying someone and soon they were far away from Lorim

City. He looked down at the white-haired sibling he carried. Azra'il's whiter-than-white skin looked impossibly paler than usual and Israfil wondered why the council would have felt a need to induce a coma in him.

Azra'il would *never* do anything to harm his people. Surely, they knew that?

When he and his charge finally arrived, everyone was still where they had been when he had left, as if no one had dared moved a muscle. They all watched, wide-eyed with wonder, as a handful of Hantsushept's assistants entered the room to assist with Azra'il's care. Sheely was brought in by the old Kurr, Miriam, and the minute she entered the room, she finally smiled. It was as if she sensed Azra'il was there and Israfil figured that was precisely what had happened.

Mikhail wasted no time as he approached Israfil and asked, "Did you have any luck locating Sarah? Is she heavily guarded or do you think you can get in to get her?"

Israfil held up a staying hand, then motioned for Mikhail to sit. Choosing his words carefully, he said, "I discovered the location of your mate. I also discovered the cause of Suri's vision." The others sitting nearby switched their attention to him, curious now as he continued. "It appears the strange void we detected when we were tracking them before was actually the energy coming from Sarah as it was being manipulated by the binders."

"But the binders were not activated," Mikhail interrupted him to say. "I checked."

"Someone there had secured them onto her wrists and fully activated them by the time I arrived," Israfil told him.

Mikhail thought for a moment. Finally, he asked, "So how do I get her out of there, Iz?"

Israfil slowly shook his head and said, "I do not know, brother."

"Did the binders affect you at all while you were there?" Suriyah asked.

Israfil nodded, explaining, "I could feel painful little vibrations coming from them the closer I got."

"But you wore them before, remember?" Mikhail pointed out.

"I know," he said, "and they did not affect me thus when last I wore them." He shrugged and said, "I cannot explain it."

All except those working on Azra'il were silent. How could they get near enough to Sarah to rescue her?

"What if several of us go and take a Kurr or two along to assist?" Mikhail asked.

Israfil shook his head, saying, "They have her in the main council chamber. There is no way to grab her without being noticed."

"But, maybe if we…," Mikhail began.

Israfil interrupted, as he placed a sympathetic hand on Mikhail's shoulder and soberly said, "Brother, she is guarded by 'The Three'."

Mikhail turned a frightening shade of gray as others around the room could be heard gasping. Sheely let out an ear-piercing scream all of a sudden, but everyone was in shock. If "The Three" guarded her, it could only mean one thing: death was imminent.

Finally, Mikhail stood and motioned to one of the lower Kurr. "Please fetch a pair of binders and take them to my study immediately," he instructed.

"Wh-What are you doing?" Israfil and Suriyah asked simultaneously.

Mikhail barely even looked at them on his way out of the room. "I am going to find a way to get back my mate," he said determinedly.

***

Suriyah knocked and waited politely. Had it just been Baphomet she would see, Suri would have gone ahead and entered the house without bothering with propriety. But since Lisa was with him, Suriyah took the extra time for human niceties.

It only took a moment or two before Baphomet answered the door. He smiled broadly at first sight of her, but as he looked both left and right *and* behind her, his smile faded and he said, "Oh, gods! Something has gone wrong with the migration."

Suri frowned and said, "Let me in, you dolt!"

Baphomet stepped aside and then escorted her to the study where Lisa and he spent the majority of their time these days. Lisa was there napping in a wing-backed chair by the fireplace. However, she awakened immediately as Suriyah and Baphomet entered.

"Suriyah," she said with a smile. She was surprised to see her Lori sister back from the human world so soon, but she was pleased as well. She had grown to discover that being pregnant was not all it was cracked up to be. But what was worse was having to deal with an over-protective Baphomet's presence non-stop. She loved him and felt connected with him more than with any other person on Earth, but he nearly drove her up the wall sometimes with his constant questions and constant chatter.

I can *hear your thoughts, you know?* his voice in her mind suddenly asked sardonically.

Lisa looked up at him as if he had lost his mind and said aloud, "So? I have a right to be frustrated by your constant nagging. How do you feel? How's Cabal? Do you need anything? Do you need a nap?" She rolled her eyes, saying, "It's enough to drive me crazy!"

Suriyah chuckled softly and lightly punched Baphomet on the arm. "Well," she smirked. "It certainly looks as if you have things well under control here, dear brother."

Baphomet flashed a sarcastic smile her way and then took his usual seat next to Lisa, taking her hand in his so they would be maintaining physical contact again – a thing which was necessary between the two of them.

"Please have a seat," Lisa offered to her sister. Suriyah took the proffered seat and made herself comfortable. As soon as she was settled, Lisa asked, "So, has my mum driven you crazy yet?"

Suri frowned a little, but then realized Lisa must be joking and she chuckled once more, saying, "Not quite." She leaned forward in her seat and said, "I have come to update you on the status of the migration, of course, but I have also brought other news for you." She explained how Lisa's mother was dutifully gathering as many Ngarinyin Aborigines as possible who wished to migrate from the human realm to the Loric Realm. The old woman was also gathering any and all from other Aboriginal tribes who wished to make the crossover to the Loric Realm in order to avoid whatever coming danger the Aborigines had warned everyone was on its way from the sky.

Then she let them know what had happened with Azra'il and Sarah.

"No!" Lisa exclaimed in shock several times throughout Suriyah's recounting of events, along with several gasps and oh, my goshes.

When Suri was finished speaking, Lisa asked, "So what's Mikhail planning? To run experiments on the binders until he finds a way to break their hold on Sarah?"

Suri shrugged and said, "I guess so. I just know I cannot stay any longer or I would help him. From what Israfil said, Sarah is dead if no one gets to her soon."

Lisa gasped suddenly and lumbered clumsily to her feet only to turn with her hands on her hips to face Baphomet and declare, "You absolutely will *not* go and put yourself through that again!"

Baphomet stood and faced her, toe-to-toe, explaining, "It would kill two birds with one stone, my love. You wanted some time away from me and Mikhail needs someone strong enough to wear the binders. It would be the perfect solution."

Lisa crossed her arms and tapped an angry foot on the floor. "And just how do you propose we do this?" she demanded.

Baphomet immediately saw her point. The two of them had inherited a peculiar quirk as they had transformed: they could not be physically separated for long periods of time without suffering great psychic distress. The only way they had found to be apart for more than a few minutes had been to have Israfil around. He was somehow able to create a buffer around one of them while the other was absent. Still, this left the other in danger of succumbing to a wall of voices so crushing there was no escape.

"I could go for short periods of time until Mikhail found a solution," Baphomet suggested.

Lisa reached up to cup his cheek with one hand. "I know you want to help, my love," she said. "But Cabal needs both of us and this is simply too dangerous."

Baphomet turned very serious all of a sudden as he gazed down into her beautifully-glowing eyes and said, "My heart, this is Sarah we are talking about – *Mikhail* and Sarah. I can no more abandon them in their time of need than I could you or Cabal."

After a moment, Lisa nodded and said, "You are so much my hero, you cannot even imagine." She looked down at the lump of her belly, rubbing it a little. When she finally looked back up, she sighed and said, "Well, perhaps Israfil could wait in another part of the Main House with Cabal and me? That way, he could be there in a flash should you need his energies?"

Baphomet looked toward Suriyah. "Would that work?" he asked hopefully.

Suri shrugged and said honestly, "I do not know, but it might be worth a try."

Baphomet looked back down at Lisa's upturned face.

He loved Lisa so much it nearly blew his mind when he actually thought of the depth of his feelings for her. But Mikhail and Sarah trusted him and they were his family, too.

Finally, he sighed and bent to place a swift kiss upon his mate's forehead, declaring, "I shall speak with Israfil to get his thoughts on the matter. If he agrees to this plan, then we shall offer our assistance to Mikhail."

Suriyah offered her services by stopping in at the Medical Facility where Israfil would hopefully still be so she could let him know he was needed back at the Main House. She then said her good-byes and was on her way.

Lisa stood staring up at her mate's glorious glowing eyes. "You are such a wonderful creature," she softly told him. "I feel truly blessed whenever I realize I get to spend the rest of my life with you."

Baphomet sucked in a deep breath and hugged her tightly to himself. "Do not ever leave me, sweet Lisa," he implored. "I would certainly die without you in my life."

Lisa hugged him back as fiercely as her pregnant state allowed.

***

The Kurr Razzia moved slowly back from the main entrance to her assigned seat in the chamber. So, the Outlanders had broken in to retrieve poor Lord Azra'il? Well, it was obviously too late for him to be saved. She said a silent prayer to the blessed Great Designers asking them to have mercy on his soul, for she had done all a Kurr could do to save him.

Her thoughts were interrupted as councilwoman DiJarre, a younger Kurr who had become a council member only a few thousand years ago, approached and asked for a moment of Razzia's time. Although exhausted, it was not in Razzia's nature to be unavailable to those in need and she smiled and indicated the open seat to her right.

DiJarre sat and immediately asked, "How much longer must the council suffer because of that *human*?"

Razzia narrowed her eyes upon the younger Kurr as she studied her. "Is it not our duty to feel pity for the poor creature?" she asked.

DiJarre looked obligingly contrite as she blushed and hid her eyes behind lowered lids. "Of course, Madam Councilwoman," she replied. "It is simply a matter that I worry for my two small children. They are at home with my mate and he is... well, less than a genius when it comes to babysitting them."

Razzia genuinely laughed for the first time since this whole ordeal began. The rest of the room quieted, first in astonishment at the older, highest-ranking member of the council laughing aloud the way she was doing and, second, in order to hear her response to the younger Kurr's question.

"Now that the unfortunate creature is no longer among us," she announced, "we must remain quarantined but twelve more hours, I should think. Our immune systems by that time should either have saved us or failed us, allowing us to succumb to the disease."

The chamber once again erupted in conversation and, after politely thanking the councilwoman, DiJarre stood, bowed and moved away, leaving Razzia to her own thoughts. No one in the City would doubt Razzia's assessment when it came to a medical issue, for she had trained under the best. It was too bad Hantsushept, who was known far and wide as the very best physician to be found within the Loric or human Realms, had chosen to flee the City with the Outlanders months ago. Razzia wished he hadn't and wondered if he had yet succumbed to the dreaded human disease.

***

Suriyah stood alone in the practice clearing. She had alerted both Mikhail and Israfil of Baphomet's decision to assist in figuring out the mystery of the altered binders, so she was now free to return to her duties in the human realm with the rest of her Jinn assisting the Aborigines with the coming migration. She propped a foot upon a thick stump for a moment as she looked upward at the crystal-clear night sky. Those lighted patterns had changed a bit since she had first walked upon the planet, but never had she felt such a fear as that which now coursed through her at the sight of them.

The visions she had had so many years ago had been dead on thus far, and she wondered if there was anything that could stop what she had seen was to happen next.

A single teardrop gently crested the rim of one eye and tracked slowly down the planes of her cheek as she recalled this particular portion of the vision. For years after having had the vision, this one part of it, the next to the last part, had been the most difficult for her to accept. Another tear snuck out of the other eye and Suriyah squeezed them both shut as she whispered, "Please…"

***

"I should get going," Israfil finally said. He had been spending a little time with Djibril and Chris at the Medical facility, in part congratulating them on the conception of the twins and checking for himself that everything was as it should be with them – physically speaking – and in part in apology for having left so quickly and without explanation earlier. Then Suriyah had come with her news.

His heart had felt much lighter at that and he felt much more optimistic about the coming rescue operation. Baphomet and Mikhail would figure out how the binders had been altered and then they would be able to disable the ones Sarah wore when they rescued her.

If Israfil could have his way, after Sarah was rescued and safely returned to the Complex, every pair of binders in existence would be destroyed so nothing like this could ever happen again. Of course, if he could have things the way he wanted, he would already have…, no. He reigned in his thoughts, as usual, not allowing them to travel down the forbidden pathways in his mind. Not now and not ever again would he allow that to happen, as he had promised himself so very long ago. It was definitely time to go.

Djibril stood when Israfil did and turned to assist his beautiful mate, Chris.

Then Djibril froze.

Chris' gaze was somewhere far off in the distance, her eyes focusing on some location other than the room where they were now. Slowly, Djibril positioned himself in front of her and leaned down toward her face. Before he could speak, she frowned and then her gazed cleared as she looked up at Djibril and softly said, "I've lost her. They may have moved her or something, but I've lost her." Djibril made to speak, but again, she cut him off, saying, "I cannot even detect the void now. It's as if she's just… gone."

***

Thomas' mouth and throat were very dry and he swallowed to wet them. He immediately succumbed to a spate of coughing and thought he would choke to death. Someone softly whispered, "Sh-h," and rubbed what felt like an ice cube across his lips. He opened his mouth and was grateful when the cold cube ended up in his mouth. He tried opening his eyes, but found that to be too taxing, so he just lay there quietly sucking on the cube of frozen water.

After a while, he realized a voice was calling to him

from somewhere. "Talis," it called. "Talis… Talis!"

It took some doing, but he finally managed to drag open his eyes and to focus them.

She sat right beside where he lay. She was staring at him again, simply staring. He could feel her every breath and, all of a sudden, he knew her thoughts.

That's when it happened.

Every bit, every second, of his past, from the time he had first been born to his own time with Nera, to their life together, to his first lifetime away from her and then to his life as he had known it as Sarah's son, and finally to the first time he, as the human Thomas, had met Nera. It was all there, as was realization, and with that realization came emotion and he collapsed in tears. The sense of loss, of tragedy, was overwhelming and he doubled over from the force of it. His friends, his grandparents…, his mother! As he fought to keep the sobs inside, his body jerked in agony. It had all been an illusion!

Nera's heart melted as she watched him go through the malaise that accompanied the return from time spent away from their small world. She did not know it for herself, for Talis had never allowed her to travel beyond her body to assist any of their crops, but she was linked with him, so she knew of his suffering. She was glad he had finally returned, though, and she held onto his hand practically willing him back to health, as well as back to a good mental state. She stayed there by his side, rubbing his back, silently comforting him as he dealt with memory after memory.

Thomas had been through this before, and he recognized it for what it was. It only took a few minutes before his training kicked in and he reached out to Nera, pulling her in close and holding onto her like she was his lifeline. The past was gone, but she was real, solid and here with him. He would put away thoughts of all he had lost, as he had done before, and concentrate instead on what he had.

His thoughts then turned back to the present, and in a flash, he comprehended the full scope of their situation. He knew he had to rise, for there was much to be done. But he wouldn't put away the images of his time on Earth completely. Those were what would see them all through this and Thomas knew they would need every bit of luck they could get to survive.

He heard the sound of the automatic door opening at the room's entrance and turned in time to see a tall figure with moving white hair and brightly-glowing eyes, as he now remembered everyone on board had, enter the room.

The figure approached and Thomas went to sit up, but then had to lean heavily upon his elbow and shook his head. He was Talis, not Thomas!

He looked back up at the creature standing before him and quietly said through his raw throat, "Brother."

Lokai nodded once to his brother without a change of emotion, but inside he heaved a huge sigh of relief. He had been half out of his mind with worry since Talis had fallen ill after this last awakening. They were running very short on time and Talis was their only hope. Not to mention the fact that Nera had been driving him crazy!

Talis levered himself back up into a sitting position, swinging his legs over the edge of the thin bed where he had lain since the start of this journey.

"Whoa!" both Lokai and Nera immediately cautioned, as Nera reached to assist him.

Every part of him hurt and Talis squeezed his eyes shut to block out the spinning room. It didn't help. Colors swam in dizzying circles behind his lids and he opened his eyes again. It was better to have something to focus on than to feel like he was just spinning out of control in the darkness.

Nera moved to stand between his legs facing him. "Concentrate on me," she said.

The door to the room whispered open again and Talis could see someone move into the room and approach the bed. As the figure moved behind him, Talis made to turn so he could see who it was and what the individual was doing, but Nera's hand on his cheek stopped him.

"Let Jairs do what needs to be done," she said.

Suddenly, Talis felt a searing pain down the length of his spine and he threw his head back in a gut-wrenching scream. The pain lasted for barely a second before disappearing and Talis immediately remembered what was going on. Though that didn't make it any easier to take.

As soon as Jairs finished up and moved on, Talis, with a lot of assistance from Nera, slid off the high bed to stand shakily on the cold metal floor. He straightened his back and then threw his head back with his eyes closed, as he brought out all six of his ke – what those on Earth had called shields. He stretched them as far as they could reach, feeling the protein punch Jairs had injected into his spine now coursing throughout every portion of his body. Even his hair was soaking it up and soon it had managed to wrap Nera into a tight hold against his long, lithe body.

Finally, Talis wrapped his ke securely around his mate and himself and kissed her soundly on the lips, eventually coercing them apart and then plunging his tongue inside for his first real taste of her in a very long time.

After only a second, Nera pulled back from the kiss, her face all scrunched up and her tongue poking out, as she blurted out, "Blah!"

Talis only smiled and hugged her closer. "Sorry, Nene," he whispered, using the pet name he had called her almost since the time when they had first met.

Nera sucked in a breath of relief, but said, "Yes, well, I believe you are recovered enough that you can get yourself cleaned up and meet us upstairs shortly." She pulled away, but was then forced right back up against his chest by his tightening hair.

As she turned irritated, inquiring eyes upon him, he looked down at her and said softly, "Thank you... for everything."

Tears quickly sprang to her eyes and she hastily blinked and nodded, saying, "Let us get this done."

Talis placed a light, but tender, kiss upon her forehead and then stepped back. His hair immediately dropped, along with his ke, which returned to their resting place along his spinal column and Talis took a deep breath. Indeed, he had recovered and now his mind was replaying every scene of his life on Earth as Thomas Baker. The information he had gained throughout his short lifetime on the planet was extremely valuable to their mission, but there was one thing missing and he could almost kick himself for his stupidity.

Sarah's visions.

She had written about them in her blog, which he hadn't ever bothered to read while he had been there. She had told him about them on several occasions when she had had no one else to talk with. Of course, he had simply tuned her out as she had talked, nodding every now and then so it would appear as if he was actually listening.

What an idiot he had been! The key to their success possibly lay within her visions and he had completely ignored everything she had tried to tell him!

You know, you did not exactly have full control of your faculties, Nera's voice echoed softly through his mind. *Give yourself a break, hmm?*

Talis sighed heavily without answering her. He still felt like he should have known better.

Well, he knew now and he was going to fix this issue once and for good. As he cleaned himself up in the suite that belonged to Nera and him, he worked to contrive a plan. All he had to do was to contact Sarah and discover from her the information he and his shipmates needed in order to correct the situation. And contact her he would, just as soon as he finished cleaning himself up and got back up into the control room to his station.

Nera's voice suddenly trickled across his mind, though this time it sounded different, almost afraid. *You had better get up here fast*, was all she said.

Talis frowned as he exited the room, wondering what could be wrong now.

***

Israfil sat next to Lisa on the settee. The two had been sitting silently, each wrapped in their own thoughts, just down the corridor from the Master suite where Mikhail and Baphomet tested the binders in hopes of figuring out some method of removing the ones from Sarah, now that they knew where she was being held. Israfil was completely absorbed in thoughts of what had happened earlier at the Medical Facility.

He had not yet informed Mikhail their new sister had lost track of Sarah's location, but Israfil knew it would not be long before his powerful brother's mind picked up on it from one of their other siblings' thoughts. Israfil would hide the information from Mikhail until he could no longer, hoping some explanation could be learned before his brother discovered something had happened, for he knew his own mind was safe from Mikhail's. He simply hoped Djibril and Chris would find Sarah before the Mikhail found out.

Azra'il's fate also weighed heavily on Israfil's mind. He had not yet awakened, last Israfil had heard, and he wondered if Sheely's energies would be able to help his brother fight off the induced coma. The old maid, Miriam had taken Sheely to be with Azra'il just after Israfil had returned with his brother and Israfil believed the two to still be at the Medical Facility at this hour. He wondered how much longer it would take for his brother to finally regain consciousness, and a deep sense of concern settled onto his mind.

Lisa appeared involved in her own thoughts and was just as silent as he. Israfil's leg was casually touching hers, which apparently provided enough energy to keep her powerful mind in check, for she appeared to be having no difficulties with the wall of voices that would eclipse her mind without being protected. Baphomet had been gone almost twenty minutes so far and Israfil could feel the tension building in Lisa as more and more time slipped by. Although she had Israfil's energies to "substitute" for her mate's while they were apart, Baphomet had none and his mind was much too powerful to be left to its own devices for very long.

"I-I think you should probably go and help him now, if that's all right," Lisa finally suggested, interrupting the silence.

Israfil asked, "Did my brother contact you requesting my presence?"

"No, but it feels like he's fading fairly quickly in there," she replied as she monitored Baphomet's thoughts.

Israfil scooched forward on the settee but didn't rise. A moment later, he asked, "What is your connection with Baphomet like?"

"You mean between our minds?" she asked. At his nod, she explained, "I would imagine it's like when you mind-link with another person, except ours is permanent."

They both thought this over. Then Lisa said, "I've heard Mikhail and Sarah are able to block each other out or keep certain thoughts from one another." A slight shiver stole down her spine. "You know, it's kind of strange, but I've become so accustomed to him being here," she said as her fingers tapped her temple, "that I think it would be just too weird without Baphomet's thoughts being constantly intermingled with mine."

Israfil opened his mouth to respond, but just then both Lisa and he caught Baphomet's desperate plea for help. In a flash, Israfil's shields were out and he was gone. Lisa stayed behind with Cabal, rubbing the little shining spot on her abdomen. Something had gone wrong in there and there was no way she was allowing Cabal anywhere near the room where those awful binders were. She wished now she hadn't allowed Baphomet to convince her to allow *him* anywhere near the things!

He was in so much pain, she could feel it. She knew when Israfil finally reached her mate. But why were they not removing the blasted binders? Lisa frowned furiously as she stood and approached the door. The master suite was locked up tight and that's where her mate lay writhing in agony, yet no one was helping him!

Baphomet struggled for each breath. The binders felt like metal claws digging deep into each forearm. From there, stinging pulses of electricity were sent up along the axons in his muscles, causing his nerve endings to feel like they were on fire.

Someone do something. Please! he called out with his mental voice. He could not draw enough air into his lungs to be able to speak, but he knew others would be listening. He only hoped Lisa would not show up, trying to be brave. He didn't want Cabal or her anywhere near these things!

The pain increased and Baphomet vaguely recalled in between the sharp pulses of electric shock how he had whined about the wall of voices that would descend upon his mind if his energies were left unchecked. Now he knew what true punishment was!

Another spasm shook up through his arms and he knew it wouldn't be long before the electricity pulses reached his spine and then... his brain.

He gasped. *Mikhail! Help me!*

"Let go of me so I can help him!" Mikhail shouted desperately at Israfil. Baphomet was in very real danger. Couldn't Israfil *see* that?

"You cannot help him!" Israfil shouted back. "We must get out of here!"

Mikhail looked at Israfil as if he had lost his mind. "I shall not leave him here to die," he ground out between gritted teeth.

"We are not leaving him. We are going for help and getting you to safety first," Israfil explained in a rush as he continued pulling his uncooperative brother along.

Baphomet moaned uncontrollably, in unabashed painful agony.

Suddenly the door opened and there stood Lyss, the human who worked at the Medical Facility. She took a quick assessing look around and then went directly to Baphomet's side. Mikhail and Israfil watched in amazement as she reached down and simply deactivated and removed the offending metal binders from their brother's wrists. Although she looked as if she wanted to stay behind to tend to the injured Lori, she hefted up the heavy binders and quickly left the room.

Seconds later, Lisa rushed into the room. Mikhail and Israfil were already helping Baphomet to stand, but Lisa nearly knocked them over as she grabbed her mate in a fierce hug. Tears streamed down her face as she held him tightly to her. A moment later, she stepped back and framed his face with her hands, yelling, "Don't you ever do anything like that to Cabal and me again!"

She then hugged him again and Baphomet stood within the circle of her arms and hair, drinking in as much energy from her as he could get. As soon as he felt he was able to speak, he raised one corner of his mouth and said, "I did not know I was doing anything wrong, sweet Lisa, but I shall happily avoid ever doing *that* again, whether you order it or not."

He hugged her close.

The experiment had failed miserably.

Israfil put a consoling hand on Mikhail's shoulder – normally, this was a dangerous move because of Mikhail's wicked-sharp, overly-protective hair. However, today Mikhail's hair lay almost dormant.

"We could try again later with me wearing them, since they do not appear to affect me quite as much," Israfil offered.

Mikhail immediately shook off that idea. He would not put any more of his family members through the pain caused by the wretched binders. Sarah certainly wouldn't approve, he knew.

"No," he said. "We shall simply have to discover another way."

Baphomet and Lisa turned to leave the room, but Baphomet stopped and turned back. "I am s-sorry, brother," he said, choking on his unshed tears.

Mikhail held up a hand and shook his head as he moved toward them. This was not Baphomet's fault. "You do yourself a disservice, my brother," Mikhail told him. "You have shown us just how dangerous the binders truly can be." He clapped Baphomet on the shoulder and saw the couple out the door.

When they were gone, he didn't close the door and Israfil quietly asked, "Will you be all right alone?"

Mikhail's only response was an empty chuckle.

"I could stay, if you wish?"

Mikhail looked at his brother. There were so many secrets behind those ice-blue eyes, so much pain, and Mikhail wondered how he made it through each and every day, but he said nothing. He merely shook his head and held the door for his brother.

The immediate future looked to hold sleepless nights and nothing more.

Mikhail went to check on Sheely, but he knew he would not stay long with his daughter. She was too much of a reminder of Sarah. Besides, she was with the as yet still unconscious Azra'il and he needed her more than Mikhail needed her company. What Mikhail really needed was to be alone with his thoughts so he could come up with a plan to free Sarah, assuming she still lived. Until she was safely back home with him, he could not rest.

He watched from his open bedroom window not long afterward as the moon set over the Nameless Bay. Even the lowing sounds of the Labi could not soothe him and Mikhail wondered if he would ever see his mate again.

***

Talis entered the control room and immediately realized all but one of the spots was occupied at the main control panel station. It was good to see that, since up until now Lokai's and his mate's spots had been unoccupied. They had both been off tending to one of their own batches for quite some time and Talis recalled how worrisome those emptied spots at the control panel had been to him while he had been working with the humans and Lorim of Earth. Only his spot currently remained unoccupied.

Taking position there now, Talis quickly pulled up his virtual screen and asked Nera, who was at the spot just next to his, "What is the problem?"

"We cannot locate your class three," Lokai answered, instead.

A chill stole over Talis' body. "What do you mean?" he asked, as he started a trace on Sarah's particular energy patterns. Each trace program came up negative and Talis' heart-rate increased with each new result.

This was impossible! Sarah's energy patterns had been programmed in since they had started this whole thing, just in case Nera lost track of Talis' energy patterns through the device on board the ship controlling his physical body on Earth. So why were they now unable to locate them?

A dreadful thought occurred to Talis and the blood drained from his face. He recalled the last scene involving Sarah he had witnessed as her son and the idea that she may not have made it through that ordeal had him reeling. He needed information from her, to be certain, but he was also alarmed due to the fact that he liked both Sarah and Mikhail and he knew that her death would have a tremendously negative impact on Mikhail's state of being, both physical and emotional.

He pulled up Mikhail's energy patterns. They appeared on the screen without difficulty. He was right where he was supposed to be – at the Badlands Complex. The only problem was he was alone. Talis thought he could see a yellowish hue coming through on the scan and that meant Mikhail had already begun suffering the effects of the absence of Sarah's energies.

Mikhail was alone, Talis had failed to obtain the information they needed while he had been there, and now it appeared he had missed his chance because Sarah was nowhere to be found. What more could go wrong? The very second he thought this, he cursed himself a thousand times a fool, for he knew things could always be worse.

Sure enough, just as this thought passed through his head, things became worse.

"Look sharp, everyone," Lokai commanded. "They are almost upon us."

Epilogue

The entire audience was tense as they waited with bated breath for me to continue. But I had no intention of saying another word, for I realized that Ana had just reached her destination.

I'm all right, *she whispered in my mind. The distance was great and I still felt a chill from the knowledge that there was nothing I could do to ensure her safety from this distance.* Trust me, *she implored.*

Jarba interrupted my thoughts as she finally realized I was not going to continue. "Where is Sephor Sarah?" she demanded. "And what is the creature Thomas, er, Talis? And who are these others?" She stood and rushed toward me, livid and desperate in her desire for answers. I knew she believed Talis and his group to be the cause of all the problems and that she thought I was finally getting to the information she sought. She made to grab me, but then thought better of it as she caught sight of the thin strips of scabbing along the back of her hand.

"Tell us the rest," she barked instead, without touching me.

I did not care what she thought. For my own peace of mind, I needed to concentrate on what was happening with Ana right now. I raised my eyes up toward the curtained seat where I could feel the Prince sat in attendance and I said, "I fear I have spent too much energy for one day. I must rest now."

The glance the Joss *had thrown up toward the Prince's seat had not been lost upon her and Jarba understood his meaning. What choice did she have? If the* Joss *was anywhere near as capable as the* Jess *had been, then she knew there was nothing but the* Joss *himself keeping him here and that she had to trust that he would keep his word and remain close to protect the Prince until his* Jess *returned.*

Resignation was not an easy thing for her, but so much was riding on this one creature's tale. Jarba nodded and watched tight-lipped as two guards led the Joss *back to his chamber. After he had gone, there was much talk around the room, but Jarba ignored it all. She had made arrangements for guards to be both inside and outside the* Joss' *bedroom chamber, as well as extra eyes monitoring the whole scene throughout the coming hours.*

She herself would see to the Prince's safety throughout the coming nights to ensure the Joss kept his word.

She would also go over everything she had learned this day in hopes of discovering something – anything – that would help in getting her people back to the forefront of the battlegrounds. Her only fear was that they were wasting too much time and that by the time they found a way back, there would be nothing left.

www.ingramcontent.com/pod-product-compliance
Lightning Source LLC
Chambersburg PA
CBHW020936260626
47169CB00006B/1745